NEODYMIUM BETRAYAL

NEODYMIUM BETRAYAL

The Neodymium Chronicles

JEN FINELLI, M.D.

WFP
WordFire Press

EBook ISBN: 978-1-68057-285-8
Trade Paperback ISBN: 978-1-68057-284-1
Dust Jacket Hardcover ISBN: 978-1-68057-286-5
Case Bind Hardcover ISBN: 978-1-68057-287-2
Library of Congress Control Number: 2022935719

Cover design by Janet McDonald
Cover artwork images by Adobe Stock
Kevin J. Anderson, Art Director
Published by
WordFire Press, LLC
PO Box 1840
Monument CO 80132
Kevin J. Anderson & Rebecca Moesta, Publishers
WordFire Press eBook Edition 2022
WordFire Press Trade Paperback Edition 2022
WordFire Press Hardcover Edition 2022
Printed in the USA
Join our WordFire Press Readers Group for
sneak previews, updates, new projects, and giveaways.
Sign up at wordfirepress.com

DEDICATION

Dedicated to JE, to whom I owe the universe, and to all the brothers who have left the Paradox. With deepest thanks to James Beamon, who prevented the half-a-box-in-space. This book's first gift was finding me a mentor like you.

CHAPTER ONE

Jei

SOMETIMES WE BLUR THE LINES BETWEEN PRODIGAL SONS AND REBEL heroes returned.

Tonight, my sparring partner would come home. I paced behind the line of combat tanks facing into the jungle dusk; I couldn't stand still. All my senses strained for signs of arrival. The low, distant chatter of other soldiers trickled to me in the dusk like the murmur of a stream as people made the best of packaged dinner conversation from the open lids of gunnery pods. Someone's tinny wristband transmitter leaked thin strains of music. Everything in the siege line smelled like damp leaves, metal dust, and motor oil.

I was anxious. I didn't know if she was returning for punishment or reward, and after all this time I didn't know how to help her or just—I just wanted to see her alive. I leapt to crouch on the nearest tread, peering into the coming darkness. But the shadow slinking through the underbrush wasn't her. Or an enemy soldier, either—just one of those weird, feathered cats.

Bloodseas, after four months apart I hadn't figured the last twenty minutes would be the worst. How she planned to break through the siege, or why she'd left in the first place, I didn't know, and I tried to brush my other questions away like I batted off the flying bloodsuckers flitting around my ears.

Like the bloodsuckers, the question persisted.

Maybe she disappeared because of what the slave said.

Four months ago

The last time I'd seen my fighting partner, four months ago, we were running a sabotage mission on the northernmost continent of my homeworld, Alpino. Seemed simple enough: break into the weapons manufacturing plant, steal its last shipment, arm the slaves, and blow the place to bloody stardust. The Growen slavers wouldn't expect us—their segment of the continent sat surrounded by neutral territory, and you can't get a military force worth talking about past those neutral zones without breaking a few treaties.

You can, however, get in two teens with electromagnetic powers in a small one-man spaceship.

"You've just got ugly all over your face, man." Lem gestured in a washing motion over her own disguised holographic visage as she scowled at mine. Her gloved finger traced invisible lines on the window as she turned her gaze to the stars outside. She shivered. "It's freaky, even if we've done it before, you know?"

I nodded. She looked unnerving, too, at least from a human point of view, with three fuzzy spider-leg-like growths sprouting from each corner of her mouth and coarse, black hair bristling across her skin—but I looked worse: with the orb-shaped helmet and tight-fitted human body armor, I looked like a Growen soldier.

"You can't just nod, man, you gotta talk," Lem said. "You just nod, and it's like I'm stuck in this tiny space with a real live blitzer."

"What do you want me to say? Yes, I look like a child-killer." I smirked, knowing full-well that whatever she might say, neither of us minded cramming into a one-man fighter together. It wasn't like *that*. Just … when you had something as infinite and—and *swallowing* as space around you, it was good to huddle against another warm body. It was not good for a man to be alone.

"As long as you say something. The hologram's just so freakin' realistic," she said.

I glanced away from the compuwall—the small, pad-like computerized control system in front of me—to my reflection in the window. The globe of silvery helmet, the shadowy muscular gray armor, the make of the weapons strapped across my chest—it all screamed Growen blitzer. Lem and I could thrash these guys now, easy, but that didn't mean we'd forgotten the terror of watching hundreds of their number march through the flaming ruins of our homes as the faces of our dead and broken family members reflected in orange on the glimmering orbs of their masks …

"Did the bounty hunter ever ask us to give these disguise projectors back?" I asked.

"No …" Lem paused—the imaginary spider-leg-lips pursed together and twitched as something new occurred to her. She looked at me. "Actually, wait, yes. You better gimme yours when we get back from this mission. I'll give it to her when I see her."

"That's too bad." These sweet disguise generators had been the first of our secrets as Paradox Warriors. Command didn't even know we had them.

A tan-white dot appeared in the distance. The white mohawk of feathers on Lem's head bobbed as she nodded toward it—as if she needed to remind me where my home planet was. In seconds the dot grew to the size of a marble. Lem checked her reflection and adjusted the short mace that hung in staff-form from her waist, bracing for atmospheric entry as my hands slid down the compuwall before us, guiding the ship toward its landing course. *Slow. Even. Smooth …*

Lem sucked in her breath.

I stiffened as her muscles tensed against my side: a shadow blocked the light from the stars against our port window.

A Growen ship floated beside us.

Lem spoke low through a tense throat: "Get into neutral airspace. Go!"

"If we run it gives us away."

"Man, we're in a Frelsi Blastercraft, I think we're about as given away as it gets!"

"We'll follow protocol."

"Why didn't they show up on our screen before we saw them? They're hiding. Hunting!"

"We've got Growen entry codes. They won't chase us. Command intended for us to go incognito." We could already see the shimmering pale white rings of a Growen Maggot as it floated, compact like an oblong striped egg, toward us. I could've thrown a stone at it. "Our heat tracker probably didn't pick them up because they've got signal scrambling on. Like we do. They probably don't want a fight either," I reassured her ... and myself.

Right.

Except the Maggot popped into attack position. Weapons burst like pustules out from between the sliding rings; the egg hatched as its plates separated to elongate the ship into a worm —a Growen Feierspitter.

Lem reached over me and slapped my computer. Fire flashed around us as we jerked into high-speed and my head slammed against the seat behind me and the stars screamed past us and Lem's elbow dug into my gut as she urged the ship onward with her palms on my compuwall, and we careened toward the planet below and the Maggot spiraled after us in pursuit and "*Bloodseas*, Lem, slow down! We're going to crash!"

"No stopping now, my guy, you gotta land this thing."

"I can't land at this speed!"

"Well you got a better shot than I do!"

The tan dot was a circle, now a sphere, now a detailed pearl streaked with bands of flax and blue, a wide expanse of nation-shapes, now a flash of brain-rattling atmospheric fire, now a snowfield smashing toward our windshield *oh shyte oh shyte the Maggot was still right behind us—*

I shouldered Lem to the side and swiped my palms up the compuwall. Our ship swooped up—a treetop snapped off on our underside—Lem yanked the eject tab—cold air sliced across my face and my stomach plummeted into my pelvis as we burst out of the ship. A metallic crash, and then a heavy boom, sounded behind us; heat singed the back of my neck as a shock wave rocketed me across the frigid sky.

My automated jetpack deployed with a *whoosh* and an awful, startling halt. I turned to see the debris filtering through the air with the scent of sulfur and burnt rubber ... the Maggot had crashed into us. We'd pulled up too sharply for it to stop.

Well.

Without Lem around to screw up my driving I eased my jetpack to a soft landing in the snow. Then I sighed, brushed myself off, and sat down on the warm shell of a sleeping snow-turtle to eat a protein bar and watch as ash flitted down around me like black snowflakes. An engine smashed into a tree in front of me; thundering hooves, and then whinnies and the pounding of enormous wings echoed over the snowy expanse as a herd of woolly pegasi took off. The protein bar was Smungwurm-flavored, and I wasn't even mad.

This was how Lem did things. I rolled with it. It was funny sometimes, and at any rate *this* particular mess was probably inevitable. I didn't see any pilot eject from the Maggot, and it'd attacked us without a single attempt at contact, unprovoked. And orbiting in silence over a neutral nation on a contested planet like this? It had to be a Ghost. These rogue robot-piloted ships haunted quiet regions throughout the galaxy, shooting first and asking questions never to take out saboteurs like us and keep the civilians afraid to travel. Locals around the universe had different legends and scientific "singularity" explanations for Ghosts, but Lem and I had seen the Growen manufacture them. At any rate, Lem's fault or not, a Ghost wouldn't have given up chase until our ship was destroyed.

Bloodseas, though, what a mountain of paperwork awaited us at home now. Ghosts are the homework-eating dog of off-planet missions gone wrong. "Uh, um—a Ghost did it!" This could mess with my spotless record.

For now though, I didn't care. I was busy smiling. Space-ninjas who grow up on jungle worlds don't often see snow, and the first time Lem saw snow was *now* as she tumbled ten meters on a broken jetpack, spinning out of control to—ooooh, ouch—smash into a deep bank.

Powdery white splashed up around her impact. "Jei, holy shyte man, you okay?" sputtered through her lips as she sank and tried to "swim" and found herself flailing. She righted herself somehow—drew her neodymium mace—and yelled for me again as she swung to smash and slice the material around her, only to watch it pack and melt instead of breaking.

"Welcome to Alpino," I laughed behind her. She whirled and looked up to where I stood above her on the ivory turtle's back.

"Shyte, man, what is this place?" she asked.

"Dunno. I've never been here. I don't own the whole planet."

Lem scowled and threw snow at me. "Man, look at you all joking when I don't even know if I need a gas mask on. Is this shyte poisonous?"

I laughed, shying away as her unpacked snowball sprinkled over my tunic. "Let's go," I said, hopping into the air a good distance away from the turtle before igniting my jetpack.

She stood back, still sinking into the snow far below me. "I gotta walk," she said.

I landed beside her to check—yeah, there was no fixing her pack in time. We'd find the nearest slave caravan faster on foot.

"So you do," I said, and so we walked, carrying the wings that should've carried us.

CHAPTER TWO

Jei

LIKE I SAID, THAT WAS FOUR MONTHS AGO.

Now, I sat on the tank tread of a Bradley 9000 on Lem's jungle-ridden home planet, leaning back against the warm, warped metal of the wall that shielded the soft whispers of the vibrating engine inside. A wrapper crackled as I drew a protein bar from my uniform's chest pocket and ripped it open with my teeth.

"Why won't they tell me what happened to her?" I asked.

The oblong jade leaves of the nearest bush shook, but I heard no answer.

"You've been quiet lately," I said, ripping a chunk of hard goo off the bar. It squished as I chewed.

The leaves rustled again, and now I *felt*, rather than smelled, an earthy perfume floating from the ground up toward the stars that struggled to peep through the thick jungle canopy. The stars winked at me, like *he* knew something, but didn't want to tell me yet.

"Do you like her better than me," I said, rather than asked. "You talk more when she's around."

The branches bristled in the canopy above me; wet droplets shimmered as they fell from the shadowed coin-shaped leaves to trickle over the rough cloth on my shoulders. I looked up. A message? Perhaps. For my energy-being friend outside of time, every moment, past or future, was *now*. He could indeed flick a planet in the past to butterfly-effect a breeze right where I needed to see it in the present.

But not everything was about me. I knew that. She never did. She saw a message in every weird pattern in the tree bark, and every lumpy rock in a creek bed.

"Did you send her something she thought was a mission, Njandejara?" I nodded his name into the evening. "Is that why Lem left?"

My commanding officers had told me she had gone on extended leave, but I'd never heard of anyone taking four months of leave in the middle of essential wartime operations. Her parents thought she was going somewhere with me. I didn't know what to tell them.

Must be on some mission only upper command knows, I told myself again, again insecure, wondering why they would assign her alone, without me.

A cold voice—high like the cry of a feathered cat and fluttery like the wings of the flying lizards it hunts—interrupted my thoughts. I groaned but didn't turn around.

The tinny heels of a female soldier's boots clicked against the tank tread as the unwanted voice jumped down behind me and repeated her question.

"Who are you talking to?" she asked.

I'd already told Lt. Seria to leave me alone. I'd only requested the post near her tank tonight because I thought Lem was coming home here.

"Don't you have the gunner position," I said, rather than asked. I wanted Seria to get back into the tank and let me be.

"It's standard to take a breath outside for ten minutes every hour, for our health," she said. "You forget protocol."

"Mm." Somebody had forgotten protocol, but it sure wasn't me. Platoon romance was against regs, and ever since I'd become a star Paradox Warrior, platoon romance seemed to be Seria's one and only goal. The slim muscular figure didn't burn my eyes or anything, but I didn't like the idea of *any* figure climbing me to success like a disposable ladder.

"I thought maybe you could show me how your mace works," she said. I didn't bother to ask whether or not that was innuendo. She hopped down from the tank into the mossy dirt around it and paced into my line of sight. Some kind of seed had made its way into the fruity center of my protein bar, and I spat it out as Seria walked by me.

"I was talking to an interdimensional," I said.

Theeere we go.

Seria's horrified face brought a smile to mine. She coughed, and brushed a strand of blonde back into her helmet. "Well—ah—why do you think you're doing that?"

Overall, an attempt at tolerance. Annoyingly enough, now she'd earned an answer. "Because he's my friend," I said.

"He? It has a ... gender?"

"Yeah. I guess, if I have to think about it, he's the Yang, and our dimension, and all of us, are Yin, so he's the he and we're a she."

"You're—a she?"

"Bloodseas, no, just in comparison with him, our universe is a dark emptiness, a soft warm holding, and he's an entering li—you know what, that sounds stupid." I clenched my jaw and tore a loose string off my uniform, avoiding eye contact. "It's hard to explain if you haven't met him yourself." My embarrassment made me grumpier, but now he decided to let me hear him, loud and clear, as he asked for an introduction.

No way.

He nudged at my elbow.

Ugh, okay, fine. "Would you like to meet him," I grumbled.

"Ah, no, I'm good, thanks." She rocked on her toes and twiddled her fingers through each other, coughing again. Good, she was embarrassed, too. Maybe the weirdness of my invisible friend would turn her off. Maybe I should say something weirder.

"Lem thinks the universe is about to go into thermodynamic collapse, and our interdimensional—his name is Njandejara—is the key to saving it," I said.

She flinched. "Yes I—I figured she might have something to do with it."

"What's that supposed to mean?"

"You're not like her. You're a rational guy, and a model soldier, so ..."

"So I don't talk to invisible people?"

Seria backed up, palms raised. "Look, I don't get it. But I'll always defend your right to speak to whatever ectoplasms you choose." She raised her wrist and pulled back her sleeve to reveal a fraying twine bracelet. "We all have our oddities."

Ah. The bracelet meant she hailed from a pale-skinned tribe of humans who lived on my homeworld, Alpino, on the opposite pole from where I grew up. They wore dragon-skin there, and ate only vegetables and reptiles, and the Growen took issue with the low safety standards and deregulated environment of their creature-centered lifestyle. Her people sent a yearly contingent to the Frelsi Coalition, but most of them stayed on Alpino to defend their tribal grounds. Seria was clearly on the fast-track for promotion if she took deployments this far from home.

I nodded to her, understanding. We all believed in this diversity, in our own way—heck, we had to.

But before she could speak again I turned my back, tapping my wristband to scroll through my messages. She hesitated once, as if to apologize once more, and then her tin-tinny boots finally left me in peace.

I never felt awkward, or had to hide my interdimensional, around Lem. He stayed with us like a silent third friend; moved, through us, like a bonded force. I could still hear a comforting echo of his breath in that last mission, four months ago, in the crispy *crunch-crunch* of underfoot snow ...

Four months ago

Lem marched beside me across the snowy plain, hunching her shoulders against the cold with her hands tucked inside her puffy cold-weather suit. The bristles of her face seemed to twitch in the breeze. Presently, she turned to me.

"Ghosts make me sad," she said. "They've got some kind of a brain, you know. We're all programming after all, biological or not. Can you imagine being alone out there, forever, in the big … forever …"

The big forever.

Her eyes widened suddenly. My lips froze. "Oh shyte, not again."

We looked around, our eyes scrambling for cover like rodents for burrows; we'd left the clump of trees behind to cross the open plains, and it had only just hit our minds that we stood now in the midst of a blank whiteness that expanded in all directions, forever. Above us shimmered a reflective, onyx sky, opaque and harsh, measuring infinite, and I could rationalize it —say the black sheen here in the northern continent came from the magnetic field playing with the light from this planet's rare-earth metal moons—but it seemed so much more true to say the void of space had swallowed all its stars, and now opened its maw to consume us, too.

Lem and I gripped hands. We stood for a moment both keenly aware of the panic attack about to ensue. Here it came … here it …

My chest ached and thumped; I could feel my lungs squeezing in on themselves, pulverizing and choking me because the sky, the wide sky over us, around us, was eating us. My temples pulsed with fire. My face seemed to freeze, and my vision blurred as the sky chewed my eyes and a fuzzy sheen overtook all things …

"Breathe," I coughed, both to Lem and myself.

And it passed. We coughed, like every time before, and

brushed our sweaty hands off on our uniforms without a word as we trudged on.

This was the most important thing Command didn't know. The kinds of mind-torture that produce fear of open spaces aren't kinds of torture you talk about with anyone but the battle-buddy who went through it with you.

"Ghosts make me sad," Lem repeated, like nothing had happened. "I'm sad I killed it. It's not like it's free to choose who it attacks."

I was more bummed about the loss of our ship, but hey. To each his own.

We found a slave caravan without a problem using the known trade routes. Escaped slaves and the helpful Growen "do-gooders" who caught them were a common sight in this sector, so no one questioned me when I loaded Lem and her spider-face into the fur-covered wagon and insisted on sitting next to her. The reward for her capture was mine, after all.

Lem kept her eyes downturned like a good captive might, but I still caught the smile that twitched at the corners of her mouth with the first beat of the wings of the pegasi pulling the caravan. The creatures' shoulder muscles writhed before us like engine turbines as their wool rippled in the wind, and with each massive flap a gust of cool air blew back into the covered wagon. I missed this. Living on Lem's home planet I never got to see snow anymore. I wished I could take off the helmet now and feel the winter's breath on my face.

We smelled the industrial complex before we saw it. Oil, aluminum dust, and feces. When we saw it, it was a black blotch sending blue smears into the sky.

At the steel checkpoint gates Lem had no problems—slaves didn't need names and numbers—but they couldn't find my made-up ID number in the system for some reason, and to my surprise they "detained" me and sent me to wait for "the magistrate" in a dingy fenced-in courtyard around a hut made of fur.

"I told you you should've stolen your identity from one of

the prisoners back home," Lem whispered as she waited with me.

"I didn't have time to interview some Growen murderer."

"Growen are people, too."

I laughed, but the joke didn't seem like her, and now it sounds ominous to my memory.

CHAPTER THREE

Jei—Four Months Ago

I DIDN'T HAVE A PROBLEM SCHMOOZING THE MAGISTRATE ABOUT MY outdated Growen ID; I'd become separated from my platoon, you see, abandoned for dead in these snowy wastelands, living for months on pegasus flesh and frozen smungworms, and finally when I'd found this spider-faced Baricella slave I'd forced it to tell me the way to civilization. Oh, and my transmitter broke so I couldn't call home. If I could borrow one and get passage, please—?

I spent most of the day faking complicated arrangements to get home and keeping Growen soldiers distracted; meanwhile Lem rallied the slaves, analyzed weak points, and picked an assault plan from the templates Command had suggested before plausible deniability required cutting off communication with us.

Now, starlight glinted off my helmet, sparkling on the tin shed behind me and washing the white crest of feathers on Lem's head with a soft glow as she emerged from the narrow shadows of the fur-covered slave-huts clustered in the dirty snow. I stamped my feet and rubbed my gloved hands together as she neared the fence.

"Thirty-two women in an unmarked grave," I said.

"Never forget, and never lose hope," she said back, identifying herself with our password answer for the evening. I turned to pace outside the perimeter of the fence, and she, inside, followed me trailing a spindly, fuzzy fingernail along the rusted metal barbs.

"Are they ready?" I asked.

"Almost. They're rounding up their kids near the back gate right now."

"Good." Once we broke into the weapons storehouse under the weapons factory, we'd arm the adults and start a skirmish to draw the blitzers to the front gate. The kids would escape out the back and hide in the woods until the fighting stopped, and I hoped in this twilight the naturally nocturnal spider-face people —the Baricellas—would have an advantage against their day-hungry human overlords. Easy freedom for them, and one less Growen-controlled weapons complex for us. Even if the Growen tried to come back, as long as the Baricellas technically owned this place the Frelsi could defend them. Maybe we'd even negotiate a new arms contract for ourselves with the slaves-turned-owners.

The steel of my heated knife glowed orange-red and sizzled through the wire fence; Lem squeezed out and trotted ahead of me with a soft *cr-crun-cr-crun-cr-crun* on the old snow. My boots thudded behind her, slow and heavy and armored, and I couldn't wait to get out of this thing. The slave-captor dynamic turned my stomach.

No blitzers yet. Most of the guards would stay away from the slave compounds and cluster around the factory. We'd fight them there.

Cr-crun-cr-crun-cr-crun ...

The shadow of a wide, tapered tower stretched toward us across snow that otherwise sparkled in the yellow glow from the light over the metal shed at the tower base. *The weapons storehouse.* There was another, smaller shadow, in front of the door.

A single slave.

"Ambush," Lem whispered, reaching behind her back for the

short staff wrapped under the sash around her waist. "He's bait." Like her, I armed myself and checked my peripherals as we slowed our approach.

"What do you want here, human?" announced the slave as loudly as possible.

"Shhh!" Lem lowered her palms as if waving down his volume dial. "He's with us!"

"Not him, you!"

Lem kept advancing, looking around for the inevitable trap. "Wow, good call. Yeah, I'm wearing something like a hologram projector."

"I can't even tell," he scoffed. "We can't see in that light frequency. If you wanted to fool us you should've altered your heat signature."

"Well, I'm not trying to fool you, I'm trying to fool the humans. Enter the code and open the door, let's get this revolution started."

The slave's face appendages crossed. "No."

Lem looked around again. I raised my weapon, watching behind us. "Are you kidding me?" Lem whispered.

"Just because you would not choose this way of life does not give you the right to come in here and overthrow our government."

"Government? These guys kidnapped your parents and forced them to work for free! That's not government we're down with." We were close enough for Lem to check the guy for wires, chains, some kind of explosive device holding him hostage; I hung back and watched our six, wondering why it was taking her so long to find the trigger point. She looked back at me and shook her head in confused near-panic. I approached to check for her—he couldn't actually mean what he said.

"You underestimate my age, human. I remember what it was like before the Growen. I remember crawling through the underbrush of the orange leaves, licking the dirt for the husks of dead grubs to soothe my aching belly. Now I eat meat every day."

The X-ray pointing at him from my Growen helmet came back negative. No explosives, not even inside him. The hell?

I started to stammer, caught myself, and said: "We're just trying to give you some agency here, sir."

"Agency? Do you really think we need two humans to save us? Do you really think we can't rescue ourselves? It's not our freedom if you give it to us."

"We're working with over a hundred of your own leaders to make this happen!"

"They are fools. Young fools." The slave backed up to where we couldn't touch him, still blocking the entrance to the weapons depot with his body. Lem looked at me as if asking for permission to knock him out. I waved her down—two humans attacking a Baricella could look like betrayal to the others hiding in the shadows. He went on: "Our free healthcare, our safety, our food supplies all come to us from the Growen. There was a revolt here twenty years ago and within a month of that anarchy everyone almost starved to death."

"So you leave, and move back to your homeland—where they stole your parents from, if you remember," Lem gritted her teeth.

"Our homeland? Our homeland?" The slave burst into loud, boisterous laughter that made me raise my weapon. We needed to get into the weapons depot before the blitzers poured down on us. "Most of the people in this camp grew up here," the slave said. "The homeland they imagine is a polluted forest of fools in constant war with nature. If you want to send us back to the darkness, you shall have to go through me."

Lem and I stared at each other at a loss. She looked terrified in her perplexity, but I put on a knowing face, as if I had an answer to his every claim. He was out-voted by his peers, and vote or not the Frelsi needed this weapons depot out of Growen hands. Saving my home planet mattered, too.

So I waved Lem to the side, to block the view with her body, and I stepped up and shot him myself.

He collapsed as the stun cartridge delivered a sudden

exhaustive blast to the sarcoplasmic reticulum in his muscles, draining them of the calcium he needed to move; I propped up his falling body to use his claw to buzz us into the weapons depot.

But his claw didn't have access to the building. He smiled, and opened his palm as he went limp.

A silent alarm trigger clattered to the ground.

"We have a problem," Lem and I both said at the same time as a mob of blitzers approached from beyond the wire fence.

Shyte.

I tried the stunned Baricella's claw on the sensor again as hurried Growen footfalls crunched in the crispy snow. Blitzers shouted from the shadows of the squat, fur-roofed concrete buildings around the fenced-in factory field—

With no answer from us, they opened fire. Lem squeezed against me and the doorjamb for cover as she fired back; colorful, oxidizing kill cartridges pinged and zapped around us. The blitzers couldn't cross the empty lot without leaving cover, but we weren't in a great position ourselves—"Try it my way!" Lem shouted.

Ugh, fine. With a long sigh I fired my weapon into the door—it blasted open around me with such suddenness, the stunned Baricella and I fell on top of each other through the entrance.

Icy concrete floor slammed against me. Above towered conical walls honeycomb'd with weapons shelves ... all empty.

The weapons depot was empty?

Shyte. Lem slipped into the tower after me; a blitzer charged behind her. I rolled off the Baricella, flattened my belly against the cold floor, and steadied my aim with my elbows.

"Looks like we've been played," I said as I fired.

"Someone has," Lem said.

The blitzer fell forward, and behind him—

"Oh, that's why it's empty in here." I laughed in relief, flopping over onto my back. "Whew."

The blitzers were surrounded by Baricella armed with enormous, glowing blue tentacled cannons.

"We figured Major would betray us, so as soon as you brought us your promise of alliance we set him up," the youngest Baricella rebel called out to us with the biggest, twitchiest spider-face grin as the blitzers raised their hands. "I mean, come on, he took a human name."

"He had a choice of names, and he chose that one?" I shouted back.

The rebel let out a joyful *whoop*—more of a stinging creak, like fingernails on steel, to human ears. I winced, laughed, and threw up my hand for a high five to Lem, job well done.

She did nothing.

"Lem?"

Lem looked at the Baricellas rounding up the blitzers, at the occasional execution shot, and at the unconscious body lying on the ground beside me.

"Hey. Lem."

She shook her head. "Yeah. It's all good. I just realized something, is all."

"Hey, we liberated the camp. We can contact Command to get resources to the freed Baricella. We saved the day." I whacked her boot with the back of my hand. "Lem, you can take off the spider-face disguise."

She touched behind her ear, and the tentacle-face appendages faded away, leaving the mahogany, small-chinned, wide-eyed fighter, staring down at the unconscious traitor.

"What do you do when they don't want to be saved?" she wondered aloud.

I didn't answer. I knew she wasn't asking me.

CHAPTER FOUR

Lem

LEM BENZARAN CREPT THROUGH THE FOLIAGE OF HER HOME PLANET, her chest tucked low to the earth, her fingers clawing her way forward through leaf litter as sweat dribbled down her lower back. She was a day late for her meet-up with Jei. Not her fault: blitzer troops had accountability rules that made it hard to slip away.

How long had it been—four months, now?

With one more furtive glance over her shoulder Lem drew back the sleeve of her armor to reveal the Frelsi wristband she still wore. It was gutted, and no longer told the Frelsi Command her location, but it could still get in touch with her battle-buddy. She dimmed the light as much as she could, and then scribbled with her dirty fingernail on its smooth surface:

"You enjoying your company?"

He responded almost instantly. She stifled a giggle under a satisfied smirk as Jei exploded at her with a string of funny curses: he *knew* she'd chosen a meeting point near Lt. Seria on purpose.

A pang of pain, and guilt, shot through Lem's chest as she joked with Jei, teasing him about his would-be lover and dreaming with him about Njande. Man, she loved this—the inside of the shell he kept everyone else out of. She savored each scolding retort … because once she let this go, she'd never get it back.

Maybe she wouldn't get caught. Maybe she'd die a good guy. Hope, like bird-puppies, was cute or whatever, and worth looking at. But it was a whole lot more likely that this was their last conversation before he hated her.

She almost needed him to.

Well. She couldn't bury her head in her elbow and cry into the soil about it. The musty scent of underbrush wafted around her as she dug her fingers into the earth to pull herself forward, knees pressing into the ground commando-style. She had a universe to save.

But she couldn't kid herself into thinking Mr. Too-Military-For-A-Name would forgive her for what she did next.

Jei

My wristband lit up with text—I almost fell off the tank tread in my rush to answer. It was her! Lem Benzaran, still alive enough to light up the night.

"You enjoying your company?" she asked.

"You know damn well I'm not," I texted back. "I've tried everything to get Seria off my back. Even told her I talk to invisible people."

"Funny that didn't work. She stopped hanging out with me over it." I could almost hear Lem laughing. "Guess you get a free pass for insanity if you got washboard abs."

"*Ha. Ha.* Seriously, don't set me up near her again. She's so distracted she almost shot herself earlier."

"Oh, I see it now! Fumbling with her gun as she bats her eyelashes as you … accidentally fires the tank into the wall 'cuz you roll up your sleeve to flash some bicep … the entire base goes up in flames and the Growen weaponize pictures of your pecs to conquer the universe ..."

"Such a morbid sense of humor." I smiled.

"Eh, can you blame me?"

"I blame Diebol." My tone darkened. I wasn't really joking. My fingers ached to crunch around his throat and crack his—

She snapped me out of it with one of her characteristic paragraphs, the wildness almost palpable in the lettering: "Oh really? You blame my crazy on the guy who electrocuted me every day for a month? The reason our friends call us mutants? The guy in charge of the army that's statistically likely to kill us before age twenty-three? Naw, can't possibly be his fault."

Harty har. "Hold up, now, I only said I blame Diebol for your *terrible sense of humor*. I'm pretty sure you came with the *crazy* pre-packaged."

"Psh, you know me, evil incarnate with a gorgeous smile. S'why your boy's wild about me."

Ech, no, Diebol was not "my boy," and she didn't know, like I did, the truth to her statement. I waved the bugs out of my eyes and spat another moonflower seed into the distance, blinking to keep ... no, the memory came anyway. Jared Diebol's agonized clenched jaw, his shaking hand as he showed me the video of what his father ordered him to do to her, the near-terror in his eyes as he almost begged me to save her ... even in the heat of the jungle I shivered with the chill of the interrogation center.

Enough of this.

"Why did you take leave?" I texted. "Is everything okay?"

"I can't tell you now. What about you? You still good with Njande?"

My skin warmed again with a sudden flush. I glanced around at the shadows gathering under the dark green leaves. "Well, he's still invisible. I'm still not. People are still trying to kill me for talking to him. Not much change there."

"But you're talking to him?"

"He's just kind of here. I don't hear him talking that much when you're not around."

"You just have to listen differently. It's hard when your inner voice is too loud. And anyway, 'sometimes it's okay to just be together in quiet,' right?"

Mm. I hadn't forgotten that mission, either. But waiting with the bloodsuckers had tired me, and not every memory of Lem made me happy. "Did you text me just to talk about our respective stalkers all night, or are you actually going to give me an ETA?" I asked.

"Yeah, just need that password to get through the EMP shield."

I glanced at Lem's name over the top of her texts, shining in soft emerald to reassure me: yes, her wristband was reading her biometrics, and this was my friend, not a trick from our Growen enemies. The EMP shield was the one thing keeping their enormous gun ships from flying over and decimating our tanks—and without our tanks, those gray foot soldiers might actually have a shot at infiltrating the outer wall that domed over our base like a translucent pearl. Even without the wall, the gunships couldn't just carpet-bomb the jungle without getting in range of our anti-air defenses—but no wall, no tanks.

And no tanks, well. Kids under fighting age would go to the gas chambers. The Growen would divide the soldiers above thirteen: those of us who talked to invisibles could look forward to a swifter, mulchier end, and non-talkers like Seria could expect concentration camps, starvation, and, if they didn't convert, ultimately a needle in the brain.

It's what you get for opposing intergalactic peace, the Growen would say. They'd gotten more aggressive about killing kids now that Bricandor, the Growen leader, thought Njande could use our minds as portals to enter this dimension.

But not today. My wristband vibrated again with Lem's question: "The shield's Password Challenge asks: 'Out of the eater came something to eat; out of the strong came something sweet.' What's the answer?"

"'What is sweeter than honey? What is stronger than a lion?'" I said.

"Ooh, nice. You set that one, didn't you?" I could almost see her flush with happiness—I'd gotten the snippet of prose for *this* password from one of the aged manuscripts she and I had unearthed on our personal mission to uncover more about our ethereally ancient invisible friend.

"Yeah," I answered.

"Man, I can't wait until he breaks in," Lem gushed. "I wish we knew how to open brain portals."

I flinched. I'd grown friendlier with the being, and studying his ancient scripts lit up my brain with questions, statistics, curiosities I found almost as enjoyable as a good tech readout. Still, though, an unease gripped my chest when I imagined anything traveling through my head. "I think I'm good for now. And you don't know for sure that's how Njande works."

"It's gotta be true, though! How else is he gonna save the universe from heat death?"

"We don't know that's it at all. The manuscripts aren't so scientific that way."

"Psh. *I* know."

I smiled. "Like how you *knew* how to rewire your air-rider last summer?"

"Pbhtl\$!!@#" I chuckled at the stream of random characters: she'd whacked the watch. "Well if you woulda *helped* me!" she said. "You're the tech guy, Bereens, not me. I'm the people person."

"You're the people person?" Wow. "Lem, if you're our people person we're a PR nightmare."

"Duh. Why you think everyone always wants to kill us?"

I laughed out loud, not because she was particularly funny but because her silly spirit made me ... joyful? I paused, biting my lip, and glanced up at the open tank hatch where Lt. Seria's head poked out at the sound of my rare happiness. Yeah, I never laughed.

But screw it, I didn't need to be stiff with Lem. "PR person or not, I've really missed you, cadet."

"Yeah, I wish things were different." Then, with uncharacteristic abruptness: "Over and out."

Well *that* sounded ominous.

I dimmed my watch and slumped back against the tank. A breeze tickled my sweating nose; something tightened in the base of my chest. I guess I sighed.

"She's never going to put out, you know," Seria sneered from above.

Watching my texts over my shoulder, now? I let my silence shame her unprofessionalism as I hopped off the tank tread to pace again, hoping Njande's voice could still my growing unease.

Whatever my reservations about our invisible friend, I kept one place in my mind only for him and me. This seat of my will, this throne room full of cinnamon pie and colorful blown-glass figures—it haunted my happier dreams. There I was really me and he was really him. I had first accessed it years ago during my captivity as an eight-year-old, when Njande led me there by the hand in my unconscious stupor to protect my psyche from what adults can do. Now, in moments of meditation, I could stare up at the stars, wrap the color green around my shoulders, and sink into the *feeling* of that inner room: a strong hold, a hug, maybe, from the older brother I never had.

"She's late, you know," I muttered to him, trying to access that feeling now. I never knew if he could hear me, but like a blind man playing darts I'd learned to guess and throw. "Even the day lizards finally shut up."

Njande didn't answer.

I sighed. Maybe his species of interdimensional time-traveling energy being didn't mind awkward silences. Maybe he enjoyed them. He left me in that answerless pause, and with the singing reptiles gone to sleep, the whole planet seemed to hold its breath.

Like Lem, the planet couldn't hold its breath for long. Its glowing lilac twin rose in the sky behind me, brighter than a full moon, and the night lit up with growls, primate-shrieks, and orchestral frogs. This gaudy place never allowed a man any peace.

Seria whispered through my wristband. "Hey Bereens … do you hear that?"

A faint, mechanical buzz began to drown out the blood-suckers humming around us.

Shyte.

My sweat iced. Even Seria feared that sound enough to stay inside the tank. It sounded like a warship fleet. Floating gray rectangles, sky-cities with cannons and blocky underbellies for carrying slaves, cages, and the newest technology in genocide while their bombers covered the sky like monsoon clouds—

"Call it in," I spat into my wristband. "I'm going to get a visual."

My air-rider shuddered as I leapt behind the tank line to mount it. My legs slipped past its metallic, egg-like exterior to seat me on the bike inside; my body rumbled with my ride as the egg coughed to life, and I leaned forward, hands against the windshield to tell it to go. Like a bull escaping its stall the air-rider bucked forward. I squeezed my legs tighter around that internal bike, urging it faster, faster …

Lem always said our air-riders looked like sparrows in a dive.

I pushed mine now above the treetops for a better look as the leaves slapped me, first giant oblong leaves the size of my vehicle, then bushy clusters of small round ones, all different blackish greens in the darkness. Spiderwebs flickered across my face and broke. That threatening buzz intensified—and as I shot out of the hot, tangled canopy, into the moonlight, I saw them.

Thirty warships blocked out the stars.

My heartrate broke into a thumping sprint. I lifted my hand —the warships were about the size of my palm now.

Shyte again. I raised my wristband to my lips.

"Grey Fox, this is Tank Watch 3. We've got 30 L-42s en route, about twenty minutes away by visual estimate, well within the shield."

"Warblepiss!" The Hoernig-species NCO swore with a lippy gurgle—his made-up word would've made me laugh if I'd never seen him impale a man with his face. "I'll call out the sky runners. Scout for foot soldiers, report, and return to your tank line. Understood?"

"Roger, Sergeant. Over."

"Get." He didn't bother to follow protocol with an over and out: Sergeant Commander Strong was as gruff and hard as the horn sprouting from his long snout, and as slippery with decorum as his shiny skin.

I never disappointed him.

I snatched a pair of infrared goggles from under my seat and dove back down into the jungle. Bugs splashed against my goggles with nasty thwicks, stinging my cheeks; leaves slapped me harder now like a halfhearted scolding as the steam thickened over my wet skin. My air-rider covered ground with patriotic hunger, weaving in and out of the tight tree trunks now as I neared the ground.

If my radar didn't pick anything up, my eyes soon would. Silver mirrored orb helmet, gray body in camouflage, anything out of place—I didn't have any kind of spiritual oneness with this blasted jungle, but I knew how to look for the shapes of my enemies. How'd the airships get in? Maybe a hidden electrical station, buried under the roots of a sprawling Bangla tree, opened a gap in the shield? Or I'd find a Frelsi border patrol soldier, my comrade, bleeding against a tree trunk, hanging mutilated from a limb after torture …

Had someone overheard my transmission with Lem?

Filking shyte. A bloodsucker slammed into my snarling teeth. I spat it out. Tasted like rust. Like everything tasted right after electrocution.

Diebol …

I clenched my fists against the windshield, breathed in green, and released. The memory disappeared. I could handle these flashbacks like a pro now. I forced a hateful grin and slipped my head back into the game with the honed focus of a targeting missile.

Yup, there. Enemy scout: gray, mottled uniform with a bullet-shaped matte helmet like a seal's head. Far into the distance behind him I caught a glimmer, a glint, as light from the planet in the sky glanced off the silvery orb helmet of a much more heavily armored blitzer.

Two Growen soldiers. I wheeled to return to base to spread the news. *There are two hundred where you see two.* My mother used to say that about cockroaches.

I raised my wristband to my lips—

The invisibility screamed at me to duck.

Something whizzed over my head—the scout had fired. Not ideal, but I could manage. I leaned in, embracing my metal ride as the landscape blurred by me in infrared streaks and I urged faster, faster, glanced over my shoulder, and drew my pistol behind me. With a deep, slow breath I sensed the electric field of my enemy's body with my fist, and drew the barrel of the gun toward his center of mass ... even moving like this, without a good sight picture, I could aim dead on. I squeezed the smooth grip and tightened my finger on the ice-cold trigger with another perfect breath—

What the bloodseas? The guy had a neodymium mace!

The glowing length of the mace's staff lit up the forest. Spikes on the mace's laser-ball leapt in and out like sine waves, casting shifting red shades across the scout's armor like water as he spun the weapon into a magnetic forcefield in front of him. He rose into the air like a demon from the inferno, strange fire lighting under his boots, and then, like a falling morning star, dove at me to give chase.

Not your run-of-the-mill blitzer scum.

A rush ran through my shoulders, my chest, my lungs; my teeth gritted in a nasty smile. There were maybe six living people who could handle a mace's forcefield like that. I was always hungry to take on the five who weren't me.

"Grey Fox, this is Tank Watch 3, we've got blitzers coming in under the warships from the north, about six kilometers out—they've got a mace warrior with them, over."

My mouth did its job, but my eyes scanned the scene, analyzing terrain for the impending duel. Not much space to swing a mace. The scout could fly with those jet-boots, so I should keep him in the tangled canopy below the tree line to limit his movement. I wanted this mace-man to be Diebol, oh man I did, but I didn't sense Diebol's em-field, so probably not, but you never knew—

"What do you mean, mace warrior?" Strong snapped back. "Electromagnetic, Stygge, what?"

"Sergeant, all I know is I got a flying guy chasing me with a glowing stick, and for some reason we haven't had the chance to break out the teacups for a nice get-to-know-you. I'll be right back after the icebreaker." Chit chat was over. I could barely hear the call anyway over the rushing wind, the bugs, the leaves slapping my arms, and the flying demon gaining on me.

And—now.

I dropped my hand back to the windshield and slid both palms violently to the left. My air-rider whirled to face the scout head on. I drew my mace like a jousting spear. My hand warmed; the short bamboo handle shot out into a full-length staff and light, lasers, and heat washed over the weapon. I leaned in, reached forward, and breathed. Ohhh yeah.

Collision imminent; *get skewered, scum.*

The mace-demon stopped short, hard—if air screeched, his rocket boots would have—and dashed up out of my way. He struck down at me, flipping over me—

One hand blocked over my head with my mace. The other stopped my ride midair; I jumped, stood on the seat, and leapt off of it, outstretched like a lemur to tangle with my enemy in the air—

We plummeted, him first, our maces clashing and flashing around us in the darkness like giant fireflies. He gripped his mace wrong, like a club instead of a staff, and swung at me too hard, and I wanted to correct him like I always corrected Lem—

"You're going too hard out of the gate," I would tell her, *"Skill over strength!"*

But when we landed on the soft soil and I tripped him and he stumbled and I slammed my mace down onto his helmet—well, that was the end of that. He tried to block; he only softened the blow as he crumbled.

A chunk of the enemy scout's helmet split off.

I almost choked.

"Hey."

Lying below me, her braid pinned in the earth by the end of my staff, chestnut skin gleaming with sweat in the starlight and eyes laughing, was Lem Benzaran.

CHAPTER FIVE

Jei

I RIPPED THE INFRARED GOGGLES OFF MY HEAD. THE WORLD SEEMED to spin as my training partner scrambled to her feet, removing her damaged helmet to tangle her long fingers through singed hair.

Lem spoke first, and fast. "Man, it's good to see you. I'm really really sorry about all this, really sorry—my whole platoon, back there, they saw you, and I had to do something about it. I'll let you go now, though, now that they can't see us." She twirled her helmet in her hands, then looked from it up to me. "Look at you being a rebel out here, riding your air-rider with no helmet on," she said. "Here, take this one. You gotta keep everyone safe —yourself, too."

What? She dropped her helmet in my hands with a sad smile, and then whirled to run.

"Wait!" My hand shot out on its own to grab her by the arm, and when she struggled against me, my confusion flared into odd anger. Without thinking my emotions powered an *em-pull*— my negative charges, the chlorine in my nerve cells, flipped to the rear to polarize me like a magnet.

I froze her in place.

"Hey, what the hell, Jei?" she snapped. As if I were the one cavorting around in a Growen uniform.

"You can't just run in and then run off and—" I breathed. "Look, I didn't know it was you! You could've gotten seriously hurt! You have to give me some kind of signal, or—bloodseas, I cut you on the edge of your helmet, Lem."

I relaxed the em-pull, letting her go, and reached to check her forehead—

She batted my hand away, twisting her eyeballs upward as if she could see the blood trickling down her brow. She blew at it and shrugged with a goofy grin. "Eh, I've seen worse." Weird pause. "Hey, uh … you should go now. You got a base to defend."

I narrowed my eyes. "Come on, Lem, you lose duels all the time. No need to be awkward."

"Haha, no. No, that's not why it's awkward. Step back before I turn my boots back on and fry your pasty ass."

"You should have told me you were going undercover. I could help."

Her eyes softened, and for a long second she stared at me with such deep sadness I thought she might cry. She drew a long breath … "I'm not undercover, Jei."

The world became hell.

The warships—the warships broke through the EMP shield right after I texted her. Here she was, scouting ahead for a mess of Growen soldiers, and here I could not believe the conviction in her voice. No. No, she valued her freedom too much, she'd been *through* too much. Quit playing. Punch her playfully in the arm, make the joke go away …

"No more games, Lem," I growled softly.

"You're running out of time," she said. "Go take care of my family before Diebol does."

And with that, flames whooshed around her boots.

I leapt back to shield myself from the licking heat as she hurtled off into the sky, and I scrambled for my air-rider to follow—

"Tank Watch 3, this is Grey Fox, where the strangledip are you?" yelled Sergeant Strong.

Where the ... that ... indeed. I glanced after Lem's disappearing light in the night sky—no, screw it, *screw her*—I glared at the broken headgear she had left in my hands, its visor fractured like the eye holes of a human skull.

Wait.

The scout's transmitter was still intact inside the helmet.

I shook myself off, reawakening with gritted teeth as I ran back for my air-rider. "About twenty seconds away from the tank line, Sergeant," I answered into my wristband:

"I have a way to neutralize the ground forces."

I counted distance on the windshield of my air-rider as I zoomed back to the tanks. With the airships now through the EMP bubble, our anti-air lasers and skypilots might hold them off the base directly, but as soon as they bombed our tanks their overwhelming ground forces would swarm in and wipe us out. I already heard their air-riders whining in the distance behind me ...

I gripped the transmitter from Lem's helmet with my teeth gritted. A quick glance over my shoulder for the incoming ground troops—no, nothing yet.

Seria already knew what to do when I got back.

"Toss it here!" she yelled, popping out of the tank with arms outstretched. I threw Lem's helmet up to her and whirled back into the jungle toward the blitzer line. My eyes darted from earth to sky and back. The buzzing had become a thunderous rumbling: soon the warships would be directly above the incoming blitzers. With the thick jungle canopy below them, the pilots couldn't see the soldiers below, and our shields still blocked their locator signals. They needed their scouts for radio communication.

Or, in our case, for miscommunication. Fight fire with fire, Growen with Growen.

"Seria, you get through?" I shouted to my wristband as the hot jungle "wind" picked up around my air-rider.

"Affirmative! They bought it." Sweet, with that garbled helmet-piece she sounded just like Le—like the scout I'd robbed. "They're ready to fire when I give them the location."

"The blitzers are about six hundred meters from where I am," I answered.

"Be more specific. Hurry before they get a visual!"

More specific? *She better not get me shot.* I leaned in, ducking toward the blitzer line, cursing the loud hum of my air-rider over the singing of the creatures of the night. There—a blitzer's reflective mirror-like helmet. Coordinates?

The blitzer's head swiveled toward me. I pressed my wristband with my mouth to send Seria my location. I didn't have time to check if she got it: with a familiar *zip*, radiating colored shots lit up the jungle around me like I was tonight's victory fireworks. The closest blitzer was shooting flayer cartridges at me.

I didn't return fire. I heard a whine, a distant unlocking *click* of giant doors creaking open far, far away, as the misinformed Growen warships prepared to bomb their own soldiers instead of our tank line.

"Get clear, Bereens!" Seria's voice crackled as she yelled.

Yes, thank you, contrary to appearance I didn't enjoy showering in explosives.

The first bomb hit in the distance. My snark evaporated like shower steam. The forest shuddered as ancient trees splintered behind me in the shock wave and Lem's planet groaned under our crossfire.

Lem.

I changed the channel on my wristband with my lips as another bomb hit, this time closer. The wind of its impact pushed me forward. "I don't know if you heard that, Benzaran, but you better get out of the woods if you don't want to die in Growen uniform."

"Don't worry, I'll make it to twenty-three," she replied. "Standard life expectancy."

She always said that, always reminded me we might not even live past our teens. She usually said that to excuse her need to pack in as much wildness into every day as she could.

I always felt, though, that if tomorrow is uncertain then today should focus on working to make it sure, and as another shock wave threw me forward, this time—shyte! Almost into a tree—I swerved, swerved again—bomb, bomb, another bomb, like the first rain-drops, and then the full storm fell, obliterating everything behind me as heat seared the back of my neck and I shot out of the jungle and tumbled off my air-rider, thrown, rolling in the dirt to duck behind the tank line as our fighter ships took off above me like a swarm of bees toward the warships and blinding light blew past me—

Seria texted me, "high five." Yeah, she was right.

We'd earned ourselves one more day toward twenty-three.

Starlight streamed through the small oval window over my bunk as the entrance to my barracks *splooshed* shut behind me. The sharp, clean creases on my still-made bed warned me dawn was still hours away.

We'd lost a number of tanks to the air raid after the shield opened. You couldn't just pull tanks back away from the line, back into the base under the anti-air guns, not with blitzers on the way: no one wanted the friendly fire hell of a ground fight in the middle of our refugee barracks. But once Seria and I tricked the Growen into demolishing their own ground forces, and we *knew* no blitzers were coming, the tank battalion had been able to move into cover. And the Growen were forced to retreat with colossal losses. It still wasn't safe to, say, fly in to Retrack city to watch air acrobats, but supplies could get in again.

We'd ended the siege.

A black hole settled into my chest, crushing my lungs. She was a blitzer now?

I avoided my bed, closed the porthole cover over my window, and saw the grime on my hands. I couldn't go to bed like this. *Just cleaned these sheets ...*

That wasn't why.

It was too dark. No explosions, no screams, no more orders or debriefs ... I would choke on my own thoughts in here.

I went back outside to walk the base's shadowed streets. Clarity didn't come. I leaned against the white wall around the base, fists clenched—needed to do something, to beat something. Ran to the garages to fix my crashed air-rider. As I twisted and re-set its body I plotted.

We did well, taking out most of the Growen foot soldiers using their own warships. Of course, we still would have lost the fort if not for our crack swarm of fighter pilots and fantastic anti-aircraft lasers. But that wasn't my part to play. We each did our part. We all survived.

But Lem gave up passcodes that could have killed us all? Lem, who couldn't keep her mouth shut when anyone needed telling off, wanted to join the Unification Cause to control all speech? She ranted for hours about the right to be different. She had trouble toeing the line in *our* army; I couldn't imagine her choosing one that wanted to remake the universe into one homogeneous, watered-down culture.

My fingers slipped in the grime around my engine. "Stupid new coating," I spat. The scent of ground metal and oils met me as I wiped my nose ...

If the Growen had entered our fort, they would've taken all the refugees we guarded, sorted them by species, and gassed them. That included Lem's little siblings—babies, almost, kids we trained to become deadly weapons because otherwise the Growen would slaughter them like a rat infestation. What did she say? "Take care of my family before Diebol does?"

She had to have lied about being undercover. Maybe someone was listening.

Dangit, of course. Of course she'd lied, the crazy girl believed connecting to Njandejara's energy would save the universe from impending thermonuclear collapse. Diebol would never let her join up with that kind of crazy. There wasn't room for fanatics and weirdos in Diebol's vision of the universe—there wasn't room for anyone *but* weirdos in Lem's.

I yanked another bent metal panel off the air-rider's back end. "Is he monitoring you?" I asked into my wristband.

I waited several minutes for a response. When I'd almost given up, she texted instead of speaking. "No. This is real."

I closed my eyes and leaned my head back against the wall. My throat hurt. Probably from all the smoke earlier. That, not a complete loss of control, was why the question, as I squeezed my fist over my wristband, rumbled in a low growl: *"Why?"*

Another long pause. Knowing Lem, it meant she was typing a colossally long answer.

No. It wasn't long.

"You don't actually care why."

"Try me."

"There's no answer you'll take to justify joining people you call kid-killers."

"I call them that because *they kill kids!*" I hissed. It was good she wasn't there in person. I wanted to fight, and I wanted to fight hard.

She … didn't. "I'm sorry. I'm really sorry you caught me. I didn't want this. I wanted to just keep talking."

I laughed, and it wasn't a happy laugh. "What do you mean just keep talking, Lem? You were going to keep sending me messages, pretending to be away somewhere, until how long?"

I could almost feel the shame radiating off the text. "Until 23."

"Until *I'm* twenty-three, you mean, because you just tripled your life expectancy by switching sides."

The next text returned like lightning. "I get it. I'm stupid. I just thought, you know, *because you kept talking to Diebol for years.*"

I couldn't even answer that. The forced, sick, painful connection I used to surveil the guy I hated most? That she would even pretend to be jealous of that, to want something like that with me, when she knew me and knew I hated it—

"I'm sorry. I'm sorry, that was messed up to say. I'm so sorry. Here, you want a why, here's a why." The block of text appeared so fast I wondered if she'd copied and pasted it. "Maybe I just got tired of the hypocrisy back home. We talked about freedom, but the Frelsi Command controls your every move. I know it's for 'safety,' but with the Growen, we promote safety all the way. Throughout history the most dangerous cities have always been the ones with the most divided, different populations. No more different, no more hate speech, no more war."

They were Diebol's words. "Okay, is he listening in on you?"

"Jei, come on, you know he'd never let me join, not with Njande and stuff. I stole one of our prisoners' identities to get in."

Smart. Skip basic, show up with a little intel as a hero. Now her statement four months ago about getting to know the prisoners as people meant something.

I took a violent wrench to the back of the air-rider's engine. "Njande and stuff?" My teeth clenched. "You really think Njande's okay with an organization that kills kids?"

"I think I can reform the Growen, Jei. Just gotta get high enough. End killing, and instead capture and educate everyone in the way of peace, you know?" Beep. Before I could answer, another text, again as if copied and pasted. "Remember when we first talked about becoming so powerful we didn't have to kill to stop anyone from hurting us? I got it figured out, man. It's all in our heads! Once I get into everyone's heads, no one will want to hurt anyone else. And the Growen's got the best machinery in place to make that happen."

I laughed again—again, not a happy laugh, just a sound to let out the steam and scorn building in my chest. Sure, this, this explanation sounded insane enough. This sounded more like her. But like her in a terrible way, where it was no longer *haha Lem you're so crazy* and more like *oh shyte, Lem, you're actually crazy.* "So you're gonna take over the Growen single-handedly," I said.

"Nah. I'm gonna use the Growen to take over the Frelsi. Then I'll use both to save the universe from heat death. That was my job, right?"

Oh my freaking—"Lem!" I yelled into my wristband. "Drop the pretty language, you're talking about murdering your family!"

"Njande will protect them."

"You almost got our entire base killed! We lost tankers today, Lem, bloodseas, I thought you were joking about blowing Seria up, and here you almost made it happen!"

"Eh, you don't like her anyway."

"Holy shyte Lem," I breathed. It disgusted me, deep in my core, to read that name, to see *Njande*, and in the next text watch her joke about the death of one of our own. I couldn't couple this disgust with her, with my friend; I couldn't fathom, I just —this was—

No one said anything for a long time.

Finally, she turned on voice. "Jei?" Her voice wavered. I couldn't do anything but listen; I was too angry to talk. "I'm really sorry," Lem whispered. "I never wanted to be on opposite sides. I missed you and thought I could see you today, make sure when everything went down you didn't get—get—please, you gotta trust I just don't want you to die. I had to give them those codes. But I knew you'd find a way to out-strategize me tonight. That's what you do, man. Now they'll move me somewhere else and we'll never fight each other again."

"You're telling me you're betraying us for our good." I wanted to say that she'd used me, but I couldn't. That sounded so weak.

"I'm so sorry. Jei …"

"What?"

"Njandejaratanderovasaa." She had the gall to say a blessing from Njande to me. Like a code, to tell me she was still on his side. As if he could side with anyone who aided our enemies.

She ended the transmission, and the engine dropped out of my air-rider onto the ground with a clang.

CHAPTER SIX

Lem

LEM BOWED HER HEAD AND BIT HER LOWER LIP, DUCKING TOWARD the shadows as the groans of the dying met her at the entrance to the Growen transport. The metallic scent of blood blended in the air with cleaning fluid, hot steel, and men's sweat; she stepped over the wounded, squeezing by the benches lining the walls, to sit as far back in the corner as she could. The floor shook, and rolled, and the transport lifted off.

"Zej, what the hell are you doing back there? Get over to the door, last one in guards the hatch."

"Yes sir." But Frank Zej—Lem—groaned inside. The projection on her face only lasted a few hours without her helmet, and Lem was notorious enough for her Frelsi work to know that the instant her disguise faded she'd meet a new friend named "big burning hole in the chest."

Can't escape your past, Lem grinned. It wasn't a real grin. It was as fake as the rest of her thoughts these days.

Hush. She was sweating. Why was she sweating? She'd made it out alive without ruining too many things or killing anyone she loved. The atmosphere roared as they left it behind to plunge into the twinkling stars where space sprinkled ice crystals on the windows. Too cold to sweat. Shivering. Shivering and sweating at the same time. *Bloodseas, Jei.*

It felt like fear. Like fear about to explode and make her do something stupid. *Nah, girl, just gotta let off a little steam.* She turned to the blitzer beside her, a blitzer she liked because she knew something about him he didn't: he'd helped kidnap her last year. "Hey, Banks."

He turned his head. "Yeah, Zej?"

"What'd the ghost say when the waiter got his order wrong?"

"I dunno. What?"

"I was ex-spectre-ing better service."

"Man, that's horrible," Banks sighed. But the corner of his mouth turned up. She'd raised his spirits. They weren't hard to raise: in one offensive last month, when both of them had been stuck in a canyon together with a dead body for days, they'd kept each other sane by making morbid jokes at it until rescue.

And, although Banks didn't know it, she made him laugh back *then*, too, when she was Lem Benzaran his prisoner instead of this pink-haired albino with an untamable five-o-clock shadow. She and Jei didn't get along at all back then, but—

Shyte, Jei.

No, keeeeep talking. "Okay, Banks, I got a question for real now. Like a riddle."

"Go ahead."

"Girl discovers she's got an evil twin. Well, not a twin exactly. But someone just like her, only cooler, stronger, better. Then she finds out her twin's gonna eliminate, like, a million innocent people."

"Wow, alright."

"So girl goes to stop this twin, but she's hidden, right—the only way to find the twin, to ask her why, to get her to stop, is to join this weird murder-cult. But they got people in the murder-cult who can read your mind, so you gotta brainwash yourself to get in."

"Whoa." Banks gripped his hair with both hands, literally sitting on the edge of his seat. "Like the Frelsi."

"Sure. So here's the question," Zej leaned in. "How much self-brainwashing you think you could handle before you actually changed your mind?"

"Whoaaaaaa." Banks whistled, and shook his head. "Q-psh," he said finally, making an explosion sign with his hand by his forehead. "Your mind, man, your mind is crazy. You always make me think, Zej."

Lem nodded. *Answer the question, dammit.*

He didn't. "It's good to have someone like you around to bring a little oddity into terrible situations, Zej." Banks sighed, patting Lem on the shoulder. She returned a sad grin for his sake, and then they both turned to look at the floor with folded hands.

Shyte, shyte, shyte, why won't you just answer the question? How slow did this dang transport move, anyway? Did it take *that* long, really, to get to Alpino? The air conditioning blowing on her face made her feel so naked. Everyone else had a helmet on, and she was the one person who actually needed one. The thin plastic sticker behind her ear, the tape holding her holographic lie in place—she wanted to touch it, to make sure—

She stopped herself. *It's still there. Messing with it might turn it off.*

"Commander Diebol wants to see you when we land, Zej."

"Yes, sir."

She forced herself to feel elated. She'd waited months to get an opportunity alone with him, and after how she'd gotten those codes, he had to praise her.

... Unless he knew she'd lost her helmet and caused the subsequent bloodbath.

Ugh. There was no winning here.

Jei

My morning after was like a hangover, a break-up, and a funeral all took a dump on my face—like the beginning of a bar joke leading up to a drunken pun. I couldn't sleep, so I ended up in the next day's briefing exhausted and angry at everything from the tattered brown curtains to the orange nutrient slop that reminded me of prison.

Orange is the best kind, Lem and I used to joke.

It was a working breakfast. Commanding officers from all weapons classes and job descriptions slurped glowing goo in the weak, speckled morning light of the conference room; hushed whispers covered the creaking of the dark wooden chairs carved for various alien bodies. On the holograph-studded metal table, tentacles, fingers, and pens tapped and scribbled symbols that represented people in life and death. I was reporting on what had happened in my little corner of the battlefield, and also shadowing these geniuses to learn leadership as they dug into minutia and strategy, touching the soul of war beyond her violent body.

"I say we retaliate while they're down on ground forces. That's the game, beetlekissers, that's the only game," Sergeant Strong was saying, rubbing the horn on his nose.

My commanding officer, Colonel Win, nodded. Normally it would've thrilled my blood to watch these two colossal Hoernigs go back and forth, Win's calm silence balancing Strong's colorful moods as their flat brown amphibian faces reflected light with the intensity of mammalian sweat ...

Today, meh.

Today I kept remembering my former commander, Captain Rana, and the way Lem and I bickered in front of him when he sent us on our first mission. Bloodseas, he would've loved to see the Paradox Order we'd created, would've loved the way Seria and I used the Growen forces against themselves last night. *"You're growing, growing, growing,"* he would've said. I missed that. Missed him, and now Lem, too.

I had to know.

"I'm sorry," I tapped Win's shoulder, my voice low. "Why didn't you tell me?"

"What's that, cadet?" Strong snapped. "You got something you can't say to us all?"

Win held up his bony, ridged hand. Strong laid off. "Tell you what, cadet?" Win asked.

"You knew Lem deserted. You knew it four months ago when she first left, when you started giving me the—" I held my tongue and didn't accuse a superior officer of giving me the runaround. "Why couldn't I know about my partner, sir?"

Win and Strong glanced at each other. Other soldiers around the table crossed their arms or sighed. "We're not here to smooth over your lady problems or babysit your feelings, Bereens," Strong barked. "We're here to plan an offensive. You report on what you saw, and otherwise shut up."

I smiled, eyes narrowed. It's not a good thing when I smile in public. "What I saw, Sergeant, is that Lem Benzaran almost killed us all yesterday. Because no one warned me she'd defected, I gave her our perimeter entry codes, and she subsequently let in all of the Growen ground forces."

"Strong?" a large tentacled Tridian gurgled through his robotic voice box.

"That's an incomplete picture. Everything proceeded as planned." Strong started to brief on how Seria and I then used Lem's helmet to destroy the Growen ground forces; Colonel Win tapped my shoulder, and nodded his horn toward the door as he rose.

I followed him through the polymerwall. It softened as it recognized our DNA and let us pass into the whitewashed cement hallway. Other soldiers darted like lizards out of the path of Win's broad-shouldered shadow.

Maybe here it would all make sense. Maybe here he told me I'd messed up, she was undercover, and he didn't want to blow her cover in front of the others.

We turned another corner, pushing through a polymerwall

into the office that used to belong to Captain Rana. Gone were the Wonderfrog's lush plants and wet spray-hoses that used to hydrate him; Colonel Win needed only a simple desk, and one small wooden plaque on the wall with four Hoernig letters burnt into it. Once upon a time, before the interrogation center, I would've appreciated the office's respectable simplicity.

Now the emptiness clenched my whole body. I pinned myself against the wall.

Win didn't bother to sit down. He whirled and locked the wall as soon as it *splooshed* shut behind me. "I know you don't want sympathy. I won't pretend to give it," he said. "We were taking orders from above. I questioned them—Strong did, too— but we were told because of your mental health history that your performance would suffer if you knew, and that her abilities posed no significant threat. You said yourself last year she couldn't even em-push yet."

Uh … "Sir, how did you know I said that?"

"The Paradox Project was my business for a while."

The Paradox … *Project*? "I didn't know Rana's files were that … detailed." I shivered, struggling to keep my attention off the empty room as my brain processed. Lem and I had started the Paradox Order privately without knowing about any secret file, just requesting missions as we saw fit; heck, I thought Command just called us "Paradox Warriors" as a joke.

Maybe Lem left when she discovered her Paradox Order had a Big Brother.

Wait. "I'm sorry, *was* your business, sir?" I asked.

"Before Benzaran defected the Project moved under other supervision. Your everyday military duties still fall under me. Your Paradoxes do not."

My head spun. The room was so empty. So very, very empty. I gripped the color green close to my chest and coughed. *Focus.* "If I ask who supervises that … program … now, would you tell me, sir?"

"Your father."

"The admiral?" I gripped my hair in my hands. "But we're just cadets!"

"You don't believe that." Win crossed his arms with a half-grin. And he was right: I didn't. We'd run what, fifty-six world-saving missions, since we escaped the interrogation center? And Lem wasn't even seventeen? No wonder we'd caught the Admiral's attention.

But ...

I rubbed the back of my neck and stared at the floor.

"You look unsatisfied," Win said.

"I can't believe Strong's briefing *right now* that you let me give Lem the codes on purpose to ... what, trap the Growen? I don't believe that's true, and even if I did, it's—weird." I swallowed. "I guess I was hoping to get chewed out for blowing Lem's cover. I don't want this to be real."

"Sorry to disappoint, cadet."

I forced an exhale, still staring at my boots. My voice sounded small to me when I spoke again; I took a deep breath to force back some bass. "Why did she defect, sir?"

He didn't answer. I looked up, and suddenly realized he looked deeply uncomfortable. His smooth, hairless brow twitched, and his lips turned down. He tapped his thick, padded fingers against his ridged knuckles like tiny drums. "Your father was the last person to talk to her," he said. "He might know."

I started. "Wait, the Admiral took over our account, and *then* Lem disappeared?"

He nodded with uneasy, narrowed eyes, as if guilty about giving me hope. "You're wondering if your father sent her on an undercover mission I don't know about," he said.

"And kept it secret from me so a fight between us would legitimize her to the Growen." I gritted my teeth. "Diebol tried something similar last year."

"The thought's crossed my mind." Win admitted. "It's just ... it's not likely, Jei. The admiral will be on Luna-Guetala next week if you'd like to ask him what happened."

A week? What would happen to Lem within that week?

"But I assume you're able to call your father before then," he added.

Yeah, he assumed a lot. The last time I even thought of the Admiral as father I was splayed out delirious under torture. "Sir, who told you I'm related to the Admiral?"

"You just did. I guessed." He stood up straight. "Let's go."

I followed him out of his horrid empty office with a backward glance at the illegible plaque. I didn't have to ask Win not to spread talk about me and the Admiral: we both knew "star soldier" gossip would make the Admiral vulnerable and screw with my apparently all-important "performance."

And blasted bloodseas, what had the old man said now that made Lem leave?

Had to be something undercover. She'd dropped her helmet for me on purpose. That's what she'd said, right? *"I knew you'd find a way."* She'd just played such a good mimic she'd almost fooled me, caught me off guard. I wouldn't normally believe over-honest Lem could run this kind of charade, but hey, like she said, in four months, a person can change. Right?

A heavy hand fell on my shoulder, pulling me very suddenly out of my grieving denial.

"Jei," Colonel Win said.

"Yes sir."

"I'm sorry about what you're going through. I can't pretend to feel what you're feeling, but I know if Sergeant Strong or any of my other close battle-brothers went AWOL, I'd hurt. And honestly," he paused, and sighed. "I would have told you, if it'd been up to me. It seems heartless to play two kids off each other."

"Thanks." Eh, I should probably look him in the face when I said that. I did, and the sad, sympathetic smile on his porous cheeks almost made me smile, too.

CHAPTER SEVEN

Lem

CLINK.

A drop of sweat rolled down Lem's nose to plop onto the shimmering visor of her bowed helmet.

"Supply told me you requested a new helmet immediately after the battle."

Shining black leather boots planted squarely in front of her face. Tiled marble floor bit her kneeling knees. Aching heat screamed at her to tear off the stuffy armor and run from the rough tenor of the voice she still heard in her dreams.

But she didn't.

Lem stared straight ahead at the boots and regal office beyond them, as if looking up into those green, green eyes would give her away. After a year away from him, and four months of sneaking around under his nose, she was once again in the presence of the Growen's rising star.

Commander freaking Diebol.

He continued: "Your helmet's interesting to me, you see. Ask me why."

Still no eye contact. Focus on the knees, focus on the knees ... "Why, sir?"

"Well, it's interesting, because when air command bombed

our troops—our own soldiers—the coordinates they received came from your helmet."

Lem sucked in her breath. *Whaaaaat, no ...* A jittery attempt to feign surprise flitted over her hidden face for any mind-readers listening—

No. Stupidity was easier: "So *that* was how they pulled that off," she breathed aloud, visualizing the bone jutting out of the hamburger meat of that one blitzer's charred leg to create real, visceral horror in her voice. Her stomach churned. "Sir, my headgear must have been stolen. I was attacked by a Frelsi scout shortly before the bombing—my platoon-mates can confirm—"

"They could confirm, perhaps, if they weren't all dead," Diebol sneered. Lem cringed. While she never loved her platoon, the Paradox way was to defeat the enemy without killing, if possible—to become so powerful fighting became pointless. That ... wasn't always possible.

"My armor's biometrics should have a record of the fight," Lem added—hopefully?

Diebol didn't reply. The silence wailed. *Dear mind-readers*: she was a loyal Growen soldier and couldn't recall losing her helmet. If she did, by chance, give her helmet to anyone, she did it in a moment of fluttery stupidity, joking around with an old friend for forgetting his headgear—no malice, she didn't know what would happen, she swore! *Shyte shyte shyte shyte shyte ...* "I can't believe I got played like that," Lem muttered. "How do I take responsibility for my failure?"

Still no answer. Lem struggled not to fidget from her kneel. *Shyte, what do I do? Do I offer a punishment for myself? I'm a loyal Growen soldier. I regret what happened with my gear, believe me, Captain!*

"I don't *dis*believe you, soldier," Diebol said.

"Soldier"—Jei talked like that. *"I miss you, cadet." "I don't disbelieve you, soldier."* Was Diebol mimicking Jei's inflections on purpose?

And she looked up.

Diebol's emerald eyes twinkled in his ashen axinite face; the spiked gauntlets on his wrists cast long shadows over the sheen of his black leather vest as he crossed his arms. He was smiling.

"Sir?" Lem asked.

"You like that word," Diebol smirked. "Soldier."

Why—oh, biometrics. Diebol pulled up her armor's readout on the screen beside him, toggling between Growen profiles to show her without a word that he *knew* the beat of every warrior's heart. Blood pressure, sweat output—her old Frelsi commander monitored that stuff, too, to check health in the field.

Hush, brain. The Frelsi were dead to her. Now it was just her and Diebol. And also this woman-shaped chair beside her. And the glowing compuwall beside Diebol, and the marble floor …

"You have a beautiful office," she said, interrupting whatever he was saying.

"Ha!" His fingers flickered over the edge of a knife, spinning it in his hand as he sat down and leaned back with his boots on the shining black desk. "It's repulsive, isn't it. All this obsequious flamboyance, while our soldiers bleed, struggle, *die* to birth a new galaxy … I would strip it down and sell the materials to pay for better armor and food for the troops, if I were High Command."

Wow. Not a hint of bitterness in his voice—just simple facts everyone knew, as easy as introducing himself. This was who he was. The reformer.

"But Bricandor believes in control via imposing and impressive imagery." Diebol nodded toward the High Commander's silver statue behind him. The long train of the robe, the bowed bald head, hands raised as if in prayer, eyes closed like a meditating monk, all belied a kind old man trying to become a religious icon.

"I like the statue," Lem said. "It reminds me of what we're fighting for—universal peace."

Diebol scoffed and jumped to his feet. Man, why couldn't this guy sit still? What—

He leapt over his desk. Midair he pointed his hand and a chair zipped across the room, drawn by his em-pull to slide under him. He landed in it to sit right in front of Lem's kneel, facing her.

Gulp. No space, no division between, only equality and the horrible, horrible memory of sitting this close, across from him, with electrical lines strapped to her feet as he tried to brainwash her and those green, green eyes pleaded with her to join him and he steeled himself against her screams and she could feel his desperation and her own and sweat drenched the both of them and her need to escape ached within her—

"Don't be so intimidated, soldier," Diebol whispered.

Breathe! That's not who we are anymore. Lem glanced at the compuwall. Her heartrate was up, way up. She sighed and brought it back down.

"I'm sorry, Captain, I just—we lost so many today, and it's all my—"

"Shut up." Diebol leaned back and folded his arms. "I saw your biometrics jump when I mentioned the dead. I don't doubt it makes you upset—whether because you're in trouble, or loyal to your fellows, I don't know, but for the moment, I don't care. Listen."

Lem closed her mouth. So ... she *wasn't* in trouble?

"I like you. Your failure to maintain control of your helmet means you're not long for this force, or maybe even for this world. But I do like how you got those shield codes. So I'm going to tell you a secret."

Okay, so she *was* in trouble. He knew she'd talked to Jei? She should run?

Diebol leaned forward. His eyes seemed to burn through her visor into hers. He folded his hands, hands she *remembered* gripping her wrists, struggling to *control* her as he yanked her against his chest. She wanted to scream and push him away—

Movement fluttering through the edge of her visual field showed her heartrate skyrocketing to the top of the compuwall's chart. *Breathe!*

"This war isn't about peace," Diebol said at last.

"What do you mean, it's not about peace?" Lem said, shoveling hot air out her mouth to let off some of the building pressure in her chest. "We're trying to end hateful relationships between people, cultures, and worlds, by turning everyone into one unified whole. With careful government control and education tuning from elite experts, we can have perfect cooperation in all economy, science, and culture. That is peace!"

"Bla bla bla," Diebol spat. "When I want you to recite the indoctrination courses I'll ask you to do so. Until then, I said shut up."

"Yes sir," she blurted.

"That's not shut up." He raised his eyebrows and flicked his fingers, impatient.

Her heart leapt into her throat. "I believe it's shutted up, in the past participle, sir." Silliness—a nervous defense mechanism —used to save her ass all the time with Captain Rana. And hey, a guy can't shoot you if you make him smile, right?

Unless you annoyed him. Diebol narrowed his eyes, fighting the grin on the edge of his lips with a fist.

Lem shut up.

Shyte, as the half-grin flitted across his face she could see he remembered the odd togetherness—*she* remembered, in his stare, the cold floor across her back, the shackles on her wrists, the tension in her muscles as the taut chains pulled ... and the respite. He had been this close to letting her go. *"If we don't hate each other, then what are we?"*

And then with that terrifying energy, the violent spark of murder in his eyes, he popped up to his feet again, hands clasped behind him to walk. "You're not just another screw in the machine," he announced. "I met someone last year, someone who showed me homogeneity, while an easy pathway to peace, isn't always the goal. Some people are unique and have qualities everyone else does not need. It's an exception to the rule of course—uniformity matters. But I realized, soldier, that uniformity isn't the most important thing."

He whirled and twisted his way back to her. She wanted to throw up her arms and protect herself—she steeled herself, still, as he spun around her. "The most important thing!" he shouted.

He leaned over, hands still clasped behind his back, to whisper to her mask. "The most important thing is freedom."

Breathe, Lem, breathe.

She wanted to burst into tears or punch him away. Was he trying to trap her into spouting off Frelsi ideology? She didn't believe that stuff anymore, she—

"There's a being out there consuming minds," Diebol said. "He keeps people from seeing reality as it is—he lodges in your —I guess it's your frontal cortex, I don't know." His fingers twitched; he clenched them over his forehead as he whirled away from her. "He gets in there." He spun back and jammed his fingers into her helmet. Lem jerked away, but he gripped her head in his hands; his breath misted her visor; her heart threatened to explode. "And until I defeat this being ..." His hoarse whisper made her mouth dry. "The universe is doomed to become forever enslaved."

Lem's lips fluttered. *Say something, say something!* Lem didn't even bother to control her vitals now in the panting silence as Diebol gripped her helmet, his face inches from hers on the other side of the visor—you'd be crazy *not* to respond with terror to this erratic flurry. "What—what's the being called?" she squeaked.

"Njandejara," Diebol whispered.

And he unclipped the safety that pinned her helmet to her uniform.

Click.

The air-tight seal whistled open. Lem's hands leapt to catch the mask by the rim, but Diebol snatched it away—she brushed her finger across her ear—no, wait, no!

Welp, the helmet was off now.

Diebol stared, his head cocked to the side, clearly not expecting the face he saw. In the nakedness Lem forced herself to believe that meant the transparent projection was working. Her mouth ran with Frank Zej's masculine rasp. "Sir, I need my helmet for combat. I'm—I'm not going to lie, sir, I'm very uncomfortable with this level of personal space. Are you—are you into me, sir?"

"What?" Diebol snapped, jerking away from her. *Yup, let's roll with weird.*

"You're all up in my face, sir. With the freedom thing, are you trying to tell me that you're—like, into me?"

"Aaalright you're dismissed. Go report to disciplinary and legal for processing for court martial." With an embarrassed, mumbling growl the Growen commander yanked Lem to her feet, slammed her helmet into her arms, and shoved her toward the exit. The polymerwall softened to let her pass and *schlooped* shut behind her as it hardened, locking her out in the hallway.

Blood rushed to Lem's face so fast she almost passed out.

She'd survived.

CHAPTER EIGHT

Jei

I PRESSED MY FINGERS TOGETHER, FORCING MY MIND INTO meditation, reaching out past the cool darkness of my bedroom.

Don't check the Diebol-channel.

I opened one eye. That was weird.

Don't check your channel to Diebol, the thought repeated in the whoosh of the air conditioning, and the beat of my heart. *Don't do it.*

I shook the thought off my shoulders. That couldn't be Njande—seemed so illogical. Had to be just my own self arguing with me.

Diebol

Jared Diebol awoke, sweating and clutching his sheet.

Someone was trying to enter his mind.

He blinked in the darkness of his sleeping pod for a moment. No light. No noise. Nothing but his own breathing sounded in the capsule buried beneath the prairie. After the long day sorting out crisis response, he needed sleep, and no one in the Growen Army dared disturb him here.

No, someone *else* had awakened him.

Oh, *yes.*

Diebol smiled. "Haven't heard from you in so long, Jei," he murmured, laying back down to stretch and fold his hands behind his head. "I'm not even sure I still remember how to do this." He closed his eyes and dreamt of the color green …

Diebol's consciousness blinked into his "brain-radio," the mind-channel he shared with his worst enemy and only friend. It was as if he'd never left. The same ivory walls graced the long hallway that led out of Diebol's mind and into Jei's; at the end of the white hall floated the same dark space of nothingness, and, beyond the darkness, the same wooden cage gathered dust.

Diebol's smile grew. He could just *feel* the glowering from Jei's hallway on the other side of the cage. Diebol stood, brushed himself off, and straightened his black leather vest with a snap. "So many memories," Diebol growled, cracking his knuckles as he walked.

The hallway had healed. Last time they'd talked, the wall's cracks had oozed blood, smoke graffiti'd across every surface with dark scenes, names, and codes. Now Diebol could almost see his own scarred face gleaming in the polished white; his boots didn't even squeak on the clean floor.

No squeak … hmm, *too* quiet. Diebol blinked, and changed the sounds in the channel so Jei could hear him coming. There: the rustle of pants, the soft *thwup, thwup* of bootsteps. Good.

It *was* Jei. It wasn't a false alarm. Something pounded in Diebol's chest with each soft footfall. Something stole his breath. He refused to doubt; it wasn't in his nature, he told himself …

And at the end of the hallway, oh sweet universe, Diebol was not disappointed.

In the cage, grinding his teeth and spinning an illusion of his mace, paced Jei Bereens.

Oh, a stressed Jei Bereens, the best kind. His flaxen hair clung wet to his bronze forehead; anger marred almost every feature in his bitter mutt face, from hard chin to soft nose to rudimentary teenage five-o-clock shadow. Jei always kept *something* of the miserable eight-year-old whelp he'd been back when Bricandor captured him the first time.

Diebol opened his side of the cage and stepped inside.

Jei charged before Diebol could even close the door behind himself. Diebol slipped to the side. Jei raised his mace overhead—

Then stopped himself, as if suddenly remembering where they were. He stepped back with a restrained curse.

"I didn't know you could dance," Diebol laughed.

"Where is she?" Jei snapped.

Oh dear. Bricandor the Mind-Reader said he'd heard that question in the ether a great deal lately; the Growen couldn't afford to expose Her.

Diebol pursed his lips and chose his words carefully. "You don't expect me to just tell you like that." He nodded toward the game board scratched onto the floor in the center of the cage. "Sit down. Let's play."

Jei scowled.

"Bricandor's not torturing me this time, Jei," Diebol added with a soft laugh. "You can't just overhear sensitive information from me anymore."

Jei's glare could've started wars. He stepped away, over the game board, and sat down cross-legged by the pile of twigs on his side of the cage. His suspicious eyes never left Diebol's face.

"You say that like it was my fault. Don't try to play me," Jei said.

"Oh, but it is your fault. Every time I've been whipped, electrocuted, cut, or burnt, it was because you'd shown up." Diebol sat across from him. "And I thank you for it. I wouldn't be the man I am today if my Teacher didn't use the lash to inculcate his lessons." Diebol nodded toward the twigs, and the game board. "Go ahead. Make the first move."

Jei dropped the first stick diagonally across the middle square on the floor. "What are you doing to make her like this?" he asked. *Make* Her? Ha, as *if* Diebol could have created Her. He wished. Bitterness surged between his clenched teeth like sour spit—*my new favorite*, Bricandor had called Her. Bricandor, the father of them all, who betrayed his loyal sons by cavorting with invisible monsters like a common Contaminated fool …

Diebol responded with another stick, diagonally, across the space beside Jei's. An aggressive move, for sure: the goal was to rope off the most territory while making diamonds and triangles to rack up extra turns, and when Diebol felt happy, he almost always played his pieces close to Jei's side. Goodness … how long since anyone had played with him? He would ask Jei, but the Paradox Warrior was busy prattling on with inane questions about Her as if game time was snitch time.

"Are you drugging her?"

Six months, at least? His life had been work, sleep, eat, for six months? *Did he just ask if we drug Her?*

"Is it blackmail?"

No, seven months. *Goodness.* Diebol really needed to get out more. For his health. Let's see, if Jei put his piece there … Diebol could then …

"I know if anyone could convert her you could. I just can't believe—look, I need to know how." There was pain in Jei's voice.

Diebol crossed his arms with one brow raised. "Will you take your turn or not?"

"Answer at least one question!"

"You know this doesn't work like that." Diebol wasn't about to discuss sacred Stygge affairs with his mortal enemy. He was here for one thing, and one thing only: to play the game.

"Come on, like you don't want to gloat," Jei prodded.

"Why would I gloat? We've only just started," Diebol laughed. With a nod toward the board: "Take your turn or I'll take it for you."

Jei slapped down another stick, going for a triangle to buy an extra turn. "Playing dumb isn't your style, Diebol," he growled.

"No, it isn't." Diebol sighed as he laid his twig in the far-left corner, near Jei's foot. It wasn't Her Jei wanted, it seemed, after all. Diebol tested a theory ... "Remember when Benzaran played this with us?" he asked. "Your hurry reminds me of her."

"*Benzaran?* Didn't you always call her Lem?" Jei's eyes burned. His hand hovered just above the game board, clenching around his next stick like a knife.

Eff. Diebol looked away into the nothingness and rubbed the back of his neck. He hated himself for the knot in his throat. It was nothing: over the past year he'd learned to swallow it. But that was because she was Benzaran, not Lem. "Distance, Jei," Diebol said. "I need distance."

"Could've fooled me," Jei scoffed.

Ah, there it was. Well, that was what you got for being distracted. Diebol saw Jei properly now: the spoilsport glowering, the grouchy hurry, the violent mental construct of the mace burning into the floor beside him—the Paradox Warrior was *jealous.* And the soldier who'd stolen the Frelsi codes, and then lost his helmet?

I knew it.

How delightful. Diebol suppressed the urge to chuckle. He rubbed his hands together with reserved glee instead, because not only did Jei know nothing about Her, Jei was miserable enough to betray his hidden partner.

Wait. After all that spectacular teamwork, Jei would betray his undercover partner?

Possibly a trap, then. Best play this next move carefully ... let Jei keep talking until all the cards hit the table. Diebol placed his next twig closer to his own side. "Are you falling for your partner?" Diebol teased.

"Funny question coming from her boss."

"I wonder what my 'employee' did to make you so angry," he said.

"Oh man, I wonder," Jei growled. "Guess that riddle just really meant a lot to me, and I couldn't stand to share the joy. What do you *think* Jared?"

"I think it must've been one good riddle," Diebol said. "She didn't pass it along. Mind sharing?"

"If you win. We won't be re-using it, and you're three moves away anyway." Jei slumped against the cage wall with another growl. "I guess I was looking forward to your evil monologue of triumph, or whatever," Jei said. "It would end things. Maybe you know that. Maybe the worst thing you could do is what you're doing now, leaving me in the dark, so I'll never know what happened to my friend." Jei sat up and dropped another stick on the board, leaning toward Diebol.

Diebol didn't lean away; Jei's teeth flashed in his face like the glint off the barrel of a murderer's gun. His voice lowered: *"But at least we both know what's going to happen to you."*

With that last threat, Jei vanished, leaving Diebol alone with the burning mace on the floor.

CHAPTER NINE

Jei

HOT WIND SURGED ACROSS MY FACE AS I LEANED FORWARD, SHOVING my hands against the windshield of my air-rider to urge it on through the Luna-Guetala jungle. Sergeant Strong said we attack first, while they're down—something along those lines, right?

Well then, they could call this taking initiative.

I leaned into the heat as I ducked under a series of thick vines and burst through the humid canopy to soar above the treetops. The closest Growen Transport Center was just another mile ahead, the perfect way to draw Diebol out. His Alpino Command Center might be the brain of the operation, but the Luna-Guetala Transport Centers were its lifeblood, and with the siege lifted and nearby ground forces decimated, I now had a straight shot to cutting an artery.

Landing pads, food-ships, armor-depots … *crush them, starve them all*. It was as if the transport center itself had stolen Lem.

I didn't actually think I'd find her there. She might have passed through here, maybe, if they retreated some of their forces to the neighboring planet, my home Alpino. That wasn't the point. She was dead, and this was my funeral pyre.

I dove back under the treetops. Leaves beat my face as if the forest wanted me to turn back. Something in the back of my mind told me this wasn't me.

But I didn't care. We'd done the impossible before, the two of us, so often, that now I needed to know the impossible could still happen.

I needed to prove Njande was still with me even when she wasn't.

I whispered his name. My shoulders lifted as if I had wings. I raised my hands: thirteen other air-riders in the jungle below me sped up as the weights I'd rigged against their screens pushed them forward. I still couldn't see them, even here, above the thick jade leaves—I trusted the soft pull I felt, from each one, on my wrists, on my fingers, as if the electromagnetic field I controlled was a series of silver threads. I bounced my palms in the air, testing the weight of the crude explosives I'd rigged to each bike's engine. I wove the bikes through the trees like needles through thread, as easily as tracing my fingers along the trails on the map I'd memorized beforehand.

"Njandejara," I said, aloud. Anger drained from my body with every letter of his name, leaving me only with grief, pure and liquid, sparkling through me across dimensions into the Invisible Man, and then, through him, over a thin green thread of memory to someone else at another time. I was connected to the whole world on a crystal stream.

"Njandejara!" I roared, raising my hands as the blue-gray bubble protecting the Growen Transport Center appeared. I didn't know the code to get in. It didn't matter. I'd read the blueprints; the layout of the little fort was open, bare to my mind. I barreled toward the blue EMP bubble amidst screams and gunshots from sentries I barely noticed; from my chest I felt a *pull* as my neurons rearranged their polarities, and I redirected this magnetic em-pull with all my will through the bubble wall to pierce it with a brief, *felt* pop of charge. I couldn't fit through the bubble, but an atom-thin needle could, and like an invisible finger, my concentrated plume of power wove through the shield, past the buildings, the people, through this and that polymerwall as I closed my eyes. It was like feeling through a bag I'd packed myself, only the bag was a city, and in a second I found that room, in that security office, and that computer that controlled the wall I was hurtling toward.

Yank! I em-pulled the switch—the shield protecting the camp flickered off just before I hit it.

Suddenly the transport center was all around me. I gasped for air like I'd just come out of the water—wow. Wow, I was in.

Growen blitzers spilled out of the buildings in waves as I arrived with my thirteen explosive air-riders. Shots flew past me, got caught in my magnetic field, and fell momentum-less to the ground. *"This isn't me"* flitted through my mind as the concentration, the spirit within me covered me, and I was "underwater" again. I ignored the blitzers, brushing them away like toy soldiers with a wave of my hand as I rode my air-rider above them; they tumbled to the side before my invisible em-push. I twirled my left wrist and pointed—*boom*! An explosive air-rider hit the supply depot. I hurled with my right hand, like throwing a grenade—*crash*! The armory went up in colorful flames. *Clap*! Security center exploded as another bomb found its mark.

I reached forward, clawing, and dragged a handful of kicking and screaming blitzers through the air, out of their barracks, saving their lives before flattening that building, too. No deaths today. Yesterday was another day, but today, everyone would live to *see* me build Lem's pyre.

When the buildings were all burning, when I had no more bike-bombs, I went for their ships. The air molecules around me practically sizzled as I lashed out for their largest transport, the one as big as a whale. It became my club—I hurled it up into the air, closing both fists as if actually holding the thing like a bat from a distance, and—*crack*! I swung my arms and the transport-turned-club crashed into the fleet of smaller transports on the landing pad. I lifted the gargantuan ship to see metallic debris raining down on the broken vehicles underneath it. I swung again. Again. The groan and squelch of titanic, protesting metal ground in unholy symphony for my funeral march.

This wasn't me. This wasn't me at all. My grief was the cord connecting me to a remote control, or some stealth program aching within my DNA, and—

And I accepted that it wasn't me. I'm a killer, just a soldier, but keeping them alive, that was Njande, and he was something else. He was sad, and his grief outweighed mine. It wasn't just this loss. It was all the losses. He felt *their* bereavement, too, Growen and Frelsi ache alike, and through him I felt the weight of the sorrow of the entire war on me—so no deaths today. My fists could clench to crush their bones, but sharp pain in my fingers would stop me; burns in my palms screamed, *pull that man away from the fire, save him!* He wasn't going to die today.

I leapt from my air-rider and let it crash as I knelt to slam my palms against the dust. The last buildings flattened, and it was over.

I rose, and breathed.

Men cowered away from me in the smoldering ruins; no one tried to shoot me, even though now they probably could. The heavy, low scents of roasted rubber and melting plastic filled the air; no one said anything, but the constant crackling of ongoing fire was punctuated with moans.

Something like a thick, invisible cloak, something heavy and covering, fell from my shoulders, and I was just me again: just a grumpy teenager, sore all over, spent, hot in the face, sweaty as a frog in a crockpot and miles away from home without a ride.

I sighed as I rolled my head to stretch out my neck, and with slouched shoulders trudged into the jungle for the long walk home.

"Wish you'd kept me from destroying my own air-rider," I muttered to Njande. I guess that was asking a little much, after what we'd just done. You get a miracle or common sense, not both.

Presently, after about ten minutes of picking my way over fallen logs and climbing mossy rocks, Frelsi ground forces zoomed up on air-riders. I wasn't surprised to see them—the explosions had to have set off alarms on all frequencies.

Sergeant Strong barked and raised his fist. The Frelsi halted behind him. Everyone stared behind me at the smoldering debris of where the transport center wasn't. They could see the destruction, and see me walking away, and no one could say anything.

I didn't feel like explaining.

"Good morning, Sergeant. Fellas," I nodded my greeting and walked right on through their floating herd.

"Dang, son, that's some work, alright," Sergeant Strong muttered.

"Looks like your partner needs to go AWOL more often," I heard Seria chuckle.

I stepped back, twirled her off the air-rider, whirled her into my arms like I was about to kiss her, and held her there for a second as she panted, shocked—and then I smirked, dropped her on the ground, leapt onto her air-rider, and took off back toward Fort Jehu.

CHAPTER TEN

Lem

ONLY THE SOFT SOUND OF MEN BREATHING PUNCTUATED THE SILENCE of the dark barracks room as Lem Benzaran shifted her weight to the edge of her bunk. She had a habit of sleeping in her full armor—an odd habit, but not completely unheard of among the most battle-hardened Growen ranks. Banks, poor dude, assumed she'd picked up the habit from a hardcore ranger unit, and teased her every morning at mess while they downed that ridiculous orange slop.

The best kind is orange, Lem remembered as she stretched her foot down the ladder past Banks' head now. Not a creak.

But the armored foot-gear still clicked on the crisp cement floor in the dark, no matter how she tip-toed every time. She missed her soft worn leathers.

These are better for the kind of combat we do, she corrected herself. She might have her preferences, but she didn't dare doubt the Growen manufacturers had her best interests as a soldier in mind.

As she reached the door, and the soft blue light of the hallway fell over her companions, Lem took one last look back at the bunkmate who'd laughed at her jokes the last couple of months. The other guys in the barracks didn't mean much, but

Banks just had that familiarity and naivete. Look at him now, sleeping with his mouth open and neck exposed like an idiot. A really lovable idiot. Nobody really looked that tough sleeping, after all.

She choked on her sigh, and closed the door behind her.

Commander Diebol was on to her. She'd played the conversation over in her head too many times already, and the more she lay awake thinking about it, the more she risked exposing herself to the Mind-Reader. So even if Diebol *wasn't* on to her, and she was just being paranoid, the paranoia would give her away if she didn't change identities ASAP. And having a court martial on the table wasn't exactly incognito-juice, either.

"It's not fair," she muttered aloud as she crept down the hallway toward the bathroom. "I serve the Growen. S'not my fault I grew up with Frelsi loyalties. I just don't want to get kicked out. I want to help unify the galaxy. I shouldn't have to change who I am to do that."

Liar.

Oh no, not again!

Lem gripped both sides of her head as her heart fluttered in her chest. *There is no lie,* she answered the Accuser. *There is no secret, no lie, no nothing!*

Shyte. She knew better than to use negatives. "There is no" only made you think of the thing you wanted to stop thinking about—like saying "don't think about naked mole rats" made you think exclusively about naked mole rats.

And now Lem was thinking about naked mole rats.

She closed her eyes as she squished through the polymerwall to the restroom and let her should-thoughts reverberate through her brain. *I'm here to help you, Bricandor. Diebol. Whoever else might be listening. The only secret is that I am ashamed of my past.*

In the bathroom, Lem stripped off her chest-plates and gauntlets, allowing herself a wink in the mirror at the handsome pink-haired bandit-man she'd become. She liked Zej. She could've kept him up for years, maybe, if not for Jei. She'd reworked all her ideals to create this honest loyalty to the

Growen without betraying Njande, this careful balance—and now she was *hearing* again.

I found you, it hissed, vibrating through her skull. Lem steadied her breath as the wave of terror traveled through the bone, down her back … she clutched the edge of the sink, choking on thoughts as opaque and rich as oil, and wondered if in the mirror she'd see *Her* peering back.

I found you, found you, nana-nanana, I found you …

Aw, man. No, it wasn't Her. Just It. Just the same old invisible monster that'd hunted her since the day she joined up with the Growen: the twisted *ba-eater,* the ephemeral brain worm Stygge Bricandor kept flitting over his ranks seeking brains to devour and *chi* energies to slurp out. Who would've guessed that the army that wanted to wipe out invisible friends had one in it.

Sometimes it disguised itself to mimic her conscience.

On bad days she thought it was Njande hating her.

I know, I know, I smell like Jei, and you're mad you didn't get to eat him last year, Lem grumbled inwardly. *You probably found me because you recognized him when my platoon got close, and when I engaged, well—you put two and two together.*

She sighed, shaking the monster off her shoulders like a fly as her mind continued its task. She'd considered ending Frank Zej with a fake suicide but didn't want to do that to poor Banks. Instead, from her seat on the porcelain throne, she bit her lip, wet her pencil, and scribbled a different confession on the back of the take-out menu pressed against her armored knee.

Frank Zej told his buddy Banks he couldn't take the guilt of their last mission and wanted to defect to study a different way of peace. Not to the Frelsi—just to freedom. She wove a metaphor for Njande in it and left hidden clues for Banks to discover Njande's voice on his own. She smiled. Maybe one day Banks would search the old Biouk settlements, or plumb the archives of the messages on the extranets …

The cold, invisible slime seeped up her back to her earlobe.

You really think you can bathe in all this evil, just wade right into my territory, covered with just a thin sheen of memory?

Ugh. Lem clawed off the rest of her armor and yanked the chlorinated cleaner from the maintenance hatch in the wall. She doused everything to remove her real DNA for Plan B while she drew on interdimensional biology 101: smaller invisible beings avoided the territorial scent of the biggest one.

So Lem stuffed her head full with her own giant interdimensional, Njandejara: his giant, hammer-wielding human form looming over a bloodstained battlefield; his chimeric lizard-lion Crajk beast form leaping to rescue her friend; his wind-and-fire spirit whispering through the jungle; his still small voice itching at her ears ... the messages he'd left her. *I will never leave you*, her favorite, and another: *The one who overcomes will become a pillar in my house* ... "I would love to help you build your house, Njande."

The memories pushed the ba-eater off Lem like bug spray to a bloodsucker. If she held them tightly enough, she became completely invisible to it, hiding under the shadow of Njande's wings, and the ba-eater couldn't find her. For now, the offended energy being hung snarling in the bathroom air around her like a cloud, filling the small space with its scent: doubt. *Soon enough Njandejara's smell will wear off you. Then I'll get you. I'll wrap you up like a spider wraps a fly, and suck your little brain dry ...*

"What a cute rhyme," Lem said, crouching now to wash her uniform in the sanitizing bin. A few more minutes of meditation and the Accuser would completely miss her identity swap—he wouldn't see where she'd gone, or who she'd become, and he'd have nothing to tell his human pal Bricandor.

Now, in more physical matters, Lem still had to solve this problem of cameras. The Growen believed in security over privacy, so right now, while she did her bathroom business, a camera watched from the top right-hand corner of the waste cubicle. It saw Frank Zej scrubbing like a murderer; she didn't want it to see him transforming into Wandla.

Yeah, wash that uniform. Wash it good, the ba-eater taunted. *Someone else wore it to kill children.*

"Njande is my shield and my *ezer kenegdo*," Lem chanted her safety spell. She felt the Accuser fading further and further back into his own dimension …

Hm. She'd have to switch identities right as she passed through the polymerwall. Both identities had access to this bathroom, she hoped. Of course. Of course they did! If not, the wall would harden mid-transformation and lock her in place to suffocate.

Oof.

Lem stood, stretched, and faced the door, stripped down now to her tank top and her jump pants. She shook herself out, rubbed her hands over her bare chestnut shoulders, and glanced up at the camera. Alright. Just not thinking about metallic ceramic forming over her face, filling her nostrils and eyes in those silent terrifying minutes in airless darkness before she finally lost consciousness and died …

Sure, I can't see you now. But I will. I will see what form you have taken, and when I do, I'm going to tell on you. I'm going to tell little old Grand General Bricandor, and he'll tell little Diebol, and little Diebol will shoot little you before you find Her, and …

"Well then at least I'll be alive outside this wall, huh?" Lem smiled.

She put her hand just behind her ear, index fingernail just under the edge of the strip that projected Frank Zej's DNA, middle finger poised to activate the new girl.

"Whew. Deep breath."

And step.

The soft wall embraced Lem's skin. She made the switch, peeling off Frank Zej and pinching him in her fingers to keep from losing the valuable sliver in the liquid wall as Wandla awakened.

And through the wall, in the dark hallway, a fat shadow emerged from the bathroom. *What was I afraid of? Of course the janitor has access to the bathroom.*

In the darkness, the hallway camera couldn't make out the details of the being that slipped a note under Frank Zej's barracks' room door and slunk away.

CHAPTER ELEVEN
Diebol

So Jei had demolished the Transport Center near Fort Jehu.

The up-and-coming Growen leader strode through the hallway, multitasking like a master. Lights bloomed by his feet as the floors recognized the unique leadership RFID on his passing pendant. He scribbled electronic orders into the air with his transmitter pen as he marched: with one stroke, he sent two Stygge trainees to Frank Zej's room to catch the undercover impostor, and with the butt of his blaster across the walls he rattled the doors of the upper officer quarters.

"All officers to the conference room," he sang.

It was at once utterly delicious and horrible news—the enemy had awakened in full-force at last, and Diebol licked his lips at the chance now to crush him at his strongest. Diebol had pestered his technicians non-stop around the clock to salvage some kind of workable Frelsi computing equipment from the Fort Jehu siege; now, one of the air-riders Jei had flung into the supply depot finally gave them a repairable computer. And that computer had just arrived safe and secure at the hidden space station.

She was awakening.

Jei

I was naked when the world went insane.

Four hours. That's how long it took Diebol to respond to what I did. Enough time to get back to base, tear off my sweaty uniform, and hit the showers. I was sore everywhere. I had a headache, and I still needed to process what had brought Njande so close to me that we could work in tandem like that; my mind felt so full, and I needed the hot steam against my skin and some quality wet alone time to evaporate away all the tension.

Someone yelled at my mind.

I ignored it.

Something sunk in the pit of my stomach.

Oh no.

My eyes closed against the spray from the showerhead; I trotted down the white hallway in my mind to the cage Diebol and I shared.

There, casting amber shadows along the mottled wooden bars, my mace lay, still burning through the ground.

Beside it, seared into the floor on my side, was the riddle I'd written.

Out of the eater, something to eat

Out of the strong came something sweet.

What is sweeter than honey? What is stronger than a lion?

I stooped and rubbed my finger over the blackened wood.

"Classy," Diebol's voice echoed around me. I looked up, around—it was an essence, a voice mail in the mind. He wasn't here. "From the old histories, before the Great Migration. I believe I tried to stop you from gathering some of those records. Of course I read every word myself."

A knife appeared over the wooden floor, scratching a pattern under my words. A whisper surrounded me. "You can't just throw a fit and break the world, you know, Jei."

My eyes widened as I saw the response he'd carved to mine.

Busy "plowing with your heifer." Remember the next part of the old story?

Hint: it involves fire.

Then my shower shut off, drawing me back into the real world with a rush of cold.

"What the—"

The lights flickered out.

Darkness brought silence, a weird silence without the humming of the polymerwalls or the constant high-pitched singing hiss of electricity, or the trickling of water. Utter silence.

Then the screaming began.

My adrenaline spiked, my every hair on end as I dove to the rescue into the shower's polymerwall—

And fell back, head throbbing, to slip almost comically on the ground. Bloodseas, it wouldn't let me through? How had the polymerwall locked? I palmed the wall in the darkness for the emergency release that could liquefy the wall. I heard the cries of little kids above the din, terrifyingly easy to recognize when you grow up in the glorified refugee camps we call bases—shyte, I had to get out to the kids! My fingers grazed the emergency release—

And then everything turned on again, and the wall slurped the release away from me. The lights seared brighter than inter-rogation flashlights, and boiling water plunged over me. The drain at the bottom of the shower tube sealed. The locked stall was already filled to my knees and rising, as if the room itself wanted to drown me in scalding water.

I always took my weapon into the shower with me. Two cuts from my mace tore open the wall. I stumbled out into the main restroom, sputtering.

Then I felt the burns.

I bit back a scream and cringed, limping as I ran from stall to stall, slicing each one open with the laser-staff end of my neodymium mace. Water spilled across the floor as I checked the bodies tumbling out behind me. Living kid with too many ques-tions. Dead guy with several burnt holes through his chest.

"Bloodseas, what the shyte happened to him?" the kid asked, grabbing his glasses as I put on my pants.

"Claustrophobia," I answered. Looked like the man freaked out and fired at the wall over and over and over—and the walls deflected gunshots. "No burns on you?"

"I climbed the walls as soon as the water got hot. I'm so light I'm filking effervescent." The scrawny younger teen human fumbled for his pants and yanked back the slide on his assault rifle, cursing like his older sister—

I shook her out of my head; we ran into the hallway, Reise Benzaran's bare feet platt-plopping behind me. A thunderous crackle sounded outside as alarms *wooo*'d over ground-rocking explosions.

"You got my six, Benzaran?" I asked-slash-ordered.

"Yessir," said Reise. He better. He was what, fourteen, if I remembered right? Old enough to go out on offensives. So he knew the emergency protocol like he knew how to count. The kid's hunched shadow fell before me in the dimly lit hallway as he backed after me, weapon raised, swiveling right and left.

Sight did nothing in this mole tunnel, and the sounds were horrible. Crunching? Thumping like giant footsteps, like the water pumps and fuel machinery at the center of the base had turned on for some reason? The screech of drones whistling through the air, the rat-tat-tat of turrets, some kind of—of squelching?

"Um um—um my wristband isn't getting any orders, sir ..." I could barely hear Reise's awkward half-question as we rounded the corner. Damn this screaming.

"Mine neither," I yelled. "The whole intercom system must be down, too—loudspeaker's not saying anything."

Couldn't see anything outside. I was brushing my hand over every clear-wall or window we passed, trying to get them to turn transparent, but they remained opaque as if my DNA no longer mattered. I wanted to rip the building open, but exposing us to what?

"Sir, what's your assessment?" Reise asked.

"Bloodseas, Benzaran, you've got a lot of questions. You'll know as soon as I know. Keep your eyes up." Something moved ahead of us in the shadows as the lights flickered again.

Bloodseas, the flayer cannons! The hallways morphed and splattered as the barracks' defenses popped out of the walls—and aimed at us!

"Stay close!" I pulled the kid behind me as I spun my mace in a figure eight around my hand. Its neodymium magnetic core created a forcefield that deflected the volley of gunshots that now lit up the hallway.

"Sir, if you raise your shield up higher I can fire underneath!" Reise shouted. I raised it; he dropped to his belly by my ankles and steadied his rifle to take out the cannons one at a time. It took him a while. *Let's speed this up.* I raised my right hand and flexed my fingers to rip the cannons out of the wall—

A sharp, tingling pain coursed from my fingertips down to my elbow. "Agh!"

Nothing else happened.

Bloodseas, had I completely destroyed myself taking out that transport center?

"Njande, help me," I whispered as the kid finally took down another cannon.

Rest.

"Njande," I hissed through clenched teeth. "I can't rest now, something's wrong!"

"Done!" Reise leapt to his feet, grinning wide enough to show off *all* his braces. I hated when Frelsi kids smiled in combat, but I knew he couldn't help it. He didn't know any other life. I nodded and flicked two fingers in the air to signal him to fall back in behind me as we hugged the walls and rounded the next corner. Almost there—almost to the barracks main exit.

"Sir, should we take the side causeway? It should contain less weaponry," said the kid.

"Good thinking." *Someone's been studying. Good for him. "Causeway," though?* I glanced back at his "bespectacled" face for a second as we dashed across another hall. I thought he talked like a thesaurus during mass assemblies to sound smart around his friends—no idea that was normal for him.

We finally reached the barracks exit. Silver scratches marred the walls; burnt paw-prints scarred the green on the exit door. Machinery dangled around us like jungle vines and mangled defenses lay scattered across the floor like dead metal limbs. Whispers and hushed gasps echoed around us.

Reise crouched; I raised my mace.

"It's the desk," I said. The whispers in the flickering darkness came from the huge jade information desk by the lobby's back wall, to our right. The desk faced the exit; it was tall, thick, and wrapped around on three sides to almost touch the wall: excellent cover.

A paw waved out from behind one of the compuwalls built into the top of the desk.

Reise raised his rifle—I shoved his muzzle to the floor.

"It's one of ours," I said.

"Oh, no, sorry," Reise cringed so hard it looked like his shirt might eat him.

"Better be." To the paw's owner: "We see you. Clear to cross the room?"

The chestnut-brown Biouk space-lemur poked his head out from behind the compuwall.

"Oh, Cinta!" Reise groaned. "I am so stupid, sorry I—"

"It is good, be sorry later," Cinta shouted over the constant blasts. He held two pistols at the ready as he returned eye contact with me again and nodded his nose toward the desk underneath him.

We stepped closer, following his gesture, to find twenty kids of all species squished against each other under the counter. Two older teens guarded the outer edges of the desk, assault rifles ready, one commando-style on the ground, and the other kneeling to aim over his buddy's shoulder.

"Holy crap, I'm being outdone by a muskrat," I muttered. Biouks don't hit puberty until fifty, so at 27, Cinta was the oldest child out of any of us—but as a newer Frelsi recruit he let my disrespect slide. He scampered to the edge of the desk to stand level with my ears.

"This is everyone alive in this barracks," he said. It was impossible to whisper over the sounds of the alarms, but he sure was trying. "Five adults dead at the entrance to children's quarters. Ten fighting age and adult dead in the kitchen." He lowered his voice further. "The refrigerator killed them."

"Yeah the shower tried to kill us; it's a bad day for homemaking," I said. "Why didn't the little kids just go further down the children's quarters into the safes?"

"The safes does not open," Cinta said, stress, perhaps, melding his Grenblenian grammar with that of his native Biouk language. Alarm had his giant face-sized ears standing straight up on his head, casting shadows over the triangular blaze of black fur streaking down his muzzle.

The safes wouldn't open?

Oh, shyte.

I looked over the little kids, feeling their panic in my chest. Ears leapt to attention, spines bristled, scales changed color, and little humans trembled. *The safes, lock yourselves in the safes*, was the rule drilled into us until we became teenagers, and even then it only changed to *lock your little siblings in the safes*—and now we had none of that? The safes were magnetically sealed: if I tried to break into them they'd shut off my mace's lasers and deflect weapon shots. So if they wouldn't open on their own—without my powers? I could do *nothing* about it.

But all these upturned faces were lower ranked than I was. With no orders on our wristbands, and Cinta still only a year in ...

I was now in command.

CHAPTER TWELVE

Lem

MIDNIGHT COMMOTION ECHOED THROUGH THE GROWEN COMPOUND as Lem crept through the barracks hallways on her way to her new identity's bedroom; suddenly light cascaded down the hall in rapids like a river down a canyon, driving with it a swarm of high-ranking Growen officers—right toward Lem.

Her heart became a pulsating fruit lodged in her throat. If masters of genocide came in playing cards, these were the kings.

And ahead of them strode Diebol, mouth running and leather jacket flapping as the light followed his footsteps.

It's cool, it's cool. I'm a land-walrus janitor. I'm invisible. She hunched her shoulders and focused on her waddle, continuing down the hallway toward the closet where they kept the cleaning robots. *Besides, these guys aren't the monsters my parents made them out to b—*

"Move, bucktooth." A heavy palm blew into her chest with the slur. Lem fought the urge to throw the man across the hallway and fell submissively against the wall as the brass breezed past. This was a once in a lifetime chance to touch a general. Her eyes followed the offender's wrist up his black uniform sleeve to—oh man, basically the most boring human face she'd ever seen. Bland eyes, tiny chin, small bump for a nose, boring.

General Johnson. *Unusual name, extremely boring face. I'll remember you.*

And with a touch of her paw behind her ear, as her fingers brushed his disappearing hand for DNA, she guaranteed that memory.

"Bucktooth?" Diebol scoffed. "Gentlemen, I've warned you not to use that kind of slur around me." His singsong voice trailed behind him as he raised his hand, still walking. He drew a subtle finger across his own neck, and Johnson stiffened. "We're all here for the cause," Diebol said, as if he hadn't just threatened one of the most powerful people in the galaxy for a maintenance worker. "Anyway, as I was saying, now that *She* is activated, you'll all be pleased with the new state of Fort Jehu." He whirled ahead of them, turned to face them, and threw out his arms. "Hurry up!"

Lem barely noticed his terrifying energy. Shyte, *Her*, finally, after all these months?

Her, in Fort Jehu?

Oh no.

The back of Lem's throat tasted sour. Lem needed in. She had to get in that room. Or, more correctly, she had to replace someone in that room.

She had his DNA, she just needed to get rid of him.

Jei

The chaotic thumps and alarms continued to blare outside the trashed barracks lobby where Cinta and I conferred over sniffling children.

I left Cinta to guard the kids with one of the older cadets, a small, quiet, human by the name of Nathan Horn, about fifteen and clearly Contaminated like I was with Njandejara. He seemed to have his head on straight. For scouting, I took Reise and his friend Gideon, a pale-ass hulk four years younger than me and still larger; thesaurus-boy hadn't failed me yet, and I figured without powers I couldn't go wrong with a steroid giant.

Outside the barracks, ashen wind met us with the taste of burnt plastic in the darkness. Everything computerized on our base had gone insane. One of our mechanized small arms towers stalked the street in front of us, firing at random, its three legs spindly like a spider's and red auto-aim lights glowing like eyes. In the distance I saw a handful of our own sky-ships doing battle with our anti-aircraft lasers. The screaming would not stop. Bodies piled at the entrances of the nearby barracks buildings, limbs thrust through polymerwalls that had opened and shut on the escapees. There were faces stuck in melting walls.

A group of younger girls, pre-fighting age, huddled by the tread of a blasted-out tank. The oldest one, a dark-skinned blonde about ten or eleven, had her hands over the other two girls' mouths, one a Biouk and one a Wonderfrog, as they sobbed.

The mechanized tower skittered toward them—

Reise rushed forward. "That's my little sister!" he hissed, firing on the tower.

Yes, I knew that, thanks. You didn't do fifty-plus missions with someone without meeting their family, and now the arms tower whirled toward us at Reise's sound.

"Move and fire!" I ordered, blocking the incoming flayer shots with my mace's spinning forcefield. Gideon and Reise dashed in opposite directions and lit up the night with colorful cartridge fire; I ran across the street for the girls. The heat from my mace drew the tower's attention—

But so did the heavy storm from my gunners. The tower jittered.

"Those things really aren't meant to be fully autonomous," I muttered, sliding to the girls in a splash of mud as the tower's frenetic fire sprayed over my head.

"Injuries?" I asked.

Juju pointed with her chin to the Biouk, not daring to relinquish control of either child's mouth. "Her head's bleeding," she said, wide-eyed. I tapped, and felt sticky ooze matting the cub's fur.

It wasn't flowing, and the cub followed my face with her eyes —looked stable enough to move.

"You can run?" I asked the human.

Juju nodded, eyes wide.

But—

"Let go of their faces, soldier."

She shook her head, eyes still very, very wide.

Her arms trembled, stiff. I peeled her sweating fingers off her companions and scooped up the Wonderfrog in one arm. She was so young she still had a tail between her back legs; it whacked me, wet. The Biouk clung to my shirt instinctively, infantile tree-dweller claws raking my skin. And with my other hand I dragged the human after me.

My gunners more than covered our retreat across the street; the tripod tower exploded behind us, toppling like a tree as we dodged back into the building.

"Hon, I'm home," I quipped, practically throwing the three girls at Cinta. "Something's happened to everything that's got a computer in it out there." I turned as Reise and Gideon re-entered. "We've got to kill the wireless router in the central communications tower so our wristbands fall back on the satellite network and everyone can actually talk to each other."

"Is there perchance a possibility of similarly eliminating the generator to this building, so the safehouse doors will unseal?" Reise asked, actually raising his hand.

The hand-raising seriously stopped my train of thought. "This isn't a schoolroom, Professor Wordsworth. And no, the power source for the safehouse doors is inside the safe itself."

"Reise? Reise, it is dangerous back there," Cinta said, apparently much more afraid of Reise having ideas than I was. "This is not like your *thing* last year. Every person in *there* is *dead* who is bigger than this tiny runt-man," Cinta pointed at Nathan, who winced, then shrugged. "We?" Cinta waved his palm over everyone behind him. "We all got out through the cooling system in the floor. Your brother almost did not fit. Your Gideon? Big monster boy? If he did not get stuck out here before it happened? Dead."

"Never been so glad to show up late to curfew," Gideon whistled, cocking and checking his weapon. It really was weird for me how *coldly* he and Reise took this compared to Cinta and me. Would I have turned out like that if not for the kidnapping at eight? Just another simulation, just another video game, another schoolhouse drill forced on them by the jerk teacher called life?

"So right now it's a bigger payload for us to risk our butts out there than in here," I said. "If everyone can start communicating we can start coordinating evac. Let's move out."

"Evac?" A human boy cried. It was a stockier, twelve-year-old double of Reise, and wide-eyed and bushy-haired he was *straight up panicking.* "What about Mom? Reise, don't let him leave Mom!"

"Jake, shhh!" Reise waved his hand, looking at me with full, teeth-clenched embarrassment.

"Reise!" the boy cried.

"Cinta's got it," I said, waving my gunners after me, although it looked like actually Nathan had it. Not a great day for *Jake*—he'd probably get held back a year before he joined the fighting ranks, if we all lived. Cinta stuffed Jake back under the counter while Nathan consoled him, and I'd normally scold the kid for failure to act like a Frelsi trainee, but at this point I couldn't really blame him.

The burnt plastic and ashen air met us outside once again as we took off toward the communication tower, hunched shadows in the grass of a now mechanical world.

Lem

Wandla the janitor was not like Frank Zej. She was neither a war-hero nor a scoundrel like the presumed-dead Growen prisoner Lem had interviewed back at Fort Jehu; Wandla required no glorious come-back and escape story concocted in her honor like Zej had when Lem assumed his face.

No, Wandla just earned civilian worker money doing civilian worker things, like maintaining the Growen sanitation equipment and occasionally helping out with extremely mindless administrative tasks. A Luna-Guetala Bichank from Lem's jungles, lonely Wandla had moved to Alpino because she liked cool weather, and because at her advanced age, with most of her people owned by Growen scientists anyway, she wanted adventure.

So when Frank Zej offered her a paid vacation, she took it. The day Zej returned from his failed offensive on Fort Jehu, instead of keeping his legal appointments he spent hours getting to know the pudgy land-walrus. Holding her giant paw, listening to her jokes, complimenting her enormous tusks ... she had no reason to believe the handsome, authoritative human *hadn't* actually spoken to her aloof supervisor about a paid vacation, and he helped her on a sky-bus bound for the city that same day.

It wasn't ideal, but hopefully by the time the real Wandla figured anything out and came back, Lem would be someone else, and in the meantime, she had the Bichank's phone number, so she could call and ask her to stay away longer if needed. Lem didn't mind doing a sanitation worker's job for free—she still had Zej's entire life savings in her bra.

Precious little good any of that did her, stuck outside this meeting room, though, while the Growen leaders conferred inside about the fate of Fort Jehu. Lem paced as two giant trash-bots followed her back and forth like pets. The cool metallic floor tickled her bare toes as her feet plop-plop-plodded like land-walrus paws. Her heart pounded. She didn't dare *think* of the reason she needed to get into that room.

"No, I just wish I was at Fort Jehu because I'm so dang loyal to the Growen, and I hate missing the action," Lem muttered to herself, erasing the word "family" from her consciousness. "Just like I'm disappointed I dropped my helmet and we didn't wipe everyone out."

Gah, she hated these fake thoughts right now, she hated them! How could she get into the filking room? The polymerwall had a small, round window in it. Lem had been careful not to pace in front of it, but a quick peep …

Inside, Growen top brass all sat around a smooth, obsidian table. Diebol was angled and pushed back from the table—yup, that was Diebol, Lem smiled: he left plenty of strategic space in case he needed to fight everyone in the room. These armchair bureaucrats had built the Growen forces together, but everyone knew Diebol despised most of them.

Well, Lem would just have to do him the favor of replacing one.

General Johnson was facing the window. He looked up for a second—Lem waved at him, and then ducked away. No matter how big Johnson's ego, a rude land-walrus wave would not justify a mention to peers in an emergency meeting. If it was rude enough, though, it might justify a quick "excuse me while I literally hit the latrine." Right? The kind of guy who shoved people and dropped anti-Bichank slurs even in front of known Bichank sympathizer Stygge Diebol—that kind of speciesist would want to come out here and punch her real quick for daring to disrespect him, right?

Lem checked again to see Johnson glaring at the window. She stuck out her tongue and bent down her paw to mimic a human hand in rude, three-fingered salute.

He looked away from her in disgust, but did nothing.

Yeah, you didn't get rank without learning how to take down names and have someone else do the punishing for you. Come on, she couldn't wait for this …

Lem looked behind herself at the empty hallway, hunting for the exact location of the surveillance cam. She couldn't see one … ah, there was one flat, oval imprint of a camera directly above the conference room entrance. If she should get really close to the polymerwall, it wouldn't see her face.

You know … A terrifying doppelgänger was worth slipping out of an emergency meeting, and insane enough that he wouldn't tell anyone.

Lem stood by the window, staring at Johnson, and when he was looking up, she lifted the edge of the Wandla sticker behind her ear, defaulting to the newly gathered DNA on the other sticker: the general's own genetic code. For just a second, the general saw his own face on the land-walrus head, before the land-walrus smirked at him, and disappeared.

At least, Lem hoped. She held her breath …

Oh yes. The polymerwall squished as it started to activate, and Lem scurried away from it toward the supply closet. As the general stomped out of the meeting room through the wall, his wrinkled jaw clenched in seething insult, Lem threw him another rude salute and jumped into the closet.

The general dove after her. "I'll skin you, Bichank witch—" was cut off by a stun cartridge from Frank Zej's still very useful gun.

Lem breathed and wiped her brow as the Growen general crumbled at her feet. In the second it took him to fall butt over boots she regretted using a stun cartridge.

Because now she had a living person, completely helpless at her feet, and no way to hide him. Should she kill him? She didn't know much about the next guy in line for his job—was he worse? And what if she needed this guy to come back to life later so she could switch identities?

"You're overthinking this," she muttered. She needed a general. She needed to get in there right now. Why would it ever be a bad thing for one of these guys to be dead?

It felt different when he was totally helpless. Just like someone's really stupid, clumsy dad on his face.

"Njande, I really wanted to do this awesome Paradox thing where we are so powerful our enemies don't want to fight us anymore, but I am not there right now," she whispered.

It didn't take long to rip out the insides of a cleaning robot to stash the body.

CHAPTER THIRTEEN

Jei

I WAVED HULK AND PROFESSOR WORDSWORTH DOWN IN THE TALL grass behind me. We were on our way to destroy the router in the comms tower so our wristbands would default to the universal data network instead—then, maybe, everyone could call for help.

My eyes shot around to every shadow; here, on the slight hill in the center of the base that supported the communications tower, the trees and shrubbery thickened. That didn't just mean cover for us.

Below, behind us in the starlight, tanks rolled over rubble as some of their crews ran in and out of barracks trying to rescue people—and in other cases, just straight blew stuff up. Scattered evac vehicles posted at the perimeter, trying to escape the bubble wall that was now a prison. I couldn't shake the sound of the little kids screaming.

Reise swiveled at a moving shadow. "Identify yourself," Gideon hissed.

The shadow fired. Reise fired back; someone cursed, and gurgled. I waved Reise to stay hidden in position, and Gideon and I dashed to our attacker's position.

A pink-haired pale man in prison uniform lay dead there, a

wound through his chest smoking as blood seeped from a ruptured aorta. Gideon threw up a thumbs-up for Reise to see.

I took the man's stolen flayer gun, barely noting the nametag *Frank Zej* on his chest. Shyte, the prison had opened somehow. Were they responsible for this whole mess? Had they somehow taken control of central computing? *How* did they possibly know the access codes?

Another flayer shot almost took off Gideon's upheld hand, this time from closer to the communication tower. Gideon dove down under the bush by me and returned fire; I swiveled to block the laser knife plunging down toward my back.

Correction, the laser *knives*. A ten-tentacled prisoner jumped back as I parried his first blow with the staff of my mace and with the second blow made his number of limbs more equal to mine. With the third blow he didn't have a head anymore.

"Sorry," I said, not really sorry at all but still trying out this whole Paradox Warrior "respect for all life." The body crumbled to the ground like floppy seafood, environmental suit hissing and sputtering water.

I ducked down beside the prisoner, searching for a communicator, my head on swivel watching Gideon's back and checking Reise's location—

Someone was moving behind Reise's bush. I aimed Frank Zej's pistol, breathed, and squeezed. With a cry a shadow fell to the ground.

I signed in Frelsi visual code for Reise to move toward the tower. He shot back a thumbs-up. "Cover Reise," I told Gideon, still watching his back as a couple more prisoners tried to take the hill toward us. Aim, breathe, fire. Aim, breathe fire ... both prisoners ate oxidized cartridge and tumbled down the hill.

The grass by the nearest tower leg rustled in the night breeze. I couldn't see Reise moving—but that meant neither could anyone else. Lem or I would've done a quick dash, but it was probably best for Reise to follow protocol and take things low and slow in the tall grass.

I saw him when he reached the tower.

"Stay down!" I yelled. He lay flat. The crisscross metal leg wasn't good cover, and someone would have to climb, exposing themselves more: I chose myself for that. "Cover me," I told Gideon with a pat on his shoulder blade.

"Roger," he said. I ran to the metal spindle, trying to see if I could draw fire with my glowing staff—

But the hill was quiet now; all the screaming and shooting was far away. I waved Reise to stay down here at the foot of the tower, and motioned with my head for him to watch Gideon's location; the scrawny kid nodded back at me, moonlight glinting off his glasses by my boot. From here they could cover each other and my climb, with enough distance between them to stay hidden and report back to Cinta if something else went wrong.

I tugged at the rope ladder that dangled against the tower leg. Seemed solid—with one more glance around I started my climb. I just needed to smash this tower's wireless router with my mace so our wristbands would fall back onto satellite data, and then our leadership could get orders out to us. And our communication tower didn't use polymerwall protection. I'd heard plans for the past year to upgrade it, but our leaders had focused on safeguarding the kids' barracks and fortifying the perimeter instead. So when I reached the top of the ladder I just had to push open the cold, dew-misted trap door above me—

Shyte. I'd forgotten about the sentry bot. It fired the instant the hatch opened; I felt the steel door reverberate against my arm as bolt after bolt thudded and twanged against it. I didn't have a good angle to get out around the door without getting shot: I couldn't spin my staff into a forcefield in the tiny, body-sized doorway.

"Grenade, please!" I yelled down.

Reise tossed it as high as he could, and a very weak em-pull on my part made sure it ended up in my hand.

Just the slightest em-pull effort made my head implode with agony again, like giant knives stabbed in all directions into my skull. I clenched my teeth, clicked the count-down on the grenade through blinding, pulsing white pain, and tossed the egg into the tower. As the explosion rocked the tower, I held the hatch shut above me, cringing into its vibrating heat.

And with a soft hum, my wristband shone green with new messages.

Lem

Seated now at the onyx table in the Growen meeting room, Lem folded her hands in front of her with the poise of a *general*.

But adrenaline pulsed through her temples. Sweat stung her palms; she could barely hear over the unbearable galloping in her chest as Diebol talked through the video embedded in the middle of the table.

The video where Fort Jehu's machines were slaughtering its inhabitants.

Lem didn't bother fighting the intense emotion. How could she? Best to reframe it in her thoughts as excitement. She was excited. Excited. She was General Johnson, speciesist against Bichanks, and she loved this.

You hate this lie, you're terrified—

She. Loved. This.

"I don't understand," said a shy-voiced human with curly white hair and wide green eyes. *General Cabalero*, read his uniform. He tapped on the video on the center of the table, switching it from grainy feeds of carnage to a full real-time strategy map of Fort Jehu. Assets under Growen control shone blue—and the entire page was a wave of giant blue squares and circles eating little red Frelsi dots like candy. "This is amazing, but how is she doing this? Is she a computer program?"

Diebol smirked. "What She *is*, is a Stygge matter, for Bricandor and myself alone. What *you* need to know is that we're cooking the Frelsi like mollusks in their own shell. And I need you to strategize logistics and reconnaissance. For tonight, we need to clean up stragglers and bolster supportive forces around

Fort Jehu, and then we need to find access ports for Her on other bases."

"Why couldn't we do this during the siege?" interrupted a gruff, deeply critical voice, from the general with the large purple-black beard. "Seems like someone's been holding out on us, gentlemen." Lem couldn't see his nameplate from here, but this general clearly didn't like Diebol: the purple beard seemed to flare like a wolf's scruff as the man leaned forward to shoot eye-daggers at the young Stygge across the table. "It *almost* seems like you cost us billions of drachma in resources for no reason."

Diebol scowled and crossed his arms. "Take it up with Bricandor," he said. "She wasn't ready until Bereens destroyed the transport camp; we needed the right Frelsi computer system."

Jei? What did Jei do?

"So you're not really in charge of Her." Purple-beard smiled. "As usual, you're just the messenger."

"So shoot me," Diebol growled, leaning forward like he really, really wanted the other man to try.

It would have been interesting, but Lem's eye strayed to a crescent-moon shape chasing ten red dots on the table, her vision tunneling as it grew closer, closer …

"You couldn't *find* a Frelsi computer?" Purple-beard jeered as the half-moon ate someone—maybe someone Lem knew. "Aren't you the one who cares so much about the working conditions of our men? But you let Bricandor hold out on us, and we lost thousands this week on Luna-Guetala alone!"

Diebol spat some retort about research that Lem didn't hear as the half-moon rolled over two more little red dots.

She couldn't take it.

"Gentlemen!" General Johnson thudded his fist down on the table. Lem didn't know if this was how he normally behaved, but this was how he was going to behave today. "Are we here to talk solutions with this brilliant weapon, or did you get me out of bed to watch you two compare laser-staffs?" She threw in a huff and a dramatic hand-wave.

Everyone stared at her for a second. Yeah, she sounded weird. But the half-moon had eaten five little red blips now, and *she had to make it stop*. Think, think: "Have we completely shut down their evac platforms?" she asked.

"Yes," Diebol pursed his forehead and blinked, as if very pleasantly surprised by Johnson's reaction. He traced the perimeter of the base with his finger on the screen. "They can't get out."

"Wait," White-haired Cabalero sounded panicky every time he opened his mouth. "Wait, why did those just turn green?"

Everyone leaned over. The red dots were flashing emerald in waves across the screen.

"Because they got communication back up!" Purple-beard snarled. "They can call for help from other bases now!"

"It means nothing," Diebol shot back. "All the help in the universe means nothing if they're dead before it gets there."

"What do you mean, nothing, comms is everything! Comms is what cost us the siege!" Purple-beard sprayed angry spittle across the table.

Lem massaged her temples, trying to shut out the argument. *Focus. You're here for* Her. *Focus!* Sure, the dots were green now, they had comms up. But the crescent moon had eaten all the little dots in front of it, and now it started down the street toward ... shyte, the boys lived there, and Juju lived over there ...

"How are we getting Her into the next base?" Lem asked. "If She attacks the nearest base at the same time, there won't be 'help' for Fort Jehu at all, right?"

Diebol made that face again, the surprised, almost apprecia-tive face, but shook his head. "At this time She can only take out one fort at once."

"Can't She just lower intensity or whatever?" Purple-beard argued just to argue. "Half-strength on two bases, instead of full strength on one?"

"You sound stupid right now," Lem muttered with the Growen part of her brain: a flying anaconda succeeds by targeting *one* guinea pig, not chasing two at a time. But Lem's almost subconscious whisper of a soul latched onto the idea; dividing Her attention might save some little now-green blips. "What does She need to get into a second base?" Johnson asked.

"We need an access port. Any access port. Any stolen computer, any kidnapped Frelsi soldier who remembers their login from the system you're targeting," Diebol said. "That's how powerful She is."

Shyte! Lem almost choked, and turned the choke into a violent cough. Three blue squares devoured another huge handful of little Frelsi greens.

"Are you alright, Johnson?" another general leaned over and whispered while the others kept talking. "That cough is getting nasty."

Lem waved him off, trying to sort out the assets on the field. If no one could get out, could something match Her strength? "What happened with the Bereens kid, again?" she asked. "I must have zoned out—"

Purple-beard practically roared in frustration. "Pay attention, Johnson! That was the first thing we discussed! Crazy Stygge-kid blew up an entire transport camp on his own but for some reason didn't kill anyone. Millions of drachma in damage!"

"Money is what's most important, isn't it," Diebol sneered.

"No, we can fund a war with heart and magic, Diebol," Purple-beard snapped.

Dang, Jei. A whole camp on your own? Lem pursed her lips and nodded, deeply impressed and not hiding it. A Growen general could be impressed with raw power, why not? A pang shot through her chest: she would've liked to see that.

And Jei was a master at strategy. He should be here, not her. He should be doing this weird sneaky-around stuff, lying to himself—

I'm not lying to myself. I am a loyal Growen dangit *how do we make this stop?!* The green blips were drowning in a blue ocean, fading to black in clusters as She ate her way across the map. Lem hadn't been this flustered since the interrogation center. Agh, like that stupid triangle-map game they'd forced her to play against Jei then ... that pure, distilled strategy she sucked at. When Jei and Diebol played, they would often give up smaller pieces to each other to trick each other into losing large swaths of territory.

Okay. So what smaller pieces could she give up?

"Everyone wants to get Her into a second base, before or after we finish with Jehu," Johnson said, thinking aloud. "And the Frelsi have a central hiding place in that sector where they evacuate their forces for every loss ..."

"They do?" Everyone looked at her.

"Yeah," she choked. Shyte, they didn't know that? Filking shyte! "It's why they bounce back so quickly, and the same threats seem to recur again and again." *Lean into the Growen general role*: "Like cockroaches. Where there are two, there are two hundred. Because they have a nest."

"How do you—"

"We need to call a cease-fire," Lem blurted. "Need to give them a chance to set up their evac platforms. Then we follow those platforms to the Hiding Place. If you can get Her in *there*, every Frelsi base in the area will be vulnerable." Welp, she'd done it, she'd played her cards. She felt her underarms getting hot and wet. Maybe she'd ruined everything and killed everyone.

The generals stared at her, then at each other. Purple-beard thought this was the stupidest idea he had ever heard, but the others argued with him. "They'll suspect something's up if we just call off an attack while we've got the upper hand," Purple scoffed.

"I like the idea of finding their evac nest, though."

"No, we should eliminate this base completely first. If She really is that powerful it'll be a piece of cake to find Her an access point for the next target. Take no chances."

"But it would be faster if we could use this victory as a stepping-stone to the next target, especially if we wouldn't otherwise be able to access the Hidden Base—"

"Is the intel good, Johnson?"

"Yes," Lem heard herself rasp. "Local contractors and bounty hunter data."

"It certainly explains the challenges in that sector."

"It's not worth slowing down an almost certain victory."

"The victory's clearly certain anyway!"

Diebol said nothing as the other humans argued. He, like Lem, watched the table, his fingers stroking his chin.

More little blips blinked and disappeared ...

"We have to do it soon," Lem snapped, trying to stifle what was starting to feel like panic. "If they're all dead there won't be anyone left to lead us to their hidden base."

Dead. Holy crap, that really made it real. Another handful of green flickered and disappeared. Who? Who were those dead blips?

She felt him watching her ...

Yeah whatever anyone else said, whatever trouble these generals gave Diebol politically, he was still the most important voice in the room.

She knew what to give Diebol to make this thing stop.

CHAPTER FOURTEEN

Jei

I PACED IN THE BOMBED-OUT COMMUNICATION TOWER, MY BOOTS *clonging* on the hollow metal floor as I choked down the instinct to scream at my commanding officer's boss.

"They thought it would be best for you to hear it from me," the Admiral said, his grey-blue eyes shimmering with hollow sympathy over the video feed on my wristband.

"Well, *sir*, they thought wrong," I spat. "It's a trap." I heard my voice rising, and I could not make it stop. "You have to know it's a trap!"

"Of course it's a trap, but the risks have been calculated and they are acceptable."

I nodded, licking my lips. Sure. Maybe this would buy some of the little kids a little more time. I closed my eyes for a second as the whips and the cages came flooding back to my memory. I wanted to hang up, fight, pretend somehow there was some other way, but every second the screams outside grew less and less as our voices were snuffed out …

"Where do I report?" I asked.

"South gate. You can leave now; your scouting soldiers have already received their orders to help with evacuation procedures."

I stuck my head out the hole in the wall that served as a window, and signaled Reise and Gideon to start making their way back down the hill per their wristband orders; they slunk in sync from bush to bush, covering each other as they moved.

I started down the ladder. "You'll have safe passage through the whole fort," the Admiral was saying. "After what you did to the transport center they want you alive."

"Well yeah, they need the propaganda video for the independent planets," I said. "I'll be the biggest hit since they executed Misty Snow."

"Son, I—"

"Don't call me that," I said. "And don't worry about me. Worry about the fact that they're going to be tracking the evac transports to the Hiding Place."

"We're following that possibility," the Admiral said. "Not that I need to justify myself to you, but the Burburan elections are tomorrow, and Bricandor may be trying to reverse some of the anti-Growen sentiment vis a vis child-killing. If they can demonstrate that we're magical terrorists who blow up buildings with our minds, and they're kindly herding our children off to safe houses, they may win Burbura's support."

"But you're not going to direct the evac platforms straight to the safe house, right?" My boots hit the ground and I took off running down the hill.

"Lieutenant, I'm not going to tell you what we're going to do," he said. "We have young ones who need medical attention *now*, so who knows where I'm sending them." That irked me, and it shouldn't have irked me, and I knew that—I knew the Admiral wasn't stupid, and I knew I *shouldn't* know anything now, not right before capture, but—

"This is your fault," I said. "This has something to do with Lem, and whatever you said to her when you took over the Paradox Project."

"Don't be a fool," he said. "She defected over an extremist idea about the thermodynamic collapse of the universe."

"Are you sure?" I leapt a small bush and dashed through the

hollow corpse of a bombed-out tank. "Because when I get out of this—which I will—I'm going to destroy her. This is your chance to tell me if she's undercover."

"No, if you escape, you are to return and report immediately to the nearest Frelsi base. You are not to endanger yourself or others by chasing a lost cause."

I snorted, but said nothing.

He doubled down. "Is that understood?"

"Yes sir, absolutely." My nonchalant response didn't have a thread of truth.

"You realize I'm only putting up with this conversation because you're family."

"Well don't, sir," I said. "I don't want different treatment, sir, and I'm not known for an attitude. I'm known for winning. If I'm doing something that would keep us from winning, you let me know, sir."

He didn't have an answer to that. I knew he didn't like how much I called him "sir," but I didn't know what he *did* want from me. I didn't want to think about it. I could see the gate now, a thin outline in the giant outer pearl polymerwall.

"The wall will accept your DNA, and no one else's," the Admiral continued. My boots hit the familiar, rubbery pavement of the physical training track; then the strip of dirt where people kept saying we'd eventually build a cultural hall for refugees to sell handmade art; then the long strip of hard cement where I'd once crashed my air-rider. "Both sides have agreed to do the exchange at the exact same time," his creaky voice droned. "You go through the wall at the same time as our transports escape, not a moment earlier."

I slowed and looked behind me at the hellscape now visible in the early morning light of the red sun. "Let me help load the transports, then," I said.

"No. They want eyes on you through the camera at the gate."

"So I have to wait there on my ass just—"

"Yes."

I growled and threw up a rude three-fingered insult at the

camera on the wall. Within its view, I paced, crushing the grass under my feet, planning ...

The admiral didn't hang up.

"Don't you have, like, admiral stuff to do," I said, rather than asked.

"It's been too long, Jei," he said. I answered his accusation with silence. "Of course, I understand. I know I haven't always been there for you. But Jei, I did hope to hear from you more than once in the whole year you've been deployed to Luna-Guetala."

I crouched down in the grass and almost laughed out loud. It wasn't as if he'd called me, either. "Would that be why you took my Paradox file, sir? You miss me?" I asked.

His voice became a note or two higher and ten times harder as he flipped from the mistreated parent to the famed and hated military leader. "That's purely strategic. The Paradox Project developed into a resource too powerful to ignore. I wanted to manage those assignments directly."

"Is Lem on assignment?"

The admiral sighed the longest sigh since the invention of windbags. I heard the creak of a chair, and footsteps, as if he'd gotten up to pace. "Enforcer Benzaran told me she had personal matters to attend to," he said.

"And ..."

"And then she told me she had a duty to single-handedly save the whole universe from thermonuclear collapse." *Oh, Lem ...* "She said to tell you, actually."

"But you didn't."

"No, I didn't." The chair creaked again. "I didn't get a chance to send her to the infirmary for her crazy-talk before she went AWOL, either. I'm running a force over several planets, you don't get to decide what you need to know," he snapped, and then had the unmitigated gall to switch back to the gentle parent, full of remorse: "And it's not important right now. What's important is you, and—" He coughed and cleared his throat. "I'm staying on the line until they pick you up. I want to say you don't have to do this, but—" His voice cracked like he wanted to play some "feel-my-pain" shyte. I bit my teeth and tuned out. Even with parent-mode, I couldn't hang up on the Admiral over three planets of soldiers. I wasn't going to let him screw with my perfect record. But that didn't mean I had to listen to him. I stared out across the base I wasn't allowed to help, watching the distant explosions in the pink dawn. This was her home, her family. I remembered when the Growen came for mine.

Things seemed to have quieted down—no more tripod or tank battles on the main causeways. I forced myself to turn and look at the wall.

Then: "Jei, I know this is hard for you. I want to—"

"This isn't hard for me," I said. "I have one request, though."

"What is it?" he asked.

"I want Frelsi shackles." I didn't want the Growen binding me. I didn't know why. "Our shackles are lower quality," I quipped. But that wasn't the reason.

He froze for a few seconds—maybe what he was doing finally hit him. I didn't know, and I didn't blame him for this exchange. If he were trading anyone else, I would hate him. But I felt like I'd dug myself into this.

I would hate him if he botched it. The Growen were only allowing a *brief* cease-fire to load children—and only children— onto the evacuation platforms. Diebol wanted to make an example of me. So maybe, possibly, if they played this absolutely perfectly, Frelsi upper leadership could salvage something.

"I'll send someone over," he said.

When I hung up, in the gut-twisting solitary wait, I suddenly realized what he'd actually wanted to say.

Lem

After the other generals left, or signed off the conference call, Lem sat alone in the meeting room staring at the map on the middle of the table. The blue squares and circles weren't moving anymore. The little green dots had begun to gather into groups and organize.

And beside them, the screen wore the still shot from the video capture of Jei flipping the camera a vicious three-fingered salute.

Lem breathed. And inhaled. And breathed again. *What did I do?* She ran her hands over her face as the pressure in her stomach threatened to birth tears.

She'd had to stop the slaughter. They'd stopped the slaughter together, kind of. She knew Jei, knew he wouldn't hesitate to give himself up to save even one other life, and of course Diebol couldn't resist the idea. It showed dominance, it punished the Frelsi for the transport center, the execution would make fantastic propaganda—and Diebol cared about no one so much as he cared about Jei. She'd actually studied this kind of warrior exchange in human history class.

Jei's green-blue eyes burned in the still shot, his jaw set. He looked so … determined? Angry? So miserable. She almost reached out to—what, touch the picture's face?

Lem shook her head, gripping her hair. She'd bought them time, but she'd basically given the Growen the Hiding Place. She had to stop the ambush. That she had caused.

Or rescue Jei?

Oh bloodseas.

She choked, hand over her mouth, and blinked before her eyes could wet. No, Lem needed to find *Her* before She could act again. If She could control Frelsi technology only one base at a time, She had to be within some kind of standard computing transmission distance from Luna-Guetala. Lem had never been taught in school how transmission technology worked, or how information traveled across the galaxy with only a couple of days' lag time, but she knew if there was no lag your call came from the same solar system. That meant for right now, She was somewhere between Alpino here, and the neighboring double-planet. Maybe—

Oh gosh brain please shut up. She had to figure out how to mask these thoughts. *I only want to save Jei because he would make a great asset to the Growen someday. And it's not in the cause's best interest for public affairs to kill off children in the safe house. The United Growen Front will survive better with Diebol in charge, not Her. I'm trying to help. I promise, I'm trying to help.*

Lem jumped to her feet as someone splooshed through the polymerwall. *Shyte, Diebol, not now.*

He was a whirlwind. "Johnson, I don't have much time, but I just wanted to say I appreciated your input tonight," he said, just tapping the table. "Thank you for trying to let bygones be bygones and thinking big picture."

"Absolutely," she said.

He tilted his head with the same almost quizzical face, tapped the table again and turned to leave.

"Wait, Diebol—"

He turned and paused. "Yes, Johnson?"

Her mouth hung open. She wanted to just ask him what to do. Where She was. How to fix this. But now she knew even the top generals didn't know Her.

"Is there anyone at the table that you trust?" she asked finally.

"No," he shrugged. "You?"

"I don't know," she said. "I don't know."

CHAPTER FIFTEEN

Jei

THEY SENT AN ACTUAL ARMY JUST FOR ME.

The instant I stepped through the polymerwall, someone shot me with twelve sarcoblasting stun cartridges. I had half a second to see rows and rows of orb-shaped mirroring helmets before something black covered my head, and I passed out.

When I awoke, dizzy and tasting metal, I was wearing a power-inhibiting collar—the kind we'd worn in the interrogation center, the ones that block calcium release from the sarcoplasmic reticulum in your skeletal muscles, so you can't move.

Still afraid of me, they'd also bolted my arms and legs down with iron bands soldered to the wall behind me. And the wall was in a cage. Which was inside another cage. Which was surrounded by blitzers actually all staring at me.

"He's awake!" someone screamed.

Another round of stun blasts sent me back to darkness.

In the world of my dreams, I laughed. I couldn't stop laughing. I wanted to leave a message for Diebol, laughing, thanking him for thinking so highly of me, but I was laughing so hard I couldn't find the hallway.

The best part of the whole thing was the pure irony, the

complete unfoundedness of their fear: I couldn't even em-pull an inch without almost blowing up my brain.

"Are you sure?" asked a strange voice.

A woman's voice. I turned in the darkness—she sounded musical, like the bird-clarinet I'd heard in Retrack City, the day I saw the colorful acrobats dancing from the sky-ships as feathers and ribbons fell over the crowd.

"Hello?" I asked.

"May I see the door?" she asked.

"No," I said. "That door belongs to him."

"I meant the other one."

"So did I."

But when I found the door, inside myself, to the room of cinnamon pie and blown-glass figures, I couldn't work up the courage to open it anymore. Carved runes bled green from the door's living wood, soft to the fingertips like the paper of an Alpino beech but solid like Luna-Guetala jungle oak. I traced the runes, the story of my scars, but couldn't touch the giant white-gold handle. I didn't know why. As a little child, when they captured me, when they hurt me or asked me questions, I ran into this room—a playroom, then—and pressed a green button on the wall to make all pain go away. We'd decided, my physician and I, that this must have been a construct of some kind to trigger my brain's natural enkephalins: the human body's drug a thousand times stronger than morphine.

But Dr. Patti didn't talk to interdimensionals—she wasn't Contaminated—so I didn't tell her who showed me the room, who had led me here by the hand every time.

I traced the vines springing from the hinges, thorny plants with purple flowers fluted like wine glasses. I wanted to find this room, again, in the interrogation center last year, and couldn't. Njandejara likely knew if I did, then, alone, I'd never leave it; now, I was allowed, but wouldn't let myself enter.

He lived in there. I often heard his voice through the door. Sometimes light, and sometimes shadow, would pass through the cracks, and if I looked through the keyhole, sometimes I caught a glimpse of a lizard-limbed, golden-maned Crajk beast, or a colorful tree with infinite branches, or a baby bird playing, or a man made of thorns. This was his room—in a mind that should belong to him completely, it was the only room I'd really, truly given him, because he'd given it to me in the first place.

"You should come in," his gentle bass rumbled through the wood. "Come in and rest."

"I can't rest," I said. "I need to kill Lem. Or turn her. I don't know. I'll know when I get there."

"You need to rest."

"I can't."

"Trust me; you're leaning on a limited understanding."

"This understanding's all I've got. Come on, I do trust you."

"Not with all your *lev*."

"What is that?"

"In humans, some combination of the programming in your basal ganglia and the chemical compote you sometimes call your gut."

"So like," metaphorically, I thought: "The heart?"

"The thing that makes decisions, but also feels the deepest meanings to you. Not the frontal cortex, or the calculation centers, but the construct that compiles their data."

I heard myself laughing, somewhere in the distance of the dream. "You know I can't trust anyone with the entirety of my—well, anything."

"Well, you must. If you fail to rest, you will die."

"Tell me then, why do my powers work again?"

I awoke with a jolt.

But this time, I had the good sense to keep my eyes shut. I felt the solid floor vibrating under my feet—we were in a transport vehicle. A subtle twitch of my limbs met the resistance of those firm iron bands, bolted and welded to the wall. Just a gentle tug —the Frelsi restraints on my wrists remained there, next to the iron bands ... comforting.

And for some reason, everything felt like paper.

"Do you think he can read minds, like Bricandor?" someone was whispering.

"As long as he doesn't wake up, we won't have to find out," someone else said.

The rushing wind outside told me we were on a planet, somewhere, not in space. How far in the air, I wondered? I wanted to open my eyes and look, but I remembered from my first awakening we didn't have windows, anyway. The scent of cinnamon and steel reminded me of the inside of the transport I'd smuggled myself into to rescue the Biouk tribe last year … so likely a space-capable transport that had to travel fairly near the ground when in atmosphere. No sounds of crashing trees, though.

So we weren't on Luna-Guetala anymore? Both planets of the double-planet system were covered with growth. Heavy Growen transports like this one left large scars and trails through the woods—easy to track and disrupt—so this model would spend most of its time carrying prisoners and supplies from LG to Alpino, nearby.

Were we in space when I first woke up? I didn't remember any wind, then …

A heavy thunk-ka-splat—the kind of sound to make you cringe.

"What was that?" someone squeaked.

"'Nother one o' those stupid pegasi, most likely," someone else said. "They're too thick in the air here." More thuds, and wet explosions: "We've hit a herd."

We were on Alpino, my home planet.

And that was my cue.

My left arm ripped out of the restraints and thrust forward like a claw. Eyes still closed, I could *feel* the other beings in the room, feel their electrical pulses surging into the air like I was a living long-distance EEG machine—and I could *yank* the polarity of their spinal cords toward mine.

With screaming *thunks* their backs hit my cage. I opened my eyes to see their comrades firing wildly but hitting only my human shields. My left hand held the men there as my scalp shrieked at me; I gritted my teeth and ripped free my other arm, then one leg, then—stomp—I stood unchained.

Right hand's turn. I ripped the collar from my throat, almost choking, feeling the wiring scratch skin and draw blood. Then, a raised palm: electrons surged through the metal of the cages. The bars felt like an extension of my fingers. I closed my fist: the bars bent with it, wheezing a high-pitched groan that echoed in my pounding head. I clenched my jaw against the screeching pain—

And then I tore out the right side of the airship.

We all fell through their screams into the feathers, bones, and pelts of pegasus remains, plummeting as the transport spun out of control with the sudden imbalance. My flailing hand grabbed and cut on some bloody hard—

"Huh." I was holding a pegasus jawbone.

There were three transports in the air, not more than ten feet off the ground. One crashed, cracked open like an egg by my escape. The other two started to circle back around toward me.

Just as my boots grazed the tall grass I reversed my system's polarity, threw my negative charges to my front, and like a magnet shot back up toward the metal side of the lead transport. Metal, it was all metal—I could touch and control it all. My hand was one with the pilot's door, and then the pilot's door ripped off to stay with my hand, and then, as I shut off the electro-magnet of my palm, the door fluttered away below me.

The pilot soon followed.

I jumped in his place and sliced my hands across the compuwall, turning the transport sharply left.

The transport crashed into its neighbor as I leapt clear.

I landed, kneeling, my back to the explosion as its shock wave flapped my tunic.

Today was not a day for grief. It was one thing to show mercy when I charged into their camp, an equal, fair game, but now I felt him, again, and he was angry, angrier than I was or had ever been. He was walking the ruins of Luna-Guetala like a towering ghost, bending to touch his hand to the foreheads of fallen children to store and save the electrical patterns that made them who they were, their software, and all those angry little patterns boiled, surged in his being, and every injustice from the dawn of time seemed to scream through my veins—

I stood and roared.

My fingers curled tighter around the pegasus' bloody jawbone. The blitzers who'd survived the explosions charged me. I'd taken out at least a couple hundred in the transports. There was barely a platoon left.

My hand extended toward the wreckage; my mace flew to me, twirling itself into a shield.

Its handle slammed into my hand, and it felt good.

I plowed into the platoon. Cartridges scattered around me like sparks from a welding saw; my right hand kept that neodymium staff spinning, my left wielded the jawbone like a sword—

In the storm of cracking ribs and shattering helmets, the fire in my skin began to overtake the power underneath it. As each blitzer body thudded to the ground with a puff of dust in the prairie grass, I felt a part of myself weakening. A joint, a limb, a segment of my spine …

When the last one fell, I fell beside him. The ground hit my back with agony worse than anything I'd felt at the interrogation center. I heard myself scream, and didn't know why, or what I'd done. My skin was fire, and my tongue a desert moon.

"I really don't know how my power works," I realized in a groan. My spine arched. I couldn't make it stop. The smell—gah I hated the smell, this burnt cinnamon and steel, the simmering transport fuel and smoldering remains. I hated it! I struggled to roll over—

Njande could make all the pain go away. It was the thought I'd had in the center and it was the thought I had now, the thought that despite months of study, despite everything I'd learned about interdimensionals and free will and the butterfly effect of interference *oh gosh*—

I ordered myself not to beg.

"I don't understand," I growled, heaving myself up to lean back on the nearest body. My spine! The bright sun overhead seemed to burn my eyes through my closed lids. "You're so mad, Njandejara. I know you're so mad. I can't hear you, I can't see you, but damn I can feel you. You cared about every single casualty at Fort Jehu." I coughed on the dust and smoke. "So why didn't you help me?" The cough became a hoarse scream. "Why didn't you help me save them?"

The wind in the grass carried with it no answer. Red, wet pegasus feathers fluttered around me as another piece of equipment burst in the distant flames. I was only good for destroying things, not saving them.

The sync was over.

"So now what, I served my purpose, now I can just die of thirst?" I scoffed. "You can't talk to me? I only experience you when I'm a tool in your hand?"

The dead were the lucky ones. He said he took the saved energies of his fallen friends and transferred them to his dimension, to rebuild us in a place of happiness. The flipside of *that* was that in this moment, with my lips suddenly cracking, and my limbs shivering in the weird hot and cold chills, I could imagine a situation where he let the Growen kill us so he could take us home. He didn't wield the scythe, but he picked up the harvest after it, so why stop it? But then, of course, it's not okay to be a scythe, so someone had to punish the scythe, the Growen. And maybe that someone was me. Maybe I was the axe that rendered the wicked harvest tool into kindling. And next someone was going to come along and beat the bloody shyte out of me, to make *that* fair, and we were all playthings in the hands of a child collecting bugs to show at home …

"I'm sorry." I opened my eyes, and saw my palm pressing wiry, stiff grass into the earth, and my other hand still clenching this jawbone I couldn't let go. Everything blurred. "I'm sorry, Njande, I don't … I don't want to fight you, I just—"

Rest.

I could not. Like the spider, after it's crushed, still keeps twitching, inching away on just the one working leg, I could not sit still in the ache.

"Hey there, whoa there, whoa," a gentle voice; the scent of the red plain-berries my mother used to mix in pegasus milk flowed around me as a rounded form knelt beside me. I wanted to thrust the pegasus jaw at her, push her away. *Don't touch me!* Her soft palms gripped my wrists, and squeezed, and I released my weapon. "It's alright. You're going to be okay. Let me help you."

Her fingers cupped the back of my head, and a coolness spread from my scalp, down my aching spine, and in little rivulets to the tips of my fingers, along every nerve. I blinked through the blur, and saw the woman from my dream, before I fell asleep.

CHAPTER SIXTEEN

Lem

LEM DISCOVERED VERY, VERY SOON THAT GENERALS HAD HIGH-ranking assistants. And entourages. And over-eager underlings who wished *they* could come to top secret meetings with Stygge Diebol in the middle of the night. Bloodseas, it was all she could do to keep these people from *dressing her* while she emptied the general's go-bag out on his fancy floating bed.

What was the point of a bed that floated off the ground, anyway? *This would cost Frank Zej's entire salary ...* The purple sheets practically flowed under her fingertips, as soft as sunset clouds in a little kid's imagination.

"Sir, you simply can't go," the tiny male human insisted, stomping his foot now. "You have contractor meetings all day today!"

"I'm sure they'll understand an urgent military operation takes precedence," Lem hissed. Man, General Johnson's go-bag had nothing in it, basically.

"Sir, that's what your lower-ranking soldiers are for!" cried the tiny male.

"What kind of general stays home on his ass in meetings while his soldiers die?" Lem snapped back.

The five other humans in the room stared at her like she'd sprouted extra heads.

"Look, I understand keeping the brains of the operation safe and all that," Lem said. Some extra uniforms ... one sad little flayer pistol ... what the heck, General Johnson? "But it's not like our battle suits have rank on them. From the gun rig I'll be plenty safe. We're attacking an envoy of children, for shyte's sake." Alright, she found a gas mask ... she needed a way off the rig to stop the assault, so might be a good idea to get her hands on some grenades? Had to keep that mouth running while she thought ... "Soldiers will die for the leaders they respect, and no one can respect a coward. All the greatest generals of history fought beside their armies, and historically, societies that stopped doing that waned into collapse."

The tiny male interrupted her half-distracted lecture with a compupad *thrust* into her view. Lem scowled. Oh no, the check-list of important names, placed right before her eyes, might hypnotize her into obedience!

It only obstructed her packing. And Lem despised obstruction.

Well, let's stay true to General Johnson's style, then.

General Johnson shared his feelings with a shove. The little assistant went flying. "The next coward to tell me what I can and cannot do will be joining me on the battlefield," Lem spread her teeth into a broad snarling smile. "You expect people to eat the bread of death for us if we're not willing to take the first bite? Take me to the armory."

As the entourage left the curtained and carpeted leaders' wing to whisk through the rest of the polished metal barracks, word of the general joining his men-at-arms traveled faster than his feet. Lem saw smiles and nods in the underling salutes as she passed; a light, airy cheer pervaded every hallway, and every-one's backs seemed a little straighter. Months as a Growen grunt had taught Lem this was *not* normal. Fear, not respect, controlled big armies like this one.

Being Frank Zej had taught her exactly what Frank Zej wanted in a leader.

Lem shivered. They were outside now in the cool Alpino prairie sunshine, climbing onto what looked like a hovering dolly—a lift—to float toward the armory. So many extra floating things with these Growen ...

Something in her own mental intonation reminded her of Cinta.

Ache gripped her chest and doubt trickled between her shoulder blades. She should be looking for *Her*, not rallying the troops for the ambush. But of course to save the Growen from finding the Frelsi safehouse, she had to be there to stop the ambush ... and she couldn't call it off, since she'd suggested it ... and the Luna-Guetala contingent was bringing Jei *here* to Alpino so maybe on the way ...

I'm getting a headache thinking in so many circles.

A yellow flower caught her eye as its petals fluttered between blades of roughage in the breeze.

Aha. Lem pointed to a cordoned-off section of empty field. No one would tell her, as Frank Zej, what lurked in the field—just that if she set foot inside the red rope she would die.

But now she had the authority, she hoped, to ask: "What's over there?"

All four assistants stared at her again. Man, she felt like she was just *sprouting* heads, on every shoulder. Like zits on a preteen up in here. "It's a quiz," Lem snapped. "Give me an answer now. Or have you forgotten?"

A thin lady in a tight dress clutched her compupad against her chest as she stammered. "That's ... Commander Diebol's field, sir."

"Very good. And what does he do there?" Lem asked.

"No one knows but—well he sleeps somewhere underground," said the fattest assistant. "Some of us think he has a tunnel from there into some of the buildings, the way he gets around. Is that what you—is that—what you're asking, sir?"

"That's good enough." Lem didn't dare keep pressing.

But on the way back from the armory, she sent each assistant off with a different task—one, to survey the blitzers on their food preferences, another to establish a committee to push a "happy birthday" program to each blitzer's watch on his special day, and so forth.

Finally alone, Lem steered the floating lift along the main thoroughfare now, the silver dome of the armory distant behind her. Tall grass stretched to tickle the tips of her boots as the flat platform rode the prairie like a raft on a pond. The curious cordoned area came up on her right ... Lem stopped the vehicle, and hopped off into the knee-high grass just outside the scarlet rope.

She couldn't see, from here, any cameras, or traps. And no one was around for at least a few acres: most of the troops had already collected weapons and boarded their transports, leaving the path to the armory quiet for now.

She glanced at her wristband. She needed to board that transport herself in thirty minutes if she wanted to make the ambush.

But Diebol's quarters had to hold some secret about *Her*.

Wind brushed through the general's greying hair. It was too cold for Lem to sweat. She hadn't used her abilities in a few months—and *really* used them, the ones Jei compared to an electric eel with action potentials in plates or whatever. The abilities she'd discovered in the interrogation center.

She hadn't pushed herself that hard in a long time.

Could she electrocute whatever traps lay here?

Njande, don't forget me. She knelt. The amber waves hid her as she dug her fingers into the pale, silted soil. She took a deep breath. She remembered exploding through the door in the interrogation center. She thought *harder*.

A discharge flickered from her fingers into the ground with a flash of blue.

And then four small explosions burst up in front of her.

"Holy crap I triggered mines," she squeaked, scrambling backward into thicker, greener grass. Two gun turrets popped out of the earth, smoking, and dangling like broken arms with a damaged metal creak.

So yes, she disabled the traps.

But suddenly she saw Diebol emerge from nowhere, striding through the field and snapping at his communicator pen: "—No, Father, it is not alright! You are underestimating Bereens and this entire facade undermines me! No, it's not big picture, it is insane! You never understood—hold on, I think General Johnson is trying to assassinate me again. Yes, I know you don't believe me. You never believe me about any of these armchair assholes. Good afternoon, sir. I said good afternoon!"

Three scenarios flashed through Lem's brain: one, he walked up and saw her sitting here on her ass like an idiot. Two, to face the music, she stood up out of the grass. Three, he didn't see her, because tall grass was tall.

I am too dark for that nonsense. But hell, she tried. She didn't know what to say to him, and so she would do everything in her power to say nothing at all. She scrambled further back into the grass, flattening herself out in the shadow of a shrub.

The rough, pale foliage here was a far cry from the cool, shadowed leaves back home. She wasn't hidden. *Agh everything I do is stupid.*

Lem rose. "Commander Diebol!" she said, with her most swaggering confidence as the man approached with his hand hovering over his sidearm. "I will be joining the offensive today, and I'd like to ask you to handle my contract meetings since you're staying behind. I wanted to talk to you personally before I leave."

Diebol raised an eyebrow, and looked around at his disturbed field. "Excuse you?"

"Is that a yes?" she asked.

He looked around again, eyeing the two smoking gun turrets. "Did you use *another* EMP blast in my field? I have told you a hundred times, Johnson, that I don't have any records or files out here. I sleep in a capsule in the ground. You won't find information on Her here."

Wow, Johnson had tried to have Diebol killed *and* schmooze with Her? More leadership drama! Lem liked.

Lem *didn't* like that the flayer pistol came out of its holster as Diebol looked around again. "You might notice we are alone," Diebol said.

Shoot, Johnson was about to be killed for the second time today.

Reise

Reise Benzaran stood on the deck of the Frelsi evacuation shuttle with both hands in his pockets. The wind blasted his coffee face and trickled through wispy brown hair quite different from his siblings' tightly coiled black locs and puffs. Waves of green and grey grass rushed by his sight, forever, off to the horizon where winged horses fluttered in the evening sun. In the distance, a single volcano rose from the plains, filtering soft smoke off into the clouds.

Alpino was beautiful. He'd always wanted to see it. He'd heard his older sister's training partner talk about it.

And he never wanted to go back to Luna-Guetala.

The familiar clunk-plop of Jake's uneven steps approached behind him. Anyone else would have worried about the unsteady twelve-year-old on the moving platform, but Reise was used to his younger brother's handicap, perhaps even a bit unsympathetic. Jake had walked that way for ten years; the insert in his boot helped keep the leg length discrepancy from worsening, but there was no denying the permanence of his infanthood war injury. At least he hadn't had a seizure for a while.

"Have you forgotten your insert today?" Reise asked.

"I didn't have time to get it," Jake said, stumbling to the railing and gripping it hard.

"You were supposed to leave it in your boot," Reise said. "There was no reason to remove it."

"I don't know, okay! I don't know."

Reise felt a cold smirk crawling up the skin of his neck to tug at his lower lip. He didn't know why. "You don't know what?"

"I don't know!" Jake yelled.

The wind carried his cry behind them, muffling and smothering it until it died behind them on the plains, meaningless and small.

Reise leaned his chest on the rail, flexing his biceps as he stared at the hypnotic lines of grass speeding beneath him. Green, grey, yellow. Green, grey, yellow.

Presently, he said: "Jake, Jerusha-Lem's captured, I think."

"*We* almost *died*!" Jake cried out.

"I think Mom and Dad would tell us if she'd died, so I think she's captured again."

"Why couldn't Mom and Dad come with us? It's terrible, it's just kids here, it's terrible!"

"Juju and Jaynes and Jos and J'miah and the baby—they'll all be safe at the Hiding Place—but I want to do something about this."

"I'm asking you a question! Why couldn't they come with us?"

Reise stopped talking. The wind rushing in his ears made everything feel a bit insane. He turned his eye sideways at Jake. "The Growen wouldn't let anyone out but kids."

"But you're above reg fighting age, and Gideon and Nathan, and you're all here!"

"Adults are people older than cadets. Old enough to wed."

"Mom said in some cultures *you're* old enough to—"

Reise didn't know why he was suddenly arguing with his brother about what an adult meant. It didn't matter, but he couldn't stop his mouth. Something was *wrong* and he needed it to be *right*. They went back and forth for he didn't know how long; a part of him wasn't even listening.

A tap at the back of his knee finally closed the conversation.

"Into the hold, both of you," Cinta said. "We are near, and no one should see the location of the Hiding Place."

Jake pointed at Cinta. "Reise, he's twenty-seven, and he's here! Why couldn't Mom and Dad—"

"Biouks aren't adults until fifty Luna-Guetala revolutions!" Reise snapped.

A sting in Reise's thigh stopped him; Cinta had whacked both boys on the back of the leg. They trotted ahead of the space-lemur in silence, and with a squeaking, scratching groan dragged open a metal panel in the middle of the deck. Every Frelsi child knew how to open the secret compartment in the front top of an evac ship. The false, main hold, with the actual hatch-door, always traveled empty.

Reise let Jake go ahead of him on the ladder down into the darkness and helped little Cinta start to yank the huge panel shut above them. Just before the last stripe of sky disappeared, Reise scanned the crowded compartment for Nathan and Gideon. They made eye contact with him and nodded.

With a loud clanging *thunk* the panel closed, and black darkness erased them all.

Reise's fingers splayed out from the ladder to the wall welded to it; he followed the wall around to the corner where Nathan and Gideon sat. Jake's fist clenched on the sweaty back of Reise's uniform, and the *ker-klunk* footstep followed close behind. Reise sat, and Jake with him.

"I want to ask a favor," Reise said. "During the ambush ahead."

"We're listening."

CHAPTER SEVENTEEN
Jei

"You're real."

My lips muttered this as I awoke cradled in her arms, rivulets of flowing dark hair cascading around me ...

I sat up suddenly; my hand shot out, and my mace flew to it as I rolled to the side. I tangled with flapping, rustling canvas—a tent entrance? I spun myself through it onto my feet in the prairie grass.

There I crouched, one foot outstretched, one hand in the fibrous silt, as my other hand held my mace out at the ready. Alright, I was still on Alpino—nothing around as far as the eye could see except myself and this tent. My mace activated under the stroke of my thumb; its false bamboo handle grew to full height, awash in green laser as spikes of light leapt from the weapon's orb'd head like electrons orbiting an atom.

I waited, breathing evenly. I didn't ask who she was. She would tell me.

The unknown woman followed me out of the silver tube tent and pulled the ripcord along its top, collapsing it. She was wearing a sleek, black sleeveless jumpsuit, with no pockets, under a thick metal utility belt with many pouches. Her hair rippled down her shoulders almost to her mid-thighs. I watched her tan face, searching for expression on the sculpted brow above the graceful lines of her slightly upturned nose.

She knelt to roll the tent into her pack, saying nothing; a bit of a smile tickled the edges of her lips. She didn't fear me—she held no weapon, and at times, even turned her back.

I rose from my crouch and lowered my mace.

"I am one, too," the woman said.

I am one, too. Her voice was the light, tinkling woman's voice from my mind: *May I see the door?* she'd asked. My heart raced now as she swung her pack onto her toned shoulders, and held out a short bamboo staff. "This is my neodymium," she said.

"You're a mace warrior, you mean," I said.

"Not just that," she said. "A Paradox Warrior."

I raised an eyebrow.

She laughed. "You didn't really think you invented them, did you? Many others have found the manuscripts you studied, from the human homeworld."

"That would make you Contaminated, not a Paradox Warrior."

She shook her head. "Not only friends of Njandejara peruse that archaeological data. There are many who see the universe as a source of deeper metaphysical paradox, and many others who study the biology of electromagnetic beings like you and me."

I tilted my head, still gripping my mace warm and unsheathed. "But Lem and I didn't know about Njandejara's archaeological history when she came up with the Paradox Order," I said. "I know some basic biology, but—I mean, we have our own special creed and everything." My throat tightened; I felt a shadow pass over my forehead. "Well, had. We *had* our own special creed ... and everything."

She raised her eyebrows and pursed her lips knowingly. "She betrayed you," she said.

"Yeah." I turned off my mace; the light faded off it in a wave, and it compacted itself back to a short bamboo staff.

"That, then, is why the ether called me to help you," the woman said definitively, pulling a nutri-bar from one of the pouches on her belt. She held it out to me. "I'm Mera."

"I'm … Lieutenant Bereens," I said, gingerly taking the food. "Thank you, for uh … you did something to my scalp with your fingers earlier?"

"I just triggered certain electromagnetic points along your spine to cool down your sympathetic nervous system overload, that's all," she said. I nodded—the technique seemed sound based on what I understood of electromagnetic physiology, although I didn't know how to do it myself. "Then I rehydrated you."

"Thanks." I wanted to ask more technical questions but needed to get back to my mission. "Where are we?" I saw plains, and distant volcanoes, but no sign of the smoking transports and pieces of pegasus.

"About twenty kilometers north of Samwen."

That was extremely far from the Growen base on the northern continent, presumably where they'd tried to take me— if she was right, we were actually closer to the Hiding Place now.

"How'd you carry me this far?" I narrowed my eyes.

She smiled and sang a single note.

A pegasus literally flew out of the sky, enormous wings thundering through the air. It alighted with a violent snort beside her.

"I met this handsome fellow at the scene of your crime," she laughed. "He was glad to give us a ride."

I shook my head half in awe and half in confusion. "Pegasi aren't … sentient," I said. "How did you talk to it?"

"A side effect of my particular electromagnetic ability," she smiled.

I was impressed and intrigued, but I didn't have time. I shook my curiosity off and cleared my throat. "Well, I'd love to —chat—more—about abilities—" I parsed my awkward diction. "But I need to intercept a Growen ambush in Sector 52b. Do you know how I can get there quickly?"

She patted the pegasus' shoulder.

"I think we might."

Lem

Cool wind whispered over the Alpino plains where Diebol had caught "General Johnson" near his restricted quarters.

Lem breathed as Diebol's pistol floated near her belly. "Diebol, I need to get to that ambush," she insisted.

"Why?" he asked. "I don't buy this change of heart, Johnson. You always have some manipulative little coward's trick up your sleeve."

"And aren't you curious to see what it is this time?" she smiled.

The same face he'd made during the meeting flashed over his features—that vague confusion, almost excited by her retort, but like he couldn't allow himself the momentary pleasure. Things he liked or respected couldn't exist in this general he abhorred. His jaw clenched as he drizzled her with sarcasm: "You don't have anything better to do, at all."

"Do you?" She knew, at this range, she could easily twist left, knock the pistol to the side, and let him fire off into the sky—she was more worried about his other hand on the short bamboo staff perched on his belt. A flick of his thumb, and the staff would extend into a fiery mace, impaling her through the belly. "The problem, Diebol, is that if you're wrong about me, and you kill me, you will create such a chaos through the ranks Bricandor will have you executed himself."

"I think you'd be surprised. He understands *culling* to create a controlled breed of leader."

Lem could *feel* the minutes escaping her. She had to get on that transport. "No. To avoid the scandal you'd need to make it look like someone else did it."

"That's easier than you know. We have traitors." Diebol

smiled; was he imagining pinning the murder on deserter Frank Zej? "In fact ..."

Uh oh.

Diebol's eyes glittered in the cool sunlight with the glow of a new idea. Lem shivered as he feigned a look at his watch. "Oh, would you look at the time, General! You're going to be late. Let me give you a *ride*."

... And that was how, before Lem could really think, within a hurried fifteen minutes, she found herself on the way to the ambush. Only now, she was seated beside Diebol on the top deck of a bullet-shaped gunship made to look exactly like a Frelsi evacuation platform. The black plating gleamed beneath them in the sunlight as faux Frelsi soldiers closed the bottom deck; the enormous hatch hummed shut with the mechanical whir of smooth modern gears, so different from the *clunk-clunk-clunk* of the old bootleg mechanisms Lem knew actually ran the Frelsi platforms. The ship rumbled to life, its quiet roar dwarfed, it seemed, by the rumble in Lem's belly.

As the ship shot across the plains Lem's stomach stayed behind in the Growen base. What ... was happening? What was she doing? What was ...?

Diebol leaned over to whisper in her ear. "You're right, you know. I can't take the risk that I'm wrong." Lem's ear burned. Did he know? Did he know who ...? "But the way I see it here, the Frelsi children might respond to our ambush with a stray flayer cartridge or two. And one of those stray cartridges might just *happen* to kill a certain Growen general who has always put his career goals over the cause."

Lem forced her head to face him with fake indignation. "Is that a threat? I will have your rank, Diebol."

"No need to trouble yourself, General." He smiled, patting her on the shoulder, and letting the pat linger. Her skin tingled; she tried to shrug him off with a scowl to cover up the return of her creeping terror. "I have another hunch anyway; one so strange I cannot afford to voice it." He leaned in again. "But we'll talk about that after you watch Fort Jehu's children die."

Jei

Time to go rescue Fort Jehu's children.

Wind picked up over the plains. My elegant new companion swung herself up onto the pegasus she'd summoned, hooking her knees over just in front of its wings as she hung her backpack on her chest and gripped the creature's mane. I eyed her movements, trying to figure out how to copy them so I didn't look like a drowning feathered cat from Luna-Guetala trying to claw my way up this thing.

My turn. Mera smiled at me, patting the pegasus' back behind her. Her gentle hand didn't even make a sound; I could imagine Lem, by contrast, slapping the creature's rump with a hearty, *Hey, you're the one in a hurry, man, get up here.*

I spat the thought into the long grass in disgust. With both hands on the beast's back and a heavy swing of my legs, I managed to mount the pegasus without looking too much like an idiot.

I was suddenly keenly aware of Mera's warm body pressed back against mine, the curves of her spine traced by my chest and belly.

"Let me take your pack," I said. "I don't know much about pegasi but I know it can't be comfortable steering with all your luggage hanging in the way off your front."

"Are you sure? I don't want it to bump you," she said.

"No, please." I smiled and reached for her bag decisively to place it between us; I didn't want her to be uncomfortable, shimmied up against a male with all the motion of the creature under us.

I wasn't wrong: the pegasus took off with an uncomfortable jolt, its entire body bouncing with each flap of its wings until it finally hit an air stream and stretched into a glide. Every movement of its enormous muscles reverberated in my seat and thighs, and every turn or dive pressed Mera back against the pack in my arms. I balanced behind her with my legs, trying not to grab her shoulders too much.

Before long we saw a string of four Frelsi transports.

And from the last transport in the convoy, an invisible green thread seemed to tug at something deep in my chest.

My enemy was here.

CHAPTER EIGHTEEN

Jei

MERA AND I STOOD ON A HILL OVERLOOKING THE VALLEY, OUR forms masked by fog over the waving grass. She kept her hand on the front shoulder of the pegasus, as if steadying the wild creature, and watched me. The mists wisped about us like breakers against rocks; the cool, wet fingers of the wind tousled my flaxen hair. My faded tunic flapped, tugging as if it had a life of its own, and only my still form kept it grounded.

I was counting transports. We'd circled several times from the air, looking for gunnery hidden in the hills, or other signs of ambush, and found nothing. It would've been almost impossible for a Growen operative to bug the transports on their way out, since the walls had remained intact during the entire night-marish attack—the better to keep us in, boiling us like water-spiders in our shells—

I ground a seed between my teeth and spat it out with cold viciousness.

So maybe the best way for them to track us to the Hiding Place was simply … to follow behind. It would explain the weird feeling I had about that last transport. I didn't dare call in on my wristband to check the number of vehicles that had left Luna-Guetala, in case the Growen had bugged my transmitter while I was unconscious; I didn't know why else they would've left the watch on me. Shyte, *age* was only thing keeping the evacuation ships safe from whatever computer magic the Growen now controlled: the slow, hulking black bullets had long ago lost all communicative computing to fighter ships that needed it more.

"Let's check out the last transport," I nodded to Mera.

"Are you sure you want to get close, Lieutenant Bereens?" she hesitated.

I shot her a querying look.

She glanced down, biting her lower lip as her eyelashes fluttered. "I didn't want to say this before, but well … aren't you worried you're being tracked? *You* could be the thing that leads the Growen to the Hiding Place."

"I'm not going there. Besides, I don't think Diebol counted on me escaping."

"But wouldn't he—I mean, wouldn't *you*—have a contingency plan?"

I looked at her, and at the disappearing black bullets cutting through the mists toward the horizon. My jaw ground. Maybe. Maybe I was supposed to obey the Admiral and go straight home now that I'd escaped. He wasn't stupid. He probably had a plan of some sort himself. But …

The green thread that'd connected me to Lem since back in the interrogation center tugged—painfully, now, like there was a hook in my intestines dragged by the departing landships. She was here, and up to no good. I shook my head and reached for the pegasus.

But it shied away from me; Mera jumped back as the creature's enormous wings beat once, almost knocking her over. It whinnied, and its hooves lifted off the ground—

No! It *could not* fly off. I reached for it—"No, Lieutenant, it'll hurt you!" Mera cried.

But she didn't know me. I threw a hand toward the ground, shoving negative charge toward the electrons in the earth. The em-push shot me up at the creature, knocking me across its back on my stomach. I gripped mane, feathers, whatever, swiveling my legs over to get a tighter grip as it bucked and gained altitude—

"Let go, it wants to leave!" Mera called.

"Well, we can't all have what we want," I said, hooking my heels under the wings. The pegasus barrel-rolled in the air—I threw my positive charges backward and made myself like a bio-magnet against its spine. It made as if to throw its back against the hilltop; I kicked my leg over the left wing, pushed down, and veered the flight off-course.

"Listen, buddy," I said in its ear. "We're going this way." I pushed down the other wing, turning the pegasus sharply after the transports. This way with this leg—that way with that—I maneuvered the wild beast's wings like aircraft fuselages. It could have thrown me easily if it would just close its wings, but instinctively, it stayed airborne when frightened.

Poor beast—it *was* frightened. The creature's rough back sweated against my belly despite the misted breeze; I felt panicked ribs heaving against my thighs. "I'm sorry, man, there are kids in danger."

I could see them, in my mind's eye: huddled against each other in the dark false holds, strapped to the humming metal floors by simple safety belts. The littlest ones laughed, playing with the screens on their wristbands; the oldest picked at the sleeves of their thick yellow camouflage, or hugged themselves in silence, as if trying to keep warm.

It wasn't cold in those ships.

We cut through the fog, the pegasus and I, gaining on the last black bullet in the convoy.

"Njande, please help me," I whispered. "Every shivering child old enough to understand wants to know where they'll find themselves when the lights come back. Or whether or not they'll ever return home. You remember I wondered the same thing. Please don't let my powers fail."

I didn't hear anything. That was fine. I was minutes away from finding out the answer.

Lem

He dropped out of the sky like an angel.

Diebol and Lem-slash-General Johnson were the only Growen soldiers still outside on the back of the last evacuation transport in the convoy to the Hiding Place; the other blitzers were prepping weapons down below. They all wore Frelsi uniforms now, complete with Frelsi space-hoods and atmosphere masks. "If anyone asks, dear General, we're Skraeli from one of the gas giants and don't breathe well here," Diebol had winked as he slipped his on.

Well, someone was asking now.

"Soldier, can I get your operating number?"

Lem and Diebol both whirled to see *Jei Filking Bereens* standing behind them, his fingers drumming on the short bamboo staff suspended from his belt.

Diebol looked flabbergasted even through his mask. "Where the—bloodseas—did you come from?"

Elation, and then terror, welled up within Lem with the simultaneous thoughts *oh shyte yes Jei can fix this* and *oh shyte no, Jei, this is Diebol and he will kill you.* She needed to tip Jei off without giving herself away; thinking fast, Lem stepped between Jei and Diebol, arms out as if shielding Diebol with her body, and spat off her mother's old operating number.

"That's a woman's number," Jei smiled. "You sure don't look like a woman to me."

Exactly. "We're escorting refugees to the Hiding Place," General Johnson answered.

"Are you now." Jei glanced ahead of them to the horizon full of smoking volcanoes. "Why are you both topside, then?" Within thirty minutes after breaking Alpino's atmosphere all Frelsi evacuees had to go below-deck to make sure no one saw their secret destination except for the one pilot in the very front of the convoy.

"Visual target confirmation," Lem said—again, the exact wrong answer, on purpose.

Jei's lips spread in a dangerous grin.

Two things then happened at once.

Diebol fired his pistol under Lem's arm just as Jei drew his mace. The colorful cartridge whistled through the air—

Instead of deflecting off the mace like normal for Jei, the shot exploded in an electric arc down its length into his arm.

"Why the hell would you use a shock cartridge?" both Lem and Jei screamed at the same time—Lem in character as she dodged to the side and pulled her own flayer gun, and Jei in an agonized groan as he grabbed his arm and swung his mace at Diebol's head.

Diebol dodged with a stylized side-wards roll, yanking back the slider to switch his weapon to kill now.

"Why wouldn't you use a kill cartridge first?" Lem repeated to Diebol. *And not even a stun cartridge, either, just straight up, old-fashioned electric shock?*

"You'll see," Diebol smiled, tapping the side of his mask as he fired again to add: "All units topside, we are under attack."

Lem fired haphazardly in Jei's general direction, assuming a high-ranking armchair officer like Johnson didn't have much target practice. Jei spun his mace to deflect the shots back at her—

Oh shyte, they're gonna see my field. Unlike Jei's neuropolarity em-pushes, the static charge from Lem's biocapacitor-cells often gave visual tells like sparks. Lem slid behind Diebol as her instinctive electromagnetic field repulsed Jei's shots away from her. Hopefully she was hidden with the sunlight and the colorful bullets zipping around them like rabid fireflies—

The top hatch slammed open between Lem and Jei; Growen soldiers scrambled out to fight. "We need to keep this quiet or the transports ahead will see!" Lem shouted to Diebol, trying to say the opposite to Jei. Lem continued firing toward Jei, feeding him ammunition to deflect back at the new contenders—

"Stop shooting, idiot, he's using your fire!" Diebol shoved

her to the ground. "*This* is how you take care of an over-powered electromagnetic."

And with one simple flick of his wrist, Diebol threw an em-push that hurled Jei off the back of the transport.

Everyone stared at the space where Jei had been. "What happened?!" Lem cried, for real, with both her identities, as she ran forward. A tiny em-push like that? Jei could always block that, no problem!

"That's why we use an electric shock first," Diebol said to the nearby blitzers, casually striding after Lem as she raced across the deck. "Not a normal sarcoblasting stun cartridge—just pure old electricity. It disables their powers and it breaks instead of deflecting. Something I only learned recently after culling a few of our own Stygges gone rogue. Should be standard protocol, but your Stygge masters don't want you normal soldiers knowing how to kill us. The Frelsi only have two electromagnetics, after all, so why teach you something you'll never encounter?"

Lem heard, but didn't give a shyte, about the hints of rebellion in Diebol's speech. He had to be over the moon, showing up his arch-rival like that without even a real duel, but she was on her belly, staring down into the mist behind the transport as her heart pounded in panic against the deck. Fog, and grass, and shapes in the fog ... shyte, where was he? Had he been sucked into the engine?

Diebol was coordinating behind her. "You two, get down to the cockpit—check for signs that the transports ahead noticed anything. It doesn't seem like it, from here. I'll kill the intruder."

Lem shimmied further on her belly, hanging almost all the way off the back of the bullet now—ah.

There he was, hidden under the overhang of the transport's large back door. He'd stabbed the staff of his mace into the door on this way down, and now hung from it with both hands, dangling. The fog cut and filled in around him, but Lem could just catch the glow from the engines below the transport door—centimeters from Jei's boots.

Another wisp of fog, and he was gone. There was a hole in the back door, still burning from the neodymium mace.

Lem heard Diebol's boots by her hips; she began firing erratically down into the mist, as if she saw something in the foggy grass below.

"He's inside the transport," Diebol said, arriving just a second later to see the hole. Diebol's fingers closed around Lem's bicep; she tensed, and almost pulled away into the mist. He doubled down and yanked her to her feet with a hiss: "Wouldn't want you falling off, General," he hissed.

Lem couldn't help believing that he knew.

CHAPTER NINETEEN

Diebol

DIEBOL DID NOT KNOW.

He didn't know how Jei Bereens had escaped or how he'd materialized here; he didn't know how General Johnson planned to screw him over this time; and he didn't know what had become of the traitor Frank Zej.

Deserters "happened" all the time. Except for Jei's little hissy-fit in the mind-channel Diebol had little evidence for anything but a run-of-the-mill Frelsi conversion, so he kept his suspicions about a hidden Benzaran to himself: despite the strange feeling during their interview, Frank Zej, unmasked, was just another idiot face. If Diebol miscalculated based on unprovable nonsense like clones and shapeshifters because "my brain-dreams told me so," the High Council would have his neck.

But now that same strange hint of memory hung around General Johnson like static in the air …

So *although* it made sense for Diebol and Johnson to split up to catch Jei, Johnson forward and Diebol through the hole in the back, Diebol refused to let the general out of his sight. It wasn't the slowness, bordering on incompetence—that was par for the course for an officer who'd never served among the enlisted ranks before his commission.

No, you couldn't trust a man who used his body to shield you from your attacker just weeks after ordering you assassinated. Diebol dragged the general after him down the metal hatch into the hold, ignoring the blustering protests and threats of demotion.

Dim yellow lights threw soft shadows throughout the rounded belly of the faux Frelsi evacuation ship. There wasn't anywhere to hide, really—the ship's cylindrical body was only as long as a standard airbus. Blitzers in Frelsi garb fanned out, weapons at the ready, running to and fro from the rust-colored cockpit doors ahead to the decontamination chamber in the back.

Diebol slammed shut the sliding door to the cockpit. "No one enters the front," he shouted. "The intruder's somewhere in the ship. He burrowed into the decontamination chamber and he's likely headed for the forward comms unit. With his powers down he requires backup; he cannot be allowed to send any transmission."

"Why wouldn't he just use his wristband?" Johnson asked, finally pulling away from Diebol's grip.

"Because he's smarter than you, General," Diebol answered through a clenched smile. Louder, to the soldiers: "I'm going into decon. Every soldier unmask, now."

Everyone obeyed, ripping free of their masks with such terrified enthusiasm you'd think they couldn't breathe in there. Diebol stalked by them toward the back of the ship, taking in each face with a split-second glance as he passed, Jei's doom in hand—

And then the lights went out.

Lem

Jei couldn't do it on his own. There was nowhere to hide.

Lem acted without a moment's thought. The light switch was right by the entrance to the hold, and the second Diebol turned his back, a quick discharge of electricity from Lem's fingers fried the switch.

Darkness blanketed the hold.

A din of sudden blitzer shouts—an unsettling crunching sound—above it all, Lem heard her Accuser's mockery loud and clear in the darkness: *Ha stupid, now I've found you! I'm telling Bricandor!*

Lem swallowed, ducking away from the door after Diebol as people switched on their headlamps. *I'm a loyal Growen soldier*, she repeated in her head to drown out the enemy interdimensional. *It's just not in the Growen's best interest to kill kids.*

I'm telling you did this; I'm telling!

Well, shyte.

At least, thank goodness, Diebol didn't talk to interdimensionals and Bricandor wasn't here? Lem made sure to be right behind Diebol when he turned around; she struggled to salvage her thoughts as her heart raced in her throat, hoping perhaps it took some time for messages to travel to the Mind-Reader from his invisible minion. Perhaps, if Bricandor turned his mind's eye to her *now*, he would find the Accuser had lied to him. *I am loyal to you, Bricandor. It's not in the Growen's best interest to kill kids*, Lem repeated. *You wanna win that Burburan election, right? That's your pet project? This is for the greater good.*

Someone gasped.

An errant headlamp swung over a blitzer now slumped in the corner. Murmurs and terrified whispers flittered over him: his head dangled at an odd, sickening angle. Lem dashed to his side to check a pulse—

Look what you did.

"Oh, I hate this," someone squeaked.

A grunt in the darkness.

Everyone swiveled, headlamps like spotlights—

Another blitzer crumbled to his knees.

Diebol growled, drawing his mace. Eerie darklight reflected off his Frelsi atmosphere mask in streaks. A shiver ran down Lem's spine.

"He's hunting us one by one," someone squeaked.

The hush of bated breath hung in the air. Someone tried to fiddle with the lights. Lem could almost hear the terrified heartbeats echoing in the tense chamber.

"He's over here!" someone shouted—

And then their headlamp went out with a scream.

A movement—someone pushed someone—Diebol perked, as if he saw something, and everyone dove out of the way as the young Growen leader raced back toward the cockpit—"Move!" he roared. A blinding rectangle of daylight shot into the dark room as the cockpit door slid open with a groan. The blitzers closest to it raised their weapons to fire—*no, Jei!*

Lem squeezed her fists: the electric field around her surged, just for a moment, throwing off everyone's aim. Oxidizer cartridges went everywhere, glittering with color that hid the tell-tale sparks of Lem's crime. Jei's silhouette slipped through the door. Diebol hurled his mace—

Oh, shyte, more? Lem em-pulled weakly, slowing the weapon's flight—

The door slammed shut with an enormous gonging; the mace thwacked into it.

Panic fluttered in the tip of every finger. *They're gonna catch me. They're gonna catch me. I won't be able to find Her. I've got to stop helping.*

Diebol reached the cockpit door, ripped his mace out of it, and smashed it with such force the door clove in two; Jei's name rumbled from his throat like a hoarse curse from the grave.

Shyte, no, keep helping. Keep helping. She raised her arm in the darkness to pull again, praying the shadows hid her—shyte, she'd only *just* learned to mimic Jei's technique, it just wasn't how her biology worked, she couldn't do this whole hidden wrist flick thing, shyte there were sparks—!

"Benzaran ...?"

She heard Diebol say her name as she shoved her errant hands into her pockets and dove to hide by the nearest corpse. *Bloodseas, Jei, if he finds me ...*

Diebol

Diebol stood in the doorway to the cockpit, suddenly heavy, staring behind himself into the hold just for a second at the place he thought he saw sparks in the darkness. He remembered them trickling off her like stars in the frigid room in the interrogation center, and the scent of blood and desperation came rushing back with a nauseating twist in his midsection …

Oh, thank heaven for Jei Bereens.

The raspy voice snapped Diebol out of his dizziness—Jei had incapacitated the pilot and was trying to send that transmission. Diebol whirled to smash his mace down again, this time toward the head of the young Paradox Warrior in the pilot seat.

Jei twisted to block both-handed with his mace's staff; both warriors' weapons locked against each other in a glowing X. Diebol leveraged his standing position over Jei's seated contortion and showed teeth. "Something bothering you, Jei?" he teased.

"Just your continued existence," Jei groaned back.

"How unfortunate that you're powerless to fix that." With that, Diebol tightened his jaw and mustered the weight of a thousand personal torments into an em-push behind his crushing shove.

Jei's biceps shook. A bead of sweat rolled down his forehead. The compuwall cracked under his shoulder blades.

And for just one delicious moment, there was a flicker of realization in his eyes that this might be the end.

Jei

When I called for Njande, a bright lavender crack appeared in the ceiling.

A chunk of burnt metal fell under the swing of a purple mace; Diebol followed my eyes just in time to jump out of the way—and through the new hole reached *Mera*, her hair waving like a flag of hope against blue sky as she called my name.

I grabbed her arm, kicked off Diebol's chest, and pulled myself up out of the cockpit into a bath of mist and wind. Diebol scrambled to his feet, reaching for me—

Mera chucked a light bomb down at him and blew him a kiss.

For a moment the whole universe stopped as her gaze turned to me. A violent gust of wind cleared the fog between us and the transport ahead. I gripped her hand, soft in mine.

She nodded.

We leapt to safety as the explosion went off under us.

Lem

Oh, shyte no.

Lem threw herself forward as the light bomb grenade dropped into the cockpit in front of Diebol. The young Stygge was Lem's only lead to Her—the only lead, after *months* of research and skulking around, who might stop the coming electronic apocalypse.

"I can't believe I'm doing this," Lem muttered through clenched teeth. "Jei, you owe me a nightmare."

Diebol

Diebol saw the grenade drop in front of him, and then the wall of light.

But before it could crackle over his flesh and leave him a dry skeleton, Diebol found himself flying backward through the cockpit doorway, pulled by an invisible force. As the weapon's secondary blast rocked the ship, Diebol felt someone's hand on his collar—someone's body over his—the pings and clangs of shrapnel ricocheting off heavy metal right by his head—and under the arm of his protector, Diebol could see the cockpit door, now ripped free, held over him like a shield.

The firestorm had barely ended when Diebol's protector dashed off him as if afraid he might bite; the makeshift shield dropped with a ringing thud, tossed like a last-minute murder weapon.

General Johnson looked genuinely ashamed of himself for saving Diebol's life.

"You're mission-essential," the grey man grunted in excuse, sweat and blood trickling down the side of his temple. "You did most of the work anyway, triggering your powers to fly back like that. I'm only here for the accolades."

Diebol rose, animal adrenaline still surging through his burning chest with a skyrocketing heartrate. No, he hadn't triggered his powers. Someone else—he'd truly thought death—

But there was no time. "Get up!" he heard himself yelling to the fallen, mouth and muscles on autopilot. The mission, as the general said. It was all just for the mission. Whatever off-script imbecilities Morda dreamt she could pull off—alerting the entire convoy with her ill-planned explosion—they ended now. The Frelsi pilots would lead them to the Hiding Place or die.

CHAPTER TWENTY

Reise

HERE IN THE DARK, HIDDEN HOLD OF THE THIRD EVACUATION transport, all the littlest kids were finally asleep. Reise Benzaran couldn't see shyte, but he felt the heavy head of his youngest brother, J'miah, crushing his right leg. Perhaps the warm vibrations of the floor put everyone at ease.

Reise heard Cinta's hiss before he heard the boom and crackle.

An explosion? Scattered gasps—everyone stiffened—someone let out a low whine—

So much for keeping the siblings asleep.

"Ambush Reaction Team, this is Waste Convoy 15, under attack as anticipated." Cinta's sharp, crisp Biouk accent was harsh in the Grenblenian common tongue. His enormous ears perked and twisted, likely responding to instructions in an implant from Alpino Firebase Command as his wristband lit up neon green in the brown darkness.

As the light blinked off there was a rustle. "Safety protocol," Cinta announced. "Six oldest on me."

"Yay, I've never been a human shield before," Gideon quipped. He didn't sound bitter, just silly, but Reise heard a soft thwack from Nathan's direction.

"Dude, Reise's got little siblings," Nate said.

"I shall allow it," Reise said. He didn't want Jake to start crying again, but it sounded like Jake was asleep, too. Reise eased J'miah's head off his lap, sliding to the side, in his mind, as smoothly as a space ninja on ice. Nathan's cold, bony grip on his forearm helped him to his feet.

Reise's palms felt along the warm wall, boots shuffling around bodies as he followed Nathan and Gideon behind Cinta and two girls about the same age as Reise's older sister. Reise didn't have to see everyone to know who was part of the security team.

His throat tightened a bit, but not because of the job. Of course, the false holds of the evacuation transports had two extremely obvious entrances, one a front ladder from the top deck that led down behind the cockpit, and the other the huge loading door into the decontamination chamber in the back. Well, the smuggling cabins *under* these false holds also had two entrances: the first a hidden front ladder to the top deck, and the second a secret back tunnel into the decontamination chamber. The six fighting age cadets now made their way to the latter to guard their companions with the illusion of occupancy. If the Growen opened the transports and saw people inside, they were less likely to think they'd missed something—and less likely to search further for hidden compartments full of children.

Oh, the hated back tunnel.

Gideon and Reise stooped now as the secret smuggling cabin came to a narrow taper under the decontamination chamber. Reise envied short people like Nathan and Cinta.

He envied them *a lot* as the space closed in, crushing his lungs in his mind—

With a gulp Reise pushed past everyone else in the dark, tapping his way across their shoulders. They knew to let him go first, or last. Not in the middle. Shyte, everyone knew what happened if he got stuck in the entrance. He barely even felt shame about it anymore.

Reise shared an unfortunate kinship with the dead man

who'd fallen out of the shower riddled with his own bullet holes, at the start of all this.

At the back of the hold Reise gripped the wheel-shaped bolt on the wall with both hands and turned. It unlocked the circular hidden panel with a creak—everyone cringed. "Squeaky wheel gets the bullet," Gideon whispered in the jolliest tone.

Reise almost laughed aloud despite his upcoming panic. He sometimes wanted to be Gideon, when he wasn't imagining himself a Paradox Warrior like Jei Bereens. Except, he'd ditch the mace, and use a bazooka. Maybe two …

The thoughts distracted Reise pleasantly as he ducked on his hands and knees at the mouth of the exit tunnel. He inhaled hard twice, puffing out his cheeks and chest—*just go, just go!*—and shimmied into the wall, fast and slippery as a fish.

In his mind, at least.

The squeezing darkness against his shoulders, even just for that split second, was so horrifically complete. Reise's temples pounded. He could taste a beating mass at the back of his mouth. He pawed for the exit panel like a man in a coffin, his fingers missing the seams as the walls closed around his head —

Reise clenched his teeth, forcing his fingertips to recall hours and hours of torturous timed drills. Up, right, left, turn—breathe, breathe, breathe—

There it was. He pushed the lid open just slightly, scanned the dim decontamination chamber for just a couple seconds shorter than he was supposed to, and scrambled out into the air. Oh shyte yes, the air, the air.

"I die inside every time you go first," Gideon chuckled as the six chosen ones replaced the hidden panel and took up defensive positions throughout the ship. "Man, when you were screaming that one time? You sounded like a straight up giggling banshee. Like from the caves on the southern continent? Giggling banshee."

"Gideon," Nathan intoned.

The bigger teen grumbled an apology, muttered something about Nathan reporting him "again," and closed his mouth.

Everyone crouched behind various crates and barrels, weapons drawn. Reise and two of the girls faced the decontamination chamber; Nathan, Cinta, and Gideon faced the external ladder from the top deck, just in front of the cockpit.

Cinta rapped on the door to the cockpit three times; the pilot responded with two knocks.

Two? Uh oh. Reise met the wide-eyed glance of the Insectoid girl across from him.

"We've got company," Gideon's voice smiled.

Reise exhaled, cooling his head with the memories of target practice on the Lawn. He knew he couldn't hear, not through the space-capable double walls, but his ears strained for footsteps on the deck above them nevertheless.

Cinta hissed again. Reise turned to see the Biouk's ears, one perked straight up, one turned, like a satellite dish, toward the ceiling. "Fighting." He scampered out from his position behind his crate. "Stand fast."

He clambered up the ladder, high-stepping off each paw like a cat touching something sticky.

He walks kind of weird, Reise remembered saying to his older sister once. She screamed at him, threw something, and stormed out of the room.

She came back to apologize hours later, her face flushed and leaves in her thick bushy hair: *Diebol did that to him.*

Did what?

Ripped out his claws. Because of me. She pulled a twig out of her hair and crushed it between her fingers. *It was lose Njande or lose Cinta.*

And you chose Njande?

Cinta asked me to.

But did you? I mean, he's still alive.

It's complicated. She'd launched, then, into some vague philosophy that turned into a tangent for both of them—Reise took to theoretical metaphysics like a bloodsucker to, well, blood—and that became an argument.

But the arguments weren't always bad. Often, but not

always. Sometimes he told her stories. That was their game; she'd often retell them to him, with her own twists, and they'd play through the scenarios, theoretical characters fighting or complementing each other in their words ...

"Reise, Gideon, topside now," Cinta's accent crackled through their wristbands. Reise blinked out of his distraction—wow, distracted even at a time like this?—and dashed up the ladder just behind Gideon, his boots thwick-ringing against the rungs.

Metallic smoke hit his nostrils with the crisp, sweet scent of natural fuel on the breeze. Reise emerged gun first, swiveling with his knee on the ladder to scan for enemies before showing his head.

"Hoo shyte!" he exclaimed, eye-level with like twenty sets of boots. Beyond Gideon's kneel, he could see tall, tan boots that belonged to Jei Bereens, engaged in a tactical dance with like five other guys while his spinning mace forcefield provided cover for Cinta and Gideon. Beside him twirled a human woman in typical Alpino civilian garb—blue pants, white shirt, black vest—wielding a purple mace. All the other guys wore Frelsi uniform, but—"If they're shooting at Cinta and Bereens they must be bad, right?" he confirmed as he aimed, cheek to rifle.

"That's the big brain move, yeah," Gideon shouted back.

Reise fired under Bereens's glowing shield, each shot a breath and a pull. This was the only moment in life where everything made sense. The weapon's butt solid against his chest, its curve cool against his cheek, his wrist hugging the stock, forestock resting in his other palm as comfortably as a part of his body ... aim, breathe, squeeze, target down. Repeat.

The other side had more firepower, but no cover. Someone threw a light bomb toward the hatch where Reise stood—the human woman with long brown hair took her mace like a club and whacked it into the sky. It exploded over a hill at least 120 meters away.

"Holy shyte I want *her* on my stick-sock team," Gideon quipped.

She smirked back at him and blew him a kiss. It was a weird kiss, Reise thought. "How many passengers below?" the woman asked as she kicked some guy off into the mists.

"Just three," Cinta answered from his prone firing position. Reise saw the Biouk's ears flatten further against his back with the question. *He doesn't like her.*

"Just three?" Her nose wrinkled. She gave Reise, Gideon, and Cinta a once-over that made Reise feel somehow smaller—was it mocking? Scornful? It was just for a split second. Hero-woman was busy turning a handstand into a fancy flip toward—

That guy. The guy who met her midair with a *filking black-light mace in his hands.*

"Do not look at it straight," Cinta yelled, as if reading Reise's mind. "Burns the retina."

"Roger," Reise and Gideon both answered, although Reise was fairly sure Gideon didn't know what retina were.

The black-light warrior hurled the woman to the side, off the transport. She went flying with a yelp—

The black-light warrior bee-lined toward Bereens. *Shyte, if he takes out our shield, we'll have the same cover problem they do.*

But then, the Firebase Ambush Team arrived.

Diebol

Just as Diebol threw out his hand to toss Jei with the same power that'd tossed that stupid witch, a body tackled him around the waist. The air exploded out of him as his chest hit the hard deck; he raised his mace to smash the person in the head—

"Do you want to be shot, you idiot?" General Johnson roared as a storm of double-sized blue flayer cartridges whizzed over their heads. Diebol looked up to see at least fifty air-riders with cannons zooming around the evacuation vehicle, their blasts flicking his soldiers off the deck like ticks off a pegasus rump.

No! No no no!

Diebol raised his hand to rip the drivers off their bikes with a violent em-pull—

An electric shock hit him in the chest. Pain flickered through his body in waves: "What the filking—"

A thin teenager peeped out from the front hold hatch, looking sheepishly from Diebol to Jei as he literally held the smoking gun. "If it works on me, it works on you, right?" Jei shouted.

Gloating did not become him. Diebol grit his teeth, seething, about to—

About to nothing. General Johnson gripped him around the torso and rolled with him off the transport.

"No, you crazy fool!" Fog splashed over them, closing like water over a drowning man between them and the transports as Diebol roared. "We'll be sucked under the engi—" He didn't have time to finish; Johnson fired a grappling hook from his belt into one of the air-riders. The jolt as they shot through the air together seemed to leave Diebol's stomach behind somewhere in the fog—his ribs slammed against the vehicle's egg-shaped shell —the general swung himself onto the air-rider, pushed the driver off into the mist, and pulled Diebol up behind him.

Diebol reached for the compuwall windshield, teeth gritted as he gripped his painful sides: "We have to get back on that transport!"

The general gripped his wrist with a force Diebol had never imagined you could develop in an armchair. "Look!" Johnson screamed. "Look around you! It's over!"

Through the mist now mixing with volcanic ash, Diebol couldn't deny it looked that way. Their fake evacuation transportation smoldered somewhere back along the plains; it had floated on for a bit after the light bomb explosion before finally spiraling into a low hill. The gunfire was already dying down amidst scattered shouts as the swarm of Frelsi air-riders rounded up prisoners from the living.

And the three real Frelsi transports had already disappeared off behind one of the volcanic ridges without a single Growen agent on board.

"We can't leave the men behind," Diebol hissed.

"What men?" Johnson growled back. "They're mostly dead. When someone gets shot off a floating transport there's not a lot left to take captive. Maybe if you had your powers you could do something about it, but in the time it takes for you to run out your cool down, you'll die, too. If you really want to help the men, help by going back to the crash site with me to round up survivors there before the Frelsi pillage the place. Unless you want to abandon them to chase your boyfriend?"

Diebol wanted to throttle the man, but for once it wasn't because of his cowardice. He closed his mouth. Johnson slid both palms across the windshield, turning the air-rider back the way they'd come.

The Hiding Place was lost.

Jei

Bloodseas, Mera was like a magical boomerang that just kept swinging back. After I'd taken her pegasus, she'd apparently called it back to help her rescue me; when Diebol threw her off the transport, she'd em-pulled herself atop one of the nearby air-riders.

She was indomitable.

She rode that air-rider close, now, tapping the driver's shoulder to bring the swallow-shaped craft around. Her eyes sparkled at me through the mist as I trotted to the edge of the deck wiping sweat off my brow. Her gaze tickled me.

"I just can't seem to get rid of you," I laughed.

"I just can't stay away," she giggled.

The driver looked at me with his head tilted, and I suddenly felt mad—at her, for the eyelashes and tinkly voice routine, and at him, for catching me in whatever that moment was. I nodded and walked away abruptly. Best to keep whatever irrational responses I had to myself.

We'd won, for the moment, but I couldn't feel happy. I couldn't feel much of anything, actually, after the initial burst of girl-smiles evaporated.

Hopefully this would wear off soon; a numb victory was almost worse than the alternative.

CHAPTER TWENTY-ONE

Reise

AS HE'D ANTICIPATED, THE AMBUSH GAVE REISE THE LOGICAL ESCAPE opportunity he needed.

The three Frelsi evacuation transports rested now in a gully beyond the edge of the plains, hidden amidst the red-earthed foothills of the large volcano on the horizon—far, far from the location of the ambush. Reise couldn't even see the Firebase reinforcements that had rescued them anymore. Somewhere back there in the low clouds, those anti-ambush heroes patrolled on their air-riders still, cleaning up enemy stragglers and guarding against any further Growen tails ... *I wish they could just escort us all the way*, Reise thought—but then, of course, they'd all learn the Hiding Place's location, and no one but the guide pilots assigned to the refuge could know that. It was good that Jei and his friend had shown up when they did: even anticipating the ambush, there was only a narrow time and distance in which the Firebase team could reach the convoy without getting too close to the secret refuge. Firebase and Fort Jehu leadership had to be sweating right now over the razor-sharp margins on their risk analysis.

Now, all the fighting-age teenagers from the evacuation convoy stood on the top deck of the third transport, conferring in the breeze. The lone adult—the Hiding Place guide pilot who had ordered the halt—said the third transport was now "dirty" and couldn't come to the refuge. She twitched her antennae in rapid, nervous circles, chittering in Insectoid run-on:

"Any one of the Growen who got aboard could have planted a tracking device we don't have the time or equipment to run a true scan I'm not risking it."

"But there is not room for all the cubs from this ship in the other two secret holds," Cinta answered, eyeing the speck-like silhouette of Jei's friend in the mist. Cinta had demanded the woman take an air-rider *far* off into the distance while the convoy members talked.

"Then some larvae have to ride in the main holds we can't take the third ship," the guide pilot said, wiping her middle limbs across her enormous abdomen as if washing the issue off herself.

"This is gonna sound, like, incredibly shallow right now," said the pilot of the third ship, a teenage Hoernig with leathery skin—female, by her lack of horn. "But I'm signed for this transport, while my orders say to follow you to the Hiding Place. What do I do?"

"Sign it over to me," Jei said. "I'll take it over to the Alpino Firebase for you. Keep my new friend busy that way, right Cinta?"

Cinta said nothing, still watching the woman in the distance. "Thank you," said the Hoernig girl. "That way I'm within my orders."

"Well then," the lead pilot chirped, clicking her mandibles together with finality. "That's that we need to hurry before more Growen come down go let's go get the larvae go!"

At that, Reise nodded to Nathan and Gideon; they both nodded back.

It was almost time to make their escape.

Reise's knee jittered a bit, standing there, as the group leaders assigned tasks to the fighting age teenagers; he just wanted to do this already. *Gimme a job, gimme a job, hurry up and gimme a job so I can go not do it* ... Cinta was one of the fastest leaders to get organized, but he assigned Reise last. The other teens had already returned to their ships, or started lowering the gangplank ramp on the back of the third transport, by the time Reise hustled down into the hold to start moving kids to the second ship. Reise gripped the rough ladder with both hands, watching his footing—

A harsh guttural sound turned his head; he paused on the ladder, hidden just inside the hatch as snippets of one last conversation filtered to him on the wind above.

"She should not see how many cubs come from here," Cinta was snapping. "She cannot see our big numbers!"

"Mera knows," Jei answered. "She'll stay away."

"No, *you* need to make her go more far. *You* walk over there and take her away."

There was a postured pause. "Alright ..."

"And Jei?"

"Yeah. What?"

"Jaika is not replaceable."

There was a heavy boot step; a scamper backward. "Maybe if you hadn't told her she's supposed to save the universe from some kind of heat death, she wouldn't *need* to be replaced. I know you're the one who filled her head with thermodynamic fairy tales, *cadet*."

A harsh space-lemur laugh. "You know half of *nothing*. Jaika *is* the heat death. *Jaika* will destroy the universe. I tell her to stay with Njande because only stay with Njande will stop her." In his anger, Cinta's grammar broke down completely, and his accent thickened with extra consonants and lisps. "Ksh! You go back to Luna-Guetala and stay away from the cubs—you and your Stygge powers only cause problem, big destruction man."

A human scoff. "Right. See you round."

"I hope not."

Reise shuddered and ran down the ladder. He'd never heard Cinta talk that way to anyone, much less one of the most decorated young heroes in Frelsi history. It was Lem they were talking about —Jaika was Cinta's Biouk name for her—and of course, Reise had heard Lem's heat death theory in their many arguments, but neither Jei nor Cinta made a lot of sense here, out of context. Lem destroy the universe? Highly illogical and highly unlikely. Perhaps Cinta spoke in metaphor. Did Biouks do that, culturally? Reise was supposed to know, but "culture," in general, was another one of those "social things" people kept telling him he missed. Getting distracted, fear of small spaces, forgetting social things … just a lot of ways he was never good enough for the right people.

"You're in a pissy mood," Gideon remarked.

"Huh?" Reise startled, almost dropping the baby Biouk in his arms. Shyte, he had a baby Biouk in his arms. Distracted, again … "How can you tell?" he asked, carrying her down the metal gangplank out into the soft sunlight after the others.

The dry, red earth crunched under Gideon's heavy step as he followed Reise with two more small kids under his arms. "You almost dropped that other Wonderfrog on her tail, that's why. You're lucky Nate didn't drop-kick you, man. Then hit your ass with a bullying report faster'n you can say tattle-tale."

Nathan looked up at them from the open hold of the second ship; he was bent over buckling two younger kids into their harnesses, telling them something that made them smile; only the twinkle in his eye let on that he heard Gideon's jab.

Gideon lived for that twinkle, and everyone knew it. "But seriously, Reise, if something's up, man, you can talk about it," the brute went on.

"Well—"

"To Nathan, I mean," Gideon finished.

Reise laughed out loud. "That's more like it," Gideon said. "We almost set?"

"Yeah."

Gideon nodded over to Nathan, who nodded back. While the crowd still lingered outside the second transport, the three boys made their way back to the third in the name of "closing up."

They did so, however, from the inside, and squeezed back into the now-empty hidden hold.

"Are you both still certain about this venture?" Reise piped as they strapped in. "The consequences when we return will be severe."

"You kidding, man? Being around your thesaurus-brain is the only thing keeping mine from melting into my muscles," Gideon said.

Reise couldn't quite understand this particular joke; he looked to Nathan's face in the glow of his wristband. "We're with you," Nathan replied. The older teen's small, thin face seemed even bonier and more triangular by the dim glow of his wristband. "I just sent Cinta our accountability message—he thinks we're in the first transport, which just took off. We should be good to go."

In the darkness, Reise's knee began to jitter again. This was real. This was happening. "Is this poorly conceptualized?" Reise asked.

"Maybe a little," Nathan said. "But if I thought my sister was in trouble, I'd go check it out, too, regardless of the safety brief. And it's not unreasonable to believe that the person who accompanies her on all her secret missions might be on the hunt for her. We can always catch a ride back to the Firebase if things get too hot."

The cold floor under them rumbled to life, warming with those comforting travel vibrations.

"Sweet," Gideon said. "Let's go find your fam."

CHAPTER TWENTY-TWO

Lem

LEM COULDN'T STOP SHIVERING, AND SHE HOPED WITH *EVERY electron of her being* that Diebol couldn't feel that.

He sat behind her on the air-rider she now piloted back to where the fake transport had crashed. The pressure of her palms on the windshield sliding right, now left, steadying the vehicle with more weight on this side, now that—she tried to focus on anything but the heat radiating through the space between her and him, a sharp contrast against the cool of the mists. She didn't like *anyone* behind her, much less the monster who'd ripped out Cinta's claws.

He'd had his reasons. That was the saddest thing—she truly believed he thought he could save her by exorcising Njande from her soul.

Or he'd thought that, past tense. Now she doubted her life mattered to him.

We're on the same team, she repeated in her head, still wondering when the Accuser's alert to Bricandor was going to drop. *We're going to help these fallen soldiers, and then report back to base. We did our best.*

The Accuser's mocking voice played, again, almost loud

enough that Lem thought Diebol had said something behind her. *No you didn't. You sabotaged the mission.*

I did that because it's just not healthy for the Growen to kill kids!

The Accuser giggled. *You also did it to protect Jei Bereens.*

Shhh. Lem invoked Njande's name to hide herself and refused to answer any more. She didn't know the "right answer" for a Growen soldier in her situation. Jei was the enemy, for sure. Even having his name in her brain could get her in trouble. *I saved Diebol's life. That counts for something.*

It did count for something, and she shivered more. Oh, Jei would kill her. Literally kill her, if he knew. The years Lem spent with Cinta's family in the lush jungles of Luna-Guetala? Yeah, Jei lived with Diebol in a *cage* as Bricandor pitted the two against each other, creating and breaking emotional bonds to teach Diebol how to betray, how to dominate, how to love, and how to hate.

Lem's forearms were visibly shaking. She imagined covering her head, diving off into the fog, disappearing. She couldn't carry this thing through. She wasn't going to make it out the other side anyway. What if she ran away from the whole conflict, hid deep in the jungle, alone, and lived on anaconda flesh and lechichi fruit?

I just want to go home. I just want to go home.

Diebol's voice rescued her from her panic. In an instant, she was back, here, and now. "We both know you tried to have me killed several weeks ago," Diebol said. "I want an explanation for today."

"Don't let it get to your head," she growled for General Johnson. "I won't admit to knowing what you're talking about. Are you recording me?"

"I don't blame you. I would kill you, as well, if I could get away with it," Diebol said. "I just note that your grappling hook skill, today, isn't typical of the incompetence I have come to expect from you. Your terrible aim was more what I expected."

"Look, I don't have Stygge powers," Johnson said. "I don't have the thousands of hours of combat training and field work you do. I've spent most of the last several years in meetings to make what you do possible. The men don't love me like they love shimmering figureheads like you. But I can and will make it happen for the mission."

Lem stayed still in the silence for a moment while Diebol chewed that over. She maintained the slumped look, a weak posture bent over the windshield, but every muscle was ready to fire and fight; if she were a Biouk, like she wanted to be, her waiting ears would have perked straight up.

"I could ask you the same question," she added now, almost against her better judgment. "You brought me out here intending to let me catch a stray bullet."

"I gave you the opportunity," Diebol chuckled. "But you became insignificant to me the moment Jei Bereens showed up." She heard a rustle as he shifted his position. "Still, not killing someone is a far cry from actively saving their life."

"You have recently become mission-essential," she said. "There are assets in your purview that I may not have considered previously."

"Is that an apology?"

"One does not apologize for something one does not admit," Johnson replied.

Diebol shifted again, this time closer to Lem.

"This is about Her, isn't it," Diebol said. "That's what's changed, from several weeks ago."

Yes. Yes, a thousand times yes, we're talking about this, yes. "Perhaps." Johnson would have shrugged, but shrugging didn't fit into his version of military bearing.

"What are you so eager to know?" Diebol asked. "Your attempts to harness Her power would be futile."

Where is She? Lem bit back the trap for her tongue. "I imagine so," Johnson said only. *Be quiet. Wait. Wait. Let him keep talking.* Silence was an interrogation technique she had never been able to master in class …

"But you'll keep trying to get into the inner sanctum regardless," Diebol finished Johnson's presumed thought.

"Like I said, I don't have Stygge powers. But I have years on all of you … years with information that could benefit Her targeting decisions." Lem anticipated the retort: "And before you say I should be satisfied with my place on the council, I want less granular strategy. I've always preferred the big picture."

"You're convinced She's not a computer program," Diebol said.

"You said it, not me," Johnson answered.

They came up now on the wreckage of the fake transport they'd abandoned when they rode their grappling hooks onto the Frelsi convoy. Their broken ride no longer looked like a black bullet—well, one that had been fired, maybe, with the front cockpit blown open like that. Still, damage wasn't irrevocable. Not to a Frelsi eye, anyway. Jei would know better than she, but it looked like the engine structure was fine, and the only issue was the blasted-out control room. Now if the explosion had hit the fuel center, that would've been a different story …

Diebol had already called a small Growen land-runner to pick them up. It sped toward them now along the ground on six wheels, fast as a silver arrow. After four months Lem had become comfortable with a lot of Growen weapons and vehicles, but these rapid armored land-runners always looked wicked to her, with their spiked sides and spear-like fronts.

Lem unmounted and clambered over the front cockpit wreckage. It felt good to move, to get away from Diebol—she stood on one leg for a moment with the other knee resting bent on a piece of metal, and threw her arms out to breathe. *Oh, Njande.* Her spirit heard better in the jungle, she thought, but even here in the misty hills she could see her interdimensional's fingertips playing through the grass with the wind like fingers through a lover's hair. She remembered a time before she could see his trails everywhere—just like she remembered a time before Cinta taught her to read the body-prints of the flying anacondas in the earth, and the tiny claw marks of the peacock guinea pigs in the trees. Everything was invisible until you learned to see it.

The wind blows where it wishes, and you hear its sound, but you do not know where it comes from or where it goes.

She wrapped that breath of wind around herself, and hopped down into the burnt out cockpit. There waited a scattered handful of soldiers who'd been too hurt to grapple onto the Frelsi transport with the rest of the group.

This, at least, required no double-thought—just hands-on action to get people loaded onto the land-runner. Lem threw herself into the work, glad to let her brain rest.

CHAPTER TWENTY-THREE

Jei

THE WARM, FAMILIAR RUMBLE OF THE EVACUATION TRANSPORT. THE hug of the safety straps across my chest. The cool, black sheen, faded into a soft iron luster in places, throughout the cockpit.

It could all have been comforting, or at least relaxing. We'd protected the Hiding Place, for now, and as I piloted the possibly bugged last transport back to the Alpino Firebase for inspection, Mera and I now had a moment of peace.

But still the angry unease burned and twisted in the base of my chest, like a roasting smungworm turning, turning, turning on a slow spit.

Rest, Njande whispered to me again, now in the rays of light filtering in from the narrow slit of piloting glass ahead of me.

Can't, I'm focused on driving, I answered. *Visibility isn't great in these things with just that 180 slit view out the front. And without advanced computerized navigation it's a lot of manual calibration, monitoring dials for pitch, yaw, everything else ...*

Trust me, and rest.

But I wasn't about to rest until I'd taken my revenge.

A dark thought, my friend.

I pretended I hadn't thought it. "You were telling me where you trained your abilities," I said to Mera.

"Mostly self-taught. I spend my time trying to get into the cool libraries and research centers across the galaxy," she smiled, her eyes almost pinched shut by the cute rise of her cheeks. "I'm a bit of a wandering hermit, I guess? I don't like being tied down by allegiances and conflict. I'm just focused on improving myself, and wherever I can go to accomplish that, I go. Wherever the universe takes me. Sometimes it calls me to help people. Like you."

"I appreciate that," I said, unable to smile through the twinge of suspicion I had. "What do you mean by the universe calling you, though? How did you find me?"

"Let's see, how best to explain ..." She pursed her pink lips together. "Are you familiar with echolocation?"

"Yeah."

"As far as I can tell, my particular electronegative abilities are related to an adaptation in the neural structure of my inner ear. I've had magnetic resonance imaging done, and my cochlea and the cranial nerve relays to the auditory centers of my brain are much larger than normal, for a human."

"Wouldn't that just make you hear better?" I asked.

"Well, no. I wasn't able to do a biopsy or anything—I didn't want to disrupt the sensitive machinations—but it seems the extra sensors taking up that space in my head are actually a bit like the sensors in an EEG machine. Or like the ampullae of Lorenzini that sharks use to sense bioelectricity, to feel the location of other creatures without sight or smell.Only mine are far more sensitive."

"So you can pick up brainwaves, and thoughts?" I stiffened. I didn't need to know a new Stygge Bricandor.

"No, I'd need a much bigger set of receptors for that—heck, that would take an enormous amount of extra processing in the cerebrum to interpret those signals into thought, and the surface area of sensors alone ... I don't think that can fit into a standard human shape."

"Oh, it can," I said. "Stygge Bricandor, the Growen dictator? He can do it."

"I have no idea how that's possible," she said. "I'm not arguing with you, it's just—how would you keep a head the same shape? Would you have additional ports or holes to better receive signals, like I do through my ears? Would the receptors be scattered through your skin? What would the molecular structure of those receptors even look like, integrating with the human nervous system?" She tilted her head, fading off into her own questions with a finger on her lip. I didn't tell her that we had a theory, Lem and I, that Bricandor had no powers at all, and just got all his information from an enemy interdimensional. "It's curious, quite curious," Mera murmured.

She tapped her thick lips again, her eyelashes drooping as if the thoughts put her in a beautiful trance. Her other hand strayed to a necklace dangling down her chest, fingers playing with three braids of shimmering pearls that reminded me of staying on Burbura with my mother, years and years ago ... her nails clicked against the necklace with a sound that made my scalp shiver as her wrist framed the shapes of her two—

I forced my eyes back to driving. "But you don't work that way. So you sense brainwaves, but can't interpret them?"

"Essentially," she murmured, apparently no longer interested in talking. We were quiet for a while, just together in the hum of the transport and the clicking tinkle of her nails against her beads.

Presently, she shook herself with a smile. "Isn't the universe incredible? Aren't we incredible creatures?" She laughed.

"Sure, I guess." Her delight at the world around her would have been infectious to anyone else, anyone less angry and tired. I appreciated it even though I couldn't feel it—it wasn't her fault I'd become a bit fed up with people who had irrational joys—people like Lem, and Cinta. "So what makes your sensors like echolocation?" I asked.

"With echolocation, hypersensitive directional hearing allows creatures to pick up the location of objects by sending out high-pitched sounds, and then hearing what direction the sounds bounce back from," she said. "I create an electromagnetic imbalance just the same way you do, by altering the simple polarity in my nervous system, pushing negative chlorine ions in one direction and positive sodium ions in another still within the cell membrane. The difference is that I'm not able to do it as dramatically as you do—I have normal EEGs, for example, whereas I'm sure yours always looks like you're having a seizure."

"You're not wrong," I said.

"So I'm not creating that fantastic electromagnet like you do —I can, I can do some weak em-pulls, but the strongest polarity shift I get actually happens somewhere near my throat, near my voice box, where the mechanical energy from sound vibrations amplifies the electrical energy from the mild static charge. Basically, I send out a signal, and then I receive a signal back. I can use the signal I send out to amplify incoming signals from other people, and thereby triangulate their location."

"You sense electric surges, basically."

"Yes. I guess, another way to think about it, is that every action in the universe has an equal and opposite reaction, so when anyone disrupts the charges in their neurons, there's a balancing effect in the universe around them that eventually gets back to me. It's easier to sense things like ships and power plants —it's very hard to sense the location of someone with very low-level power, like a normal sentient being."

My eyes narrowed, and that twisting, roasting spit in my chest sped up. "But you can sense where electromagnetic people are," I said.

"Yes. And that's how I found you!" Again, she lit up with that peppy smile, her cheeks almost obliterating her eyes into slits of cuteness ...

... The smile weakened with concern as she watched my face. "Is there ... someone you want to find?" she asked finally.

"Yes," I said. *Don't. Don't don't don't don't.* Something, whether Cinta's harsh older-brother *jealousy* on Lem's behalf earlier, or Njande's repeated insistence to stop, to *rest*, pounded within me. *Don't don't don't don't don't.*

I did.

"I want to track down my old partner and bring her to justice," I said.

"Hmm." She pursed her lips, and looked down at her boots. Her eyes shimmered with such a powerful radiating wetness I thought she might cry. "I'm sorry, it—I'm sorry you're hurting so much," she said. "This just overwhelming sadness you have—there's so much intensity it almost gives me a headache. It's tragic when friends fight."

I laughed harshly. "That's one way to put it. I'm pretty sure she was either there on the transport, or on comms feeding info to Stygge Diebol. He said her name when he broke through the door." I turned to make violent eye contact. "Her blood siblings were on that transport, Mera. And her adopted brother. She's betrayed her own family. *Kids.*"

Mera nodded, eyebrows knit as if the pain was hers. "Is ... that why we've been driving in the wrong direction?" she asked in a small voice.

Clever girl. My lip twitched into a darkened half-grin. "I just want to stop by the crash site of that fake transport before we head to the Firebase," I said.

Her fingers strayed now to her temple; the other hand twirled in her long dark hair as she bit her lip. "May I make a suggestion?" she peeped.

"Sure."

"What if—I mean, what if you tried to call her, one more time?" she asked. "Tell her you're coming for her. Give her one more chance to turn back, you know?"

"Why would I warn the enemy?" I smirked.

"Stop that." She batted me on the elbow. "I don't know her, or you, but I can sense this deep connection you have, or had. This is maybe your best friend. Like family. There's some kind of history that warrants one more goodbye."

I said nothing.

"You love this person," she urged.

"Not like that," I said, my jaw tightening. People always

gossiped about us, among the ranks, and at one point that had actually threatened her career. "We don't break regs."

"There are many ways to love someone," Mera lowed. "You obey regulations *because* you care about her, and her future. Not all love needs sex."

I laughed. Mera was direct, but not in the bold, brash way Lem would be—in an almost ethereal way, sparkling with gentleness that put everything at ease. I could feel the spit in my chest slowing down, the fire waning to embers.

"You're not wrong," was all I said.

CHAPTER TWENTY-FOUR

Lem

JEI CALLED HER AT THE WORST POSSIBLE TIME.

Lem was kneeling in the grass with Stygge Diebol at the site of the fake transport crash, one hand on the silvery metal side of the spiked land-runner for balance and the other on a Growen soldier's neck, checking his pulse. She didn't love this part—staring consequence in the face. It made her feel guilty, as guilty as throwing that Frelsi soldier off the air-rider she and Diebol stole, even though she'd fired an em-pull to protect the guy from injury on the way down.

"No, no pulse," she said to Diebol finally. "He's gone. We'll load him up last with the others."

Her wrist itched with the silent vibration of her wristband. *I'm coming I'm coming I'm coming! Hold on.*

Diebol closed the soldier's eyes, and rose to his feet. "I need to report back immediately to brief the other leadership and regroup," he said. "I'll take the air-rider."

Itching, itching, itching wrist.

"I'd rather return first," General Johnson said quickly—Lem needed to destroy the comms on the stolen air-rider in case *She* could use it to hack into the Alpino Firebase next. "I have more experience with disaster mitigation."

Diebol laughed. "You mean you want to make sure you come out of this ahead, General. Ha, no—thank you, but no thank you."

With that, Diebol swung himself up onto the air-rider and zipped off before Lem could stop him.

But—oh, shyte, now—agh! Lem groaned and trotted off a ways from the crash site, hiding herself behind the crest of the hill to answer Jei's call.

Yeah, she knew it was him even before she pulled up her sleeve to check. It had to be, with this sinking feeling, like when Colonel Win called her into his office for stupid shyte after Captain Rana died—

Only this felt so much worse.

Lem took a deep breath, turned off General Johnson's DNA projection to let Jei hear her voice, and swiped her wristband to answer.

"Where are you?" Jei seethed.

She looked back behind herself toward the column of smoke spiraling into the air and shuddered. Why was this scarier than talking to Diebol? "I can't answer that, man, you know that ..." She took another deep breath. "... where do you think I am?"

"I think you know what I think."

"Well, we can both say cryptic nonsense for the next hour, or you could say what you called me to say," Lem said.

"I called to give you one chance to explain why you tried to kill me," Jei snapped.

Look, I didn't try to kill you, I only sold you to Diebol for the fort. Lem cringed, her face hot. She swallowed and deepened her voice to force it to hold still: "You gonna tell me what that means?"

"If Mera hadn't cut the lights in the transport, I'd be dead."

Suddenly Jei wasn't the only one seething. Who the—*Lem* had cut the lights, not whoever—! "That's not what saved you," she snapped without thinking.

"No?" The mocking tone had a hint of ... hope to it.

Oh, shyte. Why had she said that? Shyte, why? "Diebol was slow, that's what saved you," Lem coughed.

"Oh, right, speaking of Diebol." She hated the bitter laugh. "How did Diebol survive that blast? He didn't have time to react."

"Are you—are you—" Dammit, what did she say? She couldn't play dumb now. She'd just confirmed she was there. She tried to slow down, to breathe—"What are you saying?"

"Oh, just that he's got a new guardian angel. Maybe someone who's been working on turning their electric fields into electromagnetic pulls. With my technique."

Then, for the first time since they'd met, she lied to his face.

"I didn't save Diebol. It wasn't me." She choked on it—she'd spent so long creating a double-speak in her mind, telling the truth in alternative ways, that a straight lie felt like a self-violation. She forced herself to double down. "You've seen him save himself from worse!"

"He called your name, Lem, I heard it."

Filk you, Diebol, you, filk you to bloodseas. "He wasn't calling my name because I helped him," was all she could say.

"Why, then?"

"I can't answer that." She couldn't say, couldn't think, how much she'd helped him. Already she'd screwed this up—already, someone might hear. "I'm a loyal Growen soldier."

There was a boiling silence. Then: "Justify this," Jei said. "Tell me how Njande can be okay with forcing homogeneity on the galaxy."

Lem sighed, and breathed, and looked behind her again. She didn't have much time. Her throat tightened, but she pushed through it to quote from the manuscripts she, Jei, and Cinta had uncovered: "Thou shalt not sow they kerem with different seeds, lest the fruit of thy zera which thou hast sown, and the fruit of thy kerem, be defiled."

"Seeds aren't people."

"Still. Sometimes he asks for homogeneity. He isn't as simple and pro-Frelsi and pro-diversity as you think he is. He's complex."

"Lem, those are seeds! He probably had some biological reason for telling the ancients that—like something about nitrogen replacement or something, or maybe 'different seeds' means like foreign seeds because he's worried about invasive species, I don't know and I don't care because I am not a farmer! Seeds are not people!"

Lem couldn't help but smile a bit at his words—she caught herself, and told herself she was only smiling because of the simplicity of it.

Earth and grass crunched and swished behind Lem; someone was coming up the hill. "Jei, I'm sorry," she said. "I need to go."

His voice grew nearer to the watch. "You're going down, Lem Benzaran."

"I know," Lem said. Oh the trembling, the trembling lip and fluttering in her chest, she had to stop. *Stop right now.* "Hey Jei?"

"Yeah."

Swallow. "Are my siblings okay?"

He laughed—a painful laugh, full of breath. "I don't get it—how you can care about them, and work with the child-killers. I don't understand you."

"I know. Are they?"

"They're fine," he said. "You'll see them soon when I bring you back in chains."

"You know I don't do well in cages."

"It'll be dead or alive, Lem."

In the silence, neither friend wanted to say goodbye, but there was nothing else to say, and the footsteps grew too near. Lem wished she had a snappy response—something cool and heroic, maybe—but she couldn't feel anything but a tension, as if there was a string tied around her aorta in the middle of her chest, and Jei was attached, yanking it. She was glad to hear his voice—and she ached knowing how truly and completely she'd betrayed him—and that pit, that sense that she was about to get in trouble, wouldn't go away. He would really kill her. And he could. But she had to stop Her. She opened her mouth to say she was sorry—

"General!"

Lem brushed behind her ear—thankfully, under the faux Frelsi mask, the change mattered little, except for stature and voice. She fumbled her wristband, shutting off the transmission.

"We're ready to head out! There's a Frelsi transport doubling back this way, we need to move."

Lem ran down the hill with her soldier and climbed into the land-runner to return to base.

Jei

I sat for a couple minutes after Lem hung up, just messing with the hem of my pants leg as the wind tousled my hair and the cool mist beaded into droplets on the metal top deck beside me. There was a tired peace about everything, and the thoughts flitting through my head didn't really follow each other in any logical fashion.

I shouldn't leave Mera alone down in the cockpit too long.

We'd get to the crash site soon.

The world was ending, and it wasn't.

I didn't have enough control of my powers to save people …

That thought had a thread I could pull on, and I did so, as the sun began to set over the prairie in vibrant orange strokes. I needed to talk to Mera more about electrobiology and see if I could figure out my own erratic situation; Lem and I had spent a lot of time hunting ancient texts to unravel the secrets of the interdimensional beyond us, but I liked that Mera had spent time unraveling the secrets within us. Mera herself seemed like a treasure chest, open and spilling strings of gems, but lined with secret compartments you might miss, and maybe a hidden trap or two. I didn't know how long she would follow me around, or what kind of payment she'd eventually want in return, but for now, I liked the idea of rifling through the chest with her, holding various crystals up to the light to comment on their sparkle, or drape them around her neck. Her new and exciting existence blunted the sharp ache of hunting Lem.

Hunting Lem.

Don't don't don't don't don't …

I did.

I pulled my steel knife now, twisting it in the evening light. The sharp curves evoked the shape of a flying lizard; my Draconian teacher had given it to me years ago.

I slipped the blade under my wristband now, sliding its cool edge along the entirety of the band to loosen the gel that connected the wristband's sensors to my skin … I needed to cut ties. I couldn't have the Growen *or* Frelsi tracking me anymore, and it wasn't like I could really use my wristband to call anyone anyway, not with whatever tracking data or computerized phantom the Growen had likely installed when I was unconscious. Sure, I'd called Lem, just now. I didn't care who tracked her. But I couldn't call the Firebase, or the Admiral, and risk sending them whatever computer horrors the Growen now controlled.

Not that I intended to call home anyway. The admiral had told me to return without hunting Lem, and for the first time in my life, I planned to directly disobey an order. Not kind of fudge it, not play smart with the rules—just straight up defy it.

It was a Lem move. And I couldn't have the Frelsi leadership tracking me while I made it. With a flick, my blade sliced through the rubber circlet. The wristband fell to the deck with a *plink.*

I was now on my own.

CHAPTER TWENTY-FIVE

Diebol

THERE WAS NO WIND, NOW, OVER THE FIELD BY DIEBOL'S SLEEPING quarters when he parked the stolen Frelsi air-rider; late afternoon shadows stretched from the outcroppings of volcanic rock that punctuated the prairie grass.

The young Growen leader swung himself off the vehicle, his jaw clenching as his boots impacted the earth. This part of his duty—really anything that involved a meeting of any kind—he dreaded. He did remember a time before seeing these faces put a pit in his stomach ...

One must have hope. Diebol slipped his transmitter pen out of his vest and drew an enormous rectangle around himself in the air, projecting light onto the moisture in the air like an artificial rainbow. Three viewing screens appeared in the rectangle for his four-way call.

Diebol stabbed his transmitter pen into the grass and sat down on a large clump of volcanic rock, draping himself over it with his feet up. In the old days, before the interrogation center last year, he would have stood at attention in front of the camera when calling Bricandor. Now, he barely looked at the square window beside him where the old man floated in a seated, criss-crossed Lotus. The wizened Stygge stared at him intently through ages of crow's feet; Diebol kept his own eyes forward, messing with hem of his faux Frelsi pants.

"You are upset," said the old man.

"Wait until she joins the call," Diebol said.

Morda poked her head in from the side of her viewing window with a saccharine smile. Her long, dark hair framed the side of the screen like a curtain. "Hello!" she chirped, her eyes almost closed in glee.

"Center yourself in your filking window," Diebol snapped. "No one here thinks you're cute."

Morda strolled all the way into view with a lippy pout. "Someone's grumpy."

"Can he hear you, *Mera*, dear?" Diebol spat.

Morda motioned around her to the empty top deck of a Frelsi transport. "He's downstairs piloting. These old clunkers have no autopilot, so he's stuck down there unless he wants to crash."

"Good," Bricandor wheezed in that soft, weak voice Diebol despised now, not caring that the man could read his thoughts. "Well, my children, do you care to explain yourselves?"

Diebol forced himself to keep his eyes on the threadbare patch on his knee—if he looked directly at either of these freaks, he would lose his cool. And without his cool, he could not destroy this simpering witch.

"I would like to know, *Father*," Diebol spat, resenting the title sealed by the blood of others instead of biological parentage. "Why your queen of the damned here destroyed our chance to find the Frelsi Hiding Place. Before she tells you otherwise, I had Jei Bereens on his back when she threw a light bomb at me."

"I'm surprised to see you survived the blast," Morda laughed. Ugh, that tinkling high-pitched sound gave him a headache. "I thought finally I would be Father's favorite."

Diebol looked up. Really? Surprised? That wasn't her em-push that shot him out of the way of the blast at the last second? He'd believed her to be overly ambitious about winning over Jei so *she* could take credit for bagging the game—stupid, not murderous. He narrowed his eyes.

"But of course, you have wonderful reflexes," Morda waved her hand. "Since one of us can read minds here, there's no point with pretense ..." She twirled a lock of hair around her finger. "I didn't exactly *try* to kill you, but I wouldn't have minded it if you'd died, honestly. You weren't exactly kind to me in the interrogation center."

"How am I supposed to work with this?" Diebol pointed at her, eyes now on Bricandor. "Half of your upper leadership want me dead—most of them because of things *you* made me do while you play the saint. I'm cornered and undermined at every—"

"Hush," Bricandor intoned.

Pavlovian response shut Diebol's mouth like a trap. He resented the chemical terror at the memory of electricity, but had no power to resist his own reaction; Morda herself stiffened at the mere sound of the word.

"Now, children, we all want to kill each other sometimes," Bricandor wheezed. "Why, Diebol, just a few minutes ago you were wishing a blade across my throat. You remember the parable of the wolves." Of course, they both did, but they didn't dare interrupt as Bricandor repeated it: he believed repetition was the key to learning, and he believed that about torture, too. "The alpha becomes alpha when he kills the previous pack leader—his father. And the siblings must fight until that leader reveals himself. These power struggles create strength in the organization. The challenge is controlling the balance of reward and punishment to remain always on top yourself. And, of course, channeling your own ambitions in the service of the mission first. The mission deserves that the fittest survive to fulfill it. Now, Morda, my daughter, why don't you explain to us why you would bring young Bereens to our precious convoy?"

"Look, I tried to stop him. First I told him he was being tracked. He ignored that. Then I ordered the dumb flying horse to leave us stranded, and this guy decided to—" Morda flushed, and her eyelashes fluttered. "It was quite impressive, actually. He treated the beast like nothing more than a broken air-rider.

He did this leg thing to control the wings while his upper body—"

"Look at her!" Diebol cried out, swiveling to sit facing both of them now. "Do you see her face? I don't have to read minds to know she's compromised!"

"It's not like I'm going to fall for him," Morda hissed.

"Bull. Half the Frelsi humans are attracted to the man," Diebol laughed. To Bricandor: "I want her out of this. It's clear she'll be recruited by the nearest poster with biceps."

"Look, don't hate me because I'm still a filking human being instead of whatever dead-inside automaton you are," Morda snapped. "Sure, I can recognize something tantalizing when I see it. You can't control what you're attracted to. But you sure as hell *can* control what you do with that attraction. This is one hundred percent to my advantage. It makes me more genuine, and it should help me release more of the control pheromone."

"Ugh, are we on that again?" Diebol groaned.

"It works on animals, I know it can work on humans, too."

"Not someone like Bereens."

"Why, are you afraid if I can control your boyfriend I can control you?" Morda pursed her lips into another infuriating kiss. She turned to Bricandor, pleading. "Look, during my time on Beryllia I ran lab tests on the substance I emit through my skin. It's actually two chemicals, one an aerosolizable pheromone, and the other a powerful neurotransmitter. The pheromone seems to work like certain insect pheromones that promote relaxation and dampen neurological power; it also makes the nervous system more permeable."

She took a breath, and continued at rapid fire as if afraid Diebol would interrupt: "The neurotransmitter is heavy, and passed only by contact, but it's so small it can penetrate skin and even some cell membranes. It triggers neuron receptors in a pulsatile fashion, so I can literally pass my neural patterns on to the subject's nervous system—run my software, or 'thoughts,' on their hardware. It requires an enormous amount of physical contact, and I'm still figuring out where I need to touch to trigger what responses. Biological systems are complex. But I did it. The pegasus obeyed me the entire time I could touch it, and a little after, too."

She turned now, back to Diebol: "Come on, just imagine a *powerhouse* like Jei Bereens under our control! I mean, you wanna talk about shutting down bases, that's how we shut down bases!"

"Oh, I've imagined it," Diebol scowled with a pointed glare back at Bricandor, who'd dismissed that notion with such viciousness last year. "But unless you plan to hold his hand for the rest of his life, it's not practical. And there's still the problem of the Contamination. You can't just mind control away his invisible friend."

"I think I can!"

"You'd be no better than the interdimensionals if you could," Diebol growled. "Freeing minds from the Contamination requires conscious *choice*, no matter how coerced. Bloodseas, he's a sentient being, not a filking horse, at least give him the honor of death on his own terms."

"Why is it always your way or *death*?" Morda cried. "He'll be so much happier my way, and so much more alive. I can literally make people happy! What power is better than that?"

"It's a lovely idea, my dear," Bricandor mused. What? Diebol's jaw ground: was the master saying this on purpose, just to enrage him? "And I don't mind who you fall in love with as long as you make them obey me. But why, child, did you allow him to disrupt the Hiding Place mission?"

Bricandor's suddenly softer voice put a visible tremor of terror in Morda's lower lip—the gentler the voice, the more pain he might inflict. Diebol's stomach tightened just listening, and Morda was forced to pause, likely holding back a stammer. "I told you, I couldn't convince him not to intervene," she repeated. Then, with a desperate stomp, as no one answered her: "What do you want me to do, hold him down?"

"We're at war, yes, that's exactly what I'd expect you to do."

"The missive was dead or alive," Diebol growled, hoping to

push her further under the bus. "You were sent to the scene of his escape to *capture* him. Not become his best friend!"

"It takes time, you moron, I—"

"Time? What time? Shoot him with one shock to power him down, and then another one to take him home. Bloodseas, it's like you didn't even read your mission brief."

"My mission brief?" Morda scoffed. "My mission brief is missing critical new biological information—which is why *you* lost him, several hundred soldiers, and what was it, three ships? An expensive mistake, Stygge Diebol. Maybe his system hadn't matured yet last year in the interrogation center, but now I believe he's structured like—I don't know, a lithium battery. Or, no—more like an electromagnet, since they can lose their charge without power. He likely gains charge with rest and certain foods, but I suspect he gathers energy best from his enemies' electromagnetic fields, and discharges it as they die or lose consciousness. When they're out, he's spent, but having multitudes of sentient attackers strengthens him *exponentially*."

That, at least, made sense to Diebol, given the circumstances of both the Luna-Guetala camp incident and Jei's escape. He allowed the idiot woman to keep talking, waiting for her inevitable screw-up: "So, to avoid that supercharge, it's better for just one person to transport him so he doesn't go berserk like he did in your ship. I'm a perfect guard, because my pheromone can dampen his powers."

"So shock him and *then* pheromone him," Diebol said.

"What is it with you and shocking people? I don't want to have to shock him every hour, what if his timer is stress-based? He'll come along a lot more easily if he thinks fondly of me. Bloodseas, I mean, he's so suspicious of everything I thought he'd throw me out of the ship as a mind-reader when I mentioned I can receive EEG signals. You lead more flies to honey than vinegar, and this one needs a lot of honey."

"That's a fallacy, actually," Diebol smiled. "Most insects prefer the probiotic content of vinegar."

"Probiotic content, bloodseas, you almost killed him!"

"*Dead* is better than *ruined our one chance to find the hidden Frelsi base!*"

"We will have hundreds of chances to find their cockroach hole. Shyte, Sterba probably has an in already; she's damn near omnipresent," Morda grumbled, folding her arms around her chest as if hiding a nakedness. "Look, okay, fine. You don't care what I think. But *Sterba* wants Bereens to help find his partner. After what Father Bricandor overheard in the ether, Sterba's convinced Benzaran's the hunter, okay? So that's why I did the light bomb thing. Nothing's going to win him over except an attempt on your life, we need him to track Benzaran for us, so there you go, attempt on your life. For Sterba. Who doesn't like you anyway. If you want to discuss this further, take it up with her."

She looked down at the ground in defeat—likely ashamed, Diebol thought, at resorting to that name-drop for the hundredth time. He made a smug note of her insecurity as all eyes turned now to the third, silent viewscreen. The blue static blinked once. Bricandor closed his eyes, listening to something neither of the younger Stygges could hear …

He nodded.

"It is so," he said.

Morda grinned in triumph; her mouth took off at lightspeed. "Then Diebol, dear, I'll need you to run a trace from the tracker your boys put in his wristband, pretty please? I got him to call Benzaran, oh, not half an hour ago. He thinks she was with you at the convoy, so I'm going back there to see if I can pick up a trace of my own," she tapped her ear with an infantile giggle. "Keep me informed and we'll triangulate her position together. With the hunter dead, Sterba will be safe, and Growen victory certain." She clapped her hands, like a child, with real, unbridled glee. "I'm excited! Whether we like each other or not, we're going to do great things together."

Diebol resented, with all his being, taking orders from someone junior to him. He waited for her to finish, then showed his teeth with a calm smile. "It's good you have a sister to hide behind. I'm glad for you," he said. "As long as she never tires of too much worthless leeching from an empty-headed ditz whose only real assets lie on her chest—well, I think you'll have a bright career ahead of you." He relaxed the grin for a moment. "Just to be clear: you didn't em-push me out of the way of the blast?"

"No, unfortunately, for some reason the thought just didn't occur to me," she feigned a sigh, tapping on her pouted lip with vicious sweetness. "All that blood flow to my rack, not enough to my brain, I guess."

"So long as we're both on the same page." Diebol nodded to her curtly. "Father, a word?"

"Wait," Morda protested. "You can't leave me out of—"

Bricandor suddenly transformed, his wrinkles tightening, his eyes a flame, yellow teeth spewing spittle across the view screen. "We have tolerated your babbling long enough, call girl!" he snarled in an eerie double-voice. "You have claimed your work. Do it!"

Diebol swallowed, and returned, for a moment, to inspecting the faded spot on his knee. He wanted to feel triumph when Morda hung up, but being alone with Bricandor, even at a distance, did not feel like much of a reward.

CHAPTER TWENTY-SIX

Lem

BACK AT GROWEN SOUTH CENTRAL, LOST IN THE CROWD OF MEDICS unloading the injured and sergeants ordering people to debriefs, Lem Benzaran was all but invisible.

Ironically enough, any wandering Frelsi soldier could have infiltrated this gaggle of fake freedom fighter uniforms. Lem didn't even need to wear General Johnson's face; her slim black atmosphere mask and hood blended just fine. Good thing, too, because Lem's disguise projector was losing energy: the little DNA film behind her ear needed a break to synthesize more chemicals from her bloodstream into the neurotoxin mist that maintained her fake identity.

Lem clambered atop the roof of the spiked silver land-runner as if to help unload, her eyes scanning for the sparrow-like swoosh that evoked folded wings around a floating bike. She needed to find that Frelsi air-rider Diebol had brought back with him. From the milling conversations of the supply sergeants, it didn't sound like he'd turned the vehicle in yet.

He probably went straight to whatever meeting he had. But the air-rider wasn't parked outside the main briefing complex where the midnight commotion happened ...

To his field, then. *Diebol's field*—it seemed too strange and poetic, the lovechild of his ascetic lifestyle and paranoid distrust of other upper leadership.

Well, not exactly paranoid. It sounded like he'd dealt with at least a couple assassination attempts already.

Lem scampered over to a spare "lift"—that's what they called the floating-dolly-looking things—and took it zipping away down the main thoroughfare toward the armory. Ooof, just in time: she heard that mousy little man from her entourage looking for her in the crowd, chirping in panic about those missed funding meetings. She almost giggled.

Shyte, she wanted so bad just to rip the mask off her face and soak up the wind …

Clumps of volcanic rock, sporadic thorny scrub, and tall grass soon greeted her on her right. Lem couldn't quite see the air-rider, but that might be its rear, sticking out from behind that boulder there. She'd already broken Diebol's installed defenses this morning with her little electric surge; in faux Frelsi camouflage it should now be much, much easier to low crawl her way to the stolen air-rider and short out its computer system, too.

Lem ditched the floating lift by the large bush she'd almost hidden under this morning, and then brushed her hand over the side of the black atmosphere hood to shift its color to camo. She dropped to her belly; grass rustled; her uniform swooshed; she struck from her mind the sudden longing for her jumpsuit and tunic and quiet boots running through the jungle trees beside silent Biouk paws …

The wind whistled above her as she strained for other noises. Soon, she heard the hum of the idling air-rider—yup, just beyond that boulder. Even Diebol, with his egalitarian sensibilities, didn't grow up under the constant Frelsi fuel shortage that required turning all hovercraft off when not in use.

His voice trailed to her on the breeze—much, much closer than she'd expected. The air-rider wasn't the only thing on the other side of the boulder. She couldn't quite catch his …

Oh shyte. Oh shyte, there was another voice—that crooked, wheezing old voice she'd only heard once or twice before. *Don't think his name, don't think his name, don't think his name, he'll hear you* … Oh shyte, if the Accuser saw her and cackled her location to his human puppet—

Lem gripped Njande's name to her chest, hiding herself from the wicked interdimensional's eyes in the enormous shadow of her own invisible friend. Her heart raced, threatening to reveal her: she snuggled deeper into the invisible shadow and repeated the spells of promise. *My heart is hid on high with my Promised One. I'm like the wind, and no one knows where I go. He spreads his cloak over me, and gathers me under his wings like a mother fowl hides her chicks.*

He responded to her in a whisper: *You hide under the shadow of the highest being, under the cloth of the Flag of Ahavah.*

She breathed, clinging to her camouflage in that dimension while staying low to stay hidden in this one, too. She edged herself under an outcropping of the rough black rock here, trying to use the direction of Diebol's voice to guess his position.

"*You* lost her," the elderly Stygge was hissing now through electrical interference. *Sounds like some kind of long-distance call.*

Diebol's youthful tenor strained with barely-withheld frustration: "I have people investigating, but I don't have to tell you I'm waging a multi-planet war while dealing with these simpering bureaucrats you call your friends. If you really care about finding Benzaran it would certainly help for you to come down here and use your mind-reading to find her."

"I have resources already in place for that."

Uh oh. Lem shivered. Diebol didn't seem to like it either. "You have interdimensional scum crawling my men, you mean."

"How I arrange alliances for our species is my business."

"We're supposed to represent *all* species."

Lem scooted closer, shoulder against the stone, eyes hunting for—ah. She saw him now through this crack in the rock. He lounged just on the other side, his muscular form spilled atop a pile of pumice like a bored kid in an armchair, facing Lem's direction and the air-rider that floated just an arms-length beyond her. He couldn't see through the boulder, but she wouldn't be able to reach out and sabotage the air-rider with him watching.

"I do not see distinctions in species, as you do," the old man was saying. "All species are one species, and one day all will be one."

Diebol pressed the middle of his forehead so fiercely with his thumb and forefinger Lem thought he might break them. The corner of his face whitened as his jaw ground. "Yes. Wonderful, Father. Leave Benzaran to me, then. I have my own suspicions anyway. Still not worth losing the Hiding Place over. Morda is— ruining everything."

Who was Mor—Lem's heart raced. Was that Her? Maybe? Or just another rare female Growen leader? There were a few electromagnetic females from various species rounded up for the Stygge training center that year ...

Shyte, Lem had thought she'd just *know* when she heard Her name.

"And she's weak," Diebol added. *No, that's not Her then. They wouldn't dare.* "Even Sterba agrees."

"I don't believe you can read minds yet, Stygge Diebol." The deepened calm sent chills down Lem's spine. "And I believe the truth is that you're jealous Morda will accomplish your failed dream."

"Mind control is cheap."

"But effective." The old man chuckled. "You said yourself I was underestimating the value of Jei Bereens. Well, now I have him under supervision."

"Are you *insane*? You gave up their precious Hiding Place because some magic woman got jittery because you *heard from your sleep paralysis demon* that a crazed teenager might be hunting Her?"

"Yes. And you failed to locate the hunter or maintain control of Bereens."

"This was the chance of a lifetime!"

"She prefers for the threat to be eliminated as soon as possible."

"Well maybe She can't have everything She wants all the time!"

Bricandor chuckled; Lem could just barely see the old man ease himself to his feet and shuffle across the view screen for an oblong cup of tea. "Within the last five hours She demolished every single Frelsi base on Burbura," Bricandor wheezed. "All Frelsi influence, stamped out. The planet is now completely uncontested."

What?! Lem's breath stalled in her throat. Shyte, in the time they'd run the Hiding Place offensive ... *all of Burbura*?

Bricandor sipped: "With a bit of gentle diplomacy, Burbura may even join our cause now. An entire planet in the span of one planetary revolution ... well, I say She can and will have everything Her heart desires."

Shyte, Burbura ... years ago that planet of seas had represented a major seat in the Frelsi Coalition, leveraging the influence of huge trade hubs and powerful mass media centers. Public support had faded in recent years with Bricandor's careful networking and manipulative broadcasts, but even still the floating Frelsi bases had continued to serve as refuge points to protect those with unpopular opinions. With all Frelsi bases *destroyed*—well, did the elections even matter now?

Shyte, Lem had to stop this *now*. *No names, no names, don't think names, but* ... the other woman Diebol had mentioned—not the M, but the S—that woman. That one had to be Her.

The conversation faded in Lem's hearing as the blood pounded in her temples. She just—just—all of Burbura?

Diebol didn't seem to like either woman much at all.

For Diebol, then. Lem's mind grasped at *any* pro-Growen justification. *Diebol's what's best for the Growen, so for him, I gotta stop Her. General Johnson needs to complete his 180; I'll have to dispose of the original permanently. Tonight I'll ask Diebol to—*

"By the way, I've been talking with my invisible friend regarding your concerns about General Johnson," Bricandor wheezed.

Oh, no.

So this was where that boot would drop.

Lem clenched both fists against her eyes. She could almost scream. *Why* had she forgotten her mental cover when she fried the lights in that stupid transport, why? She'd been fine for months, then suddenly Jei showed up and she just—what, got emotional?

"Actually, I might have been wrong about Johnson," Diebol said, sitting up now to face the viewscreen. "He demonstrated a keen dedication to the mission today, despite his personal feelings."

"My source tells me the opposite," Bricandor said.

"Of course your interdimensional would say that. They hate me," Diebol laughed. "And General Johnson saved my life today."

"Why would he do such a thing?" Bricandor asked.

"Alas, Father, I'm too old to play the self-esteem game," Diebol half-sighed. "I'm well aware most of the men-at-arms see me as mission-essential, whatever the rest of upper leadership think."

"Exactly, and General Johnson is?"

"Alright, I'll bite," Diebol spat, standing now. Ooh—Lem licked her lips—Burbura or not, here was an opportunity to zap the air-rider. She inched closer to the edge of the stone … "How did saving my life compromise the mission, *sir*?" Diebol seethed.

"Run Morda's trace as she ordered, and hold the general for a video call with me. Then, we will speak."

"I continue to insist it would be faster if you came *here*," Diebol growled. "If finding Benzaran is so important to Sterba, then—"

"I have the Burburan election to decide. They can add several billion drachma to our weapons research. I've already found your mole. If I must *also* come do your job, then perhaps Morda is not the only one in need of the parable of the angler fish."

With that, Bricandor cut the call. Lem had no idea what the parable of the angler fish was, but it pissed off Diebol enough that he turned his back to her, snatched his pen out of the dirt, and hurled it with a muted roar.

And in that moment, Lem shot out her arm and zapped the air-rider. The soft fizzle faded in the wind without drawing any Stygge attention, and Lem belly-crawled away as fast as she could. Everything sucked, but at least now She couldn't access the Alpino Firebase.

But shyte, without General Johnson, who was Lem going to be *now*?

CHAPTER TWENTY-SEVEN

The Real General Johnson

GENERAL ROJAM S. JOHNSON AWOKE TO AN EXCRUCIATING TEARING sensation in his lower back, doubled over inside a metal container where, his watch told him, he'd remained unconscious for about twenty-four hours. His every muscle throbbed.

But Rojam grinned through gnashing teeth: he knew it! He knew the force shouldn't have hired anyone but human males. "Filking bucktooth." That species-traitor Diebol couldn't twist his boxers over "slurs" now.

Yes, Diebol. Diebol had caused this somehow, vying to expand his influence over the counsel, making Rojam miss his funding meetings—that dirty, little electric mutant would pay.

But Rojam could not, would not, in this box, admit to what had happened. Even if the smell didn't give it away, his fingers recognized the engraved brand name on the wall—he had personally brokered the military contract with this waste disposal company.

He was inside a trash-bot with its innards removed.

If the men found him here, in this disgusting receptacle, they would mock him for decades. The mere thought of that humiliation sealed his teeth shut around the scream of back pain that threatened to reveal his position.

Rojam would have to shoot the first person who found him, he decided. Shoot them, and then claim they collaborated with that escaped traitor, Frank Zej. He might even say he saw Zej fleeing the scene—the general knew how to best a lie detector with a cool head and deep breaths. He would request one, specifically. He would—he would—

Someone *plooshed* through a polymerwall not centimeters away from him. "I dunno what's going on with sanitation lately," someone said. "Both of these trash-bots should be out in the halls."

"This one's full, I think." Someone rattled something nearby.

"Full of metal or something. Shyte, it's definitely busted."

Rojam felt shaking; agony shot down the length of his spine as he swore death on this idiot. "This one's full, too," said the idiot. "I guess we'll have to empty them manually and then bring them down to supply for repair."

Wheels began to roll under Rojam; first, on the smooth, metal corridors, and then, with sharp, stabbing bumps, across some kind of rocky pavement. Where did the underlings empty the trash? Rojam had never done it himself. Was it some kind of pit somewhere?

An awful grinding sound grated on Rojam's ears, and the ground rumbled. That's right, they processed the garbage in some kind of compactor. Shyte, would they just dump him into its whirring blades *whole*?

"Help!" Rojam began to scream. "Help, you idiots, help!" He pounded the sides of the trash-bot. "Help, help!"

"My, uh, trash-bot is—holy shyte, someone's inside mine," the idiot said.

Legs, and waving grass, appeared beside Rojam as someone opened the side of the trash-bot.

"What the—"

"Here, knock it over so we can get him out." Rojam *heard* the mirth in the idiot's voice. The general yelled and screamed, scrambling and straining to get past their clammy hands out into the open air. The idiots clearly didn't understand a word he said, clearly, didn't care about his back pain—

"Hold on, sir, just hold on—"

They yanked his arm, straining his armpit; they yanked his knee, daring to touch his inner thigh. These rude fools. These idiots. These—

"Theere you go, you'll be alright, sir." Rojam caught a glimpse of a nameplate, *Banks*, as he fell out on his rump in the dirt. How dare they.

More importantly, even blinking in the blinding sunlight, Rojam saw a holster with a weapon. He gripped it, as if helping himself up by climbing up the man—

"Whoa there, General, sir, excuse me—"

His fingers unclipped the holster's safety lock, yanked out the weapon, and shot both fools in the chest.

Rojam dumped their bodies into the whirring, chomping gears of the waste pit, closed its lid, and marched off to find his worthless entourage.

Diebol

Diebol pressed his fingers against his forehead, almost squealing through clenched teeth against his frustration. This day. This was the worst day.

It was extremely clear, the moment General Johnson opened his barracks room door for the visit from Diebol and his three Stygge trainees, that this was not the same person Diebol had brought on the offensive. This General Johnson wore a sparkling dress uniform and, when questioned, had an extremely spotty memory of the day's events. A blood test confirmed his identity and a polygraph confirmed he was at least confident of the story he told about fighting off Frank Zej several hours ago, but that was literally impossible given that several hours ago he had been saving Diebol's life.

"Of course, of course I saved your life," Johnson said with the perfect, cool confidence that polygraph required. "But then, as I was changing and showering from the offensive, I was attacked."

A full accountability report, once checked and double-checked, found two soldiers missing who hadn't gone on the offensive, both platoon-mates of Frank Zej. They'd last been sent to check on some sanitation issue. And sanitation had issues. There were two trash-bots missing, the trash compactor was jammed, and the Bichank sanitation worker responsible for those units had been sent on a two-week paid vacation by someone who very much matched Zej's description.

On top of everything, the onboard computer of the Frelsi air-rider Diebol had brought back was completely fried. No data, no stored networks, nothing for Sterba to use to infiltrate the Alpino Firebase.

Diebol wanted to beat himself against the nearest wall. He'd known it. Deep down inside somewhere, he'd known it. But you just don't accuse a high-ranking general without proof, and you don't usually assume *you're talking to a shapeshifter*. Diebol had no idea how Lem Benzaran could even achieve such a perfect disguise—there were rumors, on the edges of the espionage community, about bounty hunter technology that could project appearances, and he regularly employed a mercenary who used DNA keys in his armor to get through polymerwalls, but full-on shapeshifting, like this?

"There was a bounty hunter last year that we hired, or almost hired—Lark, something," Diebol told his archivist. "A Bont lizard, I think. Find her." That was the only person Diebol could think of rumored in any kind of fairy tale or legend to pass on a shapeshifting ability. A genetically modifying virus, one rumor said. Diebol doubted as much.

Diebol was in full damage-control mode. He ordered the clogged trash compactor shut down and sent a forensics crew to sift through its deep well of materials. He had General Johnson politely detained with a rotating guard of Stygge trainees to ask him the same questions over and over, despite the general's increasingly voluminous threats regarding Diebol's career. Diebol *also* held a meeting with the upper crust to somehow explain the Hiding Place debacle, communicate the danger "Frank Zej" posed to "Her," and justify detaining one of their leading members, all without revealing too much about Sterba. That meeting did *not* go well, and a call to Bricandor confirmed General Johnson had no valuable information—at least, not information Bricandor cared to share instead of saving for future blackmail. Diebol suspected, but could not prove, that Johnson had killed the two soldiers whose remains were eventually found in the trash compactor—but why, apparently, was not relevant to the threat on Sterba.

Worst of all—in a coup de grâce of humiliation—tracking the calls from Jei Bereens's bugged wristband led to a discarded wristband in the middle of Diebol's field, lying on the ground above his buried sleeping pod. All network cache had long ago been cleared except for a single channel to "The Other Paradox Warrior."

Diebol didn't need to have it tested for DNA to know who it belonged to.

So that night, Diebol asked Sterba to destroy what remained of Fort Jehu on Luna-Guetala. It was a small consolation, for him, but knowing Lem Benzaran, it should be enough to make her emotional. Emotional people made mistakes. Speaking of …

He should call Jei Bereens.

CHAPTER TWENTY-EIGHT
Mera

THE POOR MAN HAD NIGHTMARES—NIGHTMARES THAT HAD HIM rolling, sweating, grumbling in his sleep, his jaw clenched as if refusing to give in to some unseen torture.

Mera watched him with sympathy. It was otherwise quiet, here on the cool top deck of the now-still Frelsi evacuation transport. She leaned back on her palms with a deep sigh, looking up at the stars ... hooves galloped somewhere far, far away, and every now and again something hooted—again, very far away—but mostly she just heard the rustle of grass in a soft, now warm breeze. No vehicles, no lights, no engines, just the sparkling infinity of a sky that seemed so much bigger and more beautiful than the one she remembered over Retrack City growing up.

Mera sighed, turning again to her charge. His fingers clenched now against the tunic he'd folded up under his head for a pillow, his biceps tensed as he crushed something in his palms. Mera wanted to gather him up in her arms, hold him close, and calm him altogether.

She didn't care who heard that in her thoughts. They'd taken every other part of her ... at least she could kill with kindness. Every single death they'd required of her, she'd cradled the victim to sleep, ending, with compassion, the misery of their existence.

She often wished someone would do the same for her.

But Diebol had made it clear she could not die, back in the interrogation center. Attempts to do so had been met with ... consequences. Only beautiful smiles and luscious hips had eased the torment: she'd learned the power of a submissive trembling lip.

"I understand your nightmares," she whispered in the Paradox Warrior's ear. She took a deep breath and relaxed, breathing over his cheek as she tried to summon her control pheromone to calm him, and lifted a palm to send him her thoughts through a touch on his wrist—

His hand shot out like a viper; it snatched her throat, and the other hand crushed her fingers in a grip that made her heart race. With one move, she was on her back, his knee on her belly. *Don't be afraid! He's more afraid than you are!* She made herself go limp, hands open on the cold metal beside her head in surrender. "I'm sorry," she croaked, trusting the pheromone triggered by relaxation. "I didn't mean to wake you."

It had worked with a dreadbear, a flying anaconda, and a Crajk beast—it worked with the human electromagnetic, too.

Jei released Mera with a sputter, and dashed a meter away from her as if her skin burned him. He eyed her weaponless hands—Mera recognized the flaring nostrils and heaving chest, just like the pegasi. She stayed down, no sudden movements, watching his muscles for the next twitch.

"There was a fly on your face," she said with a soothing mid-throat rumble. "I'm so sorry."

He cringed as if visibly hurt by the apology; he wiped his elbow over his face. "Don't—don't touch me without telling me," he said. "It's—" He took a deep breath. "I'm sorry I'm like this. But it's a long story."

A story with Diebol in it, Mera thought. She sat up. "You don't need to apologize. It's *your* face."

He stepped forward to offer her his hand; with a pleasant

tug, he helped her up. She tried to keep his finger there for a moment, to send a concentrated burst of thought through to his neurons, but couldn't think of what to say before he pulled away.

Jei dropped himself to the deck and draped his arms over his knees with a sigh. Mera lowered herself slowly to a crisscross seat beside him, watching his face. Neither electromagnetic said anything for a little while. He stared off over the plains. She opened her pack, making sure he could see her hands the whole time, and offered him her drinking tube. He took a sip of water, closing his lips around it with a tight squeeze, and then returned it.

"You have great cheekbones," she observed.

He looked at her sideways as if not quite sure how to take that.

"I'm not going to apologize for thinking so," Mera huffed with a little fake pout. She knew people loved the pout, but she was making it out of genuine fun more than manipulation. "You have great cheekbones, so there." She stuck out her tongue and folded her arms across her chest.

He laughed—a bit of a dark laugh, covered in half a sigh, but a laugh nonetheless. "Thanks, I guess," he said.

They sat there in silence for a while—his eyes on the horizon, and the stars, and hers on their reflections in his eyes and the fluttering of his sleeveless undershirt over his chest. *Creatures don't like you staring at them*, she remembered eventually, forcing her eyes away to the waving sea of grass.

Jei presently seemed to realize sleep was not going to return to him, and began to talk strategy. Mera listened to this boring stuff because she had to. It was her job to guide him after the other Paradox Warrior, after all. Given the short distance land-runner tracks they'd found at the crash zone, Jei speculated that the faux Frelsi transport had likely come from the Growen South Central Command Post nearby. They'd rifled through the debris for a while, but they hadn't found anything that Jei could say definitively belonged to Lem Benzaran—Mera didn't track exclusively with items like a scent-sensing animal might, but they helped her get the idea of the "shape" of the person she was hunting. She couldn't explain more. She did briefly sense a discharge of power from the direction of Growen South Central, but it wasn't large enough to make a call—for all she knew, it could be Diebol in the gym.

In the end, they'd decided to follow the land-runner grooves as far as they could through the plains.

Mera liked Jei's voice. It was a low tenor, with a bit of a rasp to it, and an occasional throatiness she could almost taste. She was sad when he stopped talking, and she tried, with questions, to keep his mouth moving so she could watch his lips.

Eventually, though, Mera felt sleep closing in around her temples. She dreaded it; she wanted to beg him to keep her awake. As she found herself sinking to the cool deck, she tried to fix his quiet shape in her mind, so that perhaps it would be him, not the violent, electric blue eyes of Stygge Sterba, that haunted her dreams.

Mera awoke to a false world floating in black space. She moaned as she pushed herself off her belly; here, on the control deck, fenced in by glowing computer screens each at a perfect 135-degree angle to the next, the color blue imprisoned her heart.

Oh, this terrible brain-radio. Mera hated that they'd bonded her together during the captivity with this soulless human automaton. They'd been friends, at one point, by necessity and loneliness, and now they were this twisted amalgamation of possession, like wires melted into flesh, and Mera despised everything about it. Bricandor had told her Diebol had a similar connection with Jei Bereens, the first dark connection the old man had forged—Mera was lucky her connection did not cross enemy lines, he told her.

Mera did not feel lucky.

"Morda," said the cold voice all around her.

Mera knelt, her stomach twisting. "I hate you," she muttered.

"You have no control." The cold voice said this with no emotion. Just judgment.

"You're more than enough of a control freak for the both of us," Mera smirked. "I'm the Yin to your Yang, girlfriend."

"If you do not control this situation, you will suffer."

Mera pouted. "Thanks, I know."

"That is not a threat."

"Right, it's a promise, blablabla. I get it."

The computer lights brightened in response to Mera's impertinence; the sharp change stabbed her eyes, forcing her to close them against the familiar looming headache. "Fine, I'm sorry!" she cried out, palms raised. The more pathetic she sounded, the more she hoped to be left alone.

But the other woman had no emotion or hormonal instinct for her appeal. "I do not mean to threaten you," she said, still brightening the light. "I am warning you that attachments cause suffering, and even if you can control the attachment, you will find suffering in it. I tell you this not as a teacher, but as a sister."

"Yeah, I get it, we've been burned. I'm not going to fall for anyone," Mera grumbled, trying to cover her closed eyes with her forearms. "Just because I'm easy on the eyes doesn't mean—"

"Your *looks* are not the reason they call you a call girl."

"Thank you, Ice Queen." Mera gritted her teeth. She didn't like the memories the other woman summoned. "Some of us didn't have *near-omniscience* to survive on. Some of us had to prove our worth other ways."

"Worth? What worth?" The other woman laughed, and thank everything, the bright light dimmed. Mera dropped her sleeves from her face to find them wet. "Are you crying now, again?"

"No, that's just my eyes bleeding from having to look at you," Mera coughed. But she was crying. She didn't know exactly why, this particular time. She felt numb all the time, except in the moments when anyone smiled back at her. Making people happy made her less numb. She would do anything to make them happy. Or maybe to make herself laugh. If she could make herself laugh, she could feel something other than sadness. "I'm going to find your hunter, I promise. Please be patient with me."

"You can track her if you *make* him show you her shape in his mind," the other woman snapped.

"He is *so much stronger than me*. I can't *make* him do anything —that's not how this is going to work!"

"He is only stronger because you allow yourself to believe he is."

She'd heard that so many times. The power of the mind. "You can become whatever you believe you are." Blablabla. She should just "think" herself happy. Control the self before controlling others. Just pull yourself up by your belt-loops, "Morda!" So many mantras that only worked if you grew up under the right biological conditions to create the right mind. Mera found herself standing, screaming the lies back at Sterba now, trying to swing at the computer screens for no reason, and finding them only mirrors, mocking her with images of what she hated most. She had no control, no control of the feelings or actions, or any of the surging pain in her lower belly and temples—

At last, Mera broke free of the mind-link the only way she knew how—by ripping off her clothes. Her ascetic opposite, disgusted as ever by the natural form of the human body, released Mera, and the younger Stygge escaped into the real world to cry under a waning moon.

Jei

In the early morning, surrounded by dew on the cold metal, I awoke again, this time to Mera's soft sniffling. She wasn't really either asleep or awake—she seemed caught in some in-between trance, curled motionless in the fetal position beside me as tears pooled underneath her face. I didn't want to scare her by shaking her shoulder, but bloodseas, I couldn't just leave her stuck in that.

I nudged her with her backpack. "Hey, Mera, wake up, okay?" She didn't wake up.

"Shyte," I grumbled. "Don't make a hypocrite out of me. I won't touch you."

I nudged her with the backpack again, a little harder. She continued to weep in silence.

"Hey!" I yelled. "Hey, wake up!"

I gripped the metal underneath me for the stability of its sea of electrons, and channeled an em-pull through it that jerked her flat on her back against the floor. With the thud, her eyelids fluttered open.

Tears still rolled down her cheeks as she stared blankly at the sky. I got up to crouch beside her, feeling immensely guilty for the rough awakening.

"Hey," I said in a softer voice, leaning over her. "Are you okay?"

She blinked, as if seeing through me for a moment, and then her pupils constricted as she focused on my face. She shook her head.

I offered her a hand. She flopped her palm into it and dropped her other arm across her face; her lower lip quivered, and she let out a trembling sigh.

"While I appreciate the high five, I was going to help you up," I said to her.

Her snuffle told me she'd found that a little funny. But when I pulled her arm gently, she let herself hang limp.

"I'm so stupid. I'm sorry for crying," said her muffled voice, through the arm across her face. "I'm so sorry."

"Nothing to be sorry for," I said. "Now if we were in battle, and you started doing this, I might have words for you. But everyone's got some terrible shyte in their heads these days."

"Not like mine." The muffled voice grew cold. Mera took back her hand and wiped off her face as if she was mad at her eyes. A glowering gaze stared into the sunrise.

"No one's is like yours," I agreed. "No one's is like mine, either. Everyone's got their own coals to walk."

Mera kept her eyes fixed on the orange and pink light creeping into the blue above us. Unlike the north continent, with its onyx sky, Alpino's more equatorial areas had brilliant, multi-colored mornings and evenings. Mera's chest heaved, then deflated in a large sigh as she blew out her breath.

"I shouldn't be such a baby. I let it happen," she muttered.

"What someone did to you, or even what you think you let someone do to you, isn't who you are," I growled. I stood, then, to give her some space, and shake off the sudden anger that came over me. I wasn't going to argue with her or prod, and while I had guesses, I didn't really know what she was talking about—I figured if she wanted to say more, she would. I retreated a few paces and crouched again to open the front of her backpack with a gentle em-push. A protein bar rolled out of the pack's front pocket; I levitated it in the air just above her, waving it at her.

Mera dropped her head to the side to look at me with a little smirk. I shrugged; she laughed.

"I'm not hungry yet," she said. "But—" She put a finger on her lips and looked sideways, as if thinking. "I think I would take a hug."

"I'm going to be really mad if you stab me in the kidneys," I answered, opening my arms as she got up with a giggle. The clouds over her countenance disappeared with the rising sun. I didn't let the hug last long—"You're breaking my ribs," I joked, pushing her away by the shoulders. I didn't really want to let her go. But the sun was up, and we had a Paradox Warrior to hunt down.

CHAPTER TWENTY-NINE
Mera

MERA WAS QUICKLY BORED WITH THE "HUNT."

It mostly consisted of Jei squinting out the narrow horizontal slit 180 degrees around them, his eyes fixed on the land-runner tracks in the plains as he drove. The clunky Frelsi evac transport was warm even for someone like Mera who'd grown up on Luna-Guetala, and the cockpit too dark, with a musty mildewed smell and an annoying hum.

Occasionally, Jei asked Mera to pop upstairs for a better visual. Mera smiled for him, but she hated underling errands like that almost as much as she hated little kids. It was the same inanity each time: slide back the heavy cockpit door with its rattling groan, step into the long, empty hold, climb the rouge-metal ladder she didn't like touching, push open the thick hatch above, and poke her head out to confirm for the umpteenth time that yes, Mr. Paranoia, they did still have the same trail ahead of them they saw through the cockpit.

There was one moment, however, when she entered the hold and thought she heard scratching under her feet.

Mera glanced over her shoulder toward the cockpit. Did Jei have someone spying on her? She removed a glove and crouched, her fingers bare to the warm floor, and lowered her ear. A soft electromagnetic "hum" flooded from her throat, into her fingers, into the sea of electrons in the metal, and her eyes closed as she waited for the return wave to her powerful inner ear …

Nothing. At least, nothing electromagnetic enough to register above the vibrating engine.

"I think your ship is haunted," Mera remarked, sauntering back into the cockpit to drop herself sideways across the co-pilot's seat with her boots on the armrest and back against the wall. She faced Jei with her knees tucked up to her chest.

"It technically is," he said.

Huh? Mera tilted her head, chewing on her lip. Did these old things have onboard AI after all?

"Not by ghosts or anything," Jei said. "I have a … Being, that …" He stopped himself and laughed. "Sorry. You're going to call me crazy. I believe some weird shyte. What, ah—what were you saying about ghosts? You believe in ghosts?"

"Oh, I dunno," she shrugged. "I don't think people's souls really float around places. But all that electromagnetic programming—the arrangement of our neurons, the patterns in which they fire—I could believe that, in some weird way, very strong programs can get trapped in the magnetic fields of certain planets and places. Like the way a laser burns patterns to a disc, or a magnetic storage media can hold memories of sounds, or a strong light, reflected through a crystal, can sear shadows into wood. Maybe if something awful happens to you as you're dying, your nervous system can have such a severe electrical response that the pattern's permanently stored in the magnetic field of that planet, that place. You're gone, but the memory, the vengeful recording in the ether, distilled rage or sadness—that program—maybe that's what ghosts are."

Mera realized she was babbling the moment the Paradox Warrior smiled. A sharp pang of shame shot through her. She was supposed to smile and woo him into obedience, not tell him weird loser stories that would turn him off. "I'm sorry," she blurted.

"Don't be," he murmured. Murmured? Mera tilted her head —Jei kept his eyes on the plains ahead of him, but she saw him shake himself as if waking from a trance. He coughed. "Or be sorry, if you want, I won't tell you what to do," he grunted. "It's an interesting theory, that's all."

Oh my! "You like strange thoughts," Mera exclaimed, glowing: better, *he likes* my *strange thoughts.*

"Maybe I enjoy peering off ledges," he said, with a tone that almost seemed to trail ... but he didn't elaborate.

"You have an interdimensional," Mera stated for him. She knew this, of course, from her mission assignment, but this seemed like the right place to "fake a guess," rip the scab off that wound. It had to be a terrible burden to carry around an enormous, universe-bending presence that fed on your mind.

But Jei smiled—a pained, almost shy smile, but a smile nonetheless. "Yeah. *The* interdimensional, actually."

Mera fought not to scowl. Jei's smile was beautiful—less beautiful were her memories of her coach from Retrack, with those sick twisted fingers ... fingers that folded twice a day to talk to an interdimensional of his own. "*The* interdimensional? Are you saying all interdimensionals are One?" Mera wheezed.

"You okay?" Jei turned his head to Mera for a moment. His eyes scanned her face before returning to the drive ahead. "No. Bloodseas, no. Most of them, they're all *ba-eaters*, as the Biouks call them: monsters that feed on your mind. They can travel dimensions in space, but not time. Mine's the only one who travels dimensional time. And the only one who feeds you, instead of feeding off of you." His cheeks rose almost into a flinch, as if preparing for someone to punch him in the face. "I'm sorry if that's—offensive," he said. "I mean, I know it is. My existence is offensive."

Mera said nothing for a moment. Jei was right—they wouldn't want him gone, in his present form, if his existence didn't offend. Jei was a walking abomination, a Contaminated danger to everyone, carrying a virus from another universe in his brain. But Mera liked the idea, at least, that Jei's wasn't the same as … whatever evil the old coach worshipped.

Mera struggled for a moment: she wanted to change the subject, but she imagined *that* happened every single time Jei dared to open up about this. How did you affirm someone with a mental illness? "I am glad you exist, offensive or not," she said finally.

"Existing a little longer because of you," he grinned. "Diebol really had me on the ropes there."

"Psh," Mera pursed her lips and blew him off, feeling a little guilty about that whole impulsive mess. "Hey, do you think you could have smungworms eating your ship?"

Jei laughed. "Smungworms bury into the ground, not electronics. You aren't from Alpino, are you?"

"I grew up in Retrack City," she said truthfully. "I was trying to guess the Alpino equivalent of singing lizards in the tailpipe."

Jei smiled. "Retrack—I saw the acrobats there once, when I was little."

"I *was* an acrobat there," Mera bragged. "The ones that twirl light ribbons and dance on tightropes and swings dangling from airships? I did that for two years—started when I was fourteen. I thought I'd do that for my entire life."

Jei gave a single nod. He wasn't terribly readable, but Mera picked up just the hint of widening in the corner of his eye, and a slight, impressed purse to his lips. *Aha. He likes sky dancers.* "Why'd you stop?" he asked.

The Growen rescued me. But she said: "I began to develop electromagnetic abilities. I left to go explore my biology." Mera drizzled the last sentence with honeyed double meaning. "How about you? How long have your powers run on enemy energy?"

"What do you mean?" Jei's eyes narrowed—not threateningly, just confused.

He doesn't know. She made her voice higher and a little weaker, to make sure she didn't come across as a know-it-all: "Well, I saw the end of that fight with the pegasus jaw … you charge, don't you, when there are lots of people attacking you? To like insane superhuman levels? As long as you're conscious?"

Jei tilted his head to the side, thinking. "That actually sounds —right, lately. It hasn't always been like that ... to tell you the truth, you probably know more about electronegative abilities in general than I do."

"Well, human brains don't really fully mature until around twenty-four years of age—about twenty-two Luna-Guetala rotations. So maybe your abilities weren't done developing yet. You're what—nineteen?" She didn't expect him to answer, and he didn't, so she continued. "Sometimes, too, you don't know what you can do until an extreme stress enters your life."

"I'm not under any more stress than usual," he said. "I've lived under Growen rule three times—*that* was stress."

She almost laughed with compassion—oh, sweetie, didn't he know? "Nothing hurts like betrayal." Her fingertips reached to trace, to soothe that angry, hardened jaw—

And then her hand jerked back to her lap as his head snapped around to face her. "Sorry, sorry," she squeaked. "I didn't—you look so miserable." She lowered her eyes.

"Don't do that," he said, his eyes back on driving.

"I won't distract you again, I'm sorry."

"No, the eye thing." A different kind of anger passed over his face—how many kinds did this guy have? "You don't have to cower like that," he added. "You're not beneath me."

She stiffened. "I—I know that!"

"Well, good." He leaned forward a little, straining to see his precious hunting trail. "I'm sorry if I'm misreading," he added. It was a foreign kind of apology, to Mera—just very plain, without any ceremony, shame, or anything to gain. "I get the feeling someone's treated you like crap and you think you deserve it. I could be wrong. You do these little things that my mom used to—just—tells."

She didn't know how to take that. She planted a finger on her lip, wondering ... maybe there was some kind of abused damsel fantasy here she could use to gain control over him?

But what he said felt too true—too *naked*—and she didn't know if she'd just realized something about herself or not.

"Speaking of you," Jei added. "Why are you really helping me?"

She didn't know how to answer that now. She'd told him her cover story, but that wasn't what he was asking. "I—I told you, I travel where I want, and help whoever I want," Mera said. She decided she didn't like these kinds of questions, and before he could double down with a "why here and me, though" she returned to a topic with less heart and more head: "Anyway, as I was saying about your power surge ... I doubt it's based *purely* on your number of enemies. But from the two major incidents I've heard about, I don't think you draw on allies. Is that because you need a particular trigger to set yourself off, and override your body's survival mechanisms—kind of like how adrenaline can override your glucose control systems? Or does your power actually have something to do with an aggression pattern in the cerebral electricity of enmity? I'm not sure how I'd figure that out."

"Ah," he said. "That's why. You heard through the mercenary forums about what happened at the Growen outpost on Luna-Guetala. You got curious. That's why me."

She rolled her eyes. "Why do you care what I think as long as I'm helping you?"

"People's reasons predict their selling price," he shrugged.

"That's a disappointing answer," she blurted. It wasn't some interest in her inner being—he just had the same cold strategy she did. She was suddenly incredibly annoyed with him. She turned in her seat to face forward, elbows on her knees and chin on her fists, glowering.

He didn't notice. "What did you mean by the adrenaline thing?" he asked.

She didn't answer.

"Mera?" he asked.

She sighed; she couldn't explain her mood shift to herself, so she didn't try to explain it to him. "Your body has normal checks and balances that control how you use glucose for energy so that you don't cause too much oxidative stress to your cells," she grumbled. "Adrenaline can override that to give you a super-human power boost, but totally tears up your muscle fibers and damages other systems."

"So maybe that's literally it. Maybe I'm just on a hormone trip when there's a bigger force against me."

"You have that long cool down, though," she said. "I heard about what happened at Fort Jehu; it's all over the rumor boards. You were there. That didn't stress you enough to trigger the power boost?"

He didn't answer; his jaw tightened again, and Mera realized she'd hit a nerve. Did he feel guilty? Oh dear. Her mouth ran apologetically to carry them both past the discomfort. "I think there's a more specific trigger," she said. "Maybe I'm onto some-thing with the patterns people are giving off. Maybe you need a certain threshold of ambient atmospheric brain energy before you can fire."

"I really wish I could predict how long the cool down lasts, and exactly how many enemies I need to trigger the power surge," he mused.

"Maybe after we catch your partner we can just go from base to base taunting armies to test it," Mera laughed.

"I know you're joking, but that actually sounds *extremely* fun." His eyes lit up over a delicious, wicked grin.

"Maybe I'm not joking," Mera smiled, tapping her finger on her lip. She liked the idea of seeing him fire full-force, his head tilted back in a laugh while the world spun around his outstretched hands …

And she wasn't joking. She just had a different set of bases in mind.

CHAPTER THIRTY

Reise

AFTER ALMOST TWENTY-FOUR HOURS HIDING IN THE FLOOR, THE boys had three problems.

One, someone had farted, and while at first, they'd found themselves in paroxysms of laughter, the air in the hidden compartment never really cleared out. It had a different ventilation system from the main hold, to prevent sentient beings with good noses from sniffing out the smuggling spaces. And over time, that sucked.

Two, Gideon required an insane amount of calories. Nathan had calculated the freeze-dried rations they needed for several days, but Gideon had eaten half of the entire supply within the first twelve hours. He hadn't even meant to. They all just looked up to find him with three empty packages besides him and a sheepish shock on his face.

Third, after hours of darkness had adjusted their eyes, they discovered twelve-year-old Jake Benzaran had never left the vehicle.

"Shyte shyte shyte shyte shyte!" Reise hissed. "Why are you *here*? You were supposed to go to the Hiding Place with everyone else!"

Jake was crying. "I di—idn't want you—to leave me—behiii-ind," he sobbed. "I got—scared so I—hid!"

Reise's fingers spasmed like claws. "But that's—gah, what are we supposed to do with you?"

Nathan's gentle voice intervened before Reise could choke his brother. "What Reise is trying to say, Jake, is that we're going into enemy territory. That's no place for someone below regulation fighting age; if you were scared before, it's going to get worse."

"But don't go to enemy territory!" Jake cried. "Go to the Firebase with Lieutenant Bereens!"

"Bereens isn't *going* to the Firebase!" Reise choked on his frustration.

"But he saaaaiid!"

"He *lied*." Reise punched his own hand. "Okay? He lied. Because that's what people do when they care about someone. He's going to look for Lem. See?" Reise beat two fingers on his brother's wristband to open a map. "We're heading *away* from the Firebase, toward this Growen outpost here."

Jake stared at the glowing blips in silent shock for a second. Then, his face scrunched—wetter and more dumb-looking in the shadows of the soft green light—and he began almost to howl. "But why would he do thaaaat—"

Gideon wrapped his bicep around the younger kid's face and held him still. "Hey bud?" he said as the twelve-year-old struggled in breathless terror. "The sound dampening on this compartment's good, but it's not good enough that you can just scream out your soul, okay?"

Jake kicked. Reise sat on his legs to prevent them from gonging against the floor. Nathan leaned in to the kid's ear. "Jake, I know this is scary. And if it were just Jei up there, we'd go right up, explain the situation, and get you back to the Firebase to take our punishment. But Jei's got a civilian combatant up there, and if we suddenly appear out of nowhere, she's going to know we have hidden spaces in these ships. Now, she may be a really nice person,

I don't know, but she's not Frelsi. That information *will* find its way to the Growen, and people *will* get hurt. So you're going to have to be quiet until we can find a way out of here. Okay?"

Jake went limp. "Let him go," Nathan said. Gideon didn't right away—"Let him go!"

"I am, geez! Just making sure he wasn't going to—"

"He needs air, you sausage-snarfing bonehead," Nathan said, pulling Jake away from the other teen like a protective parent. Reise found himself laughing at the insult, despite the situation. "Jake, we think your sister's a prisoner at Growen South Central," Nathan continued. "Reise and Gideon and I are going to find her."

"Did Lieutenant Bereens say that?" Jake sniffled. He curled up against the back wall, quiet now, holding his knees.

Reise scooted over to sit next to him. "We haven't talked to him," Reise said. "Like Nate says, he's got the civilian with him." Reise leaned his head back against the wall with a sigh. When they were little, he and Jake had played games about going off on adventures together. Now that it was accidentally happening, it was much less fun. And that wasn't really Jake's fault. Maybe this whole thing had been a mistake.

But Reise had gotten sick of watching other people just wait it out when a loved one disappeared, and then cry when nine times out of ten the person ended up dead. Frelsi recovery teams had hundreds of requests pending at any one time: if you wanted something done you couldn't trust others to do it.

Time mattered, too. When Lem escaped on her own, a year and a half ago, she returned changed after having been missing for months. Cinta came back actually crippled—without claws, he couldn't travel the trees in his native habitat like before. This time, with what Reise had overheard of Jei and Cinta's angry conversation, it sounded like his sister might be in serious danger.

And they'd *all* just lost the only home Reise had known! Why the hell shouldn't he take the fight to the jerkwads who'd started it? What was the point of the constant combat training if you never—

"Hey, Jake," Gideon said to the sniffling boy. "Remember when you used to sit on Reise and he couldn't get up?" Reise rolled his eyes: Jake was about his same size, plus a few pounds, despite being two years his junior. "Remember that?" Gideon asked.

"Yeah …" Jake said.

"So look at him. He's not scared. You can kick his butt, right?"

Jake could *not*, not with his janky foot, but he nodded, unable to see Reise's eye-daggers.

"So if the guy you can beat up isn't scared of something, you shouldn't be scared either," Gideon finished.

"Brilliant deduction, master scientist," Reise muttered. He could see Nathan shrugging in the shadows, probably wearing that broad smile that was about as close as Nathan ever got to laughing. Gideon's meaty hand made a slapping sound on Jake's shoulder.

"So we've got a mission for you, brave guy," Gideon said. "We're gonna need you to keep your mouth shut and ears open until we can get you home. And when we say it's time to move, you're gonna move. No hiding or crying or other dumb shyte, okay?"

"O–okay."

And so Jake was calm.

But now Reise had to get him back to base somehow.

Jei

We weren't far, now—and the trail *was* leading toward Growen South Central.

The wind had picked up, rocking our kind-of-stolen evac transport from side to side like a seafaring vessel. It was my turn to swap out and head topside to stretch my legs. Without a word, I looked over at Mera; she leaned over and reached toward the old control sticks on my dashboard.

"You sure you trust little me to drive this giant thing?" Mera sparkled at me.

"I trust you to tell me if you can't," I said, standing to let her squeeze by me.

When her fingers closed over mine on the controls there was something like an electric jolt—not like static, but painful, like thousands of little needles stabbed me. The same thing had happened for a brief moment when she gripped my hand earlier, but this time a thought popped into my head: *Don't leave me.*

I blinked, and pulled away with a smile, stepping back to clear the space around her. Wow, I was ... tired. Poor woman probably already got enough creeps imagining things about her without me assuming she craved my company.

"You good?" I asked.

"I'm good," she said.

"I'll just be a moment. Then we'll pull over into those dunes, like we talked about, to hide the ship, and hoof it the rest of the way."

She nodded, eyes lingering on me for a moment—"Watch the road," I said.

I grinned as I turned around and slid the cockpit door shut behind me. Whatever I imagined about her fingers, I knew I hadn't imagined that glance.

I gripped the rough ladder to the top deck, sighing with the familiar, comforting hum of the evacuation transport around me, and pushed my way through the hatch up into the full wind.

"Njande," I said aloud. "I'm here."

I am, first.

"I know." I put both palms on the deck and pushed myself up out of the hole. There was a slight drizzle on the wind. "I'm just—I'm here to see if you have anything else to say. We're almost there. I'm doing this thing." I stood with my arms outstretched, facing into the wind as my calves and soles followed the rocking of the ship to keep me balanced. I felt like I could ride through him, straight through a mist of memory and shadow that would wash away with the wind and dissolve just like Lem had. Just like my mom had. Just like Fort Jehu, Lavabase, and friend after friend. Nothing was solid; everything dissolved in time.

It was backward, of course.

Njande was more solid than Jei's rock of a clenched fist, but a limited, three-dimensional creature could not know the mist was, in fact, itself. Njande saw, with deep sadness, the days stretching ahead and backward around the Paradox Warrior, and the timelines, not real yet, that shimmered around him like waves from a stone tossed into a pond.

Njande touched the moment, and collapsed the waveform.

Jei

Trust in Me with all your heart and don't lean on your own understanding.

Only this frustrating repeating thought came to me now, in the brewing gale.

"Yeah, I get that," I called back. I could barely hear myself with the roar in my ears. "And I trust you, but—"

Lean not on your own understanding.

"I don't know what that means!"

Trust in Me.

I gripped the railing and yelled without words. I couldn't pick up the rest of the message—either because the wall between our dimensions was still too thick, or my brain just couldn't contain it.

With all your heart.

The gentle repetition gave me a feeling, at least—the feeling that, whether or not my brain could catch the meaning, the speaker cared. Maybe it just meant I needed to let that organ in my chest beat normally, without all the fluttering and pounding. *Rest*, he'd said before. Maybe that meant I just needed to meditate and hone my senses for the battle ahead.

I closed my eyes, gripped the color green in my mind, and stood before that door in my innermost sanctum, the one lined with old vines and carvings across its panels. I couldn't go in there. I wanted to—no, I didn't want to? I couldn't surrender to the urge. I couldn't fall asleep inside. I had to do this, awake, and feeling all of it, every drop of pain and rage.

You have to feel miserable? He asked from the other side. *Oh, little human, woe to you, if you don't enter this rest.*

"Woe" seemed so out of place in my head. I laughed, a tired, sad laugh, not at him, but just at that word, and sat down with my back to the door. The wood was alive, and a cool warmth, a paradox of comfort, soothed my spine.

"I can't rest. I don't know how," I said. "But no matter what happens," I promised, "I'll guard this room, just like we pledged. It's yours, and mine. Only.

"Then, even if I muck this up, I have somewhere to come back to."

CHAPTER THIRTY-ONE
Reise

THE WIND HAD PICKED UP OUTSIDE THE EVAC TRANSPORT; UNDER THE feet of the Paradox Warrior and his friend, inside the hidden secret hold, the ship's gentle rocking and vibrations from the engine eventually put twelve-year-old Jake Benzaran back to sleep.

Once the little brother revved into that familiar snore Reise knew so well, someone tapped Reise's knee.

"Nate?" Yup—after so many hours in the darkness, they'd all adapted to see at least each others' shapes and expressions now. Nathan nodded his head toward the other end of the hidden hold. Gideon and Reise followed into the cramped space at the back of the ship, under the decontamination room, hunched over, in Reise's mind, like peacock guinea pigs snacking on moss.

"I'm not in anymore, Reise," Nathan whispered. "We have to find a way to get your brother back now. Maybe we can steal the ship after Jei disembarks—he's not going to bring the transport all the way to Growen South Central and risk them dissecting it."

Reise opened his mouth—he did *not* plan to give up on finding his sister, not—

Gideon got there first. "Then we split up," he shrugged. "You stay here in the ship with the little guy, and Reise and I go bust out his sister."

"I know you think this is your workout regimen on easy mode." Nathan's gentle voice edged toward aggression. "But you're going to need more than your dead-lift record to get you into a prison."

"You're not the only one here with a brain," Gideon shot back.

Reise heard a loud rattle and a thick whooshing rumble—the floor was thinner here, under the decontamination chamber. "Silence, both of you!" he snapped, pointing up.

Another whoosh, and then a clang that shook the floor above them—

That sounded like the door to the decontamination chamber closing.

Reise's nostrils flared as he placed his ear to the low ceiling. Now—two women's voices? They had to be literally lying on the floor to be heard through here ...

Ah. The first voice, sharp and tough, sounded distorted, like through a transmitter. So Jei's new partner was relaxing on the floor while she called a friend.

Well, not a friend. Reise shuddered—the eerie calm voice from the transmitter made him feel stupid, and her icicle'd tone wasn't even directed toward him. "Why are you calling me on this line?" she asked. "I ordered you to speak in our mind portal."

"I hate it in there," pleaded the second voice, a much warmer, richer timbre. *Right, that's the electro-capable girl here with Bereens.* "I hate it, it gives me a splitting headache, and if you want me controlling people with my brain, I need to not have a splitting headache." *Wait, controlling—what?* "I'm doing my best—I promise, you're going to like the results. Your hunter's probably at Growen South Central, and I can literally deliver your present to Diebol right there."

"No. I want him brought to me."

"I don't want to bring him to you," the woman muttered.

"I will not hurt him."

"Sure. You'll leave that up to me."

"You know me well." There was something like the hint of a laugh that froze Reise's blood, and then: "You will bring him to me. I'm at the abandoned station over Alpino North East. You know which one."

"You're going to make Alpino like Burbura this week, then."

"If you do your job, yes."

The voice distanced—the woman had likely stood up, and Reise could no longer make out any words from her or her transmitter.

But Gideon was slapping Reise's arm with wide eyes. He alternated slapping and pointing up, holding his own mouth to keep from yelling his shocked excitement. Nathan had already started tracing a message to command on his own wristband. Reise's temples pounded as the pieces fell into place: *At an abandoned station floating over Alpino North East … make Alpino like Burbura this week …*

It wasn't exactly a set of coordinates. But bloodseas and sandstorms, they had information on the person responsible for the computerized apocalypse.

"We have to warn Bereens, too," Reise whispered, tracing his finger across his own wrist now—

There was a quiet pop, and his screen went dark before he could send anything.

Nathan's too.

In the deeper darkness, Reise heard Gideon whacking his own wristband with his meaty palm.

No pulsing heartbeat readout. No light. No communicator. No sound. Just a dead screen.

And suddenly, the floor went cold and still; the ship's warm vibrations died with a whine.

The engine?

There was a long creak.

Then Reise found himself sliding backward down an incline.

"We just lost power to the back levitating pad!" he hissed, scrambling on all fours back across the hold to his little brother, trying to hold on as the rear of the ship fell and in the slippery darkness directions became nonsensical and the floor was a smooth 30, 45, 60-degree hill—ow, he skinned his knee—fingers splayed, he gripped, slender form hugging the floor to climb—

"She must have set off an EMP!" Nathan shouted from somewhere on Reise's left.

Reise's brain registered the idea as "likely accurate" as his hands pawed uphill through the onslaught of invisible sliding food packages and blankets. The floor was almost a vertical wall now. "Jake, where are you?" With the ignition still running, fuel still hot, and no electricity in the rear of the ship, they were at risk of explosion if the rear hit the—

The ground. The ground crunched against the back of the ship with a deafening jolt. Gideon screamed somewhere below Reise.

"G, sound off!" Reise yelled to his friend, digging in his toes to try to keep from falling off the now-vertical floor. "Jake, where are you?"

"In the front entrance!" Jake squealed as Gideon groaned and, with a crackling hiss, blue light flickered through the room.

Reise looked over his shoulder down into the light. Below him, a slow tendril of fire snaked across the now-compressed back end of the ship; stuck between the crushed remains of the floor and the ceiling struggled Gideon as the azure flames crawled toward him.

Reise glanced up. By the firelight he could now see tiny Nathan up and to the left, clinging to the floor-wall like a gecko; in the deep shadows above them Jake dangled from the short ladder into the front secret entrance.

"Nate, get Jake and go out the front!" Reise yelled. Nate's "affirmative" trailed behind him as Reise pushed off and slid down the floor-wall.

The ship lurched—Reise was flung from the floor-wall to the ceiling opposite. His shoulder crunched against the metal with agonizing force—he bounced off, back against the floor, sliding toward the fire—agh, his ribs—!

Reise threw out his legs to stop his fall—his back slid still—shyte—his boots left a black skid-mark on the hot metal—stop stop stop—he wedged himself between the "floor" and "ceiling," screaming to a stop just above the blaze with his back on one wall, knees bent, and feet on the other. Flames licked at the butt of his uniform; he squirmed, trying to inch back up.

"Shyte, that's hot," he heard himself squeal.

"Yeah! Yeah it is!" Gideon thrashed, then groaned again; he grunted in pain with every bump as the dying ship, still limping, dragged its rear across the plains. Reise couldn't see exactly through the shadows dancing in blue firelight—shyte, Gideon's front half was sandwiched between the floor and the ceiling, and the dark gap behind him looked narrower still.

Reise pushed his feet, trying to get some kind of leverage to inch toward Gideon without falling into the fire. "Wait a moment, G, I'm a bit wedged—in here—myself," Reise huffed. Push with his quads, move this foot left, then that foot left—if he could get his arm to—well, no, that arm was hanging limp and doing nothing.

Reise propped himself up between the two walls like a tripod, balancing with his palm on one wall, and on the toes of both boots on the other. Bridging the gap like this, he crab-walked side-wards over the fire toward his friend. *I am filking effervescent,* he told himself.

"Hey, man, I don't think there's any way out for me!" That almost sounded like a scream; Gideon was breathing hard. "You gotta get out of here!"

Reise kept inching. "Just wait!"

"No, man, I'm like—even I can't bench press a ship!" Reise was close enough now to see sweat drizzling down his big friend's face. The readable panic there sent paroxysms through Reise's chest.

"Can you reach your laserknife?" Reise panted. The flames waved beside him.

"No, man, it's crushed back behind—down there!" Gideon gestured to his hidden lower half.

Reise had his knife out. He started cutting a semi-circle of metal above Gideon's midsection, struggling to balance—he had to push himself up off the floor-wall to reach, and—

"Here, give it to me," Gideon snatched it. "Get out of here, man. Go!"

"No, you're not allowed to die trying to help me find my sister," Reise said. He crab-walked just over Gideon's head and began kicking at the metal, trying to force Gideon's metal gash to open faster. The flames crawled across the space where Reise had been—

"I could say the same thing," Gideon grunted. The flames danced by the edge of Gideon's sleeve.

"You don't have a sister. Cut faster!" Kick, kick, kick—the metal tore with the strain of the heat, the blade, the kick, kick, kick, but—

"It's not working, the cut's only over my top half, I can't reach my legs!"

"Here, the metal into the decontamination room is thinner, and I'm smaller than you. Hold on." Reise crab-walked to Gideon's other side, and slid down into the dark space beside him. "Knife! Give me knife!"

Gideon handed it over, and by the glow of the red blade Reise suddenly realized exactly how small of a space he'd just slipped into. He lay beside Gideon, almost hip to hip, with the floor against his back and the ceiling touching his nose *oh shyte. Oh shyte oh shyte—*

Just like in training. Focus on finger-work.

Reise stabbed the knife above Gideon's midsection, sliding himself down around the guy as he extended the semi-circle over his friend's body to create a hole into the decon chamber. Down by Gideon's knees, shimmy down, don't think about breathing—down, down—above Gideon's shins, slip his body down around under Gideon's boots where Reise barely fit and the metal squeezed his chest as he cut, cut, cut—

"Reise, get out of here!" Gideon screamed. Reise screamed himself. He was in a coffin. A hot, metal coffin. His breath was hacking a thousand times a minute as the full-blown panic attack choked his throat—

But Gideon's scream sounded like something fleshy was about to burn.

"Kick!" Reise shrieked. "It's loosening, kick up!"

The metal began to peel upward under Gideon's much stronger blows as Reise lengthened the crack. He'd almost traced all the way around Gideon now; blue light flickered around him again, and Gideon was thrashing—was he on fire?

"Push! Push and get up!" Reise yelled. Oh shyte, he had to wait for Gideon to move before he could get out. Oh shyte oh shyte. "Hurry up and push!" he screamed.

Gideon's body disappeared from beside him as the larger boy shoved his way into the other room with a last metal *screech*. Reise scrambled after him. Fire leapt behind them. The decon chamber was about a quarter of its original size, mangled and on fire.

"There!" The gangplank-style door was hanging open a crack; they could see grass and light on the other side as the ship continued to drag itself through the plains. Gideon and Reise both slammed against the door; Reise felt heavy hands on his back and a push as the crack widened for a second—he rolled out into the grass.

Gideon leapt clear as the fire reached the fuel center, and with an enormous, multi-story *whoosh* of heat and blue, the ship finally crashed into a nearby hill.

Reise stood as wind threw cold, hard rain against his face. He squinted, gripping his chest as his heart continued to fly around wildly in there. A bit further back, along a long, gaping black gash in the earth, he saw Nathan, and Jake. Bereens, and the woman with him, were nowhere to be seen.

"Do you think they're in there?" Gideon's voice came up behind him. Reise followed his gaze to the vehicle now disintegrating like candle wax in one enormous gooey blue flame.

"If the EMP originated from her, and she intends to transport him to her superiors, then no," Reise said.

"So just no." Gideon heaved. "You always say things the long way, man."

Reise punched him in the arm—then yelped in pain. His own movement sent shooting pain down his other, more dangly appendage.

"Looks dislocated," Gideon said as they trudged back to Jake and Nathan. "I can put it back. Happens to one of my lifting buddies all the time."

"I appreciate it."

"It's super-painful, but you just kind of pull forward, like this—"

"Show me later!" Reise pushed his friend in the chest, stumbling away from him. He didn't want any extra pain right now.

It just so happened Jake greeted him with an enormous bear-hug that forced out the loudest scream Reise had ever screamed.

"Let him go, Jake, can't you see he's hurt?" Nathan admonished, peeling the younger boy's fingers off his brother. To Reise and Gideon: "We overheard them before they got clear. She 'just so happened' to see a pair of Growen salvage scouts on a gunner-bike nearby. I don't know if she shifted the course of the transport earlier to run into them, or if she called someone to send them out, but they showed up conveniently right after her EMP went off. She blamed them for the EMP, Jei took them out with his mind, and then I presume the pair left with the Growen vehicle because they're all very gone."

"We had to hang on right by the front entrance for so long, I thought we were gonna die," Jake chimed in. "It's way more easy to hear by the door than in the rest of the hidey hold."

Reise scowled to Nathan: "You didn't warn Jei? You just waited out of sight until he'd left?"

"If she sees me coming out of a hidden panel, there's more than just one guy in danger," Nathan shook his head. "I'm sorry, Reise. In a galaxy where every known Frelsi base is going to be eliminated in a matter of weeks, *anything* to do with the Hiding

Place takes precedence. The Growen somehow know it's on this planet now, so it's already going to be much more difficult for evac platforms to escape notice. We can't let them know about the modified floors."

"We're prolly gonna hafta go full underground with local friendly civilians," Gideon nodded. "Also: I called it." Gideon folded his hands across his chest.

"What do you mean, you called it?" Reise scowled again. Leaving Bereens in the hands of what was probably a Stygge still didn't sit well with him.

"I called it. I knew she was bad news," Gideon said. "Did you see her face, when Cinta said there were only six people on the transport? It was like I took her on a date to that gross Biouk place in the settlement. The one with the roasted parrot."

"Hey, my sister likes that place," Jake said.

Nathan sighed, tapping fruitlessly against his wristband again. "It was more like she was disappointed there were so few of us," he said. "Like six people isn't worth the fuel for evacuation." He straightened with another, deeper sigh, and stared off across the plains.

The others looked around, too. The rain was dancing over the hills in gusts; the grass bowed and whipped in violent patterns. They had no food, no blankets, no transportation, no communication. They were closer to a Growen base than to anything else, with no weaponry but a couple laser-knives and flayer pistols. Reise wrapped his working arm around himself, shivering as the hard shower beat first on his face, then switched to his back, then his side.

"Your wristbands wouldn't happen to have successfully sent Command our lead about the Apocalypse-Woman, and her station orbiting Alpino?" Reise asked, knowing the answer.

Nathan and Gideon both shook their heads.

"I'm cold," Jake said.

Reise nodded. All sisters aside, if the boys didn't find shelter soon, there was a real chance their vital information died with them.

CHAPTER THIRTY-TWO

Lem

LEM PRESSED HER BACK AGAINST THE CEMENT WALL OF THE SILVER-domed weapons depot, blinking against dry, achy eyes as another yawn engulfed her face. Shyte, this was taking a long time.

Maybe I should've tried stalking a food service person instead. Lem was waiting for an unsuspecting armorer to walk around the corner for a smoke break so she could steal their face. This area, beyond Diebol's field, had very little foot traffic, and a wall that faced away from the rest of the post out into the empty plains—a good place for an ambush. Lem struggled to *listen* for oncoming footsteps, or vehicular hums ... *don't poke your head around the corner to look. Wait.*

Diebol's base-wide operations had shut down both of her previous identities: Wandla the janitor was returning in disgraced confusion from her vacation, and the Accuser had blown such a big hole in the General Johnson cover Lem could see through it into the next universe. She wasn't about to make that same mistake again. She had to keep Njande on her thoughts every single moment from here on out to keep herself hidden from the Accuser.

It's tough, though, because I can't think of multiple things at once when I'm already trying to double-speak the shyte out of everything, Lem grumbled internally.

I will not leave you, he answered.

Sure, but you have this funny habit of giving me free rein over my own brain-space, Lem grinned, almost teasing the interdimensional. Ironically enough, if Njande had been a ba-eater, and just took over her brain and controlled her thoughts, this whole thing would've been a lot easier. *You do everything, and you do nothing. I still remember that Paradox.* Lem's exhausted mind wandered through the memory of that trance last year ... Njande had shown her an electron and asked her if she could measure its speed, or its mass; just as the little negative building block of matter was both a particle and a wave, so she, too, was particularly a piece in her own destiny, but also waving on the forces moving through her ...

Well, something like that—there were a lot of Paradoxes that came from that electron thing. Like the one about reference planes, where in her reference plane, every decision mattered, but from his reference plane, outside of time, all things were already fixed before him, laid out like a painting he'd already finished. *I never know which one applies where,* Lem complained wearily.

We'll have to just collapse the wave form, Njande answered.

Lem didn't know what that meant. She hadn't studied physics in months, and never more than the first levels in the refugee schools anyway. She licked her lips, watching the shadows of the long grasses twitching in the slight breeze. Shyte, she was tired. She hadn't collected any DNA last night—with the lockdown she couldn't get into the barracks to get the good identities close to Diebol—and she'd barely slept with all the skulking around. Her eyes stung, but every time her lids drooped she could feel herself drifting into sleep ... she jolted herself upright. Yeah, no, this would end real quick if someone found her sleeping here with her real face showing while her DNA projector charged. Lem rubbed the back of her neck with a sore, weary sigh, rotating her head as if to gently shake her brain awake.

The shadow of that one grey, spindly thornbush moved again —Lem twitched, her hand shooting toward her ear—

Just like the other hundred times, it wasn't a person. She'd missed the wind on her face, and drinking it in with her pores was soothing and all, but shyte did she feel naked now without a mask. She'd been able to get away with wearing the faux Frelsi atmosphere hood for a few hours, but soon everyone had turned in the disguises, and she couldn't check out a new Growen helmet and uniform without an identity; Johnson's face and build were only boring and unmemorable enough to use for a short period of time in crowded areas. She couldn't remember where she'd put the gear that belonged to Frank Zej ... *not like Imma go asking around for it now.*

Shyte, this is taking so long ... Lem had overheard snippets of more terrible news through the night during her failed foray into the laundry room. *She* had struck again. The only Frelsi loyalists left on Burbura were species that could breathe underwater when the floating fortresses suddenly took a dive.

And again. On the gas giants, only the light, almost ethereal carbon-cloud Skraeli had survived the crushing gravity when the bio-towers suddenly cracked open.

And Fort Jehu was gone.

Not surprisingly, it was much easier to take out high-traffic bases that relied on technology for life support. It wasn't like that on Luna-Guetala. There, with an environment fit for multiple sentient species, Frelsi refugees could have hidden in the jungle like the neighboring Biouk tribes. All reports said Fort Jehu was now an inescapable smoking crater trapped inside a pearl bubble, but Lem tried to take hope in the thought that, if anything did live in the mechanical apocalypse zone, it could at least still breathe.

She also tried to take hope in the fact that so far the bases here on Alpino remained untouched. She owed Jei that much— keeping his home planet safe.

What am I talking about? I don't owe any Frelsi anybody anything.

A better question, really, was where she got off thinking about hope when the balance of the war had been so dramatically shifted in less than a week ... *Man, I wish I'd found some hole to sleep in.* Her brain kept jumping around through thoughts that didn't make sense to her. She usually had no problem pulling all-nighters—what was her issue?

Shyte, she'd lived in Fort Jehu for most of her life. And now ...

Lem's chest tightened, and something hot boiled under her eyes. Lem hadn't found Her soon enough. It didn't matter how many other resources the Frelsi threw at Her: no one else would be able to take Her out. Tactical nukes ran on computers ... Jei had the whole mind-link with Diebol to give him away ... it had to be Lem.

"I thought it would be quicker," she murmured, tilting her head back against the cement and closing her eyes again. "I thought, four months ago, I'd find Her before any of this started." The first dreams, with the violent electric blue eyes, and the mirror ...

Shyte, she was thinking too much. "Please cover me, Njande." The back of her eyelids flashed with purple ...

Move!

Lem opened her eyes and rolled to the side—a lavender mace came swinging through the spot where she'd been.

"Holy crap! Who are you?" Lem gasped.

"I'm the new heroine of your story." A breathtaking woman with long, dark hair twirled the staff of her mace around herself in an elegant flower petal pattern. Lem looked around—had Njande literally just dropped the perfect identity on her lap? There was no one else out here behind the building on the edge of the fort ...

The woman swung again, overhand; Lem side-stepped and drew her own bamboo short staff, rubbing her finger along its control groove. Her staff grew to its full length as blood red neodymium laser spilled across it and a spike-ball of light bloomed from its end.

"You're alone, right?" Lem asked.

"For now," said her opponent. "My partner's on an errand for me. I figured I'd just take you out myself to save him the emotional anguish of your—"

"Look, girl, I'm on a time crunch," Lem said, jumping over a stab aimed at her legs. She blocked a blow to the belly next. "I only need the parts of your back story that are gonna be relevant to Diebol. You know Diebol, right?"

The woman squinted, pursing her lips. "Excuse me? Do you not recognize me from the convoy?"

"Nope, sorry, I was busy saving Diebol, hiding from Jei, and saving Diebol again. I'm guessing you're one of the trainees interning here under him, right?" Lem asked. The freighter explosion last year had destroyed most of the super-powered Stygge Army, but they still had remnants here and there. "You've got the mace and all. I never see you guys around the base, but I know he has some." She flipped over her opponent, stretching her fingers toward the woman's cheek as she passed—

The girl dodged back, stumbling a little. "Interning?" Her entire face scrunched in offended disbelief. "No I'm not intern— wait, did you just try to touch my face?"

"Actually *does* your partner matter?" Lem's tired brain made her mouth run while it tried to process a plan; she paced around her prey, looking for an opening with skin. "I mighta misspoke. Is your partner important to Diebol in any way? We talking romantic partner, or like work buddy?"

The girl batted her eyelashes and raised a mysterious eyebrow. "Oh, you know my partner," she giggled, twirling her staff over her head in lavish flourish that culminated close to Lem's head.

"Okay, so romantic. With Diebol," Lem smiled, ducking. "That's perfect."

The next blow wasn't lavish or pretty; the girl smashed her mace down at Lem with both hands. "I *hate* him," she growled deep in her throat—or as deep as a cute little voice like that could go, anyway. Lem laughed out loud. Oh, she understood the feeling. It just sounded different coming from someone like this.

Lem caught the girl's purple mace with the staff of her red one. The two spiked balls tangled around each other, sparking rainbows as Lem pushed both weapons up above the girl's head; the girl tried to push down and resist, but she was a *lot* weaker than Lem's last sparring partner. Lem kneed the girl in the belly, switched feet to roundhouse kick the back of her knees, and as the girl fell, yanked upward. Lem landed mounted atop the girl's midsection, pinning both of those tiny hands to the ground under the handle of that purple mace.

"I need—your—name," Lem said as the girl struggled under her. "If you're not a trainee, are you—" She paused, afraid for just a second that she might be saying a name that drew a mind-reader's attention. "Are you Morda?"

"My name is *Mera*!" The woman hissed. Lem caught a horrible blow to the back of her head and tumbled forward into a somersault.

"Bloodseas, did you kick me in the head with your boot?" Lem winced, rolling into a kneel to block another downward mace strike. "You're flexible as *shyte*!"

Mera kicked at Lem's face in response—Lem grabbed her foot and yanked her to the ground. "I coulda cut your foot off, you dummy," Lem said, trying to get a still hand on the girl's bare shin while touching the back of her own ear to store the DNA. "Don't attack without your weapon unless mine's occupied." Jei always told her that.

Mera jumped to plant both feet on Lem's chest, breaking free. Lem stumbled back onto her butt, winded for a second.

"Why do you keep trying to touch me?" Mera's eyes narrowed, more curious than angry.

"It's a trade secret," Lem flinched. She could feel her face heating as she threw herself into a kip-up to stand. "Sorry, it's—when you put it that way it's messed up. But I'm in a hurry."

"Oh sweetie, you're so pure," Mera giggled, her sleek

eyebrows dancing over sparkling eyes. "I almost feel bad having to kill you." Her expression darkened. "But you've made him *truly* miserable."

"Who, Diebol? Yeah, somehow I don't feel bad for him," Lem grunted, trying to use her strength advantage to catch Mera's staff with her own again. This was going on too long. She took a deep breath, clenched her teeth, thought *harder*—and fired an electrical charge into her opponent.

Mera fell to the ground with a shuddering whimper.

Lem reached for her face—

And suddenly flew back through the air to *thwack* back-first against the building. Before she could even register the pain, a hand came for her throat.

"Holy shyte, Jei?" Lem squeaked. She kicked both feet into his ribs, knocking him back as she scrambled away from him. Oh no. Oh no oh no. "What the bloodseas are you doing here?!"

He answered by raising his hand and hurling it back down toward the ground.

Uh oh.

Lem found herself *smashed* against the earth. She wheezed— the wind was completely sucked out of her. Shyte—*air, air come back please*. Were his em-pulls always that strong? She tried to get up—it felt like a thousand pounds on her shoulders—she pushed against the ground—no, no, no—

Jei walked up, hand outstretched to keep her pinned to the soil.

"Shyte, Jei, you need to get out of here," Lem coughed.

He knelt beside her, his hand hovering over her shoulder. "Lem. You're coming back with me."

She dropped her head in her elbow. Oh, she wanted to just give in. She wanted this whole four-month-long nightmare just to end. No more double think. No more molding herself to become someone else. No more planning her life around a certain end date with uncertain results. She squeezed her eyes shut, listening to the gentle breeze as somewhere far away a storm rumbled and here, beside her, Jei's familiar voice droned through the capture protocols she'd learned way back … shyte, back in the first year she reached regulation fighting age.

"… You will be held as an enemy combatant. You will be treated fairly. You will be questioned about Growen operations …"

She was sore. She was tired. She was up against something so much bigger than herself. And she was alone.

"… The more information you can provide, the more we can help you and those you care about. You will face trial and, depending on the jurisdiction of your actions, be turned over to the appropriate local authorities …"

She opened her eyes. A pale pink ant crawled across the powdery hard dirt in front of her; the green, slightly roasted smell of the grass seemed concentrated here in the crook of her arm. *You are not alone, little one,* Njandejara whispered.

Lem sighed. She tensed her belly. She thought *harder*.

Lem's hand shot out and gripped Jei's wrist as she fired electricity. He didn't fall back like Mera did—but the weight of a thousand suns suddenly lifted from Lem's shoulders as he powered down, and Lem leapt to her feet.

Jei didn't need powers to fight. He spun, his weight on his hands, to swing his legs around and kick hers out from under her. Lem rolled to her feet. Jei quick-drew his bamboo staff and bashed it at her knees; she jumped. He flicked his staff to the side as it extended out into his full green mace, then pounced out of his crouch to swing it at her shoulder.

Agh, that oblique backhand slash—she always struggled to block that, and he knew that. Instead of trying, she threw herself to the side, controlling her fall in the direction of the swooping blow, hit the dirt, and rolled back onto her feet to block his next slash.

Behind her, suddenly, a warmth and a shadow let her know she needed to dodge to the side as that purple mace came down again. Lem back-kicked the girl in the stomach, ducked another swing from Jei, and leapt as far away from them as she could into a dive-roll.

"Young lady, the grown-ups are talking," Lem shouted. "Who are you, anyway?"

"I told you," Mera spat. "I'm a friend of Jei's."

"Really," Lem's eyes narrowed. "Bricandor said something about having Jei under supervision. Are you the supervision?"

Mera's chin jerked toward Jei as if Lem's very words had punched her. "Is she always this manipulative with the lying?" she asked.

Lem seethed. She didn't know if this girl was Growen or Frelsi or just a hired bounty hunter—maybe not the latter, since Jei wanted to capture Lem, and this girl had started with a near fatal blow—but *shyte* if Lem was going to stand here and take this—

Remember, little one.

Njande's little tug, the little "don't" at the elbow of Lem's conscience, put a pit in her gut. Agh, she wanted to stay and fight, give Jei some kind of explanation, give this little witch an education, shyte, make sure Jei was *safe* with whoever this was—

"I have a job to do," Lem grumbled. She swung her mace in a circle around herself, forcing them both to jump back, and hurled an electric shock under her feet to mimic an em-push; the force rocketed her to the edge of the armory roof. Before they could follow, she dive-rolled over its domed peak, and lowered herself down into an open window on the building's other side.

CHAPTER THIRTY-THREE

Mera

MERA THOUGHT SHE COULD *FEEL* THE RESTRAINED TURMOIL radiating from Jei, and it made her heart ache.

They'd had no trouble whatsoever entering Growen South Central once they took the scouts' uniforms and vehicle. Mera hadn't wanted to EMP the delightful old hulk of an evac transport, but paranoid Sterba had insisted in case anyone else was hidden in the ship after all. Anyway, the explosion and combat looked good for Jei, and most importantly, if Mera wanted to keep him incognito until they could find Sterba's hunter, they needed to switch to the disguises Sterba had sent them via the scouts. Mera had had a bit of trouble convincing Jei to ditch the Frelsi transport—he didn't want it to fall into Growen hands—but in the heat of the moment, with blue flames licking its base, combat against the two scouts, and Mera begging him to hurry before someone noticed the scouts' vitals had changed...Jei admitted that once the fire hit the fuel tank there wasn't going to be anything left for the Growen to take.

Mera winced a little; she hadn't wanted the scouts to die, but Jei was...enthusiastic...

Fortunately, they'd had no trouble entering Growen South Central, regardless of the lock-down. Mera had a DNA pass almost as good as Diebol's. She merely had to present Jei to the sentry as an actual scout, and pepper in a dramatic excuse about how his burn injury wouldn't let him enter through the DNA-sensing polymerwall. She'd put on the panicked medicine show as much for Jei's benefit as the sentry's: she had to hide the fact that she didn't need to lie to get in herself.

Now, as Mera and Jei stalked the inside of the Growen armory, looking for Lem Benzaran, a pang of guilt shot through Mera's chest; her shoulders drooped. Jei was focused, his back against the shelf of boxed weapons, his head turned to the side as he listened for sounds on the other side of the enormous store-room. Jei's shoulder and arm muscles hung relaxed but ready, his lips just slightly parted with a hunter's breath. He was a majestic creature—more than the pegasus.

But his eyes seemed dead in their resolve, and there was a stressed tightness at the back of his jaw, like deep inside he was cringing away from a future pain only he saw coming. He didn't want to do this.

Benzaran was doing this to him, and Mera wanted to kill the girl for it. *Contaminated horror.* Mera knew Sterba well, and the kind of person that gave *Sterba* nightmares had to be more terrible still. More than her "sister's" nightmares, Mera resented the odd moments when Sterba's voice held a sort of admiration for the she-beast that haunted her sleep ... the kind of admiration no one had ever given Mera for anything.

Well—Jei looked back over his shoulder at Mera with a little meaningful nod before dashing across the aisle to another metal shelf—Mera might get admiration from someone yet.

Jei's boots barely made a sound. The warehouse seemed mostly empty; a couple armorers were chatting together in some distant cranny, likely down that small hallway that opened up through the far wall. A fan whirred.

Mera shook herself off, loosening the tightness in her muscles. She needed to stay relaxed: she needed as much pheromone as possible to keep Jei from going berserk and destroying this entire post once Benzaran's little electric shock ran out. Really, Mera needed to get Benzaran alone. If Mera could kill her quietly before anyone noticed, Jei wouldn't have to. Mera didn't know if there was enough anesthetic gas in the entire universe to contain the after-effects of Jei's wrath if he had to do it himself.

Mera followed Jei to the next stack of weapon shelves, watching his back, listening to the chatter of the armorers; Mera eyed the rafters of the ceiling above, and the tops of the shelves. Mera had buzzed herself into the armory using her credentials as a secret agent—"this scout's got his pin number sewn onto his sleeve"—she told Jei—but Benzaran had no such credentials. And unlike Jei and Mera, Benzaran had an entire base on high alert looking for her. She'd likely gotten in here through that small window, cracked open near the far ceiling about two stories up. *I'm surprised she fit her butt through there.* Not everyone was as slim as Mera.

Mera and Jei crossed the warehouse, clearing each row of shelves one by one; they quickly reached the back wall, and the small hallway extending through it.

Several rooms branched off the hall, hidden behind polymer-walls marked out by red stripes. One polymerwall, the third on the left, had light spilling through its thin translucence. The armorers seemed to be chatting in there. At the end of the hallway lay another open arch, into what looked like a large, dark warehouse space.

Mera closed her eyes and threw out a silent, sensing hum as she breathed, trying to recall the "shape" of the larger girl sitting on top of her earlier ... *eureka*. Something similar came back in her electric fields, like a shadow in her ear. It was straight ahead, in the dark storeroom at the end of the hallway.

She nodded Jei away from Benzaran and the darkness, to the polymerwall closest to them. "How are we going to clear these rooms?" she asked submissively, in a whisper so low she almost mouthed it. "They won't recognize our DNA."

"Knowing Lem, I'd expect more of a trail of destruction," Jei grinned. It was a painful grin, but he seemed to appreciate the memory. "No, she's through that dark arch at the end of the hallway."

Bloodseas these two. No, Mera needed him away from her. She nodded obediently, but looked over her shoulder for some kind of alarm to pull; she needed to bring out the armorers to start a fight. Jei began to slide down the hallway toward the dark storeroom. Was there a camera anywhere?

No, she needed time.

Mera threw out her arm across Jei's chest. "Wait," she mouthed, squeezing his wrist in false alarm. *Wait*, she ordered through her skin. He tensed—"Do you hear that?" Mera asked.

He withdrew his hand from her grip with one eyebrow raised as he drew his pistol, other hand still on his staff.

"I think they're talking about"—Mera leaned forward, while flicking her other hand backward to em-pull on the nearest shelf in the warehouse behind them—"Did they mention your name?" Pull, shyte this was heavy, pull—"I thought I heard—"

Finally, with great effort on Mera's part, the shelf behind them crashed over. Jei whirled to the sound; the polymerwalls bulged with alarmed blitzers like popping zits—Mera slid past before they emerged. As the fight started in the hallway behind her, the Stygge princess slipped into the waiting darkness to take out her prey.

Lem

When Lem first entered the warehouse, she had one desperate and only goal: get a new identity to hide under. She considered straight up knocking on the polymerwall to the break room and dragging the first face she saw into the darkness. Was there a way to do that without the screaming that would bring his buddies into the hallway? Shyte, she didn't have any more time to wait for the "right" opportunity. What if she just broke the door down, knocked them all out, and then "woke up" among them? But where would she put the body of the guy she'd replaced? Ah, she had no time. She ducked into the cold dark storeroom at the end of the hallway—maybe there was an empty weapons crate in here she could stuff him in? Dead, this time. She'd learned she was definitely not strong enough yet to be leaving enemies alive. How about on this shelf—was this one empty?

Shyte, Jei would be on her heels by now. This was stupid. Should she just sound the alarm herself so that people got distracted fighting the other two electromagnetic intruders?

There was a loud crash—oh, sounded like someone had already done that alarm thing. That was Jei's voice out in the hallway. Okay. So she could maybe grab someone in the confusion. Lem turned back toward the light—

To catch a knife in the edge of her shoulder.

"Oh sweetie, why did you turn around?" Mera moaned. Lem grabbed for the knife that had almost ended up in her back—still stronger, Lem disarmed the other girl immediately. For good measure she ripped the bamboo staff off Mera's belt and tossed it into the darkness.

"I'm sorry," Lem said, twisting around behind the girl to wrap an arm around her throat for a blood choke. She could feel Mera em-pushing against her, trying to pry her off as cold fingernails dug into Lem's forearm and Mera's short legs thrashed and she tried to kick up over Lem or smash her instep or get her between the legs, but Lem tightened and squeezed, bringing the girl's back tighter against her chest with each breath—

The doorway of the room suddenly widened; walls ripped open with a giant metal creak. Jei walked through, his spreading arms pushing the storeroom's opening apart like a—

"Dude, that was so unnecessary, there was already an open door!" Lem squeaked in terror.

"Let her go," Jei ordered.

"You let me go!" Lem cried back. Holy shyte what had happened to him? His hand shut into a fist and an empty shelf crumbled like paper into a ball.

"I'm not playing, Lem." The ceiling began to tear above them.

"You're going to have the entire base down on us!" Lem hissed—as if whispering would really counteract the fact that *one of the filking armories was cracking like an egg*. Shyte, Jei—she fired another electric arc at him to power him down—

He threw a metal shelf in the way, and the arc zipped into that instead. "Lem ..."

"Fine, you want her? Here!" Lem threw the *biggest* em-push she could muster and hurled the other girl at Jei, diving past them both back into the lit hallway. She touched the first neck she could find—didn't matter who—and stroked behind her ear. Then she ran.

Or not. An invisible force gripped her by the ankle, dragging her through the hallway back toward the darkness. Lem heard herself screaming as she clawed at the walls, the bodies lying on the floor, anything to try to keep herself out of the grip of the horror behind her—

"No!" Lem roared. Sparks exploded out in an orb in all directions. There was a yell of pain, and the pull broke just long enough for Lem's mace to smash open the polymerwall into the room next to her. She yanked the alarm on the wall inside. An enormous klaxon sounded. Lem smashed her way through the next wall to the outside and slipped her finger behind her ear to activate the new face, whatever it was—shyte, she needed to hide her mace—she deactivated it into a small bamboo staff and stuffed it down the front of the jumpsuit, under her breasts which—looking down—had been replaced by shapely pecs anyway. She ran around to the front of the building to find a lift and escape. How long did it take emergency response to get here, geez? Sure, this was way on the edge of base, but still—ah, there they were. A couple of air-riders were zipping their way down the road past Diebol's field. Lem hopped on the nearest parked lift and flew toward the air-riders at full speed, pointing behind her and yelling.

"Two electromagnetics!" she yelled with only a very little bit of fakery in her panic. "They're destroying the entire armory, we need medical ASAP!"

"Okay soldier, calm down, we'll—hey! Hey come back! Coward, what are you doing running away?"

"Saving your ass from destruction," Lem muttered, zooming over the air-riders and electrocuting all three of their engines behind their backs. *Slow them down, sow confusion, whatever, just get myself outta here.*

More air-riders and land-runners were coming down the road. Lem leaned into her lift, breathing hard into the wind. Okay, coming up here—

"Hey soldier, you're over the speed limit!" sounded the speaker from one of the spiked land-runners. "There's currently a lockdown and emergency siren—" Lem sped over the land-runner as oxidizer flayer shots lit up the air around her. The cartridges hissed as they swerved by her ears, repulsed by her latent electric field; she smiled—it really was the little things—and tore a hard right over Diebol's precious lawn.

Diebol's private defense grid still hadn't been repaired, but no one dared follow Lem anyway. Cowardice and speeding weren't as great evils as ripping open an armory from the inside, and messing with Diebol was its own punishment; most of Lem's Growen comrades would, instead, continue down the road to the armory. *Hopefully Jei and Mera will be okay—oh, shyte …*

The sinking feeling seemed to slow everything down; still, Lem's body mechanically stuck to the plan. She halted the lift, leapt off, and where she'd seen Diebol emerge from nowhere before, she punched the ground.

Turned out punching the ground, even if you had electro-magnetic powers, still just hurt your hand. *Shyte, I really am sleepy,* Lem laughed at herself through the sharp pain shooting into her bones. Now where … he said he slept in a hole in the ground—Lem shot electricity through the earth, trying to find a powered pod or capsule that might pop open—

Nothing.

Where the vegetation bends this way, it is planted, not natural, Cinta had told her. *You can always see a human hand if you look.*

Thank Njande for Cinta. Shyte, she missed him so much. *Cover me, Njande. Hide me under the shadow of your wings,* Lem sighed, remembering the Accuser again as her forbidden past entered her thoughts. Here, in this spot the grass perfectly matched the grass around it, except with just a little more green, just a slight over-evenness in its distribution. Lem felt around the patch, and found a latch. She pulled up the sod—it was growing on a hinge, a curved brown lid hiding a perfect white, oblong eggshell.

"I bet that shell is polymerwall, just for his DNA," she guessed, drawing her mace again to smash it open. *Crash*—the shell shattered for her—"Aw, he's got his own little nest here."

Inside Diebol's sleeping capsule lay a cluster of blankets— like her, the reformer liked bundling at night, apparently. Lem shoved his blankets to the side with all his leather clothes and rapped her knuckles on the bottom of the capsule. *Please be here, please be here*—she wanted to find a hollow sound. It made sense, what General Johnson's fatter assistant had said to her: Diebol had to have some kind of tunnel. *Probably into that building with the leadership conference room* ... despite all the weird shyte Lem had seen in her life she didn't believe in teleportation yet.

Aha—a *tonk tonk tonk* sound. Lem smashed this with her mace, too. "Yay, tunnel." A dark hole greeted her. It widened beautifully as she peeled aside the flakes and shards of broken polymerwall covering it. The flakes were shimmery on one side —likely bulletproof, too. *Just not neodymium laser proof.*

Lem reached up to close the earthen camouflage-lid over herself. The egg glowed a soft white-green in the new darkness, like the grubs Cinta used to help her find to feed the day lizards. Lem sighed, shaking her head again—*shadow and wind, holding Njande's shadow and wind over me with the banner of Ahavah*—and lowered herself feet-first into the hole.

The red glow of Lem's neodymium mace illuminated three dirt walls and a long tunnel ahead of her into darkness. Lem didn't love dark places under the earth, but this one seemed pretty cuddly, for some reason. The ochre quality to the soil, maybe.

Oh—there was—there was a little metal step here in the dark, dangling on two chains hanging from the walls. Lem fingered the cold, damp, thick iron ... the chains were affixed into long grooves, like tracks, that extended down the sides of the tunnel.

"If I were Diebol, what would I—I guess I would stand on this," she said. She stepped up on the dangling step, holding her balance with one hand on the cool clay-ish earth ...

She let go of the wall, centering herself, her hand out in front of her. "Oh shyte, what a smart way to get around," she laughed, suddenly understanding. He literally em-pulled himself from place to place, shooting around under the ground without any modern technology. Was he afraid of Her, maybe? Or was this just more of his natural ascetic flair?

Lem didn't think she had the em-pulling range, or the knowledge of the terrain, to grip the end of the tunnel and pull it close to her like he did; she knew ancient trains used to run on electric rails, though. Could she electrocute—this—

Oof.

The sparks she threw behind her knocked her off the hanging step onto her face. She laughed. "I don't know what I'm doing, Njande," she sighed, getting back up. She felt loopy in her tiredness and adrenaline, and also sore for some reason—oh, her shoulder had a sticky blood stain on it. She should look at that. Mera's blade had grazed her shoulder, right.

No time, Lem.

Lem reached for the end of the tunnel. *I am Diebol.* She'd been everyone else, it felt like, as she needed them.

Now she needed the one person who could protect her from Jei Bereens.

CHAPTER THIRTY-FOUR

Mera

EVERYTHING WAS SPIRALING OUT OF CONTROL. COULD THESE TWO not *calm down*? Their enormous power surges made Mera's head pound as her inner ear reverberated out of control, and everything was throbbing, throbbing, throbbing—

When Mera could breathe again, and the world stopped being fuzzy, she was sailing through the air into Jei Bereens. Under any other circumstance she would have relished the opportunity to fall into his arms, but hurtling into his chest she knocked him over, and while he cradled her, one hand on her throat for her pulse and the other brushing her hair off her face to check her pupils, Lem Benzaran was getting away.

"Your mission, soldier!" Mera coughed.

"Yes ma'am." Jei almost smiled, but his jaw clenched down to end that nonsense. He snapped one arm out to his right and pulled.

As much as Benzaran's scream was music to her ears, Mera, sitting up, began to realize this entire situation was not going to end well for her. Diebol would crucify her to Bricandor for letting Jei destroy *buildings* in Growen territory, and technically she'd been told to bring Jei directly to Sterba once she knew

Benzaran's whereabouts. And, for the moment, perhaps worse than all of this, Jei's power level was rattling her inner ear with increasing pressure, pressure, pressure—

Mera needed this over, now. She reached for the pistol on Jei's thigh to shoot the girl in the hallway—

A ball of sparks spread over everything, throwing both Mera and Jei back with sharp, sudden jerks of pain. Mera yelped, trying to rub the uncomfortable static off her skin as she rolled to her feet. A deafening alarm sounded. Could this headache get any worse?

Yes it could, if Jei did anything at all right now. Thank goodness Benzaran's ball of sparks just now had powered him down. "We have to get you out of here," Mera groaned. "We can't let them find you here."

Jei rose to a kneel, his eyes on the hallway to pursue Benzaran—Mera gripped his wrist with everything she had, trying *so hard* to relax even as her head pulsed with pain, and told his skin *no, we need to run.*

Jei didn't pull his hand away this time, but looked at her as she pressed her other palm in agony against her beating temples—

"We have to get *you* out of here," he said. "You're right, I've got to power back up."

Oh thank goodness. "There's a back door," Mera pointed. "Can we get out beyond the edge of the base before they all come down on us?"

"Maybe." Jei's arms wrapped around her, under her neck and knees, as he scooped her up—*oh my*—and ran for the door. The hum of air-riders outside, followed by shouting, and the rumble of land-runners, trickled after them. Mera let her head fall against his chest as he pulled her in tighter with one arm and with the other spun his mace to smash the polymerwall of the back entrance.

Outside, the breeze helped with the growing nausea—the jolting of Jei's running didn't. "I—I'm being a baby, I can walk," Mera chuckle-mumbled. "It's my head, not my legs that hurt."

"You good to run?"

"Yes."

He put her down. She hoped he would grab her hand—*come on, now, that's a little much, even for me,* she told herself, running after him. *We're trying to get away here.*

"Where are we going?" she asked. They seemed to be heading into the open plains between the armory and the base's perimeter polymerwall. That didn't seem good for cover.

"Well, this just so happens to be my home planet," Jei said. "See that mound there?"

"… No …" Oh, the light was unbearable for her head …

"Snowturtles are called that because you really only get to see them in the snow, when they hibernate above-ground. During the rest of the year they make enormous burrows."

"What—why, though, wouldn't it be warmer to hibernate underground …" Mera hated everything right now. Every step was agony. She would've been better off in his arms.

"I don't know, I'm not a biologist," Jei said. "I just know there's a burrow there."

"And if there's a turtle already in it …"

"You are just going to have to charm it with the same magic you used on the pegasus and keep trying to use on me," he smiled.

Oh shyte, he knew? Mera wanted to protest, but couldn't think of what to say through the blinding light in her eyes and that annoying rumble of the storm she thought they'd left behind them but of course it had chased them like every other disaster she'd ever thought she could escape and oh goodness the pounding, maybe she needed to get away from him …?

"I don't see this burrow," she said. "They're going to be around the building and see us any second—"

"I know. Get down." He dropped to his belly in the grass and began to low crawl. She followed. He led her to a large rock and tapped it. "Tell it to move," he said to her.

"Tell the rock to—?" Oh, *this* was a turtle? The irregular grey surface looked *nothing* like the colorful patterned shells of the tiny river-turtles near Retrack City on Luna-Guetala. Did such a rock-looking thing even have nerves? Oh shyte, everything was terrible ... Mera plopped her palm down on the hard surface—oh, it was so warm. *Move, please,* she said, pushing it in her mind as she pictured and *felt* in her muscles, the act of moving aside: words meant nothing here.

To her surprise, the rock suddenly receded into the ground, and then, like a sliding door, disappeared to the right underneath it.

"Did you also tell it not to bite?" Jei asked.

Mera stared at him in disbelief. Oh goodness, she hoped she had enough pheromone for an angry rock. "I should—go first," she said, taking a deep breath and slipping her legs into the large hollow that had opened up. She felt around with her feet away from the direction the turtle had moved, straight forward instead of right, hoping—yes, there was a tunnel in another direction.

Don't be nervous. Don't be nervous. Be calm. Be calm.

She slid into the ground like she was slipping into a sleeping bag, shielding her face with her arms in case rocks didn't care about pheromones. As her head dropped below the surface, to her right she could see the living rock-lump, and to the left a dirt wall.

Jei slid in beside her, motioning for her to move further underground. "Can you get it to move back?" he asked. Mera reached up and right, trying to stay relaxed, *totally not* afraid that the rock would suddenly sprout a face and bite her hand ... *Move,* she intoned through her peripheral nervous system again.

The living rock began to return, inch by inch; Mera forced herself to retract her hand *slowly* instead of jerking it away in fear. *Relaxation pheromone. Lots of relaxation pheromone.* She felt Jei move beside her hip, scooting further into the auxiliary tunnel —she did the same as the turtle's body began to block off the burrow entrance. It looked for all the world to Mera like a stone closing over a tomb.

Before it could close off all the light and air, Mera reached above her head: *stop*. It did, leaving a sliver of a breeze for the two humans to breathe.

For several minutes, neither Mera nor Jei said anything. The voices, and engine sounds, drew closer now. Mera concentrated on Jei's breathing chest against her shoulder blade, his hip against her leg, wondering, as her headache softened, how the galaxy she'd ended up taking a job that required cuddling with her enemies in dirt. It was actually quite pleasant ... the dark coolness felt good for her headache, and all sound from outside was muffled. Jei was warm ...

Mera found herself remembering every other guy she'd ever felt in this proximity, and couldn't think of a single one who hadn't either made some comment about her body, even at the most ridiculous times, or actually groped her. She would almost worry that Jei didn't like her, except for the tender way he'd picked her up, and the almost admiring way he'd sighed when she told him her ghost theory back in the transport, and—

"You were angry when she was choking me," Mera murmured, suddenly sleepy.

"I don't like seeing the strong prey on the—" His low whisper against her ear stopped abruptly.

"Weak," Mera finished for him.

"I chose not to say it because it's the wrong word, not because I'm shy," he answered.

She didn't have an answer for that—ordinarily, she would quip something about being prettier than the other girl, but she knew somehow that didn't fit here. It almost felt like what she looked like mattered less to him than what she ... thought? Did? Was? Oh my, she was yawning ... every muscle relaxed ... was she getting high on her own pheromone, she wondered? For the first time she could remember, even though she was in enormous trouble, even though she was underground and her hair was going to end up a disaster, even though she had an enemy combatant lying next to her, Mera felt safe.

So safe, that she fell asleep.

Jei

The search party milled above our subterranean burrow only for a short while before leaving to hunt security footage and polymerwall entry keys instead. It looked like this time, my Draconian trainer's teaching about turtles might actually pay off.

It was different last time, as an eight-year-old—the dead burrow I'd crawled into had had no turtle to hide behind, and Stygge Bricandor had literally walked over my body and read my mind through the dirt.

I exhaled. My heartrate, while regular, was fast. I didn't know if that had more to do with the bad memory, or with Mera's body so close to mine. I was a bit uncomfortable, wedged at an angle with my shoulder under her back and my chest against her shoulder blade, but it wasn't so bad once I got my right arm under my neck kind of like a pillow. She looked like she needed sleep, and impatience kills when you're hiding from someone anyway. I hoped Mera wasn't uncomfortable—I tried to give her as much room as I could, but that didn't really mean anything in this burrow.

I lay there for a while, staring at the red earth, and the slit out into the sky. It was going to rain soon. We needed to get moving before that.

I sighed.

"Njande, why is all this happening?" I asked.

I heard no answer. Figured. I was getting tired of the cryptic repetitions anyway. He'd mostly left me when Lem defected, I thought. My bursts of power had nothing to do with him, anyway; as I'd said last year, he had other things to do. Nothing had gone right since I'd found Lem under that helmet.

Well—one thing had gone right. I turned my head; I didn't dare watch Mera sleep, but that one glance before I looked away showed me her lips, parted and down-turned, and a furrowed brow. She seemed so … sad. Perhaps all the smile and sparkle of her waking face was just armor.

It was more pleasant armor than mine.

After some time, Mera stirred; her little mouth yawned as she tried to stretch, and elbowed me in the ribs. I tried to give her more room somehow, but couldn't; her eyes fluttered open lazily.

"Hello," she said.

"Hi," said I.

She giggled, and yawned again. "Ohh …" she sighed. "Hey, is it dark yet? It might be easier to hunt in the dark."

I pointed to the sliver of light.

"Ah. Are the other people gone?"

"I think so."

"Mm. I'm sorry, I don't know what came over me." She shifted a little, fist on her forehead. "It sounds like they're gone … I should find Benzaran. Hey, maybe your nerves can amplify my signal, help me find her faster—?" She reached for my hand.

I smiled, but pulled my hand back to avoid the sharp little invisible needles with their subcutaneous thoughts. "I was serious earlier, Mera," I said gently. "I'm not totally oblivious."

"What?" She blinked, the picture of an innocent.

"You know what you're doing," I said. "I'm not sure exactly how it works, but there's more to your electromagnetic abilities than just listening. You admitted it earlier with the turtle."

"Egh, that was an emergency," she grumbled. "It's not my fault you think naughty things when you hold my hand."

"No, it's not like that, it's—it feels like you're trying to get into my brain," I said.

"That's all any woman ever wants, Jei." She batted her eyelashes, deflecting again, with the armor. "Why, is there something in there you're ashamed of?"

"I know for you it probably just feels like another way to communicate with the world around you." For whatever reason, the entire fact of it didn't really *bother* me, once I figured it out; she hadn't said anything—*evil*, or whatever, through her skin—and it didn't feel invasive after the first prickly moment. "I thought I was imagining it at first. But it makes sense—I kinda figured you had to have some way to talk to the pegasus, earlier. If everyone could do it, probably no one would talk any other way."

"You ... don't hate it," Mera's big chestnut eyes searched my face.

I shook my head. "I don't hate anything about you. It's just another part of who you are."

Her lips pursed with soft surprise, and a little "hm." She looked away, staring up at the ceiling. I could almost see her brain bubbling with thought.

"But we need ground rules," I said, closing my hand over her little fist. "Don't try to hide it any more. Be honest with me. I will listen to you. I'm not like—whoever else you've been around. You can be straight with me."

She took a deep breath, looking back into my eyes again with a vulnerability and wonder that was almost painful to stare into —like a deep reflecting pool that stared back, or peering hard into a searchlight. She put her other hand over mine, and nodded. "Okay," she said.

I felt the sting again when her fingers slipped between mine —but it was a pleasant sting, quickly followed by a flood of warmth through my palm, my wrist, and then washing over my arm and up into my chest. Everything cooled suddenly with that prickly freshness like right after a good shower, and it was like my skin itself felt at peace. I was awake, with my eyes open, but the dark earth, the burrow, everything around me seemed to fade into the background as my own mind came into focus.

It's a beautiful place you have here, she seemed to say, waving to my passing memories—to the pearl gardens with my mother on Burbura, to my training with my Draconian master on the rim of the volcano, to the rare, precious moments of joy playing the stick-game in the cage with Diebol as a child. *I would love to stay here forever.*

You're welcome to look around, I found myself saying cautiously, even as another part of me begged for her to live here —specifically here, on the imagined future mountain I never dared hope for consciously, with the cottage, the library, and the distant songs of far-off day lizards far below us in the verdant mists. From here in the peaceful cool above the clouds, we could see the lights of Retrack City far, far below, and watch the acrobats through telescope any time we liked, as our fingers entwined. We would practice our powers in the bamboo tea garden, not for war training but for play, to experiment with color, laughter, and energy the way cubs and guppies did, to find the magnetic fields behind ghosts and the electricity within each other, as our signals and patterns and programming melded and separated, melded and separated, over and over in rhythm—

What's this room? she asked. *I want to go in here.*

The door no one should enter in anyone else's mind—the throne room, the seat of self, where Njande lived—rose towering above us, wooden carvings gleaming in the shadows of its thick flowered branches.

I pulled back my hand and tapped out, blinking as the real world came into focus. "That's mine, okay, Mera?" I said softly. "That's the one place I'm going to ask you leave alone. You have my consent to explore any other part of the garden, but that room, that tree, belongs to me."

Her downturned lips trembled. "You don't trust me?" Her voice cracked; there was a wet shadow to her eyes.

"I'm not rejecting you, Mera," I said. "Everyone has to have a part of their own self that's only for them and the interdimensional—it helps us hold who we are." Afraid, suddenly, that I was offending her, or lecturing her, I bit my lip. "For me, anyway. Just—let me have myself."

She looked away—she seemed to shrink into the wall.

"Mera, please. I don't know if anyone has ever—taken part of you without asking—but—"

"I'm not—"

"I'm asking you not to take something. Stay out. That's mine." I kept my voice low, trying to be as gentle as possible, but held my jaw firm.

With a deep, disappointed sigh, she agreed.

CHAPTER THIRTY-FIVE

Diebol

DIEBOL WAS IN HELL. THIS, THIS MEETING, TRAPPED WITH SIMPERING bureaucrats eating away his legitimacy, crippled by the secrecy and imbecilic little power plays of his fellow Stygges—he looked the utter fool, with three metaphorical limbs tied behind his back. And that was all the upper crust cared about—not protecting the universe from interdimensionals, not bringing all peoples together into homogeneous peace, just their own self-interested council seats, and because he'd pointed that out *for years*, they all gloated now at the chance to take him down. This wasn't the Unification Force he had grown up believing in. This was hell. His fingers squished down his forehead, against his eyes, as he withheld a scream.

"The second woman in that footage is one of our own agents," he explained for the eighteenth time through his palms. "The first one is a rogue Frelsi operative trying to take out our new favorite weapon. Jei Bereens *should* be on his way to a detention center with our agent—"

"Detention? When are we just going to kill this guy?"

I don't know! Diebol's withheld scream was bulging through his forehead. "Bricandor wants to let—"—*Morda, but I can't say that*—"the development team behind Her—experiment on him."

"Didn't *you* already try that?"

Yes! Yes I did! "It's already been established I don't have control over the majority of our Stygge assets," Diebol growled.

"Obviously."

"And instead of sitting in here explaining this to you, I need to be out there helping our men find these noxious ruinations," Diebol continued to growl.

"Watch your tone. You 'need to be' where the group says you need to be." Diebol had liked General Johnson so much better as Lem. "Your loyalty is to the Growen first, not your individual interpretation of what that means. You don't get to decide your missions. We already collectively give you a lot of slack, and—"

"We are doing well," Diebol hissed through clenched teeth to cut off the wind-bag. "We have taken two entire planets in a week. I think you owe me a little 'slack.'"

"Correction," Screlch boomed through his purple beard. "*She* has taken two planets in a week, and while this unnamed female operative is risking her life against a Frelsi saboteur to protect Her—" His thick finger stabbed the screen, where Lem held Morda in a choke. "You're talking about bringing her in for questioning. I don't know what it's like at your Stygge counsels, if they tolerate that kind of in-fighting, but here among ordinary people one might even call your suggestion treasonous."

"*I have spent the last 48 hours untangling Lem Benzaran's identities,*" Diebol was almost shaking with rage. "Benzaran wouldn't even be revealing her face for the camera if it weren't for my team!"

"How like a leader, to take credit for the work of others," said Cabalero, his white hair and sickly complexion almost gleaming in the lamplight.

The heat was choking Diebol.

Bricandor, Father, why have you forsaken me?

He had to hold it in. He couldn't just kill them all. He couldn't. Bricandor would destroy him for the coup. All those careful political favors that had funded and popularized the movement—what would the media say if the up-and-coming young Stygge leader suddenly turned on all these great men to whom he "owed" so much? *It's just narrative, just filking narrative.* He'd told them several times already that Morda was enabling Jei, but they claimed, in their apparently infinite knowledge of combatives, that you couldn't really tell that from the footage.

What could he say? The bean-counters were determined to take him down, and these filking electromagnetics had given them what they needed. He'd seen it before, from the paper-work, to the investigations, to the twisted testimonies that ended in accusations of treason. They could bury a man without touching a shovel.

"Cowards, all of you," Diebol finally grunted.

"I'm sorry, what did you say?" Johnson folded his arms across his decorated puffed chest. "You are required to maintain *decorum* here. There are charges for conduct unbecoming."

"Erratic and unprofessional behavior," someone else chimed in. Diebol didn't even care who at this point. He stood up, and turned away from the table in disgust.

"Wow, what a bunch of filking windbags."

Lem Benzaran's sneering voice silenced the room. All heads snapped around to see the young woman in black leather standing by the closed conference room polymerwall as if she'd materialized through it like a ghost, her feet planted shoulder-width apart in shining ebony boots, her hands extended by her sides to grip two huge power-pistols the size of her forearms. One of Diebol's long weapon coats, studded with pockets and utility belts, hung loose around her solid frame.

She gave Diebol an upward nod of her chin. "Let's see if decorum's bulletproof."

It wasn't.

The barrels of her giant pistols blazed; the first batch of repeating rounds pummeled two generals at the foot of the table. Decorated chests shuddered in time with the musical snare-tap of emptying magazines as Lem stepped up onto the table. She strode its length like a fashion model on a catwalk, clearing her clips into the scrambling, screaming sycophants on either side with her eyes fixed on Diebol.

He rested on his wrists, leaning on the back of his chair to watch her show with his every muscle relaxed and poised, heart pounding as his enemies slumped across the table, drooped onto the floor, and slammed back in their chairs.

Only Screlch took cover behind a high-backed seat to return fire on Lem; muzzle flares lit up around his purple beard as he roared: "Don't just scream, you idiots, fight!"

Lem's mace seemed to spin out of nowhere, blowing open her coat as the glowing staff danced across her wrists. Its force-field repelled Screlch's shots, and with a lovely backhand, she split open his skull.

Six more generals to go. She continued up the table, and with a dramatic pause, threw out her chest and hurled back her hands: her coat flew back off her shoulders as knives shot from her sleeves, skewering five necks. The coat pooled by her boots as she knelt on the table right in front of the last man sitting: General Rojam S. Johnson, a frozen statue in the chair just two seats to Diebol's left.

"I can pay you," Johnson said coldly. "Double whatever he's paying," he nodded toward Diebol, then motioned with his eyes across Lem's torso. "Plus a better bedroom arrangement."

"Oh, Rojam," Lem reached into her shirt, and drew out one more weapon: a standard issue blitzer light pistol. "I've already been in your bedroom." She pointed to a splatter of old blood on the muzzle; Johnson's eyebrow raised.

The edge of Diebol's lip twitched almost into a smile. Generals were issued more elegant, hand-fitted weapons—there was no reason for Johnson to have a lowly standard issue light pistol in his room, covered in blood.

"Is this blackmail, then?" Johnson asked.

"No. It's justice." With a flick of her thumb Lem charged the weapon. It was quiet enough in the room for all three to hear the nearly-silent hum as the oxidizer cartridge slid into the chamber. "I should have killed you the first time. Banks was a nice guy," Lem said. The sound of breathing, the rise and fall of everyone's chests, punctuated her words. "He'd done some terrible things, but there was hope for good somewhere within him. Everyone else here dies for how they treat *my* people. But you? You die for how you treat *yours*."

Johnson's chair slid as he tried last minute to jump up and run—

The report of the dead man's firearm left the general on the floor. His hand twitched once by Diebol's boots, then stilled.

Diebol leaned back against the wall behind him, stretching his arms. His fingers rested, still, on the back of his chair, relaxed but ready at any moment for whatever might come next. Unlike the armchair warriors, Diebol knew how to take her on if he had to. He wasn't altogether surprised to see her, and assumed that likely, with Jei hot on her heels, she wanted refuge. He allowed her a gracious grin: "Well someone remembered my birthday."

"You're easy to shop for." Lem stepped off the table onto a chair and crossed her legs as she took Johnson's seat.

"I'm touched you know what I like." He kept eye contact, watching her hands for tricks out of the corner of his gaze.

"Of course. You're not into skin; you want soul." The words gnashed between her teeth. She glanced at the door. "We need to go talk somewhere about your angler-fish problem."

"No, I have this room for … oh, another two hours or so." Diebol feigned a glance at the time on his holopen—he was a bit surprised that she knew enough of his private life to use Bricandor's metaphor, but then again, she was literally wearing the contents of his wardrobe. He couldn't sense his Father's eyes on him, and he'd kept his mind mostly blank and observational throughout Lem's dance for him, but now, "… Is your Contamination hiding us, right now, from Bricandor's interdimensional?" Diebol asked, before allowing himself to think anything suspect.

"For the moment," Lem said. "Can Bricandor ever read minds on his own?"

"Only when in the same location, or over transmission, or a special emotional connection," Diebol said. "He didn't used to talk to interdimensionals. I think he was offered a cross-galactic power boost and took it."

"Is he nearby?"

"No. And I have no transmitters on, obviously."

"Your emotional connection?"

Diebol shook his head. Bricandor was busy with his incessant election diplomacy today. "Cold, at the moment. That may change, but if the interdimensional problem is blocked—well, for a few precious moments, we are in fact alone."

"Fantastic. Well, I won't tell. You can harbor whatever treasonous thoughts you want. You're welcome." Lem bowed, with a little flourish of her hand.

Diebol scowled. "You mistake my feelings. While it will have to do for now, I don't like idea of using the stench of your Contamination for protection. I've managed my entire life under the old man's mind, and as much as you may spurn it, I usually appreciate his eyes."

"You *like* the double think." Lem narrowed her eyes in disbelief.

"I'm playing more of a symbiotic game than you are," Diebol said. "The Teacher knows I think about killing him, and he makes sure to keep the proper checks and balances in place to prevent that from happening. Many of those solutions end up giving me what I want. It's more complicated than I'd expect you to understand."

"Yeah, it's a filking perfect little twisted mind game you have," Lem smirked. "Or, had, until She came along." Lem leaned forward and lowered her voice. "I know you're having problems. I know She's edging you out of Bricandor's good graces, and you're losing the power struggle. I can fix that for you."

Diebol was interested, but for power's sake didn't show it; he waved his hand across the room. "Like you fixed this? These people had jobs, you know. Who do you think is suddenly going to pick up their slack?"

"Oh, don't try to play me," Lem laughed. "Now you'll promote people you believe in. You're the sole survivor of a terrible attack you can blame on me. Throw in Jei, if you want." *And pin it on Morda for failing to keep him in check.* "Only your powers allowed you to live. The others were too weak and ineffectual. You'll all learn from this tragedy to make the Growen better, and from now on upper leadership will participate in weekly combatives training just like everyone else, just as you've wanted for years. And so on."

"Because no one will ever know you came in through my secret passageway, entering via my sleeping pod. Even though you're literally wearing my clothes like it's the morning after." Diebol leaned in with a low rasp; he chose his words intentionally to make her uncomfortable.

She didn't flinch, and whispered back right by his ear. "I thought you might like seeing them on someone with the strength to actually *do* the things you just dream about."

This close, he could see the skin on her neck fluttering just below her mandible—her pulse was elevated. He smiled. "Jei really has you scared, doesn't he?"

She refused to answer, but also refused to pull away. They hung there, for a moment, almost cheek to cheek, each planning their next argument, each unwilling to show weakness, sharing breath. Diebol had his hand on his pistol, and Lem's fingers fluttered near her mace. Anything could happen, from kiss to kill.

Finally Lem stood up with a frustrated scowl. "Look, give me Her location, and I'll solve your problem. That's it. That's what I'm here for. Stop wasting my time; we both need Her gone."

"You much more than me," Diebol shrugged, satisfied with his small victory.

"About a month ago, sure. But while I'm running out of

things to lose, *you* have a new problem." Lem walked over to point at the screen where Morda still hung in her own frozen clutches. "Turns out this is the girl I saved your life from— remember that? She and Jei are wreaking havoc on your shyte, man. From saving The Hiding Place mission, to trashing your armory, it's all making you look weak. Sure, you had all these idiots slowing you down." She waved around the room. "But does Bricandor see it that way? Or are you becoming replace- able? And I know you've got another lady Stygge vying for your power, too—that Morda person, or whatever."

Ah. So she didn't know, then, that Morda was Mera. Best keep that under wraps—the call girl's bungles with Jei might yet provide useful against Lem.

Still, the Paradox Warrior was accidentally correct. Diebol was not excited about the possibility of Morda having full control of a hyper powerful Jei Bereens at her beck and call, either. "Morda is another female Stygge with plans to assassinate me," Diebol assented only, rolling his head comfortably on his neck. "It can be unpleasant to juggle so many enemies at home. But who's to say you haven't thinned the herd enough already?" He smiled.

"You're missing the point." Lem leaned on both her knuckles, her eyes burning with the passion he'd so enjoyed during her less traumatic interrogations. "The question is, really, who's better for the Growen long-term? You, or Her? Because it's even- tually going to be one or the other."

Diebol sat back down in his chair, and put his feet up on the table. His hand found his chin. "What if I say Her?" Diebol asked.

"Then I'd say you've forgotten who you are."

A slight laugh, sad and bitter, puffed through his lips. "I no longer believe you people can be cured, Lem." He pushed down the pang of pain at the memory of how that experiment ended. Bricandor's harsh electric punishment was made so much more painful with the knowledge that, really, Diebol would never be able to save people like Lem and Jei: all the most wonderful parts of their brains would disappear into the maw of that space-monster Njandejara. "I never hated you. You know that." He met her eyes, and she nodded. "But elimination is, ultimately, the only humane thing to do to you. Speaking of which," he slid his pistol lazily onto the table, aimed at her chest. "Aren't you still on the kill list?"

CHAPTER THIRTY-SIX

Lem

Lᴇᴍ ꜰᴏʀᴄᴇᴅ ʜᴇʀꜱᴇʟꜰ ᴛᴏ ʜᴏʟᴅ ꜱᴛɪʟʟ ᴀɴᴅ ʙʀᴇᴀᴛʜᴇ, ᴏɴᴇ ʀɪꜱᴇ ᴀɴᴅ fall of the chest at a time. *Hide me under the shadow of your wings, Njande.* She couldn't let Diebol see, but she was almost trembling with the effort of just keeping calm in his presence. Add the double think of hiding them both from the Accuser. And the enormous glut of adrenaline still spiking her blood …

She wanted to watch the pistol on the table: Diebol's coworkers hadn't called him erratic for no reason, visionary or not. She still remembered his fist crunching the bones in her fingers …

The thing that made this so sweaty and terrifying, however, was that she also remembered the moment he almost let her escape.

What are we, if we don't hate each other?

"I'm not gonna shyte you," Lem said, still leaning on her knuckles on the table, her eyes on his as if the gun didn't exist. "I'm at the end of the line, here. This is my last shot. Everything I've been working up to for the last four months has gone to pot. You're not the only one getting screwed over by superhumans on their own team." She allowed herself a laugh, and threw her hands in the air. "So these are my cards. Yeah, you're right. I literally walked in here and handed you an advantage. It's what I've been doing over and over again, it feels like."

"We make a good team," he said with a snide smirk.

"I'm not Jei." She plopped down into another chair, kicking a general off the table with her shoe. "I'm not gonna get mad because 'we're so similar, you and I,' or whatever."

Diebol watched the general flop under the table. "You have quite the stomach for murder, Lem."

"Oh, the Paradox Warrior thing about trying not to kill, that was never about my stomach. I'm pretty good at killing. I'm actually just trying to cut back." She looked around the room; her heart sank, but she'd known it would. Every person had died immediately and damn near painlessly, but the *panic* on their blood-spattered, wide-eyed faces almost made Lem fear herself. "Killing is a sign of weakness," she said. "I wish I had enough inner power to just change my enemies' minds, or enough physical domination to subdue them without hurting them. That's the goal, eventually. But I live in the real world, still."

"Not something you're known for," Diebol said. Lem couldn't get a read on his expression—the corner of his mouth turned up a little, like he might almost laugh. He tapped on the side of his pistol for a moment …

And finally, he shifted his feet back onto the floor and laid the pistol on the table.

Lem withheld her sigh of relief.

"Here's the situation, as I see it," Diebol said, folding his hands by the gun. "You don't just need Her location—you also need protection from your old friend. Otherwise, he follows you to m'lady, and She kills him. You need me to help you shake him. And, it just so happens, I need the same thing—whatever Mera might have told you during your fight, I can assure you she is primarily here to see me dead."

"Her, too? You just have such a way with women," Lem shot.

"I think we've established I'm an equal-opportunity offender." He smiled back. "For me, the issue is timing. Obviously, I would prefer for you to wait to kill Her until after she's wiped the Frelsi out of existence." Lem showed him flat lips. "Now, I can see that idea does not amuse you—"

"Yeah I'm not killing her *after*," Lem scowled. "*After*, I just let her destroy you. I'm not your janitor."

"You *were* the janitor, though, right."

"I was." Lem folded her arms across her chest as Diebol's eyes sparkled with merriment. Well, he seemed to be having a good time, anyway. It figured: he'd just lost twenty enemies, at no cost to himself.

But without that violent introduction proving her immediate use, Lem had no doubt in her mind that she would already be dead—Diebol wouldn't even have given her an audience. Shyte, he still might kill her.

Diebol continued: "Anyway, as I was saying, your usefulness to me vis a vis killing Her comes with a loss. The only reason it's now or never, for *me*, is that I have *your* two idiots that need dealing with. So let's talk about them. I'll give you Her location *after* you help me leave here without Mera and Jei tailing me. After all, if I tell you first, you have no reason to help me stay alive."

Lem didn't like this; it felt like selling Jei out a second time, and apparently that showed on her face.

"As you said, you don't have many options left," Diebol said. He stood, stretching his arms over his head with a yawn. Lem eyed his pistol on the table and his mace dangling from his belt —something in his body language had her on high alert suddenly.

Diebol glanced at the time on his holopen again, and then at the door. "Before we continue, we need to establish my innocence in your coup. We need footage of you entering and leaving here through the front door. And you need to fight me."

Lem stood. Mera's cut on her right shoulder suddenly stung —or she was aware of it, suddenly, as she shook herself out and drew her mace with a nervous energy bubbling in the top of her stomach. "Do I get to hurt you?" she asked.

His eyes lit up. "If you can," he said.

"How are we doing the end? I mean, how do you and I meet back up to finish this conversation?" This inner bubbling felt like a trap and stage fright all at once, made a hundred times weirder because oh yes, she very much wanted to fight him—she tried to slow things down. "It's gonna get noisy and messy."

"Leave here as Johnson, now, as if the meeting's still going—go to the latrine on the left with the badly-placed camera." His eyes glowed with conspiratorial mischief, as if this were a children's game. "Come back as yourself, and when I'm done with you, we'll make it look like you left through the back wall. But of course, you'll be in the tunnel."

"Excuse me, when you're *done* with me?" Lem scoffed. She expected a chill to run down her spine with the words, but instead found a surge of electricity crackling around her skin. "Would you like to reword that?"

Diebol's eyes widened for a split second with a spark of excited fear. He blinked it away, bowed his head, and swept his hand toward the door. "I look forward to doing so."

Lem touched the back of her ear with a grimace, keeping Diebol in her sights as she stalked around the table and out the door.

Reise

No one spoke as the four Frelsi cadets marched toward the volcanic horizon. Reise trudged behind Gideon, his teeth chattering as he shivered through the punishing rain. That one black smudge on Gideon's right shoulder blade was shaped a little like a blastercraft. Like Reise's own blastercraft back on Luna-Guetala—the one he'd just gotten assigned, the one whose AI he'd spent months working on. She was almost ready for a name. Or she'd *been* almost ready for a name, before the ship took to the air on its own to fire on Fort Jehu's inhabitants.

What was it like, for an AI, when someone else suddenly took control of the hardware it lived in? Was that comparable to possession, or mental illness? Sleep? Or death?

Shyte, it was so filking *frigid* out here.

Reise calculated it would take literally a week on foot to reach the place they'd left the main Hiding Place convoy yesterday morning. Between the four of them, they had three now-roasted protein bars that had been squished in Gideon's pockets; Gideon, ever the fitness fanatic, always had water tubes on him, but that hadn't survived the crushing impact of the ship, so Nathan was currently trying to collect rainwater in a thin, silver emergency blanket as they walked. Reise and Nathan still had their pistols, but Nate's charge wouldn't last another day. It wasn't a good situation.

But everyone except Reise would rather take their chances with the wilderness than with the Growen base in the area.

This moment was probably the thirty-first time—no, thirty-third, now, in the last few hours—that Reise contemplated breaking off from the group. He didn't believe in giving up.

As if reading his mind, Nathan spoke again. "Reise, I'm really sorry. We've got to get that information back to Command," he said.

"We could've stolen communication options from the Growen," Reise said.

"Reise … it was one thing when we had copious weapons and a reasonable plan," Nathan said. "Look at yourself."

Reise didn't; he could feel the throbbing shoulder just fine, thank you. He focused on the blastercraft-shaped smudge on Gideon's back instead.

"We can't just bring your little brother toward a Growen base," Nathan added. "And don't think I don't see that limp Gideon's trying to hide."

"Who are you trying to convince?" Reise asked. "Jake's right here, you don't have to talk like he's not."

"Firebase elements will be patrolling the area where we left the convoy. They're watching for more Growen trackers,"

Nathan said. "It won't be more than a couple days before we find them. They'll track us based on the last location our wristbands were working, too."

"Depending on how they interpret the ashes of our transport," Reise interjected.

"Sure, but we both agree we couldn't stay there like sitting ducks. Look, we'll be out of the rain soon. It'll warm up then."

"Warming up" meant something different to someone born and raised in the heat of equatorial Guetala, though: Alpino summer was the closest Reise had ever come to winter. Reise filking hated this kind of cold. Maybe he did want to go back to LG after all.

"I'm not mad about the cold," Reise said, kicking through the grass. "I'm mad because I don't believe four people are required to deliver one message."

"You can't charge into a Growen base with one arm and a pistol, you'll—"

"Yeah, I know, when you say it like that, it sounds stupid," Reise said. "We're walking the way you want to go. We didn't warn Jei, we're not helping Lem, we're just looking out for the biggest number of people. Your tyranny of the masses has won out. What more do you want?"

"I just don't want you to feel like you failed your sister." Nathan's soft voice grated on Reise's ears like a whimper.

"Oh, I don't," Reise said. "Trust me, I don't. I feel like we colossally wasted our time, filked up our good records, and got injured for no reason. I do feel like that."

"Speak for yourself," Gideon laughed, somehow without a trace of bitterness in his guffaw. "Nathan filked up my record a long time ago."

"Hey, I couldn't not report you," Nathan protested. "*You* chose to—"

"I know, I know, Nate! And I've learned my lesson," Gideon said. "Just trying to lighten the mood. You two and your debates are making the rain wetter, somehow." He wiggled his fingers by the side of his head as if scrambling his brains. "I'm this close to starting to sing just to drown you out."

Reise shoved his foot harder through the thick grass; specks of mud scattered across his uniform pants. Watching each step felt like more progress than watching the horizon. He could count the steps and calculate their total distance based on the length of his stride ... about five kilometers so far. He wasn't normally good at math, but today he felt like he needed some numbers so he could, when they died out here for no reason, spit them back in Nathan's face.

"I really did think you had a good plan, Reise," Nathan said. "I wouldn't have come if I didn't believe that. It's just that circumstances change. You'll see, this will end up being for the best. Everything happens for a reason."

"Yes, when we're all wearing our 'high value intelligence' medals at my sister's funeral, that'll be just the best," Reise snapped.

"Alright, I'm going to sing," Gideon announced.

Nathan grumbled—his legendary patience apparently finally at end with the threat of out-of-tune melodies—"No one's holding you here at gunpoint, Reise."

Reise shoved his good hand into his pocket; he was alternating between freezing his thigh with his hand and freezing his hand with the air. "Unfortunately, like you said, Nate, I'm just one person, and I'd need a team to pull anything off at this point," Reise said as Gideon began to belt out some show tune about metal skirts.

"You're being incredibly selfish," Nathan admonished.

"Yes," Reise admitted. "I'm not sorry. I don't know if you were asleep during the evacuation, but our cause isn't long for this galaxy. I'd rather take care of the people I care about than pretend I owe something to a crappy universe anyway."

"But we do owe—"

Reise heard Jake, behind him, starting to hum along with Gideon. Reise almost wanted to join, but again, something was *wrong* and it was impossible for him to think about anything else.

"I'm not saying we shouldn't prioritize the intel," Reise interrupted. "I'm saying I believe we had alternative options for accomplishing both. We've chosen your way. I'm not going to be happy about it."

"Happiness is a choice," Nathan said.

"That's something people say who have the luxury of not caring. We'll see if that's still true when it's your family getting laid down for some greater good." With that, Reise stomped past Gideon, hunching his shoulders against the rain as he marched toward the horizon.

CHAPTER THIRTY-SEVEN

Lem

SWEAT TRAILED DOWN LEM'S TEMPLE; HER CHIN TINGLED WITH HEAT and her vision seemed to grain from the black-light neodymium mace locked in an X against hers.

For once, Diebol had no snide grin on his face, only concentration. Lem kneed him in the belly, shoved like a bench press— he stepped backward, weight shifting just enough—Lem slid sideways out of the lock and popped the lower end of her staff toward his knee.

He grimaced as the heat made contact; an em-push shoved Lem back.

Perfect, she thought, sliding backward along the blood-slick floor, out through the hole she'd smashed in the conference room door.

It was a dance, a display for the benefit of detectives and political analysts. There were no cameras in the conference room, but the camera in the hallway could see Lem again now as Diebol's mace pounded overhead down through the gash. She hopped backward again to dodge, coaxing his whole form into view. Shouts, and the clunking of heavy boots, filtered through the hallways in a crescendo with the beeping alarm. Diebol slashed a diagonal toward Lem's left shoulder, and ribs; she dashed left with his force, past it, and spun around him back into the conference room with a parting slice toward his left thigh.

He grinned as he blocked. Lem didn't like his grin. It was too happy, too panting, with sweat that beaded like glitter on his cheeks and childlike energy in his eyes. It seemed so innocent, and innocent Diebol was not. He dove after her, flinging himself at her with each move—each blow, each block, each momentary lifting onto his toes. He didn't dodge and side-step—he only dashed closer, one centimeter at a time.

Jei mentioned, once, that when he played the board game in his mind, Diebol would always throw twigs into his opponent's "safe" territory, in what seemed like insane moves until he turned around and owned the entire board.

"It's all mental," Lem muttered. "Gets in your space to throw off your game."

"What was that?" Diebol whispered, sliding almost chest to chest with her, breath to breath—almost impaling himself on her mace. An em-push in his palm shoved her weapon to the side at the last minute, the glowing, dancing red spikes almost crackling against his skin as the butt of *his* staff, here inside her embrace, stabbed toward her throat—

Lem dove backward. The staff skewered the air where her chin had been. She bicycled in a twisted backflip, her mace knocking his mace above his head, her knee smashing into his jaw with a tooth-clacking crunch—

She landed in a kneel by the head of the conference room table; he doubled over, gripping his face with one hand.

"I think I'm done with you now," Lem said, hurling her staff to make the loud, obvious hole in the wall through which she was supposed to have escaped. "You can meet me in your tunnel."

And with that, as her staff slammed back into her palm with a quick em-pull, Lem slipped under the panel in the floor that led to Diebol's secret tunnel. She went to take a nap, and left him to deal with the hoard of soldiers come to rescue him and clean up the remains of his accidental coup.

Mera

Mera couldn't answer the midnight conference call with Bricandor and Diebol from inside a turtle's nest back-to-back with Jei Bereens. The pendant she wore around her neck pulsed between her breasts with bursts of heat, vibrating over and over about the missed call. Thank goodness it didn't make sound, or glow—Jei would have caught her for sure. As it was, she wanted to rip it off and smash it to make it stop buzzing against her sternum.

As much as Mera hated entering Sterba's domain, she had no other option. She closed her eyes, held her breath as if diving into a frigid pond, and exhaled as the hair on her skin stood on end.

Computer screens surrounded her at a perfect 135 degrees from each other. Sterba turned from inspecting a line of code to give Mera a cold blue stare; the destroyer was corporeal, in her projection today, standing before one of the screens with her shoulders draped in a long sapphire dress and cape, blonde hair frizzing like trapped lightning down her back.

"Do you do everything backward?" Sterba asked. "Yesterday you were supposed to call me in here, but you called by transmitter; today, you are supposed to answer the conference call, and you are in here. Do you not know what is going on?"

"I am trying," Mera insisted, grounding her boot into the floor. This time, she would not tremble, or cry. "I had her on the tip of my knife. But she is so much stronger than me!"

"Weakness is a choice," Sterba said. She didn't look up from her computer screen; her fingers danced across it, fluttering and tapping as numbers and letters flickered under her fingernails. "We just received word that Benzaran murdered almost the entire High Council."

"Oh! Is Diebol dead?" Mera's heart skipped a happy beat—

"The opposite. Diebol is the only survivor from the Alpino contingent."

Mera's happy beat stumbled over itself in her chest, leaving a tangled ache. "But no, that's—most of the military leadership is part of the Alpino contingent!"

Sterba nodded; she dragged a paragraph of code from a top corner, spun it, and slammed it into another paragraph with a spell-binding flare of her wrist. "Essentially the entire military force is now in Diebol's hands. He's already placed his own loyalists, from the enlisted ranks, in those command slots."

"But there are five other claves of generals still, on the other planets," Mera insisted, trying to muster hope.

"The Alpino contingent is the plurality, with ranking authority," Sterba said. "Until and unless Burbura offers Bricandor their own military support."

The brightness was intensifying, just a lumen at a time, and Mera's temples were starting to throb. "Is that what they're calling about?"

"I think they want to know where you are," Sterba said.

"Can you tell them I have Jei? I will deliver him to you shortly." The words stuck in Mera's throat; she backpedaled. "I—I still need him. To take her down for me."

"I can only hide you under my shadow so long," Sterba said. "We are both in danger of relegation to mere tools in their hands if we do not shift power soon."

"But you're so much stronger than they are."

"Exactly." Sterba paused her work to turn toward Mera, hands folded now over her belly. "And so Bricandor fears me as Diebol despises you."

Mera didn't dare think the thought—the feeling of it fluttered over her belly at the glitter in Sterba's eyes. There were two assassinations here.

"Can you do it?" Mera asked.

"As with the Frelsi, I need access to the computer in his room."

"You'd think this would be easier."

"His location changes often."

Mera stared down at the floor, chewing on her lip. "Jei could do it," she said.

"Prove him first. I am not confident you have control," Sterba said. A sneer pulled at the corner of her eyebrow and lip. "I see your heartrate writhing like a dancing girl in ecstasy."

Mera's face heated. "I'm not falling for him," she said. "I'm using emotion to my advantage."

"Your weakness is made worse by deception," Sterba said. "Spinelessness suits you like your skin-tight garb. How many times did you sell me out, on the rack, in the training center?"

"That wasn't my fault!" Mera cried, dashing forward—she found herself gripping the hem of the other woman's sleeve. "You know Diebol had me on drugs, I couldn't even see straight, I didn't—"

Sterba turned away. The long scar tracing her cheekbone silenced Mera's mewling. It was true; she was weak.

"Suffering makes us strong; attachments make us weak," Sterba said. "You know what you must do."

"I'll make it up to you. I'll kill Diebol," Mera snarled. "If it's the last thing I do. I swear."

Jei

Mera and I crawled out of the turtle den in the dead of night under cover of a new mist. She seemed troubled; she was caked in sweat, and a bit trembly.

"Lem seemed exhausted when we fought her," I encouraged Mera as we righted ourselves in the long prairie grass. "She's probably asleep. If you can track her now, I think we've got this."

Mera's lower lip fluttered. She closed her eyes, and heaved a large sigh.

"Are you—afraid of her?" I asked.

"No," she muttered. "I just still have a bit of a headache." She extended her hands out into the air, tilting her head at an angle like a Biouk listening; I could hear her low hum. "I'm conflating her presence with another one. Diebol *is* here," she said.

"Are they—together?" I asked. Something stuck in my throat —likely dust from the turtle's den.

"I don't know. Honestly, Jei." She put down her hands and opened her eyes. "I think we need to consider that he might be controlling her. We need to take him down, too."

I laughed. "Taking Diebol down has been my goal for over ten years. It's not quite that easy." My jaw tightened. "But there's no way he's controlling her. I thought about it. I know she had to take a secret identity to join; I'm pretty sure that's changed, and they're in communication now. But she was in complete control of herself today. She's calling shots."

Mera tapped her finger on her fluffy pursed lips. "We need to take them on two against one. I'm a little worried about triggering your full power for one, and then getting attacked by the other while you're down. But I can't take either of them in a fight alone."

"I think you're right that I need more than one attacker to charge up, though. Taking out those armorers in the hallway—I paid attention, and I could actually feel the power drain as each one passed out."

"You still had enough juice left to tear open the roof, though," Mera pointed out. "Maybe the strength of your enemy matters, too. Maybe you were feeding off Lem."

"So maybe we shouldn't split them up," I said. "Maybe we need both."

Mera sighed. "Jei, can I tell you something?"

I tilted my head; she chewed her lip. Her chest stilled with a held breath.

It made me nervous. "… yeah?"

"I need this to be a sure thing," she said. "I—I know Diebol. Last year, he—he tried to capture me for his army of electromagnetics. I escaped, but—he can't—look, if we go after him, it has to be one and done." Her lips clamped shut around her last words, ending her stuttering with uncharacteristic finality: "We can't afford to fail."

The fear was real. She didn't flutter her eyelids or play with her lips—the dead serious shadows under her eyes in the darkness didn't have time for that.

"Is ... that what you have nightmares about?" I asked. That other anger seeped into my belly—cold, like a rising tide.

"Sometimes," she said.

I pressed my fist over my mouth, clenching and unclenching it as I thought. "We will make sure it's a sure thing," I promised. "Let's start by finding them. We have a better shot if we act tonight."

CHAPTER THIRTY-EIGHT

Lem

LEM JOLTED AWAKE AT THE FIRST SOUND OF A FOOTFALL, JERKING HER head back against the earthen wall of the underground tunnel. She groaned and shifted her sore weight in the dirt.

"Light sleeper," Diebol said, standing over her with both hands in his pockets.

"Courtesy of you," Lem answered, tilting her head back to look up at him. "What's the plan?"

He nodded down at her shoulder. "I didn't do that. We need to fix it."

She turned her head to the sticky, stiff bloodstain covering her deltoid. "It's not deep."

"As if bacteria care. Follow me."

He offered his hand; Lem stared at it for a moment, wondering at how she'd arrived here. Scars traced his thumb like asterisks on fine print. This hand came with terms and conditions.

She gripped as he pulled her to her feet. "Jei's mind-channel has echoes of your belief that you can stop the universe from heat death," Diebol began, as they walked. "Well, Bricandor openly intends to cause it, in the name of his ba-eater and its friends."

If Lem were a Biouk, her ears would have stood straight up on her head. "I'm listening."

"I figured. It may be simply a myth, and the power balance has never been right for me to confront him about it. However, as you know, I am against all forms of interdimensional oppression." He stopped at a metal safe embedded in the tunnel wall and laid his hand on its surface; it popped open with a click, and he withdrew some bandages, ointment, and a needle in a sterile package. *No medbot?* Lem wondered. *Wow. I guess working with Her would make me tech-paranoid, too.*

"I would like to leave here tomorrow morning to go confront him about it," Diebol continued. "Perhaps blame this twenty-death incident on your interdimensional and his ba-eater working together—I'll improvise, but bottom line, I have options now." He sanitized his hands with a crystalline gel pod, and sat, nodding for her to sit as well, while the gel pod formed into transparent gloves over his fingers. "I would like to leave without Mera and Jei chasing me, and I'm sure you would like the same thing for yourself. So before I give you Her location, all I'm asking of you is that you board a ship tomorrow, with my face, making sure they can see before it takes off."

Lem watched his hands as they paused above her shoulder. "May I?" he asked. "Your hands are dirty."

The base of her chest knotted; she forced herself not to shudder. *Don't show fear. Don't let past him beat you now.* "Sure," she said. *Breathe. Breathe. Don't panic, breathe.*

He peeled the edge of her jumpsuit off her shoulder, revealing her toned deltoids covered in blood. Lem winced; the cold air stung the wide, open gash in the center of the bloody mess, and as Diebol slowly peeled the material away, sticky crimson pulled against the wound. She was starting to flash back to the dark room, and his grip on her fingers …

"Now, as I mentioned, I have some prior knowledge of Mera previously," Diebol continued.

"Lemme guess, you tried to force her in to the Stygge Army,

too." Lem stared into the cut, forcing herself to stay present, stay here, as Diebol began to clean off her shoulder.

"We all make mistakes," Diebol said. "I happen to know she's a tracker. Now, she can pick up multiple electromagnetic signatures, but she can really only follow us one at a time without getting a headache. She wants to kill me, remember—"

"What woman doesn't."

"—and may already have a general idea of my whereabouts. Tomorrow, we'll display you publicly as me. That way, you don't have to worry about *also* evading my men: you just lead Mera and Jei to the decoy ship we'll pretend I'm taking off from. They will follow whichever of us they see first, so we'll make it easy and make it me. I'll hang around that ship, hidden, so she reads two signals, and maybe we can flash your face through the window so they think we're traveling together. Once they get into the hangar bay, we'll have the ship take off via autopilot."

"How we gonna leave that ship to go our actual separate ways?" Lem asked.

"That's the best part," Diebol grinned, irrigating the wound with a disinfecting solution. The icy liquid felt good; pleasant, relaxed chills flooded Lem's scalp as the rivulets dribbled off her shoulder and down her side, and as Diebol traced the edge of the wound in small, hypnotic circles with a white cleaning cloth, Lem remembered how tired she was. "I have a device that masks our electromagnetic output—basically a signal dampener in a vest. We'll put those on, and sneak out."

Lem sighed, and looked away from the wound for a moment, resting her neck on the wall behind her as the world blurred, and she forced herself to blink instead of sleeping. "Why can't we just do this now? Why we gotta wait 'til morning?" she asked. "I'm at that point where I don't even care, I just want this shyte to end."

"Nonsense. You need to be in tip-top shape to murder my compatriot." Diebol smiled, such a genuine, conspiratorial smile Lem could've sworn they were just smuggling cookies out of the mess hall. "Besides, the vests need to charge."

Diebol held up a needle and thread very deliberately right in front of her eyes. "No surprises," he said. "I wouldn't normally close a shallow cut, of course, for fear of locking in infection—but where this has split, on your arm here, the skin won't close over it right without stitches because your muscle's too developed. See how it's oozing still, in the middle?" He pointed with his pinky finger at the gaping fish-mouth of a wound, and the red, striated tissue underneath.

"My muscle's too developed, huh," Lem chuckled. "I appreciate the compliment, I guess. Yeah, go ahead, sew it up."

"I don't have anesthetic," he said. "But we both know you tolerate pain." The needle pricked into the edge of wound, and Lem sucked in her breath, not at the pain, but at the familiar feeling of his proximity to it. Her other hand slipped to the bamboo staff dangling from her belt ...

"I'm sorry," he said. Her eyes flitted to his face, fixed on his work—he pulled the thread tight with clenched jaw, and he winced as the needle dove back through her skin again. He really was sorry. "You're doing well," he murmured.

The needle hit a sensitive spot a bit more central to the wound—a wave of dizziness washed against her forehead, and a gasp escaped her lips. Why, she wondered? She never had a problem with blood, or pain. But she began to shiver, and the firm, moist earth at her back seemed to be replaced with icy cement as her vision seemed to darken, and she heard clinking chains, and Cinta's yowls ...

"I'm sorry," he repeated. His voice brought her back to *here*, and she saw him watching her face. "I would have you do this, so it's not me, but ..."

"It's difficult to suture your own shoulder with only one arm," Lem grunted, leaning her head back on the wall again. "I'm fine." She stared at the irregular lumps in the dirt wall across from her, listening to him breathe beside her, feeling the gentleness of his fingers around the sharp sting of the needle ... "You ever wonder what we would be if you weren't evil?"

He laughed. "If *you* weren't evil, you mean."

"I would never mean that," Lem said—twitching as the needle penetrated again. In her exhaustion, the sheer sensory overwhelm sent shivers and tingles through her skin, and she thought, for a moment, that the pricking pain was replaced by something else more pleasant. She bit her lip, and her eyes strayed to the needle, glinting in the low light of Diebol's holopen ...

"Of course," he said. "How could I not wonder? I spent months trying to save you and Jei from your Contamination. Of course I thought about what could have been. The three of us could have overthrown Bricandor, if we wanted." He shook his head, mocking his past self. "I used to imagine game tournaments with him and—ha, *hiking!*—with you, if you can believe it."

"Jei's the only friend you ever had, isn't he," Lem said. In the shadows, as her eyelids drooped and the endorphins of the needle kept pricking her awake, her enemy looked sad. What would have become of him if he hadn't been the other little boy in the cage with Jei? Was that kid still in there, under all the blood, just wishing he wasn't so filking alone?

But the young Growen leader answered with a canned response, "Attachments cause suffering," he said definitively. "I didn't need the attachments after all."

With that, he closed the wound, and cut the thread.

Reise

The four Frelsi runaways found themselves forced to stop their march through the wet Alpino plains once the sun went down: without the digital compasses on their wristbands, or any source of light, they couldn't risk changing direction by accident and becoming lost. They sat with their backs against each other, still wet and cold and in significant need of body heat despite the cessation of the rain.

The wind, at least, had mostly died down. That made it worse, though, when grass rustled here and there—was it a breeze, or something else? In the distance, something hooted; Reise twitched.

"It's okay, Reise," Jake said.

"Thanks," Reise said back. He leaned his head back on his little brother's shoulder behind him. "When we return home, this is my fault, okay? Don't tell them that you hid with us on purpose. Say you fell asleep."

"I should lie?" Jake asked.

"You should," Reise said. "Or, you don't have to, and I can, if you want."

"My own stuff is my own fault, though," Jake said.

Reise shrugged and lifted his head to blow on his hands. "Self-determination for all," he said. Still, he detested the idea of Jake facing consequences for something that was Reise's responsibility. It was another something *wrong*.

From Reise's left, leaning against both boys' shoulders, Nathan piped up: "'When we return home'—see, you're feeling more confident now. That's a good attitude, Reise."

Reise's eyes narrowed in the darkness. "I'm interested in logic, not unfaltering positivism," he snapped.

On Reise's right, Gideon's back twitched with laughter. "Oooh, he got you there, Nate," the larger guy said. "Your shyte is *unfaltering* as *filk*! But it's positivity, not positivism, Reise."

"I don't think it is," Reise said. Before Gideon could answer, though, Reise stood—he saw a light, in the distance, over the silhouette of that hill. A light!

Nathan saw it a second later. "No Reise!" he hissed.

"You three stay here," Reise whispered, his uninjured hand on his flayer pistol already.

"Reise! No, we can't risk getting caught, we have important—"

Reise had already taken off through the grass, his back

hunched to keep his shape from showing against the horizon and the stars. In his mind, if the information they carried was important enough, it was worth any risk to get it back sooner. His pants legs swished faster as he broke into a bent-over sprint ... as the hill rose under him, he lowered his hands to the earth, keeping pressure off the shoulder that was still throbbing from Gideon's forceful replacement.

That had been *fun*. If fun meant sudden, excruciating pain. Gideon had literally yanked his arm forward, which seemed like the opposite of what Reise thought you should do, and kind of *up*—it had actually "clunked" back into place.

Reise crested the hill now ... *yes*.

Below the dune, a pale-faced blonde human female squatted by a fire across from a red-scaled Draconian who appeared, by the ridges crowning his humanoid skull, to be male. By the flickering light, Reise could see blue stripes painted across the woman's face, and leather strips of dragon-skin dangling from her wrists and ankles. The Draconian wore only metal: silver bands decorated his neck and midsection, and a light, chainmail-like weave loincloth hid his mammalian dangly bits. His forked tongue flicked through sharp, pointed teeth under a single simple lip piercing as he leaned forward, speaking, with great passion, low words Reise couldn't hear over the crackling of the fire.

Curled around them lay a moderately-sized dragon, its spiked tail wrapped around under the human woman's ample derriere, and its face smoking in the shadows behind the wings on the Draconian's back.

Reise could feel his pulse racing through his throbbing shoulder. Wow! He knew certain Alpino people groups used the non-sentient volcano-dwelling lizards as beasts of burden and food, but in real life he'd never seen—

The dragon sat up suddenly, stiff like a feathered cat, both front paws tucked in close to its seat. Its green eyes glowed in the darkness, staring at Reise with its pointed ears on end.

As it stirred, the two sentients talking over the fire suddenly saw Reise, too. They stared through the darkness, but didn't reach for their weapons, or get up.

"Hi," Reise said. Then, the code for civilians friendly to the Frelsi: "Do you have any butter?"

CHAPTER THIRTY-NINE

Jei

As Mera and I strolled through the fields on the periphery of the Growen fort, I almost forgot where we were, and why. It was so quiet. The stars weren't as beautiful here as out over the bare prairie, but even the Growen preferred to save energy at night, and only mission-essential buildings emitted light pollution. A cluster of buildings far off in the center of the base flickered with red and blue communicator lights, and scattered barracks buildings glowed with patches of translucent polymer-wall here and there, closed windows lit from within by silhouettes burning the midnight fuse.

Out here, behind us, the armory lay quiet now; only a soft glow through a few points in the wall, and a beam of light emanating from the crack in the top, hinted at the forensic specialists still working inside. Multiple land-runners were parked in the front, with guards posted by the entrances, but Mera and I took a long, long circle around the building through the fields, and no one was the wiser. Grass swished by our legs, and a few musical insects sang as we walked by.

We were following Mera's electrolocation. She would put her fingers out into the air, or into the ground, and close her eyes to hum—sometimes completely inaudibly, and sometimes a low, soft rumble of her voice box would just barely tickle my ears. Then, we would walk more.

For the first time in months, I felt … happy. Maybe even at peace. Not quite—I couldn't rest inside, not until I could taste justice, but something in the way the horizon framed Mera's silhouette, or the shadows highlighted the near-glow of her cheeks, or the way her tongue tapped on the roof of her mouth with little *kk*s and *tt*s as she thought, and listened, in the evening breeze …

Despite what I'd said to Cinta about "replacing" Lem, I'd actually never felt about her the way I felt about Mera. Lem was my battle-buddy—like my brother, but a girl.

Mera was something else. Mera made me think about the possibilities of my powers, and hers, entwined—about the neurons on the tips of our fingers, touching, and firing, lighting up the ridges of our fingerprints as the very mole-cules pressed into each other and capillary pulses synced, in a world where our abilities retired from battle and our souls, the electricity that made up our programming, the lines of code flickering in patterns in our beating, wet brains, became one story, one light, one new universe of peace.

I told myself the thought was metaphor upon metaphor, my mind couching itself in nobility to cover for something very basic and biological. But another part of me—very nearly the part that loved Njande, and, when I was alone, the occasional line of poetry from the old Alpinoan masters—*that* part said that to love someone this way, in the right place, and the right time, could be the highest calling given a man.

It was a different feeling, but by no means a lesser feeling. Like Mera said, I only hated Lem this much right now because I'd cared for her that much before. The betrayal of a brother, once ensconced in the psyche by battle and blood, often hurts more than the betrayal of a biological lover. *"Your love is better than the love of women,"* wrote a warrior-poet to his friend in the historical archives we'd found for Njande last year …

"What are you thinking about?" Mera asked me, tracing my forearm with her finger.

I sighed and shook myself off. "Stupid shyte," I said. "Lotta nonsense."

She fake-pouted. "Ah, I was hoping you were thinking about me."

"Well ..." I stepped in front of her and leaned forward with a soft laugh, almost but not quite into the space in front of her mouth, as I started to retort—

And noticed the fullness of her lips. *Why am I doing this to myself?* I squeezed her hand, and then stepped back, to give myself and her a little space.

She trotted after me and gripped the elbow of my tunic in her fist. "Hey," she said, stepping in front of me.

"Hey," I said back. My voice sounded lower, and more gravelly, than I intended.

"Jei—listen." Her voice grew higher and more bouncy as she began to put on that colorful armor again; her hip slipped out to the side, shaping her into an *S* as she planted her finger on a pouted lip. "I'd like to try something together. To see if it enhances your powers. We have a big fight ahead of us, and certain ... endorphins ... might *prime* your neurotransmitters."

She emphasized the words endorphin, and prime, with weak giggles and a hand trailing across the pearls that hung on her chest. Bloodseas, I almost hated that armor. She seemed like she was mimicking something—something she thought I wanted instead of the wide-eyed acrobat who explored old libraries and made-up scientific theories about ghosts.

"Mera, you're not an experiment to me." The words burst from my mouth before I realized what I was saying. "I'm not going to use you like an energy drink or a disposable hand tool." That sounded—harsher—than I intended, and I backpedaled quickly and lowered my whisper. "Sorry, I—am I misunderstanding something, here?"

I wasn't misunderstanding, and she was unfazed. "Come on, tell me I'm not the woman of your dreams."

She was very literally a woman from my dream. "Mera …"

"What, you can neither confirm nor deny?" she pouted.

"No, I can't deny it," I said. My voice sounded angry, and I didn't know why. "You're talented, you're sweet, you're full of these hidden thoughts and feelings and theories I just want to drag out of you and hold up to the light—"

"Also I'm perfectly proportioned, and you like ribbon dancers," she quipped, still with the filking armor.

"Yes, thank you Mera, I'm not blind. You're literally a sunrise, or an unobtainable memory, made human." I found my hands clenched by my temples in frustration I couldn't explain. Her eyes searched me in the dark.

"But?" she asked.

My throat caught; I resented myself for my overly-honest outburst. "We need to find our target," I coughed. "We're running out of time."

She deflated, and continued walking.

Agh, I resented myself for that, too. Before she could retreat too far, I strode up next to her and took her hand. "Mera, I don't want you as something disposable. I don't know how else to explain it."

"Everyone's disposable," she said. "It's no hard feelings, just how it is. That's why we have to seize the moment when it comes."

"That's—that's heartbreaking, that you think that," I said.

"It's mine to think." Her voice hardened a bit.

"Okay." I nodded, and took a deep breath: "That's true, you're yours," I said. *Kiss me*, said the tingly pins and needles sensation in my fingertips, before trickling up my arm and fading over my neck, and lips.

I withdrew my hand. "But I'm also my own person, too, right?" I said. "I am also allowed to say no."

"I don't believe you *mean* no for a moment. Not if you like me. Every guy wants this."

Yeah, I was screwed. I'd lost so many potential girlfriends over the past five years to this conversation. "I made a vow," I said. "When I started to understand my abilities, and the interdimensional world, I decided that because of my powers I'm going to kiss, and be with, just one person. I don't know one hundred percent who she is yet, and—"

"What do you mean, because of your powers?" Yup, I was blowing it. Her scowl of disapproval said I belonged in a convent, not an army.

I folded my hands like a prayer by my mouth, hoping I could explain using the inner exploration we both understood. "Okay, so we control our electromagnetic abilities via thought, emotion, will, and other neurological impulses, right?"

"Yes?" She continued walking—not away from me, but with a slow amble, kicking the grass.

I stayed beside her. "The—*physical*—part of love is a complex chemical and neurological reaction, right," I said. "It's unique in that it involves at least four electrical systems, and a hormonal system. For comparison, fighting takes a hormonal system and three electrical systems, and most of your daily activities just take one or two."

"What do you mean, four electrical systems?" she asked.

"Somatic—the moves you decide consciously to make; the sympathetic system, which ramps you up unconsciously; the parasympathetic system, which calms you down, also automatically; and the sensory system, which feels things. Right?" I walked with her, watching for her understanding nod before I continued. "There's also the reflex system, where your spine makes decisions for you, like to jerk your hand away from pain, and your gut actually has its own 'enteral' system that talks to the parasympathetic system, but can run on its own without it." I took a breath. "The physical part of love uses at least the first four *and* a system of hormones that talk between them, and every time you use a system, you invoke 'plasticity'—you change your neurons based on what you just did, to make new synapses or strengthen existing ones. It's a powerful, permanent thing you do when you supercharge multiple systems at once."

"Cool science lesson, Jei, but I think you're avoiding my

question." Mera stood up and stepped close to me again. "Why don't you just say you don't like me?"

"Well, let me finish my science lesson," I said, trying to joke. Thank goodness she laughed. "There's a lot to explain, and I really want to do it right, because ..." I sighed. Honesty sucked. "Because I do like you—bloodseas, I like you a lot, and I want to make sure you're okay with the weirder parts of what I think."

"Aw, that's sweet," she said. "Go on."

"Oof, sweet isn't a great word."

"It's better than the alternative I'm thinking right now." She crossed her arms as her slender eyebrows twisted in the starlight.

I sighed as she started walking again; my fingers absently unclipped my staff from my belt, and began whacking the tops of the grass with it as we passed. "Alright. So when we use our powers, we essentially hijack the pathways of these neuro-systems for other purposes. Some of us—like Lem, I think—have additional systems that end in different kinds of nerves. I think that's the reason she can throw sparks. Or like you, with your specialized inner ear. But anyway, the way we use our powers is tied to the way our neurons connect, and when I supercharge four systems at once, when I—when I *sync* my neurological system up with someone else—I want to make sure that intense link doesn't damage my powers."

She tilted her head back to sigh at the stars. "So what if you weren't electromagnetic?" she asked.

"I—don't think I'd change my mind, honestly," I winced. "Everyone still has the same basic neurobiological system—sex is sex. A stable, long-term physical link frees you from distrac-tions, heals the mind, pushes you to achieve, and—clears out unwanted tension." Like the tension I was feeling right now. "At best, a bunch of unstable, half-formed links decreases my ability to use that link reliably. At worst, the distraction and—*drama*—of multiple goodbyes would make the link weaker."

"You're basically saying having more partners makes you worse at sex," she said flatly.

"I don't think that's unrealistic," I said. "There's a hormone called oxytocin, the bonding hormone, which ties mother to child, and lovers together. It affects the way your muscles move and the way you think, and ties you closer to those you love. It's part of why sex is so healthy. And it's higher in people who are monogamous, and lower in those who aren't."

"Okay, okay, pause here." Mera stepped close to me again and held up both her palms. "I get what you're saying. And you know what, I'll give you this: even forgetting oxytocin, if you only have one lover in your life, that person will always be the best you've ever had. You don't have anything to compare it to. Pleasure's all in the brain, so doing it your way your psychological expectations set you up for a better experience. And of course as you get to know one person's body and preferences over time, you establish a stronger foundation for creative experimentation—lots of benefits to your way, not to mention the decreased disease transmission." She smirked and gave the elbow of my tunic another gentle tug with her fist. "But forget about sex, Mr. Horny Science Lecture. Let's talk about kissing."

"Cultural greeting kissing, or romantic human kissing? I have culturally greeted a lot of Insectoids on the mouth in my day," I laughed.

"Romantic human kissing, you butt," she said.

"Well, biologically, isn't kissing a signal to your autonomic and hormonal systems to get ready for something else?" I asked. "It's still part of my promise, for me."

Mera kicked more grass with a little skip, twirling her fingers against each other behind her back. "The distinction seems arbitrary."

"Arbitrary is what you make it. Why does a handshake seal a deal? It's the meaning behind it that matters."

She peered up at me sideways through her bangs. "It seems so strange to me that you'd suddenly limit your expression of love for others because you got to thinking too much."

"Love, and what I'm talking about, aren't the same thing. Like you said before, there's more to love than physical intimacy.

I can love as many people as I want." I whacked another tall clump of grass with my staff. This needed to be over. We needed to hunt. "Anyway, in the nonsapient world, species that are naturally abstinent and monogamous—like otters and eagles—don't seem to be restricted and repressed. They seem happy. They seem less frenzied and stressed out than the snakes or the salmon that spend all their energy mating and fighting as much as possible and then die flooded in cortisol."

"Cortisol being the stress hormone," she said.

"Right."

Mera stopped in front of me with her arms crossed over her chest and took a deep breath.

"Well, I'll be frank with you, Jei, I take a more balanced approach than either the salmon or the otters. I don't spend all my energy on boys, but I do like a little fun, a little risk. I haven't stopped myself from doing what I wanted, when I wanted."

She looked at me, as if challenging me to judge her. I looked right back and didn't. I stepped closer to her, and lowered my voice. "Is that who you are, who you've been, or who you think people want you to be?"

"I am the same person I've always been." She doubled down.

"I like that person. I don't define her based on an arbitrary number of past hook-ups. I define her by her passion, her skill, that pool of secrets behind her eyes." I clenched my fist tighter on my staff to keep my fingers from running along the curve of her chin in this shimmering moonlight. "And if that person chose to like me back, I wouldn't try to control her. But I wouldn't lie about who I am or what I need, either." I finished with a harsh whisper, "And I wouldn't love her and leave her."

With that, finally, she dropped the armor. She actually looked baffled; for a while, neither of us spoke. Her fingers danced near mine; I allowed it, and our fingers intertwined. She was different, this time—no pins and needles, no transmitted thoughts ... just her hand in mine.

And in this way, we continued our walk through the starlight, until she found our target.

CHAPTER FORTY

Reise

THE DRAGON-RIDERS DID, IN FACT, HAVE METAPHORICAL BUTTER.

Like most sapients from Alpino's more rural people groups, Sensi, the painted human, and Wiz, the winged Draconian, were both Frelsi sympathizers. In fact, when Reise interrupted their midnight smungworm roast, they were engaged in heated discussion about how the changes on Burbura could alter their nomadic freedoms here on Alpino. They were glad to give the lost teens a ride on their enormous lizard to the nearest Frelsi patrol.

Reise had never ridden a dragon before, and it wasn't at all what he expected.

"There're a couple o' soldiers who have their route just along the boundary lands this time o' night," Sensi shouted over the wind rushing in their faces. Reise, directly behind her, was fully engaged in not making a face as the woman's strong musk blew directly up his nostrils and her hair, tangled with tiny reptile bones, smacked his cheeks.

"What's the boundary lands?" Jake asked from behind Reise. This, too, was uncomfortable: even with the Draconian flying overhead instead of riding, the long dragon mount barely had room for all the riders on its scaly back, and as it side-wound through the prairie at break-neck speed, its muscles rippled under everyone in a way that jolted them together and apart again over and over, making Reise feel like he was inside a rock accordion.

"That's where the prairie becomes volcanoes n' such," Sensi said. "You are'n from here, eh? Draconians usually live near the volcanoes in the winter on account o' their cold sensitivities, while we Blues usually live there in the summer for the good huntin'. Every year there's a whole to-do when we cross the boundary lands."

Reise finally gave in to his nose and turned his head, tucking it into his shoulder to look behind him instead of trying to brave the hair of death. By starlight, he could see Nathan, in the back on the base of the tail, gazing up at the Draconian and then down at the dragon with a pleasant smile on his face, taking it all in. Gideon, behind Jake, made eye contact with Reise, almost laughing out loud at Reise's sputtering unhappiness.

"I thought dragons could fly," Jake called to Sensi.

"Common mis-con-ception, from off-worlders," Sensi answered. To the flier, above: "You all good up there, Wiz?"

"I couldn't be better, my friend," Wiz called back, every syllable clean, crisp, and accented with a grandeur Reise thought belonged in a palace or a temple. "It is a lovely night for a flight." The Draconian's bat-like wings were *enormous* unfurled —about twice the man's height in wingspan. Reise wouldn't have believed they could pack closed so tightly if he hadn't seen the leathery rolls on Wiz's back when he first approached the pair.

When the group reached Sensi's Frelsi patrol friends, Reise soon realized he would've gladly taken any amount of time behind the stink-hair over the stern debriefs. The boys got the first earful from the patrol members, who had been informed of the AWOL teens the day before, and had no problem dishing out advice to unruly troublemakers from the back of their air-riders. Then, back at the Firebase, the guys got it again from the inter-rogator who took their statements about the possible location of the force that destroyed Fort Jehu.

And, finally, the Hiding Place guide who arranged their transfer got to give them a piece of her mind, too. She walked into the colorful cushioned interrogation room with her antennae almost twirling with rage.

"Oh, hi again!" Jake waved to her as she came in. "Reise, it's the same guide who was in charge of our convoy before."

Reise tried to pretend he himself did not exist; he almost hid his face under the largest throw pillow on the plush seat beside him.

"Hi nothing," the guide chittered, her mandibles clicking together well in advance of the words from the translating voice box that hung around her thin throat. "Hi nothing you've caused so much trouble for me but I guess thank Njande it's for the best!" She threw four of her legs into the air; Nathan tried to make pointed eye contact with Reise, which he ignored. "You gave some intel that might save some lives let's see." She motioned with her antennae toward the door. "Come on Hiding Place transport this way."

Jake and Gideon stood right away, eager to finally end the late night, in trouble or not. Reise found himself hanging back, looking around at the patterned rugs and tasseled bolsters that made this room look, in his mind, more like a rich person's romp room than an artificial cave for extracting secrets. Even the inter-rogator, a plain, mousy man, had simply scribbled their intel onto his compupad and then left the room: no frantic reports, no war-room head-slamming, no good cops and bad cops and glasses of water on plastic tables near two-way mirrors—well, that wall actually probably was a two-way mirror, but still.

"That's it?" Reise said.

"I know," Nathan said, coming up beside him. "It's all really anti-climactic."

"I feel like I need to leave and try again," Reise said. "Like I was playing a vid-story game and accidentally chose the wrong ending."

He pushed through the polymerwall out into the hallway after the others, trotting up to the Hiding Place guide. "Ma'am," he began—

"I don't want to hear it you were lucky that things turned out okay," she said.

"With all due respect ma'am, we weren't *lucky*," he said. "We all escaped alive from the burning transport because we were loyal and smart and thought on our feet and remembered our training. We got the information we did because we were suspicious and cautious and stayed hidden because we didn't trust our superior's new friend. And we got back here as quick as we did because we took the right risks and leveraged our allies. Maybe we're not the heroes, but you need people like us to save the heroes' butts sometimes."

"Are you saying you're planning on running away again," she groaned.

"I'm sure as hell saying I don't wanna just cower in the Hiding Place, ma'am," Reise said, lengthening his stride to keep up as she skittered through the hall.

Gideon joined them. "You know, Reise has a point. Command is always saying we're short on combatants—there's no point in sending fighting age scouts to go hide."

"That was your original destination."

"That's a clerical matter, though," Nathan interjected, scuttling up on his tiny feet. "They were evacuating everyone they could. The more transports that go there, the more risk of exposure, so why send an extra one for buttheads who couldn't even stay on the first one?"

"We'll all be going to the Hiding Place soon anyway, if the Firebase gets hit next," Reise said—surprised that Nathan had his back but not inspecting a gift lechichi's pores. "I'd like to respectfully request to remain and assist with evacuation."

"Hey, we could be one of the supply squads," Gideon said, pointing to his companions and holding up three fingers to emphasize that they had the right number of people.

The Hiding Place guide threw four limbs in the air again and stopped walking. "I'm like a queen up here with you larvae crowding all around me."

The boys looked at each other, not quite understanding; Nathan took a step back, away from her, so Reise and Gideon did the same.

"I feel like you're supposed to learn some kind of lesson and you haven't," she said. "But maybe lessons aren't practical you're certainly a good team or at least some kind of team let me talk to command and see about getting you on evac." She looked over at Jake. "You're the one who's underage right?"

He nodded, flinching. Reise steeled himself for a dramatic show ...

"I'm going to be transporting a group of underages as soon as the order goes through you will be on board and not hiding anywhere I don't care if you miss your brother or if you are hungry or sleepy or whatever excuse is that understood?"

Jake looked at Reise. *Come on, don't do the separation anxiety thing. Please don't ...*

"Next year, buddy," Reise said.

Jake sighed. "Yes ma'am."

The relief was so palpable Reise could almost feel the air currents in the room change as Nathan and Gideon let out their breath. Reise patted his little brother on the back as the group followed the guide down a side hallway. Jake was growing! Good for him.

But Reise still intended to find a way to locate his sister.

CHAPTER FORTY-ONE

Cinta

CINTA COULD NOT IMAGINE ANYTHING *LESS* SIMILAR TO THE LUNA-Guetala forests than the Frelsi Hiding Place.

It was not as if at home, under the thick canopies, and tightly-woven tree houses, Cinta saw sky all the time, or even every day, but something about seeing stone overhead every time he looked up now had already begun to drive sharp teeth into his brain. Even if he stood in the center of this vast cavern, right under the volcano's opening, he would only see the enormous vat of molten material that hung just inside the entrance to hide inhabitants from anyone flying above. In the belly of this hollow mountain, no one's eyes tasted sky.

The space-lemur felt he would never get used to living underground. The bubbling sound of geothermal vents and water pipes had become pleasant, and even comforting overnight; less so the occasional rumble to frighten away civilians with fake seismic activity. And despite the grow-lights scattered through the cavern and tunnels for psychological and physical homeostasis, Cinta's body already did not feel morning or night.

It was night, now. Cinta panted, envying humans their overactive sweat glands as he laid down his hoe. The smothering heat of the jungle did not compare to the breezeless inferno here, closer to the top of the volcano. Rich black dirt squeezed between the toes of his paws as he scampered to the edge of the garden shelf carved into the inside of the mountain. He adjusted the grow-lamp fixed into the rock above him, and sighed, gazing out into the chasm below and above him. Food-producing shelves dotted the volcano's inside walls like honeycomb; deep below him, repair vehicles milled around the parked transports on the cavern floor, and soldiers ducked in and out of view, disappearing into the tunnels that fingered off into the earth, away from the mountain, under the plains. Every voice, hammer blow, and footstep echoed in odd, muffled patterns as sound waves spiraled up the conical subterrene toward the hidden sky.

This was the Frelsi Hiding Place. This was where the bulk of all Frelsi finances disappeared; why they could not always afford new ships, why half the buildings on Luna-Guetala had doors instead of polymerwalls, and why Cinta now understood what Jaika meant when she talked about eating orange slop.

He missed her.

Commotion below? Cinta's ears perked: soldiers swarmed a small tunnel-car that emerged from under the earth by the passageways to the command center. *Something important happening ...*

Cinta scampered onto the ladder, unclipped his vest from the hook on the grow-shelf to the hook on the ladder, and rappelled down using the left side of the ladder a bit like a balance pole for his back paws. He'd watched other Biouk space-lemurs literally just climb down the moss on the rock mountain walls, but since his ... injury ... well, without his front claws he could not grip.

At least dangling and falling by rope like this threw a warm breeze into his muzzle fur.

Cinta landed just as he got an alert to the wristband on his front right paw. "Your sister's brothers have been found. Back at Firebase. With crazy intel?" A few other alerts, from other friends, along the same vein.

Your sister's brothers. Did they question, Cinta wondered, why he had not gone looking for *Jaika*, for Lem, as they had? He had forced himself to forget even the breeze of the one sentence she had left him. He did not know because he chose not to know; only, he knew, Njandejara held her safe.

Cinta crossed the warm, shimmering black floor on all fours, but the crowd around the tunnel-car had already begun to disperse. Two Skraeli cloud-people, in atmosphere uniforms to keep their bodies from dispersing, had pulled in from a meeting down the hall just to share the gossip.

"I bet it's a Stygge, some kind of Stygge super-hacker."

"No, it's gotta just be some really tight computing equipment. There are some great salvage spots in Alpino orbit."

"They have a location! They're putting together a sabotage team."

A sabotage team, did they say? Cinta needed to join that. He could not deal with living in this mud-lump any longer. He had a good body-size for small spaces and significant experience with Growen infiltration—anyway, his resume said it that way. His mother, his *Mali*, said instead, "you steal eggs and girls."

He missed his family, too. Mali always said exactly the wrong thing about him—he had never stolen a girl, only helped his adopted sister escape. Inside, his heart laughed.

Cinta chattered in Biouk to the supervisor on the floor, grabbing the other space-lemur's attention with an upward chin tilt and a chittering sound. "Hey, I'm off to throw my name in for that sabotage team. I'll return to finish planting after."

"Winds with good scents, to you," the supervisor rasped back through his friendly front teeth. Cinta liked this supervisor; like all the permanent Hiding Place personnel, he radiated peace.

Cinta took a shortcut through the girl barracks tunnel. Many others, he thought, would want a place on this sabotage team; he needed to put his name in first. Why the decision to send someone from the Hiding Place, instead of Firebase, he wondered? Did the decision come from proximity to the destination? Or did they fear an imminent attack on Firebase? Not good.

A deep male voice from one of the barracks rooms—and a squeal from a little human girl—! Cinta skidded to a halt, ears straightened in alarm. Male DNA was not supposed to work in the little girls' rooms! He kicked the polymerwall: "Hey! Who's in there? All okay?"

The polymerwall dissolved open, melting around the door-jamb. Little ten-year-old Juju Benzaran stood in the doorway, her finger on the lock button; in her other palm stood two small figures, shimmering in the center of the light map created by her wristband's hologram projector.

Cinta relaxed with a breath. *Only a phone call.* He knew he projected his feelings for his once-little Jaika sister on her biological sibling. They looked much the same—same cherry wood skin, almond-shaped eyes, hair like vibrant, fresh sweet moss, except that Juju's was an unusual blonde, and Jaika's dark as the deepest pool in the forest. Oh, Cinta feared for them when still this slender and small. With no fur, no claws, and teeth weaker than a peacock guinea pig's, he did not know how humans survived evolutionary adaptation. Juju frightened him more than Jaika-Lem: Juju had no fight in her spirit, only the softness of a mist, and at her age Jaika already wore twice the muscle mass.

"Hey Cinta!" Juju bubbled. "Uncle Carl, Aunt Lark, it's Cinta." She pushed her palm almost in his face, showing him the tiny projections of the mercenaries that had alternately kidnapped and rescued her last year. "They may be near Alpino soon."

"How are you making this call?" Cinta's throat rasped a gentle low growl. "The signal jammer should not allow it."

"I've had a secure frequency to them since last year, silly," Juju said. "It can't be jammed. That way if I ever need them to rescue me, they can!"

"You should not make calls from here," Cinta said, reaching for her wristband. "So many security risks! These are civilians!"

"They're not civilians, they're bounty hunters," Juju pouted, holding her wrist far over Cinta's head.

"That is so much worse," Cinta groaned. "Come, come talk to Command now."

"I don't—"

"Now!" Cinta snarled. To the bounty hunters: "Excuse us, hello, good to see you again."

He knew how to herd human children bigger than him—he had managed and pinned and wrestled Jaika for years before she became tree-sized. Humans did not like sharp teeth by their ankles, and soon Cinta had Juju in a meeting cave across the stone table from their direct in-house commander. He did not like angering the young one, but he did not like everyone to die, either.

"Sure, we'll sanitize the line," the Ichthian commander bubbled through her robotic atmosphere suit, essentially an aquarium with armor and legs. "That just means, Juju, we need a second VPN on your wristband, and an adult has to call with you for OpSec."

"That's so lame!"

"Indeed." The Ichthian's sarcasm projected through the color change on her gills. "But while you have your friends on the line —are they near Alpino? Everyone knows about the exploits of Lark Scrita and the Ebon Shadow ... I was actually about to see if Command could call for mercenary assistance."

"We *could* be near Alpino, if you need us to, lass," the Bont lizard in Juju's palm grunted. Cinta did not like the way Lark Scrita's clear third eyelid washed over her eyeball. *Njandejara loves reptiles, too,* he snapped to his mammalian instincts.

"And I apologize," Commander Blawble continued bubbling into the translator on her robotic aqua-suit. "I recognize that you both have Frelsi security clearances for most planets; I know Command, and Juju's parents, appreciate you very much. But we're facing serious threats of technological infiltration. I can't have you calling here again until we've had tech install our protocol."

"Not a pro'lem, sweet'eart," said the lizard. Her human

companion in onyx armor still said nothing; Cinta did not think he had ever heard the Ebon Shadow speak. "What's the job?"

"It's a sabotage. Maybe an assassination." To the little girl, "Juju, you're dismissed. Transfer the call to me and go to bed."

Juju dropped her head as she slid her palm across the robot's palm, and shot Cinta a hard look as she made for the entrance.

"Juju, they will still let you call them, with supervision—that is better than nothing," Cinta said, trotting after her to the poly-merwall.

"I know," the ten-year-old grumbled. "I'm not mad at you. Mostly." Her bony, long human fingers slipped into the fur on his shoulder; she scratched him and sighed. "Sucks, we can't just have normal things."

"I know." Cinta reached up; she bowed her head for him to ruffle her hair, and then left.

Cinta turned to see the commander blinking at him as she talked to the bounty hunters. Her long violet tail curled around under her in that small tank, almost touching her front fins. Ichthians usually covered kilometers of underwater territory every day: Commander Blawble had to possess special skills and *unorthodox* passion to deploy here in extremely inhumane, cramped, and dangerous conditions for her species. In such a small tank, even the slightest change in water quality could kill her. Even a Merperson or Burburan biped, who could at least breathe air, would struggle with a deployment here, and Cinta had never seen either. Loneliness would be a constant food for someone like Commander Blawble, the only one here of her kind.

No one came here without sacrifice.

"I hate war," Cinta muttered, mustering his resume speech as he trotted back to the commander's table. He would get on this sabotage mission, and he would destroy whatever it took to let Juju go home.

CHAPTER FORTY-TWO

Jei

GROWEN SOUTH CENTRAL DIDN'T DESERVE THE SPARKLE OF THE stars over its quiet fields.

Mera and I waited most of the night over a patch of earth where Mera insisted she felt strong signals from either Lem or Diebol. "There's got to be an entrance, somewhere," she said. "It's an open field—there's no way we won't see them come out." She stomped around on the grass like a puppy preparing a nest for itself, and sat down in the hollow she'd made—I guess growing up in the city no one beat her over the head with lessons about not disturbing her surroundings. I smiled.

She yanked her bamboo staff off her belt with an annoyed sigh and dropped it in the grass like it stung her.

"What's wrong with your mace?" I asked, eyeing her slender hand for burns I couldn't see in the dark.

"I've been having problems with the neodymium core over-heating," she sighed. "And I don't think I should—I'm not straining the crystal lattice *that* much, I mean, I can barely em-pull, and of course the electrons in the metal are free to move. But for some reason using it for meditation has become a little difficult, and it overheats after I fight, or track, or really do anything em-related."

"May I?" I asked. She hesitated, and then handed it over. She was right—it was quite warm. "It's probably nothing wrong with the core itself," I said. "More likely the biocovering's somehow interfering with the neodymium's magnetic properties. Can I open it?"

She nodded, and I took out my pocketknife to slice into the false bamboo—really a layer of piezoelectric sensors triggered by Mera's genetic code to turn off the cutting heat wherever her own DNA touched the staff. This layer prevented these maces from burning their wielders; only the owner could hold a neodymium mace when active. They literally held a piece of us inside them—suddenly, with Mera watching me, I felt like she was trusting me to cut through her skin.

It didn't take me long to adjust the sensor inside for her. We alternated sleeping while we waited for our prey, first her, then me, and lying with my head in her lap, I had no nightmares.

Let me in, she said in my dreams as her finger traced my temple. *I let you in, now let me into this room.*

But in my mind, I still lay with my body across the threshold of that carved door that Njande lived behind, and Mera did not cross the boundary I had drawn.

"Sun's coming, Jei." Mera's soft hum roused me from sleep before the last handful of stars could blink away. "He's on the move."

I scrambled to my feet, fingers and pants stained in the rough broken grass. She crouched, a hand on the earth, and then leapt into a run. "He's moving fast!" she said. "I didn't know we had an underground tram system?"

My boots barely touched ground as I sprinted alongside her. The sensation of blood and air flooding my chest felt good, and I could go faster—the predatory sensation of *chase* flared my nostrils. "Are we keeping up?" I asked.

"Not in the slightest," she breathed. "I think it's going toward the center of the base. Shyte, it's going to be so crowded there."

"They probably have formation soon, too," I breathed back, throwing out my arms to catch a little more delicious wind. I felt rested and charged, but the timing didn't look great: formation meant crowds, as all the lower ranking soldiers stood in line to get orders for the day—an ancient military discipline I knew Diebol despised in the era of modern communication.

Mera swerved a hard right—"Oh thank goodness," she said. "It's going toward those hangar bays instead."

Uh oh. That made sense: Diebol traveled between planets often, and I could imagine Lem maybe wanted to leave this one, too. We needed to hurry.

But we'd never catch up on foot. Mera was underestimating because she wasn't Alpinoan: unlike on her home planet, here the flat purity of the prairie allowed for a clear visual at extreme distances. Sure, we could *see* the giant white tubes where the ships parked and took off, but I knew from experience the buildings appeared much smaller than they should. "That's like twenty minutes away by land-runner," I said, stopping her with my hand on her shoulder. I nodded to the barracks building nearest us: it was just starting to glow with square patches of pale white and yellow light through closed polymerwall windows as the silhouettes of soldiers rose for morning duties. "We need a vehicle."

"Oh—" Mera breathed hard, doubling over to put her hands on her knees. "I'm stupid."

"No, you just thought there'd be an opening closer." I trotted over to the side of the building, keeping my body low in case one of the windows suddenly went from translucent to transparent. Mera followed close behind. There were air-riders parked out front, but of course I didn't have any of the DNA keys necessary to pilot one.

"I think I can hot-wire it," Mera said.

"What? How? That's technically impossible!"

"Hold on. Stay here!" Mera held her palm back toward me as she crept around the corner and dashed to the nearest vehicle.

I tucked my back against the cool surface of the corner, and held my flayer pistol in both hands, ready to cover her. For some reason my heartrate seemed higher than what was normal for me in combat—the thought of someone coming out the door and hurting her tightened my grip and focused my vision. As she fumbled with the nearest air-rider, I was beginning to see her clearly, for what she was—and realized with a strange calm that I liked her anyway.

Mera

Mera could not, in fact, hot-wire an air-rider; she didn't even have the slightest idea how to clean an engine, or troubleshoot her computer back home. She just had DNA keys to any Growen vehicle she wanted.

She bit her lip, opening the front hatch of the air-rider as if she planned to do something inside it. Oh goodness, she was getting sloppy. She'd slipped up, a moment ago—said something about whether "we" have tram systems, "we," the Growen. She hoped, however, that as Jei was letting her touch him more, she could drown any residual suspicions he might have now under a flood of pleasant endorphins later …

You're such a gross person, Mera grimaced to herself. It hurt, what she planned to do to him—that he was starting to trust her.

Fire flared across her chest. How dare he? How dare he trust her? She suddenly hated him for allowing himself the injury. Fine, then, he deserved what came next, for daring to act so foolish! It was survival of the fittest—he knew that! He shouldn't, he *shouldn't* trust her—

—Even if she'd saved his life, healed him, and comforted him through one of the toughest experiences of his life. *You hit him when he's vulnerable, and now you're going to use him. You snake.*

Mera didn't hate herself for her weakness, she realized at this most inopportune time, but for her strength.

Agh, did this look real enough? She slipped her palm around to the compuscreen windshield and turned on the vehicle. It would have to do. She didn't have time: if Diebol left the planet, she may not get another chance to have Jei kill him.

Jei would be happy, she insisted to herself. She would protect him—she would let him fire up just enough to kill Diebol, but not so much that he destroyed the base and cast doubts on her ability to control him safely. He would live, then, and no one would harm him ever again. She would make him happy. He deserved happiness, right?

Right.

Njandejara was speaking in full specifics, as clear as day, to Jei Bereens. Warning signs and details flashed before the human over and over; through a complex butterfly effect of weather and nutrition, Njande even manipulated the boy's neurotransmitters to push that suspicious sense of unease, and, when that didn't work, he actually whispered into Jei's mind.

But the dimensional rifts were too thick, as thick as the human's closed, fused skull. Breaking the rift required a touch from both sides, and in his pain, Jei had stopped trying. Njande did everything short of shoving his fist through the cracking time-space continuum to force the understanding into Jei—

No, he could not do that.

If Njande's finger made contact, Jei would die, still too weak and human for that kind of radioactive touch. The "tissue" of an energy being beyond their event horizon—the kind of unstable energy that could spark Big Bangs—would instantly disintegrate anything it touched in the corrupted, decaying realm that held Njande's friends captive. Their dimension itself was doomed by a broken thermodynamic law, and in order to rescue them he needed to enter it, but he could not enter it without destroying it, but if he did not enter it he could not rescue them, but—such was the circular Paradox in which Njandejara was trapped by love, and, in a much smaller manifestation, such was the Paradox that kept Jei from hearing over and over the direct and indirect warnings screaming at him.

With enough guilt and kindness, however, perhaps Morda would hear instead.

Lem

But that wave form will not collapse.

Lem did not understand the heartbroken snippet she heard from Njande suddenly as she rode beside Diebol through his underground tunnels on his self-powered electromagnetic tram. Holding the mantras and spells of the Being over herself was becoming a habit, a tapestry interspersed with new threads and thoughts she didn't know she knew, a beautiful silver lining to the threat of the Accuser hunting her down.

But Lem was having trouble thinking of anything at the moment except Diebol's left boot, flush against her right one, as she leaned as far away from him as possible and gripped the chain by her waist. She struggled to balance on the single dangling stair, one foot on top of the other as Diebol's em-pull shot them through the tunnels.

"So I'm being you, leading them to the ship, flashing my face through the window; you're handling the technical part, setting up the takeoff, bringing me the hiding vest—then we both go our separate ways, right?" Lem shouted, summarizing the plan for the umpteenth time.

"I'm hurt, Lem, it's almost as if you don't trust me," Diebol cracked back, smiling. "Come on, this is your stop."

Lem scrambled to dismount, stumbled—fell—Diebol's hand shot out, and gripped hers. She steadied, and stood still, her heart quiet and unafraid, but her trauma-bathed mind pulsing and fluttering at the rough skin tight around hers—

If we don't hate each other, what are we?

"Aren't you supposed to collect my DNA?" Diebol asked. "I

imagine if you need a blood sample or something you'd already have spoken up, so—"

"I got you." Lem nodded, reaching up her other hand behind her ear.

Diebol

As his own face washed over Lem Benzaran's features like a distorting mold, Diebol let go of her hand, and stepped down from his self-made tram to lean on the wall beside her. A hundred snide comments leapt to his lips—"that's an improvement," or "I hate you more now," or "I always knew there was a reason I liked you"—they were all inane, and he said nothing.

It wasn't like looking in a mirror—it was far more unsettling, because a mirror didn't keep its eyes open while you blinked. A mirror didn't wear a bloodstained jacket when your own was clean. And a mirror didn't stare at you with a *biological* fear that never left no matter how much the soul inside no longer cringed.

"I'm sorry," he shrugged. He'd always done what he needed to do, what he believed was right. He couldn't stop the consequences in this mechanical world—he could only try. "Your exit is up here." He pointed at the trap door above them. "You'd better give me that jacket—I think that's Johnson's blood on it still. We don't want questions."

Diebol 2.0 handed over the jacket without a word—just a snide little smile. For a moment, the original Diebol feared he'd made a mistake—that somehow she would double cross him—but of course that smile had that effect on people. He knew that. It was his own smile. Perhaps it was *because* he knew his own smile that the thought of betrayal crossed his mind.

He was relying on the fact that it was not, in fact, himself, but Lem Benzaran under that face.

CHAPTER FORTY-THREE

Lem

LOOKING FOR ALL THE WORLD LIKE THE ENEMY HIMSELF, FROM HIS shimmering green eyes and ashen axinite skin down to his mace hanging from her belt, Lem exited Diebol's secret tunnel into a cleaning closet. The poetic justice of the young Growen leader skulking around janitorial closets was not lost on her. She lifted the floorboard above her head and scrambled out next to a few deactivated trash-bots and a mop. She tip-toed to the poly-merwall—

He said he picked his exits in areas with poor camera visibility. I guess he would have access to that information ... Still, she really didn't trust him not to lead her into some kind of trap. She glanced at her wrist, suddenly missing her chronometer for the time: he'd said she had about five minutes before that hallway became full of soldiers. She leaned her ear against the polymer-wall, hearing no one ... how did she *know*, though?

Njande—born of wind and fire, I am wind, she hoped, slipping through the goo.

The hallway was dark. "He said to take a left," Lem muttered, squaring her shoulders into a relaxed swagger with purpose. Diebol had this little dip to his walk—not deep enough to lose military presence, but enough to show he, not some arbitrary dogma, made his decisions. Not spoiled or entitled, though. More of a knees-and-back walk, than hips. His rest poses, *those* were all hips.

She reached the end of the hallway and took the stairs down as soldiers began to pour out of their rooms, adjusting belts, checking insignia, and taking final stock of boots for possible inspection. She was already outside before the first one caught up with her with a respectful, bright good morning that reminded her of Banks.

Agh, poor Banks—that whole thing made her mad. She was so filking sick and tired of—

The wind blows wherever it pleases, Lem recited internally, returning the soldier's good morning and focusing. She waved to another gaggle of soldiers gathering outside, and swung onto the nearest air-rider. She leaned in as she took off, swishing her hands up the windshield in repeated strokes to force the vehicle into a few showy loop-de-loops as she rocketed across the court-yard. She needed to be seen, and felt, to lure Jei and Mera into watching a ship take off with her and Diebol "in" it. Meanwhile Diebol would continue underground, as planned, to meet her at the hangar bay, to bring her the vest to hide herself from Mera's tracking.

You hear its sounds, but you don't know where it comes from, or where it goes. She leaned right, and zipped onto the main thor-oughfare.

An air-rider engine revved behind her with a whir that built into a nearing crescendo Lem didn't like at all. That sounded like someone speeding up in pursuit. Lem glanced back over her shoulder—

"You're early," she called to Mera. The other woman was hunched over, pressing her palms into her windshield with speed-limit-breaking intensity. Jei was *standing* on the seat behind her, lowering into a crouch like a feathered cat about to pounce, one hand outstretched toward Lem as they gained—

Lem was sorely tempted to let them get close so she could

shock their engine, but at this speed? Nah, they'd spin out and die. *Also, I'm Diebol. Diebol doesn't do that.*

Shyte, Diebol didn't do any of the things she did, when it came to em-abilities. She wouldn't be able to really fight without blowing her cover—and they *needed* to believe both herself and Diebol boarded this ship. Shyte, why did she have to play both parts?

She knew why, of course: setting up an autopilot launch with an expensive ship on a military base required a bit of precisely-timed log-management. If anything, she worried Diebol wouldn't have enough time, even though he'd been up most of the night preparing ... Lem pressed forward, urging the air-rider faster, lowering her chest close to the air-rider's metal hull to try to diffract any em-pulls from Jei into the conductive material's sea of electrons—

Nope, stomach gone, hello nausea. Her air-rider suddenly swerved straight up into the air, flipped, and dipped into a nose-dive toward the ground. Lem threw both hands toward the dust road—no! She felt that weight of a thousand suns pushing back against her shoulders as Jei hurled her air-rider into the road —*agh* with a loud cry she managed to right the air-rider just as it skidded across the ground with a burst of yellow sparks so fierce her own sparks didn't matter at all and *bloodseas up, up, up, go up*!

What the galaxy was happening to Jei? How did he suddenly get to where he could ignore metal diffraction, throw vehicles, rip ceilings open, *shyte* there shouldn't be any kind of biochem-ical reaction in one human body strong enough for this!

"I'd love to get on your workout regimen, Bereens," she shouted over her shoulder. She needed that, she needed to feign Diebol's cool head right now.

Growen air-riders and land-runners swarmed around them now, firing on Jei and Mera as everyone's favorite leader raced them down the causeway. *Don't get hurt, please don't get hurt* echoed in her brain alongside *don't kill me, you idiot*; Lem's air-rider gained some height and distance on her pursuers—through the corner of her eye she could see Jei's staff spinning in the air around him and Mera, deflecting fiery colorful oxidizer cartridges—oh, shyte, deflecting them toward Lem. Lem pulled Diebol's bamboo staff off her belt with trepidation, praying that the DNA masking that allowed her to walk through Diebol's polymerwalls was strong enough to protect her from the cutting heat on his weapon, too. She held the staff out from her body and slid her thumb over the activating ridge—

Nope, it was searing hot. It denatured the projector's enzyme mist immediately; there just wasn't enough of Diebol on her fingers to protect her. Lem switched it back off before it could burn her.

Shyte, so she also couldn't use a weapon. Her own violent crimson mace would give her away. She'd seen Diebol get around this problem in the past by levitating other people's active maces with controlled em-holds, but again—not something she could do without sparks.

Fortunately, it sounded from the traffic and gunfire like Jei was busy. The hangar bay loomed close by now; Lem glanced behind her over her shoulder again—

Hoo shyte! What was happening? Jei was standing on the back of Mera's air-rider, literally flipping a land-runner over his head with a wave of his arm. Mera screamed in what looked like legitimate surprise as the vehicle crashed beside them—

What.

Lem shook her head. Alright, hangar bay here. Diebol said it was the third one, in the row to the right—

Lem heard Mera crying out Jei's name; another backward glance, and Lem saw Mera driving one-handed while streeeetching to place her palm on Jei's back as she struggled not to crash ... Something seemed odd about that—why would *that touch* matter more than driving—?

Not my business. Lem yanked her air-rider to a stop centimeters from the ivory hangar bay wall, practically diving off it through the sloping polymerwall. *Diebol, you better have my hiding vest ready!*

Mera

She couldn't control him. He was going to break everything. He was going to be killed if he wouldn't obey her. *Stop stop stop!* She wanted to scream, beg him, please—

Be calm you worthless simp, Mera ordered herself as a car literally flew over her head, her air-rider threatened to spin out of control, and flayer cartridges whizzed around her ears. She needed pheromone to stop this. *Be calm!*

There were three emergency responses for mammals: fight, flight, or freeze.

Enough fear could force muscles to relax as if dead.

If Mera couldn't will herself to calm down, perhaps she could terrify herself into freezing?

She remembered her coach, on Retrack City, with his fist raised.

A burst of pheromone so strong Mera herself felt woozy seemed to slow down the world. She saw herself as if watching a film, driving with one hand, reaching back toward Jei's spine with the other—

The rough cloth of his tunic brushed her fingertips, then in the flapping wind she found skin.

Rest, she ordered.

He stumbled back against her, gripping her shoulder suddenly as they swerved to a stop outside the third hangar bay on the right. A strange look crossed his face as Mera swung herself off the air-rider, and Jei dismounted behind her, misstepping as if suddenly drunk. Mera grabbed his hand and pulled him through the polymerwall after her, hoping that the pile-up he'd caused back on the road behind them would slow their pursuers down long enough to let them hide.

They burst into a darkened hangar bay; rows of ships lay before them, all quiet.

Only a single cockpit light remained on, in a Maggot ship in the far back corner. Above that ship, the hangar bay ceiling hung open to allow takeoff, admitting a rectangle of sunlight onto the Maggot like a spotlight on a stage.

All this, Mera saw in an instant as she and Jei stumbled through the polymerwall into the hangar bay. He looked at her with wrinkled brow and disappointed eyes, one hand on his back where she'd touched him. "I'm so sorry," Mera gasped.

"Why would you do that?" he asked.

"You've gotta save some for Diebol, Jei," she said—whimpering for effect. "The soldiers back there charged you up, but if you take them all out, then what? I already said it before: this has to be one and done. We can't afford to fail." *Also, I will get in huge trouble if you destroy everything!* "I was hoping to be at least a little more incognito!"

"I can take this whole place down," Jei said. He raised a hand, and a clear bubble of some sort burst in a spherical wave through the room, rippling through the walls. Some kind of forcefield, to keep the other soldiers out? "I don't need to *rest.*" There was some other meaning when he spat the word. He raised another hand and crunched his fist—the Maggot in the spotlight bent in half with a screech of metal.

Diebol dove out the window with a yelp, rolling on the concrete.

A yelp? Mera hummed—

The shape was all wrong. The shadow that returned to her ear contradicted the picture before her eyes.

This was not Diebol.

CHAPTER FORTY-FOUR

Lem

WHERE WAS DIEBOL WHEN YOU NEEDED HIM?

Wire and shards of metal snowed down around Lem as she rolled across the concrete floor of the hangar bay. The cement impact stung her shoulder blades—she righted herself, staring into the wreckage—

There was supposed to be a trap door into Diebol's tunnel. Somewhere in the far-right corner? She'd planned to use it when the decoy ship took off, but now that decoy ship lay in rubble, and that rubble, engine parts and armor plates, blocked her escape.

Mera stalked toward her, purple mace spinning in a lily pattern. Lem leapt to her feet; she stepped back into the shadows, her hand in Diebol's long leather jacket, fingers curled around the handle of his pistol as she flicked the safety past kill, past stun, to shock. She paced backward, stepping on her toes around this sparking control panel, that leaking engine fluid, trying to find the loose bit of trap door floor …

Well, this is all a disaster, she wanted to say; instead, she channeled Diebol's history of attempted recruitment with Mera, and reached for a bad memory to throw her off her game. "Your mace work is getting better, Mera," Diebol remarked, sinister grin half-hidden under his hood. "I'm still accepting recruits."

"I'd rather die," Mera retorted, cute little chin up-thrust in the air.

"Leave her alone." Jei threw out a hand, yanking Lem out of the shadows—it felt like her spine was jerking through her belly as she flew through the air—Lem fired the pistol and an em-push to break free—

The electric arc from the gun missed, but hid Lem's em-push sparks as she broke free from Jei's pull with a midair flip. She fired again, landing back in her corner, still searching for that trap door—"Jealous boyfriend, much?" Lem laughed in Diebol. "We were just talking."

"She doesn't want to talk to you." Jei spun a metal panel in the air before him, levitating it like a shield to divert the electrical charges from Lem's gun. Lem felt the pistol trying to leave her hand—she em-pulled back—still her boots tapped the cement under her, searching for that loose grout …

Sharp pain in her back, and then a blinding flash of light! Lem had lost track of Mera, and as a cold metal knife-tip thrust through her skin, Lem's electrical system discharged an instinctual shock—Mera fell back, clutching the knife, as Lem's hand dashed to her own right flank.

The blood was minimal, and Lem could breathe. *Knife didn't pass rib.* Her shock had protected her—*I think?* There was no time to check. The purple mace smashed down—Lem stumbled back over a broken chair-cushion—Mera's next swing crushed the pistol right out of Lem's hand—

Lem never finished her stumble. Instead of falling backward, she found herself suspended midair, frozen, hanging with her arms out in Jei's massive electromagnetic hold.

Was there any point anymore? Lem could cry. Jei stood, in front of her, his head tilted to the side: "I didn't know you could throw sparks, Jared," he said.

"You're not the only one allowed to level up, Jei," Lem answered, mocking his inflection. Shyte, what was she supposed to do now? Diebol had clearly abandoned her. He was probably watching somewhere with great amusement … but no, he needed Mera to think he'd left, right? And he still benefited if Lem could take out Sterba—

Sterba.

Sharp, glowing blue eyes flashed under Lem's eyelids.

Oh no.

Hide me Njande, Lem begged. Oh, shyte. Oh shyte, why had Diebol told her the name, why why why—should she fight, should she hide, should she shock, should she not? *I'm a loyal Growen soldier I am I am I am I'm Diebol* but would thinking that get *him* caught for their conspiracy, but did that matter but—

Lem struggled, trying to start an em-push to break the hold but with her mind all over the place she couldn't focus. Jei turned her in the air before him now in cold inspection, one hand outstretched toward her, and the other held straight up toward the ceiling, palm flat as if holding up the sky. Her body floated down to him now, immobile, face to face with the dying embers in his eyes.

"What are you doing to the people outside?" Lem whispered —Lem, not Diebol, listening to the shouts, the muffled shots, the thuds that shook the outside of the building—

Jei smiled. "Oh, Lem." He reached around behind her ear.

"No, don't!"

His warm fingers found the strips of the disguise projectors.

"Jei—"

He ripped them off. Lem choked on a scream as the millions of microscopic needles yanked out of her bloodstream and the adhesive tore away from her skin. "What I wanna know," Jei was saying with a voice as cold as liquid nitrogen. "Is how you became such good friends that you not only *touched* him, but he also gave you his mace?"

"Shyte, the bounty hunter did say those would hurt coming off." Lem laughed through clenched teeth. She strained for an electromagnetic surge to break his hold. She felt sweat bursting from every pore, her belly burned—shyte, was she frying her insides instead of breaking free?

"Where is he?" Jei asked. "I can tell he's close." She was so warm. She stopped, she breathed—everything cooled down like a breeze—okay, surge again, try again—

"He should be in this room," Mera groaned. Groaned? Out of the corner of her eye, Lem could see the smaller woman leaning against the wall, gripping her head.

"Is she okay?" Lem asked. "She looks like her brain's imploding. Shyte, is your supercharge hurting her?"

"She's just manipulating you," Mera coughed, crouching almost in the fetal position. "Make her tell you where Diebol is, or we're screwed."

"Jei, what are you doing to the people outside?" Lem snapped.

"Using them as fuel." Jei shrugged. He tightened his fist, and Lem suddenly felt something closing around her ribs. "Your concern is touching, Lem. Wonder why your own family and friends didn't merit the same." Shyte, it was too tight. Lem just needed to close her eyes, think *harder*—she squeezed her eyelids shut—

The blazing blue eyes lived there now. *Where are you?* They asked.

Lem blinked open; a gasp pushed through her lips. She clenched her teeth, trying to focus, pushing, pushing for a surge—

"Where is Diebol?" Jei repeated.

"Right here." An electric shock fired from somewhere on the left.

As Jei suddenly powered down, Lem's repressed blast rocketed through the room.

Oh shyte.

She heard *everyone* cry out in pain, and through the near-blinding sparking air Lem finally saw her trap door.

Diebol stood waist-deep in it with both hands on a flayer pistol, elbows steadied on the ground, and chest partially hidden by a chunk of broken cannon. "Right this way, darling!" he called with only the slightest edge of pain from her static shock in his voice. Lem scrambled toward him; the young Stygge grimaced, and ducked into the tunnel.

Lem barely had time to pull the metal door shut after her and lock it before she heard Jei smashing in from the other side. "Filk you," she hissed to Diebol through clenched teeth as they ran. "You just wanted him to see me as you. That's the whole point of this."

"While I did enjoy that, unfortunately, no, you and I still have work to do," Diebol answered, waving her into a side passage lit by a single glow-orb on the earthen wall. "I have the vest ready to hide you from Mera's tracking. You'll go straight to Her—I'll deal with them."

Even over the sounds of her own boots on the firm clay Lem could hear Mera and Jei breaking into the tunnel after them. Lem was trembling. She didn't know if it was from her surge, or just anger. "You never wanted to go confront Bricandor," she said. "You just wanted to see Jei go off, and beat him at his strongest."

"Do you really think I'm so petty, and care so little for the safety and well-being of my men?" Diebol snarled back, turning another dirt corner into a small, bare room that, to Lem, looked like a dead end. "You should know better than that." He held up a huge, clunky vest covered in panels and wires. "No, you were too slow. This is your fault, and technically, you have failed our deal. But fortunately for you, there is me."

Lem slipped into the room after him and grabbed the vest, yanking it over her head. Running bootsteps on bare earth, nearer, nearer … she couldn't get the back of the vest to close … shyte, she didn't want to leave these three to fight and kill each other, but she needed to get to Her! "Are you leading him down here to fight away from the soldiers, then …?" she asked, breathless.

"I am leading them further into the tunnels, yes. I'll have to improvise after that. Here, the vest must be closed to work. Turn around." He turned her by her shoulders. "You double back and steal a ship. These are the coordinates to Her location—" He stuffed a piece of paper into the pocket of her jacket. "Plus the door code to the ship, and the entry code to the space station, when you get there." She saw his hand reach around to yank his staff off her belt. "I'll be needing this."

"Is it good, am I good to go?" Lem heard voices over the footsteps now.

"Almost." Diebol whirled her back around to face him. "I've enjoyed working with you, Lem," he said, reaching over her shoulder to something in the wall—she felt a click on the left shoulder of the vest—

Oh no.

"Don't move," Diebol whispered in her ear.

"It's a bomb. The vest is actually a bomb," Lem realized. "I'm an idiot."

"You had very little choice," Diebol soothed. "Oh, and electrocution will set off the vest, so I wouldn't recommend any electromagnetic stunts whatsoever. I also wouldn't recommend pulling away from the wall you're hooked to. Lots of ways to explode."

But—she—*why* such an elaborate ruse, though, because if he wanted her dead, then why hadn't he killed her when—but he'd given her the codes to Her, so why—she thought—

Lem could only watch with an open mouth as Diebol spun away from her with a bow.

"Oh, and you have ten minutes before it goes off on its own," he added.

"Before what goes off?" Jei was in the doorway; the glow-light cast shadows across the side of his face as he lowered his head like a bull about to charge.

"The explosives in her vest," Diebol said, sidestepping to protect his back as he waved in Lem's direction. "Obviously, any electric disturbance will set them off. Fortunately, it's a sequence you will remember well."

Jei stepped into the room and without hesitation dashed to Lem's side. Diebol slipped past him out of the room with the snide grin of a future Supreme Leader who knew something everyone else didn't.

"Mera, I'm going to need you to keep him busy," Jei called, his fingers flicking across the wires connecting the different panels on Lem's chest.

Mera's voice from the hallway was punctuated with grunts and the whirring clank of hot staffs smashing against each other. "Why can't *I* defuse the bomb and you keep him busy?" she squeaked back.

"Because you don't even know where the engine of an air-rider is located," he snapped. "I know what you're doing, Mera, but I also know you want him dead, so filking make it happen."

The sounds of fighting moved away from them, down the hallway. Sweat dripped from Jei's nose; Lem found herself holding her breath and realized she still hadn't stopped trembling. Her flank burned where Mera had stabbed it, and soon she realized through heaving shoulders and shuddering breaths that her face was wet with something besides sweat. *Jei, don't die. Please don't die.* He unclipped something on her shoulder—something began to beep—he leaned in closer to her, one hand on a wire by her waist, another on a wire on her other shoulder, and counted to three before yanking both wires at the same time. The beeping stopped; he counted to himself, tapping panels in pairs in a pattern apparently well-known to Bricandor's childhood captives.

"Isn't this the part where you're supposed to tell me to leave so I don't blow up," he muttered.

"I'm sorry, Jei." Her voice was wavering. She swallowed, and tried to keep talking, but—she looked up at the ceiling, trying to hold back the sob she could feel in her throat. She swallowed again. "Shyte," she whispered, blinking hard ... stupid, blue-eyed witch still in there ... she opened her eyes and breathed. "Jei, I have to live," she whispered. "I have to—I've been trying to stop what happened at Fort Jehu since before it happened."

"Like you didn't help cause it, giving up the EMP codes." His jaw clenched as he worked.

"That's not how She gets in, you idiot," Lem hissed.

"I thought you were undercover. I really did, and I really want to think it," Jei said, behind her now. More tapping—more wire-plucking—"I thought maybe I could explain away the fact that when you opened our EMP shield, you got tankers killed. You did give me your helmet, after all. But it's more what you *didn't* do. You were there, when Diebol went after the Hiding Place. Don't try to lie about it. You *did* save his life. Maybe he doesn't even know it, but I do. You knew Fort Jehu was going to happen? *Then where were you when it did?*"

"Jei, it's not like that, I can't—"

"You can't tell me, right," he said. "The funny thing is, you're a lot like Njande, actually. Always the thing I hated about him most. No explanations, we just have to hope he's somewhere, doing something he can't tell us for some reason. If you really were undercover, couldn't you have told me *months* ago?"

"Jei," Lem growled. "You literally have a portal in your head to the bad guy. I couldn't tell you *shyte*."

Jei laughed, in front of her again now. He didn't look at her; his eyes stayed on the patterns his fingers traced as he unplugged a wire by her knee, another by her neck. "Did you know Cinta doesn't even believe in you?" he asked in the voice of her Accuser. "He told me you're supposed to destroy the universe, not save it. He told it to you backward to keep you from making it a self-fulfilling prophecy." He ripped a wire off by her stomach, his teeth clenched. "The person you're saving us from is yourself."

Lem couldn't breathe. She couldn't—she blinked—"You're lying. Cinta didn't say that," she croaked.

"Am I?" He looked up at her through the sweaty hair falling in his face.

He wasn't.

CHAPTER FORTY-FIVE

Mera

"MY PUPPET IS SO MUCH MORE WELL-BEHAVED THAN YOURS," Diebol quipped, throwing a blow down toward Mera's shoulder. She blocked, and slid backward, glancing at her wristband. Diebol had said explosion in what, ten minutes? She needed to get Jei out of there. She ducked under Diebol's arm and dashed back toward the room.

Her hair jerked on her scalp—*ow!*—her back slammed against his hot chest as he yanked her to him. "Where are you going?" he asked, in a voice so gratingly cheerful Mera wanted nothing more than to see him cry. "I still have you for the rest of this dance."

"You can't kill him. I know you want to, but you can't." Mera elbowed him in the stomach, knocked his staff out of his hand, and bent over to flip him over her shoulder—

He caught himself with both feet on the walls and both hands gripping her shoulders before his back could slam into the ground; he smiled up at her, innocently.

"Why not?" he asked. "Technically, I'm doing your job, right, if there's a bomb in there—that takes care of both of them, right? Sterba's safe?"

"You can't kill him!" she screamed, hurling an em-push with

both hands to throw him down. He twisted his hands in front of him as he fell, as if catching her em-push—

Her back hit the ceiling with a painful thud. She broke the push with a slice of her hand and landed in the dirt on her belly.

"Ooh, I have an idea." Diebol crouched into view and tapped a mocking finger on his lips. "What if you scream for help, and we see who he chooses, Lem or you? That would save his life, wouldn't it?"

Mera snarled and threw a claw at his face, em-pulling his eyes toward her fingernails. He grabbed her wrist with an approving grin. "Oh wait, except he wouldn't choose you. No one really chooses you, do they?"

"He believes in me. He thinks I can take you," she hissed.

"After Benzaran almost beat you one-handed? I saw the video. Nah." Diebol stood, dragging her to her feet with him to —*oof!*—kick her in the belly. She clenched her teeth and brought a boot of her own up between his legs. He blocked with a downward palm and a laugh. "Prove me wrong," he said, pulling her close to him. His hoarse voice blew hot air by her ear: "Scream."

Mera clenched her teeth. He had fingers all over her skin—

Hurt, she ordered his nerves.

Diebol's chin jerked upward as he steeled himself against obvious agony, every muscle in his neck twitching and limbs suddenly stiff. He tried to unwind his fingers from her wrist —*Stay*, she ordered.

His throat made a sound like coughing. *Look at me*, Mera demanded, ready to see that smile wiped from his face.

He looked—and he was laughing.

Mera jumped back from the insanity in his eyes, her heart pounding.

"Oh, no, is it over already?" Diebol asked hoarsely, stepping after her, the grin widening until she thought his cheeks would tear. She swung her mace at him to keep him away—he threw up a palm and her weapon stopped centimeters from his hand. She tried to pull it back—he pulled, too—no, she wouldn't get close to that monster! She shrunk back, letting go of her weapon before she could think to stop herself.

Diebol hurled Mera's mace into the wall behind him. "Of course he wouldn't choose you," he croaked, still shuddering off the last waves of pain as he walked toward her. "Because for all her flaws, Lem's always doing something she believes in. She's a real person. You don't even know who you are—it changes by the lover, doesn't it?" He walked toward her with his arms open, as if daring her to come at him. "You're literally a fantasy."

She threw up her hand to em-pull her weapon into the back of his head—he ducked, and let it slam back into her hand.

"Then again, you never had a chance to become a person, did you? The dancing troupe on Retrack City made sure of that, if I remember. What was it your coach used to say, again?"

You will become whatever I tell you to become. If a client wants it, you give it to them.

Diebol didn't have to say the words to scream them in her head. Mera snarled, trying to wipe away the memory by slicing off his face—

His mace flew off the floor to block. "Tick, tock ..." he tilted his head from side to side, still advancing. "How many minutes has it been?"

No! She swung again; he blocked again, and with an em-pull too strong for her to escape dragged her throat to his hand, knocking her mace aside with his as she flew toward him. She tried to swing the glowing ball back toward his head—he pinned her weapon against the tunnel wall with his. "Never forget who saved you from your past," he hissed. "You may think he cares about you, but real love doesn't come from what you've got in your fingertips." There were two cries of pain down the hallway. "Aha! Let's go see how well I did your job."

Lem

"Then why are you trying to save me?" Lem hissed, choking on withheld tears as Jei continued untangling his way across her vest of explosives. "If I'm this super-villain you think I am, why aren't you just letting me blow up?"

"Because this is what I do, Lem," he said. "I don't know why. Maybe I owe it to you to bring you to justice. Maybe I'm just running out the clock because I'm done living in a universe where all the people I let into my head turn out to be evil. Maybe there's just nothing you can do that will make me want to let you die." He took a deep breath. "This should do it," he said, and yanked the cord from the wall.

He was repaid for his successful bomb defusing; the vest suddenly burst open, spraying something caustic over both of them. Lem cried out as Jei seized and collapsed to the ground; as she fell beside him, she saw a wall of bars pierce through the ground and into the ceiling, slamming shut over the doorway.

Then she lost consciousness.

Mera

Mera coughed as Diebol released her neck to hurl her into the earthen cell with the two fallen Paradox Warriors. "Check his pulse. Sometimes these things overdose," Diebol ordered.

She did, her vision *blurring* with pure hatred. Her hand shook, but she could still feel Jei's neck beating against her fingertips.

"Alive?" Diebol asked.

She nodded. "I thought you wanted him dead," she spat.

"I want you to prove you can do what you said you could," he said. "And while you do, you live here." He threw a hand into the cage, and unceremoniously em-pulled Lem Benzaran's unconscious body out of it. The bars slammed shut, floor to ceiling, after him.

"And her?" Mera snarled, rubbing her own neck to get the Diebol feeling off herself.

"Sterba wants to meet her. At this point, Jei's beaten her down enough that she's no longer a threat." He gazed down at the girl draped over his arm. "She's pretty, isn't she?"

"You're a creep," Mera hissed.

"Not really. Unlike you, I can recognize something is wonderful without being so overcome by it that I take it." He shrugged. His face grew merry as he turned back to Mera. "Did you really think Bricandor was going to let you kill me? Or that Sterba could trust you to protect her, after you crumbled so easily in the interrogation center?"

Mera didn't answer. She folded her arms and looked away, down to Jei's unconscious face. His jaw open, head tilted back— he *looked* dead.

"Here are the rules," Diebol said in a sterner tone. "I don't quite share your free range sensitivities when it comes to our enemies. So he'll be shocked every hour on the hour to make sure he stays powered down. I've also made sure you're both far enough underground that he shouldn't be able to register anyone here but you. No super-power-ups, no dramatic escapes. You will submit to regular blood tests as you practice on him so we can analyze your pheromone and put it to better use in mass production. When we're done, who lives depends on how well you do. Understood?"

"Understood," she repeated. This time, her downcast eyes weren't an act.

CHAPTER FORTY-SIX

Lem

LEM AWOKE IN A MEDITATION CHAMBER SURROUNDED BY BLUE. The deep blue, searing hot liquid of a gravity engine, many stories below her in what looked like the cavernous central room of a space station; the darker blue lights of multiple huge computer screens aligned in an octagon on a platform just below this one; the soft baby blue of the soothing liquid bathing her skin in the long glass tube she floated in; and the sharp, electric blue eyes of the woman with wild blonde hair standing just outside the glass of the meditation chamber, watching her.

Lem sighed into the breathing mask on her face.

She was here.

Not the way she'd intended to arrive—not in the *strength* she'd intended to arrive—but she was here. She swum to the top of the tank and climbed out. Her back still stung where Mera had stabbed her. Every inch of skin ached from being crushed by Jei, overheated by herself, and then poisoned by Diebol. Her mind was blank and fuzzy from poor sleep as much as from months of exhaustive mental gymnastics.

Njandejara ... be with me, she said for one last time.

Always, little one, he answered. She breathed out, grateful for the soft peace that rippled over her muscles, and stretched, shaking liquid out of her hair.

"Welcome, hunter," said Sterba, bowing slightly with both hands in her long sleeves.

Lem bowed back. "It's been a long time coming," she said.

"Indeed. Come, warm up and eat. Then you will die."

"Mm." Lem followed behind the long robe, tucking her hands into the pocket of Diebol's jacket. She felt the paper he'd left in her right-hand pocket … best leave it there for now.

The pair traversed a long, metal walkway with no railing, stories above the steaming blue vat of a gravity engine. The cavernous orb'd room was pierced through with multiple walkways, all converging in the middle onto three platforms: the platform Lem awoke on with the meditation tube, a larger platform below it covered in computers, or a smaller one far, far above, just under the ceiling window out into space.

Sterba walked on the air, her boots sparking, up to the top platform. Lem followed, throwing a sparking em-push below her to rocket herself up after. Her boots impacted the platform with a soft, uncertain *thunk* behind Sterba's almost soundless step. Sterba motioned with a perfect, graceful closed hand to the table in the center of the small platform. A white lace tablecloth lined with blood-red flowers and delicate blue swirls covered the table, and atop that sat two simple, cylindrical porcelain cups and small plates.

"Parrot meat with lechichi leaf, as in your childhood," Sterba motioned to two perfectly circular sandwiches as she sat down on one of the cushions by the table. "You are welcome to take whichever you prefer, after I taste it, to assure you it is not poisoned."

"It's been a while since I've had anything that wasn't nutrient sludge," Lem noted as she sat cross-legged on the cushion across from Sterba. "Do you normally invite people who are trying to kill you to dinner?"

"You are the first person I've wanted to meet," Sterba said. She bit a large section of one sandwich, then held it out to Lem.

Lem touched the other woman's cold, pale hand, as she took the sandwich, and watched her electric eyes—no, Sterba did not *do* games. She believed in direct displays of power, the Yang in which Lem lived, not the Yin of darkness and deceit where Diebol played. Or—the wound in Lem's back reminded her—Mera either. Still, feelings and dreams aside, Lem silently turned the sandwich, and offered it to Sterba to bite a different section. She did so, and satisfied, Lem ate.

For a moment, they both chewed in silence. The tender, crispy memory of hunting with Cinta hit Lem under the foreignness of the bread—something most civilizations on steamy Luna-Guetala did not make. That came from Alpino. *Oh, Jei.*

She took a deep breath to clear her mind. "I'm sorry about the nightmares," she said.

Sterba nodded. Neither girl asked how she knew she had haunted the others' dreams. Lem could not even remember hers —she just awoke each day knowing Sterba existed to destroy everything she loved. She had rehearsed a myriad of arguments to fit Sterba's harsh perfection into a Frelsi model, or to amend the Growen system. She swallowed now. "You have options," she began. "The Frelsi could adapt to a disciplined hand like yours, and Growen Unification doesn't have to mean eliminating diversity by force. For example, there's a new trade system, that you could leverage for financial unification by educating the—"

"We are above petty Frelsi and Growen politics," Sterba said, raising a hand. "This war is about morality."

"I'm getting tired of everybody telling me what this war is about like I haven't lived it the past sixteen years," Lem remarked.

Sterba smiled. "Diebol gave you his freedom speech."

Lem nodded. The sweet complexity of the bread reminded her of arguing with Jei. She couldn't imagine he was okay ... *hush brain.*

"Diebol is incorrect," Sterba continued. "Mental freedom is not enough—mental *perfection* is the goal, a Universal Law for all behavior." She pressed a closed fist against the table by her plate. "Having different moral systems across the universe causes a myriad of injustices. Right now there are tribal Alpinoans killing dragons for food—a cruel practice, for such intelligent creatures. Multiple planets like Burbura have deep economic divides between the poor and the rich; meanwhile wealthy, nomadic Insectoid species like the Vibrants evade all taxation throughout the universe with their unregulated squatting culture. Even on your own home planet women in Retrack City suffer underground businesses that really just sanitize slavery. One Universal Law will cleanse this filth."

"You do know that slavery *increased* on Luna-Guetala when the Growen moved in and your soldiers started funding the meat-markets," Lem said. "Retrack's been Growen territory for years."

"When I have further control this will end." Sterba pursed her lips for finality, as if her promise fixed it. "I will kill those soldiers. In fact, I will enforce moral natural selection everywhere, literally eliminating morally problematic people and their genes. Imagine the happy community after the imperfect are dead: no more rapists, no more thieves, no more greedy corporatists or unjust leaders—just genetically *good* people."

"So, in your version of 'happy community,' slavery's bad, but genocide isn't?" Lem broke a piece off her sandwich, really for no reason than to see it tear. "I had friends in Fort Jehu." Wow, she could allow herself to feel the pain now ...

Sterba flinched, but cool indifference returned to her face quickly. "The Contamination must be eliminated at all costs. I also cleanse evil by removing those who would *defend* the 'right' to resist Universal Law in favor of their own beliefs."

"I'm sure you're aware many of those you killed weren't Contaminated," Lem said.

"Nonaction—failure to fight evil—makes you just as complicit," Sterba said. "Under Universal Law, those who fail to report even their own families will suffer the same penalties as the lawbreakers themselves. I apply this same rule to all beings: Njandejara fails to use its power to end evil, and therefore, as complicit, must be eliminated."

Lem took a sip of the warm liquid beside her, cupping it in both hands as she inhaled the herbal steam. "So say we need Universal Law. Shyte, I'll agree the universe sucks as-is. But who gets to decide that Law?"

"The intelligent and just, selected by an algorithm I create."

"Ah. And if, say, a being outside of time who can see, well, basically everything—a being who would know the best Universal Law—*doesn't* force all people groups into uniformity to obey it … why do you think *you* know better?" Lem asked.

"I can synthesize the optimal outcomes from all legal systems, based on my advanced computing. My mind, once removed from attachments, became—well, perfect," Sterba paused. "Boasting is ineffectual."

Lem took another sip—it was grassy, and bitter but rich. "You're electrogenic like me, right?" she asked. "But you've got some kind of processing boost that makes you a super-hacker?"

"When I glance at a computer, I own it. One touch, and I can see and manipulate every electron within its wires, like the blood sorcerers of old with their fingers in human veins."

"That's cool. There's gotta be some kind of insane mutation in the structure of your brain."

Sterba allowed herself a slight smile. "Perhaps, through my superior mental control, I have simply broken the barriers imposed on all sentients."

"You think you meditated yourself superpowers?" Lem laughed. "I guess we don't have time to get out the test tubes to analyze you."

"I suppose not," Sterba said. She tilted her head and placed her sandwich back on her plate. "What is the war about for you?"

Lem wanted to say a bunch of things about morality, maybe find some common ground here … perhaps something about changing culture through free allied discourse instead of force, about the inability to know for sure one way was right, about working *together* to learn the best morality, perhaps amending Sterba's Universal Law idea to consider how it might apply *differently* in different ecosystems and work more effectively if spread through organic means—

"I will know if you try to invent compromises," Sterba said. "I am interested in *your* reason. You have spent months hiding under other peoples' truths; aren't you tired of them?"

"Only the pure of heart get in here, huh," Lem sighed. "Well, you got me. To me, the war's about Njandejara. I love him, and wanna hang out with him without you stopping me."

Sterba finished her sandwich and folded her hands. "Lem Benzaran, have you ever seen Njandejara?"

Lem's instinct was to say yes—yes, all over the place, in abstracts and concretes from the rustle of dewy leaves to the lessons the old hermits muttered under their breath, but as she began to talk Sterba laid a hand on her wrist.

"Pardon me. 'See' has many meanings. I don't mean perceive. I mean, could you draw him? Can you define his form?"

"He looks like ..." The Crajk beast, saving Jei from the tentacle'd hydromorph last year? But no, because if she said he looked like a Crajk beast, then he would have to *be* that, and he was too much like a tree, or a star, or wind, or virtue, or a word. "No, when you put it like that, I've never seen him. I think ... I think there's something in the archaeological texts we uncovered, too ..." Lem felt almost a trance cover her with the spell of the ancient things. "'Be faithful to remember: you saw no *temunah*, no form, on the day I spoke to you out of the fire. Lest you corrupt yourself, and make an image ... you heard only a voice.' Seems to me he's pretty proud of being unseeable. Like he thinks if I could see him, I wouldn't be able to *get* it—my brain could connect him with something easy and familiar, and I'd trust that thing, and let it rule me, instead of knowing him."

"As if it's about you," Sterba said. "Don't gloat—his *decision* to be unseen comes entirely from megalomania. He knows, as well as you do, that the first rule of trust is *knowledge*. You trust what you *know*. But here he comes, insisting on being unknown, and yet demanding your trust. And you find it difficult to trust the galaxy's decisions to someone like me, who you can *see*, who has *proven* their superior intellect?"

Lem withheld a laugh with such force tea sputtered on the tablecloth.

"Excuse me?" Sterba asked.

"Sorry, it's just—I don't mean to be rude, but it took you four months to find me. With your *superior intellect*."

"To your credit, not my loss," Sterba said, neither perturbed nor laughing. "I don't think you know what you are, and I feel for you, trapped under the reign of a Being inferior to yourself."

The lightning eyes did not blink. "Shyte," Lem muttered. She'd never had anyone look at her with that intense admiration, and even—"I almost want to ask you what you saw in your dreams."

"The same you saw in yours. A future that could be."

Lem sighed and looked away, cheek on her fist as she stared at the swirling dregs of her cup. "Eh. I might actually be destined to bring about the end of all things, so."

"According to Njandejara," Sterba pointed out. "But that's the narrative from the losing side."

Dark green slurry under a film of lighter liquid ... Lem tilted back her head to finish the drink, ignoring that last statement. "Sterba, the dreams alone should tell you we can know what we can't see and understand what we've never met."

"And that some things are better left unknown." Sterba leaned forward. "I can't pretend to know the mind of something that's existed for eons, but don't you find it a bit convenient that the year after Njande reveals you're supposed to destroy his future, here he sends you to me to die?"

Lem's eyes lifted from the cup. "You don't know that, though."

Sterba pressed a long finger to the table. "Just look at everything that has happened to you, because he sent you to me. You would *never* have lost your friend. Everyone dies—you would still have died one day. But you'd have died happy, arm in arm with those you love. Now if Njande cared about you, why do you think it was so important for you to die *early*? I mean, look at you, then look at me—what do you think is going to happen?"

"I'm gonna live, that's what's gonna happen." Lem smirked.

But Sterba's intense, blue stare left no room for false confidence. Lem sighed and placed her cup down on the table. "You're right. I don't know what's gonna happen. But we can find out."

"And we should." Sterba rose, sliding her left foot behind her into a ready stance as she lifted her hands. Lightning sparked between her fingertips.

Lem sighed and leaned back in her chair, rocking it on the back two feet. "I know something's wrong with me. I know I'm supposed to have this passion for justice to kill you. Maybe it's the months of brainwashing myself. But after coming all this way—shyte, girl, I don't want to kill you."

Sterba did not relax her stance. "I feel it as well. That is why it is our duty to fight. If we go on talking, one of us will change her mind."

"That's kinda the point," Lem said. She winced at the tightening in her belly. "Come on, can't you just, like, believe Njande doesn't exist or something?"

Sterba's insulted glare forced another sigh from the tired Paradox Warrior, who put her chair right on all four legs and laid both palms on the table, elbows bent. *Yup, now I gotta stand up.* Ugh. She gazed up at the other woman: "You sure you don't want to keep talking?"

"You would rather die in a glorious blaze of fire than fizzle out and betray what you stand for. We are alike in this. We know each other's souls, and will not change the glory we see in each other."

"So because we're such good pals, and we respect each other's beliefs, we gotta kill each other," Lem quipped.

"Sarcasm has no place here," Sterba answered.

"I know. I'm sorry." With another long sigh, Lem pushed herself to her feet and rolled her head around on her neck, pausing to look up at the round ceiling far above her, and the stars visible through it … *Goodbye.* She drew the bamboo staff from her belt, jerking it out to the side as she rubbed the groove that lit it up red.

"Do not be afraid," Sterba said, drawing her own mace: a blinding white. "It will be over soon."

CHAPTER FORTY-SEVEN

Jei

I FOUND MYSELF IN MERA'S LAP WHEN I AWOKE, AND THIS TIME, I groaned.

"Not how every girl wants to be greeted," she said.

I held up a finger. The red earth walls around us spun, and swill churned in my esophagus. I rolled over, palms in the cool earth, and crawled to the corner to vomit.

She crouched after me, a soft hand on my shoulder blade, and offered me a nausea gum tablet. I shook my head. "We give these to little kids when they go into space for the first time," I told her, flopping back against the wall. "We don't take them after regulation fighting age."

"You're tougher than the Growen then," she said sitting beside me against the wall. "These are essential; people don't leave port without them. But they'll get the taste out of your mouth."

"Fine." I plucked the baby-gum out of her open palm and popped it between my teeth. The burst of menthol tingled the roof of my mouth as I chewed and pulled up my sleeves to check for injection sites. I found two. "What'd they give me?" I asked.

"Something to … lower your inhibitions." She looked away from me, eyes on the ground. I let my head loll to the side, and glanced across her exposed shoulders and arms—no injection sites, but deep purple bruises marred her neck and wrists.

I reached over to feel her tiny wrist between my fingers, checking for the cracking or *crackling* of broken bone. She winced, but she could clench, unclench, and rotate her fist without issue; her limpid, grateful eyes stroked my face. She was fine, but didn't say so, and her hands lingered in mine, begging the check not to end. "How long have you been trying to get out of the Growen?" I asked.

She leaned her head against my shoulder. "It's not that simple," she said. "They saved me from some really terrible things, Jei."

"Does that make this okay?" I asked.

"No, but survival isn't about okay," she said. "I owe them and I hate them, but my feelings don't matter. It's not like they'd let an electromagnetic like me *leave*. They'd just kill me." She said it with a cold matter-of-factness I hadn't heard from her before. The trembling softness returned: "I—I've only been happy since I've been around you."

Something tickled at the back of my head … "Why can't I be mad at you?" I asked, thinking of Lem, and searching for the embers of rage and grief that had ruled my life for the past weeks, to find only cold sleep inside me. "Is that a side effect of your powers?"

"I—I hope it's a bit more than that," she said. "I hope you know there's something real here. I've really tried to help you get to your goal."

"Well, almost. You were sent to kill her. Whatever she was trying to do, you were sent to be her opposite." I stared at the ceiling, my enemy's head on my shoulder, everything too light and floating as my thoughts blurred out with the scent of strawberries, cream, and lilac. The turning spit in my chest had stopped, and I wanted it back. I wanted to feel grief and confusion and loss and question what they'd done with Lem, what *I'd* done, finish piecing Mera into it all, and I could feel *nothing* but acceptance.

"But we were working together for the same thing most of the time," she was pleading.

"And what did you think would happen after?" My fist pressed against my forehead, as if exasperated with grief, and I was wet around the eyes, but it all seemed distant—locked in here, I didn't *feel* the emotions my body seemed to remember without me.

"I live in the moment, Jei, I didn't think of after. I've never had that luxury—not until the moment you showed me," she said. She lay her cool palm against the side of my face, turning my chin to face her. "Look at me. I know you believe I care about you. It's not just because I'm a great actress, is it?"

I laughed, holding her hand. This, I did feel. "Yeah no, you're not a great actress. It's easy to believe you care about me because you're the worst Growen agent ever. You let me destroy five or six vehicles before you stopped me, and you were actively recruiting me to kill your boss. Who you tried to kill with a grenade." I closed my eyes, leaning back against the wall again. "I only realized it here at the end, when you pretended to 'hot-wire' something without wires, and stopped me from destroying everything."

"I really did want you to save your power for Diebol," she mumbled. "I really thought we could kill him and her both."

"What do you mean, both?" I asked, stiffening. There was a finality in her statement.

Her lips drew down. "She's dead, Jei. We killed her, the three of us."

"No, you're lying to me." My fingers kneaded my forehead as I shook my head; I could, even without closing my eyes, trace the path of the green thread, tug on it, and know it still connected to a living being. "She's not dead."

"She's as good as. The thing that caused Fort Jehu is meeting with her now." Mera laid both hands on my forearm. "Jei, it's over. Your war is over, everyone is gone; you can let go of it now."

I barely felt the prickling this time as her thought seeped through my skin. *Relax*, it ordered. Then: *be happy*.

I grimaced, fighting the flood of literal *enjoyment* that spread from my arm to my chest to the rest of me. I wanted to pull my arm away. I needed, I suddenly realized, the darker emotions that made me suffer. I *needed* to be unhappy. But I couldn't find them. "Why are you doing this?" I groaned, squeezing my eyes shut.

"Because I care about you." I heard trembling in her voice. "I know you don't want this, but I want you to accept, let go, and stop suffering. I can't escape, but you can. You can lay your head back and just let me take on all the pain of decisions and choices and fighting. Haven't you been through enough?" Another wave that made all my muscles relax. Shyte, I needed to pull away, but for the first time in months there was no ache *at all*. No soreness from training, no little scratch here and there, no tension from thinking too much ... just *contentment*. "And all your flailing only makes things worse. It was *your* broken air-rider computer that we used to hack into Fort Jehu—one of the ones you hurled at us when you destroyed our supply camp. Everything that's happened has been your fault anyway, because you couldn't just let go." The despair rolled over with the peace, splashing into one dark breaker swirling over me with nighttime sea-foam. I was sinking in two feet of water, and found the smile on my face against my will.

I should have gone into that room back when Njande asked me to, I realized. I should have rested. It would have protected me from this exhaustion, this overwhelming need to just fall into her arms and let her take control. She was right—I had been flailing, running after nothing, and really, it would matter so little if I just disappeared—

There was a fruit tree engraved on Njande's door in my mind. From its branches, engraved in the shapes of different fruits, hung the names of every person whose life I had saved in the past week: I'd saved the Hiding Place, I'd mitigated the damage on Fort Jehu, I'd ended the months-long siege in that area just using Lem's helmet, the deaths of the blitzers taken by the pegasus' jaw had saved hundreds of future names I didn't even recognize, and mistakes or not I'd crippled supply lines for the Growen. It wasn't all for nothing. *Is the battle worth fighting only because it can be won?*

"There are so many forces battling for your mind," Mera whispered, running her finger along my collarbone. "Jei, how do you know this one isn't a ba-eater, too?"

"By the fruit of the tree he grows," I said, blinking back to our red earth cell. "What's he asking me to do?"

"Didn't he ask Benzaran to do the opposite?" Her lips pursed in cutesy faux confusion.

"Don't play stupid," I begged. "Your brain is beautiful."

"I'm not the one playing stupid," she said.

I blinked back into my mind. I pawed along the smooth wooden door and realized, suddenly, that I'd padlocked it to keep myself out of the throne room. Why? Did I believe I didn't deserve to have peace when Lem betrayed us? Did I believe I *couldn't* win if I wasn't miserable? I'd told him *no* over and over, and now I couldn't hear him on the other side.

"You know what you are," Mera said. "You're a failure, and we failures, we've got to stick together. I'm the only one who knows what's really happened—I'm the only one who can get in here, with you, and understand you."

I fiddled with the lock. I'd told him I was tired of his repetition—rest, rest, rest, don't, don't, don't—I would've accomplished more by *not* helping, but then again, I'd accomplished so much *by* helping, that in the confused mix between working with him and against him, between him mitigating my damage and increasing it, I—

"Jei, stop." Mera put her fingers at the base of my skull, where she'd previously healed the overwhelming pain after the battle with the pegasus' jawbone. This time, a sharp jolt of agony brought me out of my mind, to her; my body seized. "You're hurting yourself," she said.

The pain ended as suddenly as it'd begun; overwhelming

relaxation now flooded through my spine from her fingertips. "Stop thinking," she soothed. "The future sucks. The past sucks. Just be here in the moment with me. I'll protect you. I'll take you to the garden in the mountains, and you don't have to know anything else."

I couldn't speak. I tried. My lips seemed dry. I closed my eyes as she followed me into my mind, and I tried to hide from her in my channel to Diebol, in the wooden cage where we played games, in the darkness between the two white hallways.

There was nothing there but a laugh. *We've only just started.*

CHAPTER FORTY-EIGHT

Cinta

No one spoke as the bounty hunters' ship approached the quiet space station floating above Alpino. It certainly did look deserted; chunks of broken material orbited behind it, and it lay dark to the naked eye. Time, now, to test the intel overheard by Reise and the others on Alpino.

Cinta checked his pistol, priming its chamber as the drop zone approached. The Bont lizard beside him stood, casting a quick eye over her own inventory: a pistol strapped around each thigh, and a long glow-whip dangling from her right hip.

"Yannow they only hired us 'cuz they don't give a bean if our ship gets hacked," Lark Scrita, the lizard, remarked to her companion. "They don't wanna risk their own hardware."

"And yet we're here," said the Ebon Shadow. Everything about him gleamed, from his smooth, one-piece helmet and mask, to the gloves dancing across the control panel in front of him. A strange control panel indeed: most modern civilians used compuwalls for navigation, but here the wealthy Ebon Shadow still pressed old-fashioned buttons like the ancient and the poor. That, and the extreme cleanliness, spoke to Cinta of a man obsessed with detail and control.

Cinta said nothing. He only wanted to enter this place, confirm Growen presence, and call down the missile strike. All else mattered little. His pacifist upbringing still left a painful taste in his mouth with every mission, as if, biting his tongue, he sat before his disappointed parents with empty paws, and only after the end did he ever feel better. *That's why you're the perfect soldier,* Jaika-Lem, had told him once. *You'll never take things too far, because you take life to save it.*

Cinta did not agree, but he had decided last year that letting innocents die without lifting a claw only made him a participant in their deaths. If he had to live in a universe with bloodstained paws, he would rather stain them with the blood of murderers.

"Target," said the Shadow. A shining black polymerwall congealed between him and his two passengers as they buckled up their jetpacks. Another reason the Frelsi had hired the two mercenaries: the gear available to them far outclassed anything the ragtag freedom fighters owned. Cinta and the lizard both slipped on their space helmets and clicked their seals into place.

"Ready, lad," the lizard said. Through the helmet's transmitter, right by his ear, Cinta found her reptilian voice somehow even more strange and hissing. It was not ugly—just strange.

"Depressurizing." The oxygen hissed out of the room. Once everything grew silent, the wall opened to a beautiful tapestry of stars.

Oh Njande, you must be happy, to see this every day, Cinta sighed. He floated after the lizard, steering his jetpack softly out of the ship down toward the ragged metal surface below. A glance back over his shoulder startled him, even though he knew to expect it: the Ebon Shadow's ship used advanced holographic techniques to hide itself against the stars, and it looked as if Cinta and Lark now floated out here in the cold alone.

The enormous broken wreckage below looked to Cinta like the shape of the ducks he used to hunt in the northern swamps. He followed Lark Scrita toward the head. "There's a cold ventilation shaft on the X," the Shadow's voice clicked in his ear.

"Aimin' for X," repeated the lizard. She possessed a readout in her helmet that synced directly with the Shadow's ship. Cinta found it strange how she and the Shadow spoke, without using any of the military radio etiquette drilled into his head over the past year.

Cinta's boots touched down on the surface of the station with such softness he thought, for a moment, he had missed. He bent to grab the repair handle next to a square hole in the surface, and looked up at the Bont lizard—she nodded. Yes, this ventilation shaft.

Cinta crawled inside. He did not like small spaces, but this was not his first time climbing into a tiny tunnel for something he cared about. The starlight was blocked out behind him as the bounty hunter followed.

"There's a slight power surge toward the X," said the Shadow.

"Checkin' the X to see if it's just some old equipment still running, or some shyte that actually matters," Lark answered. "Cinta, that'll be a left at the next branch, if you please."

Cinta ran his gloved paw along the dark wall—he felt the opening before his eyes really saw it. He turned and continued. Behind him, the bounty hunter hissed: "Bloody beans, this shyte's killin' my knees."

"I am sorry," Cinta answered. "I will go faster." His body worked well on all fours—he did not really understand how the bipedal lizard bent to accommodate this space.

"Not your fault, luv," the bounty hunter answered.

"Technical readout now indicates you're heading toward a running engine," the Ebon Shadow said. "It might just be a reactor that hasn't burned out yet. To be safe, exit the shafts at the X and take the hallway."

"That's this next vent right below us, Cinta," Lark said.

Cinta felt the rough grate below his clothed toes; through it, he could see a gentle gray light. He drew his multi-tool and undid the screws.

"I'm feeling gravity," Lark said. "I think there is something living in this station—gravity systems are usually the first to fail over time."

"Noted, updating the Frelsi," the Shadow answered.

Cinta lifted the grate and slid it to the side, looking both ways down the dimly lit hallway before leaping. Lark followed; Cinta heard a soft, almost imperceptible *plat* as she landed behind him.

"Air, too," he said. "I can hear in here."

"Love those nutty Biouk ears," Lark said. "What you hear?"

"Just your feet," Cinta said, running close to the wall, and drawing his pistol.

"Prolly don't have to tell you this, but best keep your helmet on, laddie," Lark said. "With the open shaft behind us, we're definitely not in breathable oxygen right now."

"Just waste leak from a biosupport system," Cinta agreed. "But there is biosupport."

"Right," she said.

He aimed around the corner nearest him; Lark aimed around the opposite one. She held her hand like a blade in front of her face to indicate silence. Cinta pumped his paw twice to answer affirmative. This signed protocol, at least, they did the same. Lark waved an open hand toward Cinta's corner to point out their direction. Cinta answered yes and went.

They progressed through a few hallways in this way, always checking around corners first, as the sounds of their footsteps became clearer and the light grew stronger. Presently they came upon a translucent polymerwall.

Cinta paused; two dead human bodies lay frozen beside the polymerwall in the ragged, patchy spacesuits of civilian treasure hunters, their faces contorted in horror. Cinta closed his eyes for them: *May your being live well in the afterwards.*

Lark strode right past the bodies as if they didn't exist and held her glove up toward the polymerwall.

"A little closer to the left side, Lark," the Shadow said. Lark moved her hand accordingly. "DNA key obtained. Transferring to your suits now."

Cinta's eyes widened. What? No wonder everyone feared this pair. That kind of technology only existed in most people's nightmares.

"You are go to pass," the Shadow said. Lark and Cinta splooshed through the polymerwall.

The hallway ended abruptly below them; beyond its edge glowed the burning blue liquid of a live, fully-fueled gravity engine. Above them yawned an enormous space crisscrossed with walkways that all led to a center platform covered in giant computer screens. Above that central platform hung a smaller one with a human-sized meditation tank.

And above that, a sight that made Cinta's heart stop.

"Well, at least we know there's air in here," Lark muttered.

Lem

Lightning exploded from Sterba's fingertips; Lem blocked with an orb of static shock, and with one hand threw her mace—

Lem's mace whirled back toward her in midair, under Sterba's control. Lem leapt to catch it with both hands, and twirled to swing it like a club toward Sterba's head.

They battled midair like dancing fireflies—dash in close, scent and sweat and heat—explode away, force and wind and energy —Lem had the upper hand on the ground, with greater upper-body strength, while Sterba did everything possible to keep throwing her into the air, waiting for her to miss a jump and fall.

"What are you?" Lem panted. "That's not static electricity, that's straight up lightning. That's not biologically possible."

"Impossible is what you believe it is," Sterba replied, stabbing the butt of her mace toward Lem's stomach with perfect, quick precision.

Lem blocked. "You're not wrong. But also, a little wrong," she laughed. "There are limits to what your brain can do."

"Those thoughts breed failure." Sterba threw her down toward the hissing blue liquid of the gravity engine with such force Lem almost—didn't—agh, hurtling past—*platform*! At the last minute Lem's em-pull grabbed the edge of a walkway. She ricocheted back up as if bouncing on a long, flexible rope. Sterba dashed down to her; Lem waited, felt for her approach—

With a quick, sparking pull Lem grabbed Sterba's heel, turning her midair to slam her back against the walkway. Lem landed atop her, legs around the other woman's waist, and stabbed her staff toward Sterba's chest.

Sterba's em-push stopped the staff just short of her skin as she tried to shove Lem off her; Lem held on with both legs, struggling back with pure strength—

"Do you wonder what happened to your friend?" Sterba asked suddenly.

"Oh no, don't do this," Lem groaned, teeth clenched with her force. Her tired mind couldn't win this if Sterba tugged on anything related to Jei's fate. "Please don't do this."

"We didn't kill him, you know." Sterba strained her push. "We're wiping his mind."

"That's not—possible." Lem's arms trembled with the effort to bring—that—staff—down—

"It will be more of a living death," Sterba continued. "He cannot hear your Njande anymore, you know." Lem's grip started to slip on her staff. "Because of you. You left, and his hope with it. All for what? A mission you were doomed to fail?"

Lem's jaw tilted upward, eyes closing with effort as she screamed through her teeth, straining *down*—

The massive energy field finally overcame her. She shot upward toward the ceiling; her back hit metal with a cracking pain; she fell back down toward one walkway—ugh, cushion her fall with an em-push—bounce, hear ribs—cushion again—*agh!*

Lem channeled all the pain into another em-pull, shooting herself toward Sterba through the air, mace forward like a lance.

Sterba, weakened by her previous effort, just—barely —blocked—

Lem's mace tilted upward last minute; Lem herself crashed into Sterba, and then found herself rolling down the walkway—

Her tired mind flashed with a memory of her lost friend.

CHAPTER FORTY-NINE
Cinta

LARK AND CINTA TOOK ONLY A SECOND TO STARE UP AT THE brilliant battle above, shielding their eyes from the sparks and blasts of light as shock waves rippled through the enormous center of the space station.

"Beans, that nutter's filked," Lark murmured.

Cinta wanted to argue, but could not. His mouth burst like a monsoon cloud: "We must call in the strike, this is the computer center, we must hurry!"

"Frelsi receiving your video feed now," the Ebon Shadow answered in his ear. "They'll respond with their analysis and whether or not they agree. Your ETA back to the ship?"

"That's your adopted sis, right?" Lark pointed. "The one that's gonna die?"

Cinta nodded. "We can help?"

"We can clean up the mess," Lark said. "Shadow, hold that thought on the ETA. Gonna need you to dock leech-style, just above our location. If you hurry before the fight ends, maybe super-goddess-thing up there won't notice."

The Ebon Shadow sighed. "Affirmative ... risking hull integrity now," he grumped.

"Stop whinging." Lark sprinted back down the hallway to the polymerwall that kept in the air. She began to strip out of her space-suit. "Cinta, 'member those dead blokes we passed on the way in?"

"Yes."

"Get this suit on one o' them, drag 'im through the polymer-wall. The DNA key in the suit'll let him pass."

Cinta snatched the material from her and dove through the wall back out into the cold. He tried not to look at the exposed teeth on the first peeling, fried face he saw. The frozen stiff arm—fought—his—attempts—to stuff—

"Hurry!" Lark's hissing whisper peaked the sound levels in his transmitter, hurting his sensitive Biouk ears. He winced, fighting with—this—dead—leg—

Cinta zipped up the suit and heaved, struggling to drag the body three times his size through the wall. Once he got the arm through, Lark gripped and pulled with him. She got the suit off the body and back onto herself in perhaps a tenth of the time it had taken Cinta to dress the dead man. "They still fighting?" she asked.

Cinta peeked out from the shadow of the tunnel, up to the giant room above them. "Yes." Back at Lark: "How do you know she is going to lose?"

"Use your eyes. Moon-goddess is tossin' your sis like salad." Lark squatted, and lifted the body over her shoulders. "'Sides, the good guys always lose. Best we can do in this nutty universe's clean up."

Cinta did not like the darkness in the bounty hunter's voice, but he did not argue. The hunter glanced up, watching both duelists as they took to the air again—"Now." She dashed across the walkway; Cinta followed, trying not to look down into the hot, hissing blue liquid of the gravity engine below. "Stay hidden," Lark said, as they squeezed under the shadow of the walkway right above them. Lark squatted again, and put the body down.

"It's a nutty idea, but it's our only shot, I think," Lark whispered. She seemed to be trying to keep the corpse roughly under the fight …?

"Docked above the location you sent," the Shadow's voice crackled. "Drilling now. Any sound?"

"Nah, they can't hear you. Too much screaming and whacking."

Cinta's ears disagreed—with a twitch they could pick up just a slight buzz, like a fingernail against metal, or a bloodsucker far off. *But the humans should not hear.*

"Might need you to get in here, Shadow," Lark said. "Gonna need a tractor beam."

"I like your idea less and less each moment," the Shadow answered.

"It's the Grey Ghost, lad," she answered. "Like screamin' right in my ear."

The Shadow sighed, but they could both hear the sounds of movement and rustling as he rose to comply. Whatever the Grey Ghost meant, apparently the Shadow would not argue with it.

Cinta shifted his weight back and forth, his front paws itching by his pistol. Cinta wanted to wait and see how this plan evolved, but—what if he could take a shot at the glowing pale human? Oh, he knew Stygges could deflect cartridges with their staffs, he knew any action would endanger these other two humans with him—but Jaika …! *Njande please.*

The sheaths of his phalanges ached where he had once had claws. Cinta had become accustomed to finding strength in helplessness—but waiting was the hardest thing to do.

Jei

When Diebol's door didn't hide me from the girl of my dreams, I wandered back to Njande's again. *I serve many people, but bow to only one master*, was carved there in the living wood, apparently by my own hand, in crude knife-strokes.

"After all this time, do you even think he wants to be in there?" Mera whispered.

The flooding haze stopped as she pulled away from me. We sat now, face to face in the cool earth, kneeling in front of each other. Her long, dark hair trailed down her shoulders, framing her chest, and her downcast eyes wore remorse bleeding with determination. She hated herself for this, but would not stop until I, in her mind, was safe. She was experimenting and playing with different techniques—I could see that, now, in how we'd shifted positions, how she controlled her breathing, the tensing of her different muscle groups as she touched or didn't touch my arm, or the back of my neck.

"Let me protect you, and then, when this is over, we can run away," she said. "We'll escape all of them and hide in the mountains. I'll teach you the dances I knew as an acrobat; we'll read through your library, tangled in each others' arms. Just let me in."

"There can be only one king on the throne," I said.

"He's not even talking to you anymore, Jei. He's gone, with her. Don't you feel it?"

I did. I was dizzy; the damp, cool air of the underground cell seemed heavy as Mera lowered her voice, fingers tapping over my knuckles. "Jei, you're hurting, and you're hurting others. But I can soothe that. I think I finally found out how to help you let go, to heal."

Mera held up the green thread that connected me to Lem; I saw it, shimmering emerald, as if it existed here in the cell with us, glowing sharp against the blurry backdrop of Mera's compassionate smile. She put her fingers around the string like scissors—

No!

She snipped.

And it was gone.

There was no return tug.

Lem

Lem felt something tear inside her—that thing tugging at her aorta suddenly ripped.

The green thread is cut, the Accuser giggled.

"Agh, the what?" Lem gripped just below her chest with a wince—*Jei?*

Lem hesitated.

Sterba's ankle thrust behind Lem's, and she tripped.

A burning white staff plunged into Lem's chest.

The agony purged all other voices from Lem's mind; she dropped her staff, gripping Sterba's sleeves with jaw open and eyes wide as her breath left her.

"I'm almost disappointed," Sterba said, laying her on the floor. "You look afraid."

Lem blinked, coughing, and shook her head. She could see through the scorn in the bright blue eyes, and in the blinding, eternal moment Lem suddenly understood her enemy's weakness. *Poor girl.* She defined her perfection by herself, but no living, three-dimensional creature could maintain the paradoxes required for perfection in *every* area—just a tap in the right direction would send that delicate, complex mind into a crash. The more complex, the more failure points. If only they'd continued talking ...

The pain purified Lem's loss into laughter; blood sputtered across Sterba's robe.

"Stop smiling," Sterba snapped, yanking her staff out with another burst of blazing agony. "You have failed. Die now, a slave under your invisible master's thumb."

Lem coughed; it was strange, she realized, but the insult meant nothing to her: she didn't mind being under a thumb so gentle. *Burning, burning, burning.* She waved her wrist, motioning Sterba close. Sterba knelt uncertainly, her eyes colder now than when they began—she did not tolerate proximity to failures, but she brought her ear close ...

"My right pocket," Lem coughed. Blood speckled onto the

floor in front of her; she could feel it dribbling down the side of her mouth. Sterba knelt, and pulled out the piece of paper Diebol had left in Lem's jacket. It contained only two words, penned in elegant strokes:

If only.

Oh, Diebol.

Sterba tossed the paper; it fluttered by Lem's vision, down off the walkway. *All these poor souls, flickering in a world we all don't understand* ... Lem wanted, suddenly, only to gather them all up and tell them it would be all right. It wasn't so bad, the thing they all feared.

Another flashing wave of blazing agony: Lem felt her body jostle as Sterba shoved her to the edge of the platform with both hands. Lem gripped the white robe—*still have a job to do*—

"Let go! You're done!" Panic flashed in those blues; Sterba hid it under a sneer: "Have some *dignity.*"

Lem tightened her grip on the woman's collar. One more thing. Just one more thing.

"You forgot an attachment," she whispered.

Sterba's eyes widened, and with a blood curdling scream she shoved Lem away from her. Lem choked on hot red as she hurtled over the edge—dizziness overcame her—

Njande, don't forget me, please.

All things end, as they begin, in liquid darkness.

Jei

Mera showed me a clip of Lem's death.

And she let me feel it, all of it, slamming into my chest like a land-runner crash. Everything from my mother's loss to Diebol's transformation to the moment I found Lem under that Growen helmet, every tearing, searing, screaming shred of *helplessness* to stop everyone's suffering as I gripped my head with shaking fingers—

Then she held my hand, and it all went away. "I am so sorry, Jei. But no one else can handle all that with you. I can. I want to. You've been so sweet and accepting of me, more than anyone else. Let me be that for you. Let me in. After all, do you think anyone else even wants to be in there?"

No, I didn't. Not after I'd gotten—her—killed. *I* didn't even want to be in here.

And admitting that, I suddenly felt better.

Because I knew how to not be in here anymore.

I leaned back against the cool wall of the cell, eyes to the lumpy clay floor, blinking as my fingers came into focus around Mera's. Her soft tips traced the callouses in my palms ... my way out of my head.

I sighed.

With the decision my numbness gave way to that feeling you get after you've cried until you can't cry anymore, except I hadn't had the luxury of tears. "Was this your plan all along?" I murmured.

"I didn't plan on actually liking you." Her voice wavered. "I'm sorry."

"I'm sorry, too."

I looked up at her face as she slouched beside me. She wore real remorse—no armor, no giggles. It was the sick reason I didn't cringe away when they shocked me every hour: seeing the pain on her face told me everything I needed to know about her feelings toward me. Her fingers lied, but her eyes never did.

If I could take a bullet to the skull, I would rather one that felt for me as it went in.

I rose to my knees beside her and placed a hand in the earth by her hips. Her eyes widened in dark, waiting pools as I drew near for the dive, her breath sweet with mine.

With a surrendering breath, I dug my fingers into her hair, drew her chin close, and as her lips enveloped mine, I let the bullet in.

CHAPTER FIFTY

Sterba

Sterba's hypercharged mind calculated trillions of bits a second as the body fell. What attachment? What attachment could she have forgotten? It was nothing—it was a lie, meant to fiddle with her mind. The Nightmare Queen knew she had no attachments. She worked harder than anyone to purge—

Oh no, was that it? Was the attachment to purging attachments, in itself, a form of obsession, an attachment? Attachment to perfection? Surely that was not—was she attached to the Nightmare Queen herself?

No one else will ever understand you like I do, the Queen's imagined voice echoed in Sterba's ears. *You were so attached to your dream, you killed your one chance at escaping your nightmare.*

No. No there was no attachment. There was nothing! She had killed her own *family* to purify her attachments. Surely she was clean.

Killing is a form of suffering. Suffering cannot be caused without attachments, right? What were you attached to, when you killed them?

No. It had been dispassionate. She was not attached. She could give up her ideals!

But without the ideals, how will you give up other attachments?

You cannot be unattached to losing attachment, or you will be deliriously attached.

Sterba gripped her head as the colors and sounds of the world became too loud—too blue, too gray, too silver, too many footsteps, too much electrical singing and hissing—

As the Queen's body hit the gravity engine, Sterba curled to her knees, and screamed and screamed and screamed.

Cinta

In the screaming electrical storm, Cinta's ears and eyes struggled to process anything but distorted nightmare.

Jaika-Lem's body started to fall from one of the top walkways, far, far above them.

Lark Scrita's fingers flashed behind her own ear; for an instant Cinta saw the lizard morph into his sister—then she winced, ripping something off her skin, and slapped the corpse beside them.

Now *It* became his sister, frozen in distorted horror in the shadows of the lightning.

What?!

As the Ebon Shadow snatched the falling warrior out of the air under the shadow of the walkway, Lark shoved the frozen corpse into the gravity engine. "Body-swap!" said the lizard.

The dead body hit the liquid with an enormous splash, and a hiss. The scream intensified.

"Is she looking away?" Lark asked.

"We do not have time!" Cinta snapped. "Wound like this could be aortic rupture. Four minutes before brain death!"

"Just a second—"

"She looks away! We go now!"

The three powered up their jetpacks and dashed through the storm to the tunnel. "Ship, open med-pod, deploy three med-spiders and blood transfusion for likely aortic rupture," the Ebon Shadow ordered as they flew.

Back in the hallway, a vacuum-sealed hole in the ceiling now led into the Ebon Shadow's ship. The Shadow zipped through first carrying Jaika; Lark followed; Cinta glanced back to see the lightning storm intensifying, stretching toward them now like tendrils—

Cinta scrambled after the bounty hunters as the ship's penetrating tunnel slurped sealed behind him. He dashed to the half-open med-pod containing Jaika, almost shoving the Ebon Shadow aside—biomedical, this was his world. The ship rocked, rumbling to life as the flare of the engines lit up outside the windows; with Lark at the helm, the trio took off, leaving a large, sucking hole in the hull of the space station.

But as they began to put distance between themselves and the cursed frozen graveyard, everything slowed suddenly—as if some invisible force held the ship still.

Just then, the onboard communicator warned them that the Frelsi had fired their missile.

Sterba

A missile? Child's play.

What attachment have you forgotten?

With one hand, Sterba em-pulled the polymerwall of her broken hallway, dragging the seal forward to cover the hole sucking oxygen out into space. That done—her body no longer sailing through the air toward certain death—Sterba raised her palm, eyes glowing with electrical sight, to find the spacecraft that had to be nearby. There had to be one, had to be one—ah, there, a large computational mass leaving—she clenched her fist, holding it still.

What attachment, though?

Sterba would need only minutes to find an opening into this

ship's computer. She held that thought, held the ship still, as one of her screens flashed to warn her that Alpino Firebase had fired a missile in her direction.

What are you still attached to?

Child's play. If she could intercept the signal guiding the missile, she could enter the missile's mind. Her hands, elbows, forearms danced across the compuscreens as she calculated—

What attachment have you forgotten?

She gasped as her grip slipped on the spaceship outside—the Queen's dark eyes flashed before her vision. The lightning surge returned, uncontrollable. What, about her, was less than perfect? What possibilities died in the gravity engine? Where did she need to let go?

"It's foolishness, this mind game," Sterba muttered. "I know there's nothing I've missed."

And yet, as the missile arrived, she did not catch it—she released the last attachment she could find, and let go of her reason for living at all.

Morda

He refused to just *be happy*.

Morda rose from her work with a deep sigh, stepping away from Jei Bereens to a front corner of the room as Diebol approached for the fiftieth, hundredth, whatever time with a shock charge in his pistol to keep Jei powered down. She turned her face toward the wall and clenched her teeth. She could hear it hurt him, but she'd put him into a deep enough trance that perhaps he didn't know it? Tears squeezed from the corners of her eyes; she bit her lip and brushed them away.

"He's ready," she told Diebol, eyes still on the wall.

"We'll let Father judge that."

"Of course."

The soft, sharp padding of boots on raw earth grew distant, and she was alone again.

Because she really was alone. She could make him step, sit, turn—even, in a moment of proof, she'd had him draw a sharp rock across his skin, and he didn't hesitate. But she couldn't bring back the delight from when they'd talked together in the transport. She managed a fine approximation: the wrinkling of the corners of the eyes, the brightening cornea, but she could not feel that radiating admiration. After all she was doing to protect him? Her, locked away from sunlight here, between these damp soil walls, subjected to blood tests and questions like a lab animal?

Love me, she ordered. "You're doing it wrong," she said aloud.

He drifted in and out of her daze; she tried letting him come to, to bring back his light, but she didn't like what he had to say then.

"I can get you out of here," he said, sweating out his clearing nausea. "You have to let me think of a way out."

"And let you just leave me?" Morda shook her head with a dark laugh. "No."

"I liked you," he sighed. "Why would I leave you behind? I can help you."

"I heard *liked.*"

"I'm not gonna lie to you. It could just be the cage talking," he motioned to their world of walls. "There are moments when you really make it seem real. Shyte, with the right neurotransmitters, maybe it is—maybe what you're doing is indistinguishable at the cellular level from love, I don't know. I don't think so."

"Are you kidding? I *love* you."

"No." His turn now, to shake his head. "You love yourself through me."

She crouched beside him, close enough that, even though he tried to hide it, she could see the cringe in the corner of his eye.

"So I'm not good enough. You just want to change me," she hissed. "Just like all the rest of them."

"No, that's you—you've been changing for the performance. I only ever wanted to change your brand of armor." His jaw tightened; he stared straight ahead with every muscle tensed, unable to get away from her pheromone, but daring, still, in this way to insult her.

How dare he *look* like that, like she might hurt him, instead of trusting her.

"Look at me," she ordered, fingers at the base of his scalp. "And stop using past tense."

His head swung around like a puppet's on a string, but his eyes were empty. And the more she tightened her fingers on the back of his neck, the more she clung to who they could be, the more he continued to slip away and fade.

CHAPTER FIFTY-ONE

Jei

SOMETIMES SHE LET ME FEEL THE HOURLY SHOCK, WITHOUT HER drug, just to prove that the world sucked without her. I tried, at alternate points, to rebel or to obey, to demand respect or beg for her covering—I couldn't find myself, at moments, and I wondered if this was how the Growen treated her when they first "rescued" her, or if someone before, in the name of love, did this to her. It was too practiced, too habitual, to be anything but learned over a long time.

Her fingers were so tender, cleaning and bandaging the long cut on my arm. I did manage to get her to talk about her Retrack City days, and her best performances, and the street food, and the places she'd explored—the underwater sunken temple on Burbura, the dusty library on Gas Giant 3, the labs deep underground in the tunnels of Beryllia, the ancient technological towers rising out of red deserts or bound by jungle—and in those moments she seemed just like a person, a wonderful person I wanted to reach.

But then I would have a thought; perhaps I would mention Njande or Lem or my family, and feel something, and she would shut it down with a jolt of pain to the base of my skull. She could be her, but I was not allowed to be me, and most of all I was not allowed to be sad.

"Just let me *talk*," I growled, unable even to move a hand to grip the back of my head—I could only clench my teeth against the fire shooting down my spine.

"No, you listen! You've talked enough."

"If you'd let me be—"

"Be someone who doesn't test my patience, that's who you can be," she said.

Soon, she stopped talking about her, too, because she hated how I looked at her, or tried to ask questions or answer back. "I can't trust you with myself," she snapped.

I was still good enough to kiss, but that became just another way for her to demonstrate she could do anything she wanted. I began to try to make her angry on purpose, or otherwise to bribe or trick her into drugging me out so I could fall asleep. That was all I wanted—just to disappear into unconsciousness. She could follow me only when I was awake.

"I don't know what you're hoping for, hiding from me," she hissed as the world blurred.

"*Va'aniyadati go'ali chai, va'acharon al-afar yakum,*" I muttered, a string of gibberish from an old memorization exercise.

It meant something to her. "No, he's not. He's not coming to buy you back."

The spell seemed to annoy her, so I repeated it, and closed my eyes into it as pieces clarified. *I know my go'ali lives.* The one who buys something depreciated, and restores it to its glory. It was an ancient legal term. "You don't have to accept where you are, or even what you are. You can be healed, and you don't need to be afraid," I murmured more gibberish. "Healing doesn't change who you are, it restores what you're meant to be."

A hiss, and the pain. "Stop it. Stop torturing yourself with nonsense we don't need. I accept you as you are, and I'm the only one who ever will. I love you. Relax."

The things I'd memorized still flitted through the back of my mind as she put me back to sleep to get away from my words. I couldn't hear his voice anymore, at all, but I recalled something about wings, and weight training, and how heavy wings would feel if you suddenly found yourself carrying them, before you learned to use them.

Why didn't you help me? I asked him.

We stood now, him and I, in a field of rolling hills stretching to the horizon and back, waving with the light purple and green grains many Alpinoans used to make bread.

"Why didn't you let me?" he answered.

"Stop it with that," I said. "I know you could have just made me do what I needed to do."

"What you want is Bricandor, or Morda, not me. I can control you, but I will do it through synergy, like a lead and following dancer, not like a puppet on a string. Perhaps like a character in a story. You wouldn't feel my hand forcing you." He leaned on a staff, and wore robes hiked up around his thighs as he crouched barefoot in the dirt, inspecting the bases of the plants with weathered hands. "I put everything I have at your fingertips— everything except my own identity, my own 'throne,' I've given you. You only needed to ask, instead of taking, to rest, and listen to me, instead of grasping and squeezing. Does this sound familiar?"

"It does not," I said. I stood above him with my arms crossed. "I know you're Outside of all of this. I know from Out There, you could have—just—*micromanaged* all this differently."

He did not look up from the plant. "If you know I'm Outside, then you know I know what I'm doing."

"That's the thing—I think *you* know what you're doing is wrong. Diebol should be dead, not Lem. I shouldn't have to *ask* for you to just do what's right."

His eyes flashed, jaw set; a deep roar rumbled through the earth around me as he rose, shooting above me like a geyser or a cedar growing in time lapse, or a rearing cobra. A whirlwind caught my tunic around me. "If you know what's right, then let me ask you something," he boomed. "Answer me, since surely you know!"

He threw out his hand, or branch, or gust of wind; I plunged into a deep darkness lined with scales and tiny claws. "When you micromanage the world, making everything turn out just so for you and yours, how will you answer the cry of the lizard, hatching from its egg? Will you guide it to its first meal?"

A taste of protein and energy burst into my mouth—then, a blast of fear. "Or will you spare the innocent insect, just pushing its way through the earth, just asking to live another day?"

A warm, stinking pelt, and wetness, enveloped me. "Do you know when the deer give birth? Or how instinct works, how every chemical in a spider's body guides her in harmonious, soupy synergy to create a web like her mother's?" My hands *filled* with spiders, racing amok through my clothes and hair as stars and planets whirled toward me with a vibrating string-filled song I'd never heard before. "Do you know why the laws of physics work? Don't tell me the math—can you sing me the why, the music behind the math?" It hummed around and through me, and I realized, suddenly, that while my ears needed air to transmit sound, *his*, his felt vibrations at the source, inside everything, everything close around him—it was suffocating. Out There was not an escape. Out There was more in here than in here was.

The hum became a buzz by my ears. "Would you wipe out the bloodsuckers that bite you, and kill the birds that need them for food? What do you know of the ecology of good and evil?"

I was dizzy, so dizzy, with the entire universe spinning between, through, and into my fingers. I shook my head—

"The question, you see, is not *whether* you will trust, but *who*. Yourself? Me? Someone like Morda? Everyone has a price, and everyone has a master."

Something tickled my cheek, and I opened my eyes. Soft green shoots cooled my palms. Warm dark earth smudged my tan tunic like paint on a canvas, and suddenly I thought myself very pale and blank under the shimmering azure sky above.

We were back in the field as if nothing had changed.

He stood before me now, a human in woven green, leaning

on that bamboo staff. Long, stringy grey hair clung to the sweat on his dark neck. "Jei, I have no easy answers for you. And if I did give you all the answers, it would take away your agency, your discovery of a future then predestined. In lieu of an answer, I do have a question, though."

I sighed, my hands on my tunic belt, my shoulders hunched. "Sure," I muttered.

"What do you think of my field?"

I sighed again as I squinted across the rows of almost-black earth. "I'm guessing you don't intend those plants—there." Red, thorny tangles broke up the gentle green like blood spills.

"No, those are weeds."

The more my eyes tried to take in the field, the more they strayed back to those weeds. Kilometers and kilometers of gentle green stretched in every direction—but those weeds. A noxious gray gas hovered over them, sucking the color out of everything.

"How many weeds are there?" I asked.

"Pretty much every other plant around you is a weed."

"That's so stupid. Why'd you do such a bad job?"

His dark, slanted eye twinkled. "Do you really think I planted them?"

"I guess not."

"My enemy came, a few months ago, and planted them in the night." He knelt, his fingers stirring the dirt between the roots of two small, crowded seedlings. Delicate leaves seemed to reach for his fingertips … a heaviness fell on my chest, and I found my eyes misting, and I didn't know why, or if I did know why, I couldn't put it into words.

He looked up at me with deep sadness, and gripped my hand. "Lotta weeds in your fields, too, huh."

"That's all there is," I croaked. "I've killed all the good things. Or if I haven't, someone else has." I crossed my arms, for some reason still trying to hide, to avoid the *rest*. "That's my question. Why do you allow this?" I snapped, pulling my hand away from him. "Why don't you kill the weeds?"

"If I were to pluck up the weeds now, I might harm the

greens." He patted the little plants on their tops with a flat palm, and then stood. "I wait until they're all ready to harvest, and then we'll sort out the weeds and burn them. The weeds and the greens look very much the same when they're young, and sometimes, while they're growing, the greens can look a bit weedy, too. I give them a chance to become what they are."

"Is that why there's suffering in the world?" I asked.

His black, black eyes reflected my face back to me. "Yes. Even the weeds that choke and hurt and steal and injure get a chance to show themselves as greens. Plucking the weeds is secondary to growing the greens."

My chest heaved in an aching, halted sigh. We were all trapped, then, in what could be. I hunched my shoulders against the incoming rain, and he stood shoulder to shoulder with me for a while, as it rained, and the plants grew, and I mourned.

"Njande?" I asked.

"Yes, Jei?"

"What really happened to Lem?"

"You have a slight tendency to pluck the weeds early, Jei." He shifted his weight, looking down at his bare feet. "That's what happened."

"Is she dead?"

"Nothing I love ever dies."

"But you know what I'm asking."

He looked up at me—shorter than me, now, with gentle wrinkles framing pained cheeks. "I can't give you all the answers, Jei. Every bit of information I give influences how you behave, and each little action you take changes fate. This system requires a gentle touch. I trust you to do well with the information you have."

"I really *haven't* done well, though," I said. "I don't know, when I wake up, if I'll even have my own brain. I could be doing horrible things right now, and not know it."

He laid a hand on my shoulder blade. "You muss things. But you also fix them. You know, the moment I was most with you— it's not the moment you think, with the power surge, and all. Of course I was there. But the moment we were most together was the moment you tried to defuse the bomb and save Lem."

"Even though it accomplished nothing? That was literally just a cruel trick from Diebol."

"But your heart wasn't a trick. That's why there's hope for you. That might be the moment that matters the most." He patted my back again. "You'll see."

And with another pat, he sent me back into the waking world.

CHAPTER FIFTY-TWO

Lem and Cinta

Lem did not want to come back.

A blurry world, far too bright, played out in front of her in a dream as she watched, from Outside, while Cinta, fully covered now in a sterile suit, packed another bag of blood into the black med-pod containing her body.

Am I dead, or not? she asked.

The pod hissed as its mechanism punctured the blood bag; with another hiss, and a gentle whir, it loaded into her veins.

You don't have to be dead, if you don't want to be, Njande answered. *See?*

Cinta looked up for a moment, ears twitching—he heard voices he should not. He glanced to his left, into the cockpit of the sleek black civilian ship; the Ebon Shadow and Lark Scrita sat there, unmoved, giving no indication they heard what he did.

Wait, you can just do that? Lem asked.

Cinta tapped the digital readout at the head of the med-pod. The robotic med-spiders inside her thoracic cavity had already found and closed the tear to her aorta, and, with a stapled tracto-tomy, stopped the air and blood leaking from her torn lung. Still, the minutes of intense hemorrhage had left the human's body in shock. The pulse she had, Cinta found thready, and weak.

Yeah, Njande said. *I can do that.*

The machine's long proboscis down her throat breathed for her. Cinta hoped it did not hurt, where she was.

Well, that's unfair, Lem said. *There are a gazillion other people who deserve to come back. Why me?*

Now, finished closing the burnt hole through her back, the robotic med-spiders skittered across her sternum, needles stabbing in and out at machine-gun rapid-fire speed from their abdomens as they extruded first bone matrix, then muscle fiber, and skin.

Everyone doesn't need to come back, said Njandejara. *Lives cause ripple effects through time and space, and resource limitations aside, people need a break after they've done their work.*

Cinta loaded another cartridge of healing factor into the notch just beside the blood bag. The med-pod clicked as it accepted, loaded, and injected the material.

That one—the break one, I want that one, Lem said. *I'm so done.*

Cinta lifted the med-pod's transparent lid to check, again, the chest tube he had cut into her side to drain out the air and blood from the sucking chest wound that threatened to crush the injured lung.

Lem, what are you afraid of? Njande asked.

Healing factor delivered, Cinta took out the empty glass tube, and replaced it with her last dose of antibiotic, to prevent the overwhelming gut infection from that extended period without blood to her lower body.

I don't—no, it's unfair, Lem said. *Why me, and not someone else?*

The telemetry readout flashed: her blood pressure still would not stabilize. Cinta scrambled for another blood bag.

I don't follow some arbitrary moral code of fairness, Lem. I am the Code. The Way. Have you even met me? Your rule-focused view of morality is as simple as Newton's construction of gravity; mine is closer to Einstein's relativities. Newton's equations work for certain conditions, but the truth of gravitational attraction is a broader equation. In that same way, every little rule you've ever learned works only for certain conditions as an application of a broader rule of love. So don't tell me to obey a rule you don't understand.

Cinta discarded the old blood bag and reinserted a new one.

But I might literally be coming back to ruin everything, Lem cried. *Shyte, the Frelsi won't even know it was my word that killed Sterba. I'm just coming back for trouble.*

The med-pod hummed and clicked again, reloading the new blood.

Since when were you afraid of a little trouble?

The med-spiders on her chest withdrew their needles and powered down, finished.

No—no, I'm done.

A beeping alarm sounded. Her heart rhythm devolved again into disorganized ventricular waves, for the second time in the hour, as she tried again to die. Cinta groaned. "Come on, Jaika," he snarled in Biouk.

"Shockable rhythm," said the med-pod. Cinta snatched the med-spiders off her chest and clicked "all clear" to deliver the 200 Joule shock; he pounced to load another cartridge of epinephrine in the medication notch by the blood bag, his throat rasping with unintelligible prayer—

"Why are you trying to save me?" Lem hissed, *choking on withheld tears as Jei continued untangling his way across her vest of explosives.* *"If I'm this super-villain you think I am, why aren't you just letting me blow up?"*

"Because this is what I do, Lem," he said. *"Maybe there's just nothing you can do that will make me want to let you die."*

Embedded in her repaired aorta was a green thread.

CHAPTER FIFTY-THREE

Diebol

DIEBOL WANTED JEI ALWAYS IN A STATE OF IN-BETWEEN: HE DIDN'T want the man to sink into the sweet numbness of despair any more than he wanted him to rise to victory—he wanted Jei to struggle and fail and *hurt*. It was a special kind of hatred.

So he was a bit disappointed as he walked now through the red earth tunnel with his hands in his pockets. He was fresh from a meeting where everyone brought good ideas to the table and everyone listened to him. Sterba was gone, but she'd given her life for three planets of domination—better than most conquerors, historically. With the concerted efforts of this new unified council in the aftermath of her victories, even Alpino and Luna-Guetala couldn't hold out long. With Benzaran's death on film, Morda under control, and Jei reduced now to a shell …

It was going to be lonely up here on the top.

Jei

I couldn't see. Her cold fingers on my temples had ordered my eyes to close, and until my liver metabolized her chemicals, they

373

would stay shut. Cool metal—shackles on my wrists—someone squished soft earplugs into my ears—we were going somewhere.

I'd paid attention to the patterns. She needed to stay relaxed, or her orders didn't work well. They worked better after someone injected me with something—a benzodiazepine, I thought I'd overheard. I envied the pegasus that had managed to get away, but I'd spent a lot of time thinking through how it had leapt back from her hand when I reached toward it—she'd ordered it to leave, and I'd still managed to override that just with physics. Did it really come back to her, once I released it, or had she caught a ride with a Growen scout or something, to come and rescue me from Diebol?

There was a way out, somewhere.

Njande, let me finish this. Let me die and take him with me.

We were walking—I was stumbling, a bit, on the packed earth. "Behave now," she whispered into my wrist. "We want you to live, my dear one."

I nodded, but I licked my lips, waiting for my moment. It was going to come.

The path under my feet became hard, and a cool blast of air hit my face—we were walking inside somewhere now. Somewhere big, I thought? Hard to tell without sound.

The shackles came off. *Turn,* I was ordered. *Bow.* Then—*empush.* I felt my palm open, and that blast of *weight* moving away from me. Bloodseas, they hadn't let me use my abilities in a while. It felt alright. *Lift. Crush.* My fist closed. I couldn't hear the crunch, but I could feel it.

Please don't let it be horrible. Please don't let it be horrible, what I'm doing. Please let me find—find some way to bring this building down.

It was a gymnasium, then. There was a lot of room, for whatever they were having me do, and it was inside. Likely a demonstration of Morda's power. I was a trophy, at this point. Oh well. The twinge didn't even come with humiliation anymore. They were letting me move, and stretch out into the electromagnetic world. Could I feel their spines, like when I was back in Diebol's transport before the pegasus jaw fight? They didn't want me to power up fully, so maybe the room was empty except for Morda and …

I felt my chin tilt up toward the ceiling. Something tugged. Something green.

Without thinking, without orders, I threw my hand up in the air in a fist.

What are you doing? her fingers asked my other wrist.

Pulling something out of the sky.

Stop, you'll kill everyone!

The crashing something laughed inside as it found me. An explosion rocketed around us, throwing me back with a wave of heat. I ripped the earplugs out to hear Mera screaming. Diebol was here, too—close by, fighting with something. They both sounded hurt. I felt along the wooden panels of the floor with my fingertips, trying to get my bearings—oh, there was flame nearby—

"Where is he?" Lem said it like an order, not a question.

Oh, Lem.

The wave of *relief* and shock threw my head back into an unbelieving grin.

"How did you even get—how are you alive?" Diebol was panicking.

Fingers on my wrist—I couldn't pull away, but it didn't matter. Mera wasn't going to stay calm for long. There was fire all around us, heat in every direction—the last command she gave was *open your eyes.*

I opened them. Mera was beside me, half-crushed under a support beam with flames reaching toward her, her own bamboo staff jutting through her chest. We were surrounded by the wreckage of a light fighter, in a large gymnasium torn open to the sky as fire ran over everything. Beyond the fighter, leaping through the burning ruins, Diebol dueled with a white-robed warrior I almost didn't recognize. Lem spun an ivory mace in one hand, crimson in the other, agate skin gleaming in their glow under the shadow of the flames as sparks popped around her like dying stars.

The heat kissed my wrists. I lifted the beam off Mera with an em-pull; she drooped in my arms as I cradled her and stepped away from the fire.

"You didn't have to pull a spaceship down on us to get away from me," she coughed. Her pitiful laugh made my gut twist; her big eyes teared up with pain.

"You know I did," I answered softly.

"I'm sorry," she murmured. Her head tilted toward my chest; she lay her cheek there as I held her close.

The roasting spit churned inside me; there was no medkit or doctor here, only ruin, fire, and combat, and I could do nothing but hold her as she struggled to breathe. "It's worse because if you'd just relaxed your grip I could've helped you," I said.

"You never would've liked me without it." Her tiny fist clenched against my shirt; her eyes squeezed shut in agony.

"I did, though. Who you are—without all the pretense and lying and control—shyte, I—" I put my mouth down against her forehead, my voice breaking. "I still love you."

She winced through her smile. "I wish I'd known some attachments are worth suffering for."

Diebol

Jared Diebol truly hated playing underdog to these ancient interdimensional elder gods.

As far as Diebol could figure through the flames and the pain, over the past weeks Lem Benzaran had survived Sterba, attacked the first Growen Maggot she could find, stolen it, and flown as fast as she could back to Growen South Central for Jei.

And then Jei had literally pulled her ship out of the sky.

"Just like your Njandejara to give you these insane breaks." Diebol winced, limping on a leg crushed by Jei's carelessness.

"Everyone just played their part," Lem answered, double staffs whirling like fan blades. Parachute strings still trailed from her shoulders—she'd obviously ejected from the cockpit literally the moment her ship took a nose-dive. Diebol sneered as he ducked this staff, blocked that one, stumbled back, *agh* the leg—

"Your get well card helped," Lem added. "You know there are still other 'if onlys.' This doesn't have to be our future."

"Oh, stuff it." Diebol shoved her back with an em-push as the blaring alarms of the fire crews pulled up outside.

He shoved her so hard he lost her somewhere in the fire.

Oh, shyte.

He threw debris around with random em-pushes—shyte, where did they go? There was a body by the doorway—Diebol leapt the barrier of metal plates and other ship debris, landing on his good leg with a flinch. It was Morda. He crouched for a pulse check—no, she was dead.

The roaring of the flames was punctuated with small explosions behind him as the fire found the ship's fuel reserves. Diebol dove out of the building to join the emergency crews gathering outside. He didn't see Lem or Jei anywhere.

Diebol growled through gnashing teeth. He forced himself to breathe evenly as a medic ran over to him; he heard himself shouting orders, putting the base on lockdown, sending soldiers to find the escapees, but he had no illusions. Until she knew he was alright, Benzaran likely wanted Bereens as far away as possible as fast as possible—which meant using that ridiculous disguise generator.

Well, on the plus side, at least the video call with Bricandor had cut out the moment the ship crashed on everyone. This could have been embarrassing. Now, it was just a training accident—an experiment that needed improvement. And the data was worth a life or two: they'd already started synthesizing Morda's pheromone for mass production in the bioweapons lab, and the implants division could already mimic her pulsatile neurotransmitter release with a more precise, remote-controlled skin device. Like Sterba, she'd served her purpose. What Jezebel couldn't kill, Delilah could woo, and soon all sentient life would know the touch of her submission.

In the end, mind control was cheap, but when you were up against literal demons and gods, maybe you had to cheat.

CHAPTER FIFTY-FOUR

Jei

AND HERE WE WERE.

Lem and I sat side by side in a stolen Growen Maggot ship, silent except for the familiar sound of each other breathing. Lem ran her hand across the buttons on the console to open the armored plates outside the windows; the light of a million stars filtered over us as we floated with the engine off, looking down at the planets orbiting in the distance. The double-planet, Luna-Guetala, spun around itself in left field, two dark-colored marbles gleaming under a yellow sun. Alpino, far off on the right, flickered, just a pale dot in the ether.

"Wherever we go, we're filked," Lem said, matter of factly. "I'm facing at least a court martial for desertion, even though I warned them when I left. You can probably argue something less for yourself, but," she shrugged, "no one's gonna believe any of what I did was necessary."

"Maybe it's not just the Growen that needs reform," I murmured.

"Can't really blame 'em, Jei." Her voice harbored no regret.

I had enough regret for the both of us. Three new planets under Growen control. If I had obeyed the Admiral, could Lem have stopped Sterba earlier? If I had stronger will, could I have kept Diebol out of my brain so she asked me to help? Could I have done differently than I did? My mind played, on repeat, a hundred imaginary ways that Mera could maybe possibly have lived if I had caught on earlier, avoided hunting Lem altogether, or just slowed everything down. Most of my scenarios relied on fantastic impossibilities of fate and amnesia, explosions and passionate pleas, perfect storms that magically overcame years of programming to convince her she was worth it. I didn't know how much of the touch lingering on my wrist was her toxic remnant, and how much was my own bamboo mountain dream, still held, still loved, despite her fatal flaw … I only knew her haunting would last forever.

The solar system spread before us seemed so big.

I ached.

We stared out our opposite windows, neither looking at the other. I knew Lem was staring forward, wondering about her heat death. I was still watching the past, where I couldn't have possibly *known* a crushed-in air-rider computer could get hundreds of people killed, but I hated myself anyway. Where you didn't really know *why* someone would let you run amok in the universe—he just did, with no easy answers. Where the moment you felt most right, you were wrong, and the moment you felt most wrong, you were right.

"*Va'aniyadati go'ali chai,*" I murmured.

"Yeah," I heard her muffled, as she leaned her mouth on her fist. "That's the only hope, at this point. That the restorer is coming. Maybe not now. Maybe everything's ruined for now. But no matter how much the world breaks … it will be redeemed. Somehow. I don't know how."

Something in the edge of her voice made me turn to look—I caught her wiping her eyes on her sleeve. "Sorry, I'm tired," she said.

I wanted to say she didn't have to hide around me, I'd seen her cry before, but—I couldn't expect that kind of trust now. I stared back out my own window with my chin on my knuckles.

"Hey Jei?" Lem asked.

"Yeah."

"We good?"

I looked over at her. "Yeah, we're good."

There was nothing but each other in the empty ship, and we both needed rest before we returned anywhere. Lem hesitated for a moment, and then, with a deep breath, she shifted to show me her back; I turned mine, and leaned back against her. It was a Frelsi thing, guarding back-to-back like that. We each faced down our own dark window with the others' warmth behind us, and as we fell asleep, back-to-back, there were no nightmares.

I am a Paradox Warrior.
I hunt the oxymorons in the universe,
following the creed of the electron,
and the Being beyond time.
Rest is action.
Weakness is strength.
Sadness is necessary for happiness.
Attachments are suffering …
and attachments are healing.

INDEX OF TERMS AND CHARACTERS

Air-rider: Single or double-rider hovering transport vehicle, popular among civilians and Frelsi warriors for its low cost of construction, safety profile, and ease of operation.

Alpino: Neighboring planetary system to Luna-Guetala. Its various biomes range from arctic tundra to temperate zones, but due to extensive landmass, with oceans comprising less than 50 percent of the surface area, much of the planet is covered in volcano-strewn prairie or cool desert. Bereens's home planet. Contested Zone.

Ba-eater: A Biouk term for an interdimensional being that devours the human psyche. Used to describe gods and demons of multiple religions.

Bangla: A species of wide, many-trunked, vine'd tree common to Luna-Guetala jungles.

Baricella: A species of bipedal mammal characterized by long, black, fuzzy growths around the mouth that resemble the pedipalps and legs of spiders. Habitat includes Luna-Guetala jungles and the moon of Baricel orbiting Gas Giant 3; small colonies were transported by Growen slavers for cheap labor to the Northern Continent of Alpino. Visual spectrum includes high-acuity infrared but does not include much of the color spectrum. Communicate verbally with an extremely high-pitched language, most of which is outside the range of other mammalian hearing; emotionally, communicate with motions of the growths around the mouth.

Bichank: This people group, called "land-walruses" by many humans, bear more similarity to a sentient grizzly with tusks. Habitat includes the Luna-Guetala jungles, but actually likely originated on the cooler planet of Alpino. Culturally similar to Biouk peoples, communicate verbally with a throaty, roaring language, and emotionally with eye movements and wrinkles of the muzzle, like humans.

Biouk: See space-lemur.

Blitzer: Member of a Growen heavy infantry unit, characterized by silvery armor and large, reflective, space-capable orb'd helmets.

Bricandor: Leader and supreme diplomat of the Growen Unification Forces. Human in appearance and appetites; rumored to have appeared in the galaxy, or at least developed his Stygge powers, after the Black Comet.

Burbura: Independent planet with over 90 percent of its surface area under water, a condition many scientists attribute to a past global warming crisis. Highly technological trade, media, and political hub home to most of the sentient species in the known universe—"where Burbura goes, so goes the galaxy." Independent planet/uncontested, with both Frelsi and Growen diplomatic presence.

Cadet Commander: The highest rank available to a child in the Frelsi guard, preceded by Cadet 3, 2, and 1, and Enforcer. Followed in adulthood by Lieutenant 2 and 1; Sergeant 5, 4, 3, 2, and 1; Captain 3, 2, and 1; Colonel; and Admiral. Unlike the Growen Unification Forces, which separate rank into three chains—Officer, Enlisted, and Stygge—the Frelsi separate rank only into the child and adult chains.

Captain Rana: Wonderfrog officer over the Eighth Combined Battalion in the refugee base at Fort Jehu, overseeing both children and adults in self and community defense. Former commanding officer for Lem Benzaran, Jei Bereens, and Lem's siblings. Contaminated.

Cinta: Space-lemur from Luna-Guetala, 27 revolutions old, currently studying interspecies biomedical science to become a healer. Formerly a pacifist, joined the Frelsi Unification Forces last year after capture by the Growen. Lem Benzaran grew up as his little sister for a few years, and they have since remained close.

Contaminated: A derogatory term for a matter-based, sentient being who speaks to interdimensional energy beings such as, and usually specifically, Njandejara.

Contested Zone: The areas not covered by the Spaces Treaties. On Contested planets, the Growen and the Frelsi fight for dominance. On Independent Planets in the Undecided or Uncontested Zones, neither is authorized outright displays of force. The Growen hold that all Frelsi allied-planets fall within the Contested Zone, but that Growen-occupied planets do not.

Dr. Patti Loylan: Physician assigned to the Eighth Combined Battalion at Fort Jehu. Also supervises the biological research program to improve artificial habitat compatibility, travel comfort, and optimal combat ability of diverse species. Shy. Not contaminated.

Ebon Shadow: Bounty hunter alter ego for brothers Carl and K'arl Hampt. The most feared mercenary in the galaxy, the Ebon Shadow was often hired by the Growen for plausible deniability with assassinations or kidnappings that would otherwise break the Spaces Treaties. Following the events of the Battle of Bioumatta, chronicled in *Neodymium Exodus,* and the presumed death of K'arl, the Ebon Shadow began exclusively accepting anti-Growen contracts, working in tandem with the young Bont bounty hunter Lark Scrita.

Electrogenic: An electromagnetic being that can generate electric charge, similar to the electric eel on the rumored human homeworld.

Enforcer: The second-highest rank available to older children. See Cadet Commander.

Firebase: The largest Frelsi base on Alpino, located in the South Central continent about three hours' journey from Growen South Central by air-rider.

Fort Jehu: One of the larger Frelsi bases on Luna-Guetala, about an hour's journey by air-rider south of Retrack City.

Frelsi: Conglomerate of militarized special interest groups and refugee bases organized to protect people groups punished for refusing to join the Growen Unification Project.

Gideon Horn: 15-year-old male freedom fighter, ward of the Frelsi refugee system. Orphan. Special skills in ground combat and weightlifting. Known for cheerful, occasionally insensitive demeanor. Best friend of Nathan Peter and Reise Benzaran. Contaminated.

Gray: Frelsi slang for members of the Growen Incursion under the Growen Unification Forces.

Grenblenian: Common trade language throughout Luna-Guetala, adopted by most planets with a mammalian presence.

Growen Unification Forces: Interplanetary social organization forcefully uniting all sentient beings under one centralized government. Supported by various economic and social causes, including interest groups that propose eliminating Contaminated people to defend the universe from interdimensional invasion through their brains.

Jake Benzaran: 12-year-old male ward of the Frelsi refugee system, below fighting age. Brother to Jerusha-Lem, Reise, Juju, and others. Special skills not yet known. Sustained significant childhood injury leaving him limping, and prone to epileptic attacks; as a result, can be quite skittish. Contaminated.

Jared Diebol: 22-year-old male soldier in the Growen Unification Forces, advanced early to commander status due to his Stygge training, electromagnetic abilities, and unusual voracity. Specialized knowledge of the Frelsi electromagnetic pair due to his close mental relationship with Jei Bereens. Not contaminated; obsessed with curing contamination.

Jei Bereens: 19-year-old male freedom fighter, ward of the Frelsi refugee system. One of two known electromagnetic humans in the Frelsi forces. Highly trained, with specialized knowledge of Growen systems and technology due to his childhood in Growen captivity. Arch-enemy of Jared Diebol; Paradox Warrior partner of Jerusha-Lem Benzaran. Contaminated.

Jerusha-Lem Benzaran: 16-year-old female freedom fighter, ward of the Frelsi refugee system. One of two known electromagnetic humans in the Frelsi forces. Highly trained, with specialized knowledge of Biouk space-lemur society due to childhood living among the space-lemurs. Contaminated.

Juju Benzaran: 10-year-old female ward of the Frelsi refugee system, pre-fighting age. Quiet, with talents in early communication, and an unusual protection spell from Njandejara. Sister of Lem Benzaran. Possibly contaminated.

Land-runner: A sleek, heavily armored, spiked vehicle that uses wheels to move along a planet's surface, most commonly employed by the Growen.

Lark Scrita: 17-year-old human living her life as a famed sixty-year-old Bont bounty hunter. Not contaminated, but the child of a contaminated couple killed by the Growen. Unallied.

Lechichi: A fruit common to Luna-Guetala jungles. Grows in clusters of small, translucent white orbs with rough reddish-purple husks.

Lieutenant Seria: 21-year-old female freedom fighter, ward of the Frelsi refugee system, highly trained in communication and investigative skills. Not contaminated.

Lift: A floating platform with one solitary railing and a compuwall for light transport of goods and people within a short distance.

Luna-Guetala: The only known habitable binary or "double-planet" system, differentiated from a simple planet-moon system by the sheer size of the smaller celestial body. Luna, the smaller, more temperate twin, is often mistakenly called a moon by LG inhabitants. Neighbors the Alpino planetary system.

Meat-man: Frelsi slang for perpetrators of sentient trafficking, whether through slave trade, brothel ownership, or actual sale of sentient beings for edible consumption.

Mera: 20-year-old female soldier for the Growen Unification Forces, thought to have been originally rescued from an abusive life as a sky-dancer by Diebol. Graduated from the same Stygge training program Lem and Jei rejected. Tasked with solving the problem of Jei Bereens when he becomes super-charged. Special skills in tracking electrical fields with a sense organ similar to the ampullae of Lorenzini in sharks; releases a calming pheromone and neurotransmitters that allow her to control Outgoing, insecure, warm. Not contaminated.

Nathan Peter: 16-year-old male freedom fighter, ward of the Frelsi refugee system. Recent orphan. Special skills in compassionate organization and negotiation. Known for small size and quiet voice. Best friend of Gideon Horn and Reise Benzaran. Contamination status unknown.

Njandejara: Interdimensional energy being interested in befriending matter creatures. Differentiated from other energy beings by existing outside time, as well as outside space; rumored to be the ancient origin of all life. Considered a mental illness by Growen scientists, and a dangerous invasion force by Growen philosophers.

Reise Benzaran: 14-year-old male freedom fighter, ward of the Frelsi refugee system. Brother to Jerusha-Lem, Jake, Juju, and others. Special skills in sharpshooting and piloting. Known for unusual, highly educated speech pattern. Contamination status unknown.

Retrack City: Large, cosmopolitan area occupied by the Growen forces during latter period of the Growen-Frelsi conflict for

Luna-Guetala. Most populated and culturally celebrated space-port on LG. About an hour's ride by air-rider north of Fort Jehu.

Revelon: Planet in the Uncontested Zone with fairly low gravity, mostly cool climates, and thin mountain ranges, inhabited by tall mammalians with keratinized, thick, rock-like skin.

Skraeli: Any of a number of sentient life forms comprised of complex carbon-nitrogen clouds. Require extreme gravity to maintain protocellular oxidation and life, and must wear atmosphere suits on the lower-gravity planets inhabited by most sentient beings. Language comprised of flashes of color punctuated with occasional sounds; emotions often communicated with scents.

Space-lemur: The human slang term for the Biouks, a sentient tree-dwelling race of omnivorous mammals characterized by small stature about half the height of an average human, enormous ears often as large as the head, powerful claws, a lack of tail, fangs that extend to the chest in adult specimens, and an extended lifespan often over a hundred Luna-Guetala revolutions. Divided into "moon" and "planetary" subspecies, with the "moon" species dwelling on the Luna twin of the Luna-Guetala twin planetary system. Language comprised of harsh, throaty sounds and snarls; emotions often communicated with ear movements.

Sterba: 30-year-old female soldier for the Growen Unification Forces. Trained and tortured by Bricandor to force an artificially strong bond with Mera, who is viewed as her sister. Special skills in heightened concentration and cognitive processing allow her unprecedented control over computing and machinery with incredible range. Cold, perfect. Not contaminated.

Stygge: A person gifted with electromagnetic abilities who has allied themselves either with the Growen, or with another force bent on eliminating the Contaminated.

Undecided Zones: The areas protected by the Spaces Treaty; also known as Uncontested Zones. See Contested Zone.

Wonderfrog: The human slang term for the Bwangam people, a semi-amphibious sentient group with a body plan similar to a human-sized frog. Native to Luna-Guetala, but population range also includes the Burburan swamp systems. Language comprised of rounded, guttural sounds, with frequent repetition; emotions communicated with changes in skin color and aggressive, expressive body language.

TRANSLATOR'S NOTE

The manuscript you have read was translated from a time-shifted language that appears itself to be a Biouk translation from the original Grenblenian. Therefore, the reader should understand that many idioms such as "Prince Charming" or "homework-eating dog" may not exist in the original, or if they do, they exist in rather different contexts.

The entire work caused a number of us a great deal of trouble. The original manuscripts of these chronicles appear worn and aged, but dating with radium, argon, and carbon produced wildly inconsistent and unusual values, and electron microscopy revealed the presence of compounds and genetic material not in existence on our planet. The original joke in our lab—that these volumes came here from the future, or perhaps another dimension altogether—eventually became less of a joke, and more of a conclusion, especially once it was revealed how, and at what cost, our lead obtained these documents. Nevertheless, no one in our laboratory felt comfortable publishing our results as fact.

And so, I have brought them to you, as fiction. I hope in this understanding you will forgive any apparent anachronisms in the text.

ABOUT THE AUTHOR

Jen Finelli is a world-traveling sci-fi author who's ridden a motorcycle in a monsoon, swum with sharks, crawled under barbed wire in the mud, and hiked everywhere from hidden coral deserts and island mountains to steaming underground urban tunnels littered with poetry. She was once locked inside a German nunnery, and recently had to find her way through swamp-filled Korean foothills dotted with graveyards on Friday the thirteenth under a full moon without a flashlight. On her quest to rescue stories often swallowed by the shadows, she's delivered babies, cradled the dying, and interviewed everyone from prostitutes to senators. If you want cancer-fighting zombie fiction, dinosaur picture books, scientists jumping into volcanoes, or talking cars and peyote legislation, you might like Jen. You're welcome to download some of her stories for free at byjenfinelli.com/you-want-heroes-and-fairies, or join her quest to build a clinic for the needy at patreon.com/becominghero. Jen's a practicing MD, FAWM candidate, and sexual assault medical forensic examiner—but when she grows up, she wants to be a superhero.

Byjenfinelli.com

IF YOU LIKED ...

IF YOU LIKED *NEODYMIUM BETRAYAL* YOU MIGHT ALSO ENJOY:

Jeff Sturgeon's Last Cities of Earth
Edited by Jennifer Brozek

Easy To Be A God
by Robert J. Szmidt

The Silver Ship and the Sea
by Brenda Cooper

OTHER WORDFIRE PRESS TITLES BY JEN FINELLI, MD

Neodymium Sacrifice

Our list of other WordFire Press authors and titles is always growing. To find out more and to shop our selection of titles, visit us at:

wordfirepress.com

facebook.com/WordfireIncWordfirePress

twitter.com/WordFirePress

instagram.com/WordFirePress

bookbub.com/profile/4109784512